CHAPTER 1

In the growing heat of a summer morning a column of warriors, the army of the south folk, marched along a long, straight street. More than two hundred men, making slow progress, our pace held to the slow rumble of the wagons which carried the tents and supplies that we would need in the days ahead. The street's large cobble stones, which the Romans had left behind, were covered by a couple of inches of dirt. Grass was trying to reclaim the lost ground but the way was well worn. There was no dust, the sun hadn't risen high enough to draw the dewy dampness from the dark earth. An observer would have been intrigued by the makeup of the army; Angels, Danes, Saxons, Frisians and Wealh all marching side by side. Some remained in their companies but most seemed happy to mix with their brothers of the shield wall. I marched at the head of the column. My sword and fighting seaxe were scabbarded at my sides. I was carrying my blue shield with its design of wolves and ravens, the eager followers of the warband. I wore the gleaming shirt of scale mail which my father had left me and, on my head, the crested helmet which was a gift from king Stuf of the Jutes. It was a little bit the worse for wear after taking several hefty blows, but it was still a rare piece of craftsmanship. My forearms and lower legs were encased in stout leather. Only a great warrior could be so richly attired. Close behind me walked Wyne, tall and powerful, carrying my new Wolf standard, an iron spear eight feet tall with a cross bar, inches from the top, which supported a wolf skin. The wolf's head, with its mouth wide and teeth bared, glared ahead at our foes.

I was leading my warriors to war. It is where I belong. I am a king. Death is what defines me. All warriors are surrounded by death. We carry death with us. It is our destiny to kill, it is why we live. We will meet death in war, or at the hunt, or in some dispute or skirmish. We die, in the act of killing, surrounded by death. Our gods, Tiw, Woden, Thunor, Neorth, Baldaeg and the rest concern themselves with man's trials; war, battle, the sea, justice, betrayal and death. My woman, Asfrid waits for me at my hall with our son, Toglos Wulfhelm. She will rule my people while I am away. Women are surrounded by life. Their trial is not battle, it's not bringing death. Their trial is giving life. In bringing forth life they face their own death. Their goddesses, Frige, Freya, Eostre, Hretha, Sigel and so on rule life, love, plenty, fertility, spring, the sun, all of the things that bring life to the middle earth. I am leaving the world of life behind and entering the world of death.

King Wulfhere, or Wulfhere the Mad, lord of the Wolf. That's how my enemies know me. When I first heard it I was troubled, I didn't like the name. I didn't think myself mad. Now it has become part of my war gear. Reputation can win a fight. Fear is a powerful ally.

In spite of the summer heat I will wear my war gear from now until I return home again. I want the heavy gear to be like a second skin. I practise in it every day with the men of the Wolf and it doesn't hinder me. It is magnificent and marks me for what I am. Tiw chose me, from all of the men in middle earth, to carry his will abroad and to be his sword. He has granted me wealth, fortune and victories and I honour him with the blood of my enemies. My men understand that we have a higher destiny than most men. They are led by Gram, who has taken it upon himself to be my body guard and closest companion. They dedicate themselves to war and spend their days perfecting their ability with spear, shield or sword.

Unlike most armies I march with my own waelcyrge. He came to me in the summer with his priestesses and built a temple amongst a stand of ash trees about a mile from my hall. I didn't invite him and I won't send him away. He is greatly respected amongst his kind. When he arrived I was being served by a waelcyrge who had come with me from the old land but she gave herself to him as a sacrifice to give great power to the new temple. He knows that I have Tiw's protection and for that reason he serves me, in order to serve my god. He has no name, just Waelcyrge, and like all of his kind he dresses in priestess's robes and takes on the attitude of a woman to conduct spirits to the next world. Two of his priestesses remain at the temple and two are attendant upon him on the march. His presence unnerves some of my warriors, but not my household men, my Wolf pack as Asfrid calls them. They are used to walking in the presence of a god.

The harvest is in. The granaries and storehouses are full. This is the season for war. We are well supplied and the enemy's stores will make a good prize. Eadric, my reeve, did a first rate job, working all the daylight hours to lay in provisions, build up stores of arrows, and gather the pots, tents, wagons and all of the necessities for fighting a war. He is an excellent organiser, but he isn't a warrior. Asfrid is in charge at Wolf Home, with Eadric to assist her. My younger brother, Wuffa and the Danish atheling, Sigurd have stayed at home to help Asfrid as well. Sigurd's Danish bodyguards will be at the hall with my family, but four bodyguards aren't enough to defend my land and keep order while I am away.

The man I trust to keep my family and kingdom safe in my absence is Artorius. I know that Asfrid doesn't like the young giant but he is a ferocious warrior. He is Wealh, of the Dobunni tribe, so he, and all of his companions, are mounted. They can ride quickly to any part of the kingdom where there might be problems. It might seem strange that I should trust a Dobunni with my kingdom but he has given me his oath, and I know that he is a man of honour. Taking him to war against Cynfellyn, king of the Catuvellauni would put a strain on our friendship. Artorius believes in Combrogi, the new idea which has spread among the Wealh. It is a dream that the Wealh tribes will unite to hold their kingdoms from the invaders; Angel, Saxon, Jute, Frisian, Pict and Irish. Ambrosius, king of the Cornovii, has called on the Wealh to stand together, but the tribes hate each other more than they hate us! When the tyrant, Gwrgant, king of the Trinovantes of Caer Colun, inflicted foul cruelties on his own people I granted Artorius and his followers refuge. When he is ready I will help him to try to overthrow the tyrant. If he succeeds I will have a powerful friend amongst the kings of the Wealh.

The sun rose higher and our march rolled on. We hailed the farms that we passed with their neatly tilled fields, and blew horns as we marched to assure the folk that we weren't raiders. The people left their homes and halted their work to watch the king pass by with his army. I made my way along the column during the march, talking to lords and men. All of these men were warriors. The men of the fyrd were still hard at work in their fields. If the kingdom was threatened I would call the whole country to muster, but I couldn't expect farmers to march abroad as a raiding army. These were the lords of my kingdom with their companions, and young men who wanted to make a name for themselves on the slaughter field. War offered everyone a chance to impress the lords of the land and perhaps gain a place in the hall of a great man. At the very least there would be plunder, slaves or livestock.

My uncle Wulfstan was in fine spirits marching with his hearth companions, Oswine and Snorri, and his firm friend, the Danish jarl, Ullr and their men. We had other Danish lords with us, Harald, Thorkell and Svein, and the Frisians, Hod, Brega, Vifil and Unlaf. Owain and Meredydd had forsaken their horses and joined us 'Sais' on foot and of course there were the Angel lords who made up the bulk of the army. The army was well armed and eager, but none of them could compare to the Wolf Pack. I had over forty men, forty proud, well armed, well trained warriors. The waelcyrge had painted the mark of Tiw on our shields so that even on the march my warriors stood out. With my lads at the centre of the army, I knew that we would stand firm and fight to the death rather than accept defeat.

I was confident that the horsemen of the Wealh would never breach our shield wall. My Wealh companion, Marcellus had told me that when we fought the Catuvellauni they would launch a wild charge. Warriors would immediately follow the horsemen and hurl themselves against our shields with wild ferocity. They would try to overwhelm us with the uncontrolled savagery of their attack. If we broke, the horsemen would be in amongst our fleeing men and there would be utter destruction. If we could hold their charges, their stamina and courage would fail and the victory would be ours.

We marched through the long, hot day and the laughter and jokes were still coming when the light began to fade. We halted and made camp beside the street. We were still a long way from Wealh lands but I posted watchmen just the same. We were to follow the street to Theodford where Icel would be waiting for us with the army of the north folk. Once we had joined forces we would hear from his scouts and make our plan.

We were on the march again early the next morning. I had decided that we would push on to Theodford without stopping again, with each man carrying enough food for the day. The wagons could catch us up tomorrow at the camp. The weather was warm enough, and the nights were mild. We would spend the night in whatever shelter we could find. I wanted to see Icel. I wanted to gain an idea of his strength, and I wanted to start the war. The longer we delayed, the more provisions we would need to find, and the greater the chance that the Wealh would get word of our attack. They would have spies in our kingdom and that of our allies, the Corieltavi.

I hadn't ever imagined being part of a war like this. I had fought in the past to defend our land, but this time we were the invaders. We were going to take land from the Wealh to make our kingdoms stronger. Icel and I were going to take three important Catuvellauni towns at the western edge of the great fens. We already ruled the Eastern boundaries of the vast wetlands. The new towns would give us complete mastery of the fenlands and their salt making, which would make our kingdoms hugely wealthy. At the same time the Corieltavi were going to strike from the north to recover territory which Cynfellyn had conquered from them, and take some more land to make their kingdoms safer and wealthier.

We would be marching into an enemy's land. We would have to trust new allies who we didn't really know. We would be far from home and far from help. The very idea, the very thought of what we were doing overwhelmed me with a humbling sense of history and destiny. This was Tiw's will, it had to be. The Waelcyrge had made sacrifices and read the runes and he assured me that Tiw would be with us. This was no mere raid. We were going to push the boundaries of our Angel land out amongst the halls of the Wealh. We would be sending a message of might to their kings and it was in that message that our greatest danger lay.

Marcellus had dismissed the threat of Combrogi. He believed that the Wealh tribes hated each other too much to unite. Further too that, he couldn't see how one king would ever have the might to hold all of the different peoples together over the vast lands of Britain. It was just too huge, too wild and varied to contemplate. I believed that a clear danger can make peoples put differences aside to defend themselves. My companion, Edgar, who was now dead, had told me how his father, a proud Saxon, had followed his king and fought alongside Franks, Goths and Romans under the warlord, Aetius, to defeat the savage, Attilla. Would Cynfellyn of the Catuvellauni send to the Cornovii of Ambrosius, or Artorius' Dobunni, or the Brigantes, Trinovantes or Atrebates for aid? Would our triumph be the threat that would unite the Wealh? I couldn't foretell this fate. I would trust the will of Tiw and sharpen my blade for hard fighting.

We approached Theodford after noon. Icel's army was camped in the fields outside the town. Smoke rose from cooking fires and drifted lazily above the tents. There was constant movement around the camps, and the familiar sounds carried to us as we approached. The babble of conversations and laughter competed with the scraping grind of blades being sharpened, and a smith's hammer, pounding out its metallic ring. I stopped our column and climbed onto one of the wagons, waving the army to gather round.

"We are the south folk. My brothers! We are the beating heart of this army. The rock against which the Wealh will be broken. The might of the gods is with us. In the days to come you will be forging a legend. You are the first army of the south folk. Set a mark, brothers. Set a mark which our children, and our children's children will have to strive mightily to equal. Defeat the Wealh, sieze glory, and we will live forever at the hearths, and in the hearts, of our people!"

They cheered then, and when they marched into the camp they were two inches taller, straight and proud. A warrior hurried to meet us.

"Lord Wulfhere. I am Edgard. King Icel has sent me to bring you to him."

"Good. Where can my men find shelter?" I wondered

He waved a hand at the town and the land around us. As I thought, we would just sleep under our cloaks. I addressed my men again.

"Find yourselves a dry place to rest. I must speak with Icel. Wulfstan, come with me."

With our hearth companions we followed Edgard into the ancient town to the hall of the lord of Theodford.

"Wulfhere, my brother, it's good to see you," Icel rose from his bench and clasped my hand. The modest hall was filled with the lords of the north folk. I greeted Heremod and Yrre and one or two others who I thought I recognised. The king stepped back and glanced around the faces of my companions nodding greetings until he saw my uncle.

"Wulfstan! So you are here. The stories are all true. Please, you must tell us what news you have of the old lands. The tales are so wild and so varied that it's hard to know what to believe."

Icel returned to his seat and Wulfstan stepped forward to the fire pit where all could see him.

"I'm sure that you will have heard how your brother was surprised and killed by the Franks. I see some faces here in the hall who have come from the old lands. Our homeland is laid waste. Soon it will be empty but for carrion birds and wolves and the dogs of Childoberht and Halfdan Scylding. This is now the only Angel land and you, Icel are the king of our folk. It won't be long before they are all here. There is nothing but death back there.

After your brother was killed the Council of the Wise offered me the royal helm. But there is nothing left to rule. My son, Wulfnoth, lord of the Northern Marches was killed by Danes. This must be our home now. The lands won by Offa of Angel will stand empty again, as at the dawn of time, until the Dane and the Frank have torn them apart and taken their share. The story of our people begins again in this land," Wulfstan concluded to a silent hall.

Icel eventually broke the silence.

"Not just here. We have spoken with travellers from the old lands who say that many of our folk are making new homes with Winta and the Lindisware, while others are sailing further north to Bernaccia. More of our people arrive at our ports every day seeking land and a new home. So, Wulfhere, Wulfstan, as trusted lords of our people, what would you advise that we do now? Should we delay our war until the Angelcynn have settled in their new homes?"

Wulfstan looked at me,

"What do you think, boy?"

I looked around me. The hall was hushed and waiting on my decision. I hadn't marched my army here just to slink home again!

"Should we wait for newcomers in a land that is full of newcomers? In my army I have warriors of many tribes; Angel, Saxon, Dane, Frisian, Iceni, Atrebates. Warriors from many different peoples. I have told them that in the days to come they will be forging a reputation for our people in a new land. A reputation which future generations will have to strive to match. They will be laying down a standard of courage and battle craft by which our people will be known. If they fight bravely, and cunningly, they will be winning victories for their children and grandchildren by filling our enemies with fear and doubt.

But, my lords, if we put on our war gear, and shake our spears, what message do we send if we then retreat quietly to our halls with no blood on our blades. I think that we must send forth the message that when the Angelcynn are prepared for war there is only victory, or death.

The land that we win in the days ahead, watered by the blood of our foes, will make fitting homes for hard pressed people from the old lands. The livestock and slaves that we take will ease their settling and fill their bellies. This war will bring you wealth and power my king. We stand at the dawn of a new history. Our courage and our blades will shape this land forever!"

The lords in that hall bellowed their approval, thumping the tables and shouting their agreement. Icel simply nodded, words would have been lost in the tumult. Finally he held up his hands for quiet.

"We will rest here tonight and tomorrow night, while the last of the muster is answered. At dawn the following day, we will march to war!"

CHAPTER 2: The Plan

The lords of our army drank their ale and made proud boasts of the feats that they would risk on the battlefield for their king. Spirits were high and there were clearly great expectations of victory, and plunder to follow. I was pleased that our army would take the field brimming with confidence and fierce aggression. Gradually the company drifted back to their men until there was only a small group of us left in the small, dark hall.

Icel had obviously been waiting for the chance to question Wulfstan more closely about his brother's last days and the fall of Angeln. We sat in near silence, respectful of our king's grief, while we listened to Wulfstan's doleful tale. I had heard it all already and as I stared at the rafters, and the overlaying thatch which came and went in the low, flickering firelight, my mind drifted back to the old land and showed me memories of my youth; the old hall, mother smiling and laughing in the sun, father teaching me how to handle my spear, ships at the dock, the river, roaming the woods with Ceolfrith my ever present childhood companion. Good things, warm memories, which would remain the same forever, in the old lands in my mind. The hall, the people and the time was gone, but they would always stay with me just as they were. It was a strange thought.

Time drew on. Wulfstan had finished his report and Icel had asked him all that he could reasonably be expected to know. I sensed that Wulfstan was becoming impatient, and I was too. There was a brief silence while Icel considered Wulfstan's latest answer and as he drew breath to ask another question I cut across him,

"None of us can know his fate. We might all be feasting with your brother before this war is over," I announced darkly as I put my pot down sturdily onto the wooden table. "Fate will not be changed. It is what it is. We have business to attend to. We have a war to fight and warriors to lead. Do you have a plan?"

Icel's advisor, Heremod looked a little annoyed at my interruption but the faces of most of the men in the hall betrayed the thoughts within, and most were clearly with me. There was a good deal of shifting as they straightened themselves on the benches and prepared to hear the true business of our meeting.

"Yes, of course, Wulfhere. It's strange though, thinking of them all gone."

"I know, my friend, I know. But this is your time. They've had their time and they'll be watching you, waiting to see how well you fare. Make them proud, Icel. Grasp the time that you've been given and fill it with a life that will make men wonder and regret their own wasted hours. The old lands are gone. This is our land now, our future. We must make it what we want it to be.

What is your plan?"

The plan was simple enough.

"I will take my army north from here, follow the causeway street which crosses the fenland and take Durobrivae, the northernmost of the three towns at the bridge over the Nen. I want you to skirt the southern fringes of the fens and take Duroliponte, the town at the Granta bridge. Then you will march north and I'll come south and we'll take Durovigutum, at the Ouse, between us."

"What do we do when Cynfellyn comes to get his towns back?" Wulfstan wondered.

"We sit tight behind our walls and hold him until our Corieltavi allies come to our aid. Then we crush him. If he goes after them they will send word and we will march to join them. Whatever happens we will crush the Catuvellauni between us."

"I'd rather destroy Cynfellyn first," I decided. "This way we've got to just sit and wait. We've got to garrison three towns and wait for him to make all the decisions. He might just sit back and use his horsemen to stop supplies getting to our men."

"So what do you suggest?" Icel wanted to know, a little irked that his plan hadn't just been accepted.

"I suggest that we march into his kingdom, with our allies, looting and burning and drawing him out to fight. We destroy his army in battle and then we can take whatever we want."

"That way we lose the element of surprise. What if his towns call in their fyrdmen and sit on their supplies. We can't mount a siege. We'll have to return home empty handed," Icel was annoyed. "I think my plan is best. We'll march the day after tomorrow."

I wasn't going to argue. Both plans had weaknesses. I just preferred being in control of events. I wanted Cynfellyn to come to our call, not us to his. We took our leave and went to look for our companions. We couldn't find them at first but were directed to a strange kind of fort. There was a large area of ground, slightly away from the town, ringed by a sequence of ditches and breastworks like all the Roman forts. Then, within the outer ditches were nine wooden walls, which were now all but rotted away. Then there were more ditches and earth ramparts. We went through the gateway to discover a great open meadow with a few small buildings at the centre. Our lads had made camp against the overgrown earthen rampart of the innermost ditch at the northern side of the meadow. Most of them were already sleeping soundly beneath their cloaks but I could see a few shadowy figures sitting round one of the camp fires. As we turned towards them I heard the Waelcyrge and his priestesses making incantations. They were weaving their magic by the small buildings at the centre of the fort. We ignored them and walked wearily to the camp fire. Marcellus, Wedda and Inwald were sat around the weak flames. I stopped at the fire and looked back across the unkempt meadow to where the calls of devotion were still drifting out of the timeless, all-consuming darkness of the night. I shivered slightly with the feeling that the eyes of unknown spirits were watching us from the shadows.

"What is this place, Marcellus? Have you been here before?" I asked my friend.

"Yes, this is a sacred place. It was the meeting place of the Iceni. Their muster place. Their warriors would gather here and make sacrifices before they went to war. The small buildings over there are temples that the Romans built. The Waelcyrge says that there are ancient spirits dwelling here. He's probably right. We wouldn't have come in here but the waelcyrge insisted. He says that he can call on the ancient spirits to help us. Says that our gods can compel the older spirits to do their bidding."

We listened in silence as the waelcyrge and his priestesses made their calls and devotions to the gods. Beyond the weak light of our fire they were a part of the endless night. We sat around the fire in silence and the magic of their rites carried us deep within ourselves and far beyond, to the endless blackness that hid our ancestors and the gods themselves from our eyes. We could all feel them, somehow, in that sacred place. Above all I felt the presence of Tiw. He was at peace. I felt sure that his contentment was a good sign for the coming war.

At Theodford we were about thirty miles from the Granta bridge. Icel had half as far again to go to the Nen bridge. We waited the next day for our wagons, and the last of the army of the north folk to arrive and then he left at dawn heading north west. At mid-day we left our sacred enclosure and marched south west. Icel had sent me a man named Leofa who knew the country and would act as our guide. The day had started brightly but cloud blew in during the morning and although it was too high to bring rain straight away, there was an obvious threat. I hoped that it would rain. Poor weather would keep folk inside, hopefully helping us to remain undetected until we were on top of our enemy. We trundled along all afternoon at the pace of the wagons, making steady progress through that unremarkable landscape. We forded a river, and when the light began to fade we pitched camp for the night. We posted watchmen and I was happy for the men to light cooking fires as we were still a long way short of our destination

The rain started to fall before dawn and the fires were re-kindled to prepare hot porridge so that the men would start the day with full stomachs. There was no need to rush. I hadn't planned to take the town at the Granta bridge until the morning after tomorrow. That would allow Icel enough time to take his town, and meet us on the Roman street at the Ouse. I asked Leofa about the towns that we were attacking and their Roman forts.

"The fort at the Granta bridge is no real obstacle. The breastworks and ditches are overgrown and neglected. No-one lives within them. The town has grown along the street. It must have been very impressive at one time. The fort I mean. The ditches enclose a big area. They must have had a lot of warriors inside. It's too big to defend properly, really, although it wouldn't take much to make it strong again, the ditches are quite deep. You could put a wall up and build a town inside I suppose, if you had the men."

"What about the other two?"

"They could be a difficult proposition if there are enough men to defend the walls."

"Are they busy towns?"

"More than most, I suppose. Being on the street, and by bridges makes for a lot of passing folk and traders. They make a lot of pots thereabouts, so there's a fair bit of coming and going, yes. If you stop to talk you'll get all the news that's for sure."

"So they might have enough men to man the walls?"

Leofa could only shrug. We would know when we got there.

We marched all day with cold, wet feet through that low, landscape. We were skirting the fenlands and the fields were all ditched. Where the land wasn't farmed, tufts of thick marsh grass and willows flourished between the meres, bogs and marshy reed beds. Away to the east the occasional gleam of water grasped the eye and a great grey heron flew heavily over our path. We spent another damp night beneath our cloaks and in the morning we sighted a town up ahead.

"There it is, Duroliponte," Leofa told me. Pleased to have done his job.

It was an impressive town. There must have been somewhere between twenty and thirty neatly thatched houses surrounding an old Roman building, which was protected by stone walls. There were also several outhouses of varying sizes within the walls, which suggested that at one time it had been the heart of an estate. The townspeople were fleeing for their lives, scattering into the surrounding countryside. I ran forward, calling my companions and the Wolf Pack with me. I shouted at the men to split up and skirt each side of the town to 'round up' the inhabitants.

"Marcellus!" I shouted as I ran. "Tell them we wish them no harm. Tell them they can stay in their houses, quickly!"

Marcellus began shouting in the strange, throaty language of the Wealh. We reached the town and slowed our headlong rush to a jog, and then a walk. Some of the townspeople, whose chances of escape were hindered by age, ill health or small children, had stopped at the sound of their own language and waited, nervously, to find out what this was all about.

Their houses were simple wattle and daub affairs, but I was surprised to notice that there were no work huts. If this had been an Angel town the houses would have been surrounded by the huts that we used for weaving, carving or whatever craft the owner possessed. The ground all around was worn bare. Chickens hurried around warily and two or three dogs were barking. We waited while the men who had circled the cluster of houses joined us with a decent collection of terrified fugitives.

I told Marcellus to announce that this land was now ruled by Icel of Angel. All people living here would be guaranteed the protection of their new lord, and permitted to stay at peace in their town at the Granta Bridge. When he had finished this announcement I told him to inform the good people of Duroliponte that I wanted to speak with the head man of the town.

He wasn't present. Clearly he had a good turn of pace. I did find out that his name was Cunebalin and I let it be known that I wanted to speak with him, and that he wouldn't be harmed.

The folk of Duroliponte were huddled pathetically before me. Some of the women were still weeping, certain that they were about to be thrown down and fucked by dozens of brutal warriors. A man, who must have crept back to the town to hear what was going on, scurried from between the houses and crossed the bare ground to join one of the weeping women with her children. She clung to him, wailing her sorrow into his chest. He stared wide eyed at me.

"Marcellus, tell them again that they won't be harmed. Tell them to return to their homes. This is no longer Cynfellyn's land. This town is ours and all the surrounding land will owe us feorm. Tell them!"

The bulk of the army had gathered around us and the women started to wail again. I didn't want to risk a blood bath and every moment that the men stayed in the town there was a chance that some incident could lead to slaughter. The men had been told to harm no one, but there was no point in putting temptation in their way.

I saw Wulfstan and called him over.

"Take them straight over the bridge and set up camp. Keep them busy. Have them cut stakes to ring the camp. Then practise the shield wall. I don't want them coming back here for women or thieving! "

Wulfstan nodded,

"Nothing here worth taking anyway!" He snorted.

Gram and the Wolf pack lads knew that raping or beating women brought me visions of the night my mother was killed and the women of my home town were raped and tortured for the amusement of the pirates who had destroyed my home and killed my father. I had been a young lad, hidden nearby, and the images of that night had often danced across my mind to torment me in the years since. They had seen the way I reacted to the ill-treatment of women, and they helped Wulfstan march the army across the bridge and out of town.

"Are you the king?" I turned to discover the source of the question and found a lad of thirteen or fourteen summers waiting for my reply.

"Yes, I am. I'm Wulfhere, lord of the Wolf," I answered honestly. "Who might you be?"

The lad was of Angel blood, I glanced around for his family.

"Maccus." He stated boldly.

"Who's your lord, Maccus? Who does your father follow?"

"My father sold me to Cunebalin. He tried to make a farm but the stock was stolen and the crops trampled. He sold me and my sister. Then he left. My sister died in childbirth."

It wasn't unusual for children to be sold into bondage in hard times, but I took pity on this bold youngster in a Wealh town.

"Maccus, fate has sent you to me today. Sometimes the spinners give us choices. A chance to make a change to our lives. Cunebalin isn't here and my word is law. Tonight, Maccus you can return to your bed a slave, or you can join the warriors of the Wolf and fight for a god."

"Really? Will you take the oath of a slave?"

"I will take the oath of a warrior, Maccus. Prove yourself a worthy warrior and then I will take your oath."

"I will prove myself, king Wulfhere the Wolf! One day I will give you my oath!"

"And I will give you a place in my household."

I called Gram over,

"Gram, this is Maccus, he will be joining our ranks. Make him a Warrior. Teach him what he needs to know about us." I told my dour captain

"Yes, lord."

"Maccus, Gram is your captain and you must do whatever he tells you, even if you fear it might lead to your death."

"Yes, lord."

I followed the army over the bridge. The street led away to the north of north west. Wulfstan had chosen the site for our camp, about half a mile further on. The men were cutting stakes, lighting fires or pitching tents. The wagons had been gathered at the heart of the camp and the oxen un-hitched and taken to graze and drink. Soon the air was rich with wood smoke. The camp was ringed with stakes driven into the ground close enough together to stop horses sweeping down upon us and to slow a headlong charge by warriors on foot.

With a lot of shouting and a few bashed heads Wulfstan organised a practise, with the men forming the shield wall and driving hard at each other. He kept them at it through the long summer evening and didn't call a halt until the light was beginning to fade. The tired army returned to their cooking fires to slake their thirst and fill rumbling stomachs. I enjoyed the hot pea pudding and travelling bread. I took a generous helping, and sat by the fire, shovelling it in. It had been a long day and I packed two bowlfuls away quite easily. Once I had eaten I was ready to talk. I called all of the lords to my fire and aired my thoughts.

"Cynfellyn will soon know that we are here. As soon as he does I expect he will bring his army to drive us out and protect his people, I would. Icel wanted me to take this town and leave men here to hold it. If we leave men here they'll be as good as dead. If the town was walled they could send word when Cynfellyn arrived and wait for friends to come to their aid. With no wall……" I shrugged. "So, I will keep our army together. We will push on to the Ouse and take the town there. Leofa says it has a strong wall. We will hold that town and wait for Cynfellyn."

"He'll just take this place back. We won't hold the three towns," Owain pointed out.

"What matters, as I've said all along, is to defeat Cynfellyn. Once his army is destroyed we can just march back here and it will be ours again. When we have time we can make this place a burrh, and grant it to a strong lord. We can march out and demand tribute from the nearest Catuvellaunian towns. We can do what we want, once Cynfellyn is defeated. So I won't split our army. We will stay together. We will march on in the morning and take the next town, whatever it's called, and give it a proper Angel name!"

CHAPTER 3: The Wisdom of Wulfstan

I sent the lords back to their men. Once the formless sound of chatter had receded I glanced up and saw Wulfstan and Oswine watching me across the camp fire.

"From the expression on your face you're either still wrestling with some deep and meaningful problem, or you've got wind. Which is it?" my uncle wanted to know.

We all laughed and I was glad that marching to war had obviously helped him get his old spark back.

"You'll be glad to know that I've got something on my mind," I chuckled. "I still want to meet the bastard head on and cut him to bits. I'm just wondering if we'll be better off keeping everyone together, the whole army, Icel's men and ours, and drawing him onto us?"

"Ah, well now. That's a different matter," Wulfstan cautioned.

"What do you mean?"

"Well, how are we going to pin down the horsemen if they won't fight us head on?" The old warrior mused. "They could skip around, out of reach for weeks, picking off foragers and supplies from home while we lumber around trying to catch up with them. We would struggle to feed ourselves and end up dead in a Catuvellaunian field, or going home with nothing. We need bait. A soft touch, to draw them in, and then we can hit them. And I'll tell you this, Wulfhere, if it comes to a choice between our lads being bait, and Icel's lads being bait, it's going to be Icel's lads," Oswine and Ullr chuckled grimly.

My uncle was as hard as granite, cold and unforgiving as a blade, but he was right.

"It's a good point," I conceded. "You can't get the Wealh to fight you if they don't want to."

"That's probably what the Corieltavi thought," Wulfstan went on. "We'd help them get their land back and then end up going home empty handed! Sais fools! Distracting the Catuvellauni for them while they get back their lost ground. Why else would they offer us the salt making? That's the richest part of the deal. Too good to turn down. I don't think we'll see the Wealh riding to help us. We'll have to win this war with our own spears, Wulfhere. We can do it. We can defeat this Cynfellyn. If we hold a strong place and make them come onto our spears we could beat a thousand of these Wealh."

I looked from him to Oswine and Ullr who just shrugged. I had a lot to learn from these cunning leaders of men, an awful lot to learn.

I didn't sleep much that night. I was mindful of a possible attack and I kept checking on the men who were guarding the camp, making sure that everything was quiet. In spite of, or perhaps because of, that I was ready to move on to Durovigutum at first light, having been the first to sample the hot porridge that had been prepared for breakfast.

It was an easy fourteen miles or so along the Roman street to Durovigutum. Under normal circumstances we would have been there by mid-morning but we couldn't leave the wagons unguarded, so we didn't reach the town until evening with the oxen complaining mightily.

Durovigutum was a large town with a great earth and stone wall. It was protected by a wide ditch which completely encircled the whole town except for the great gate. The gateway was a great stone arch, wide enough for a wagon to pass through, with narrower arches on either side for folk to pass on foot.

"Impressive," I said to nobody in particular as I halted the army out of bow range and examined the scene before us.

"Very," agreed Wulfstan. "Or at least it would be if they had enough men to defend those walls." He was right of course. We were in luck. There was no army here, only the townsfolk. They were strong enough to deter bandits but we could attack the walls in a dozen places at once, even before Icel arrived with his army. The defenders would be stretched too thinly to keep us out.

"Come on then, let's go and give them our terms. Marcellus! I need you, come on."

With a small group of my closest companions I approached the great gate. Marcellus hailed the men who had gathered on the wall above the gates. He told them who I was, and demanded the name of their leader.

"His name's Vordemus," he informed me, pointing out a slightly shorter figure whose long hair and beard were blowing across his face in the wind.

"Right, tell our friend Vordemus that his town is now ruled by king Icel of Angel, who has taken it from the weakling, Cynfellyn. As Icel's warlord I don't want to harm his people or his town, so if they open the gates and come down to meet me they will be treated with all due respect. If they don't, I will kill every living creature inside those walls. Every living creature." I nodded in the direction of Vordemus and his friends and Marcellus called my warning loudly enough for everyone in the town to hear.

They weren't fools. Their king was nowhere to be seen. They were on their own and they knew that they couldn't hold the walls against us. They sought assurances that they wouldn't be harmed.

"Tell them that my word is enough. If they continue to hesitate I will take it as an insult. Tell them that I'm growing impatient." Marcellus passed on the message.

An order must have been given inside the gatehouse because, with the sound of heavy beams being drawn out and dropped, the gate suddenly shuddered, grated, and swung open. After a short wait the town's leaders came out of the shadows under the great arch. They must have been afraid but they bore themselves well. I removed my helmet and my companions followed my lead.

"I am Vordemus," the leader informed me. He was a short man, barely as high as my chin, with grey strands at the edges of his long hair and beard. He led a small group of six men and a woman who were bunched behind him.

"Vordemus, I am Wulfhere, warlord of Angel, chosen sword of Tiw himself, and I salute your courage and good sense. Durovigitum is our town now. You are our people, you owe king Icel your loyalty and he will grant you his protection. You can call upon his laws to right any wrongs that you have suffered.

Now, I would like to come inside and have a look at our new town. Lead on my friend.

Leofmund, get everyone inside! Gram, make sure that everyone knows that this town belongs to the king. Icel's laws hold sway here."

The town was ours. The first part of the plan had worked. Now I would wait for Icel, and Cynfellyn. We had done well. Durovigutum was a fine prize. The town walls weren't square like most Roman forts. There were six sides, all of slightly different lengths. The houses were well kept and prosperous, with a few, small, neatly tilled fields and livestock enclosures between them. In the middle there was an open square where a number of traders were hurriedly packing their goods away.

I told the lords of the south folk to find some space for their men but not to damage property or take any plunder. Everything that they wanted would be bought and paid for.

"Would it be easier to set up camp outside?" Leofmund wondered.

"It would certainly be easier," I conceded, "but if Cynfellyn turns up, this lot will shut the gates and shoot at us from the walls, while we try to fight off the warriors outside. In here we could hold off three armies if we needed to."

The army marched in. Vordemus showed us around his town. There were some wonderful, large buildings with open courtyards, and a temple with plenty of open space and shelter. We told the men to make camp around the temple. There was plenty of room and they would be together in one place.

The walls of the town were huge. The soil that had been dug from the great ditch had been piled up to form a rampart and then a stone wall had been built atop it. The wall was half as wide again as I could reach with both arms spread wide. The top of the wall must have towered thirty feet above the bottom of the ditch. It was breath taking. I gazed out across the flat countryside and willed Cynfellyn to come at us here.

By the time we got back to the army there was some sort of discontent afoot. I could hear raised voices and we entered what

Vordemus had called the old forum to discover an argument between Gram and some of the lords. The men were gathered about the steps to the high columned building at the back of the courtyard, and there was a good deal of bad tempered shouting going on.

"What's this all about?" I demanded as I strode across the yard.

The noise fell away to dark muttering and the men stepped back and cleared the way. I climbed the steps two at a time and halted at the centre of the argument. Wulfstan and Oswine were alongside me. Marcellus was joined by his companions and they fell in behind with Wedda.

"Gram?" I looked to my hearth companion for an explanation.

"Lord Wulfhere," it was Ithamar who, with Hygsic and Harald, seemed to be leading the argument. "We need plunder, lord. We need to reward our men. This is a rich town. These are our enemies! We have marched this far, lord. This town should be our prize!"

I knew that there would be anger among some of the men at our lack of reward. We had taken two towns and they had nothing to show for it. It was bad enough that they couldn't have the women. None of them really understood why I forbade it, but here they were, with two great victories and no loot. I was surprised at these three though, I hadn't expected to be questioned by them.

"You are right of course, Ithamar. There will be plunder. There will be livestock. There will be slaves. But not here," I addressed the whole army from the top step. "Do you think that I would bring you to war with no intention of rewarding your loyalty and service? Do you think that I would return home myself without filling my wagons? Have patience. There are great battles yet to be fought, but this place isn't a prize. This town is worth more to us as a town than as a ruin! This town is ours now. We have made it part of our kingdom. All the land that you can see from the wall is our land now. These people are our people. We don't loot our own towns. We don't steal from our own folk. We have taken this town in order to draw Cynfellyn forth to battle. When he gets here there will be plunder. Plunder from the corpses of his army. There will be horses, war gear, treasures, the plunder of the slaughter field, and once their army is destroyed we will claim tribute from the Catuvellauni. Don't worry my lords. You will be rewarded. But remember this, all of you. It would not be wise to question my decisions a second time!

Now, light your cooking fires, fill your bellies, sharpen your blades and no more arguing amongst ourselves, my brothers."

Calm was restored. The men started to return to their campfires.

"Ithamar, Hygsic, Harald!" The three stopped and turned to face me. "Have I ever failed you? Have I ever let you down? Ithamar, when I received word that you were threatened by the Trinovantes was I not there the very next day to stand at your side? Hygsic, how much land do you have in my kingdom compared to what you had in the old land? Harald, did I not grant you the right to a share of all the catches made by all fishermen along the coast from your hall to Dommocceaster? Why do you question me now? Go back to your men and remember that I will be watching you in the days ahead. I would hate to think that you might let me down again."

Cowed and shamefaced they turned to leave and came face to face with the waelcyrge who was walking slowly up the steps with his priestesses at either side of him. As he came he took in the scene before him, searching the faces of each of the penitent lords who nervously returned his gaze. They shuffled nervously aside and stood respectfully, waiting for him to pass. The waelcyrge didn't pass them. He stopped, on a lower step and addressed me in his strange, falsely high-pitched, mimicry of a woman's voice.

"Wolf lord, chosen sword of Tiw, I wish to make a fitting sacrifice in honour of your victory here. It must be worthy of Tiw's generosity, in order to mark his help in your triumph and to keep his favour in the trials that lie ahead."

As he spoke he eyed the three sorry lords, who glanced nervously in my direction. I surveyed them coldly. I wanted to chill their blood. I wanted them to know that with a word I could have them hanging upside down in an ash tree waiting for the cold blade to be drawn across their throats. I could be generous, I would reward loyalty well, but there was a price for disloyalty as well. When I was sure the lesson was well learned I turned to the priest with his gaudily painted face.

"Waelcyrge, I will have Vordemus send you a prize bull, and a ram, and we will hold a feast in Tiw's honour."

Icel didn't arrive until after noon of the following day, tired and short tempered. I went out to meet him with Vordemus and my companions.

"Wulfhere! It's good to see you. Any sign of the enemy?" He asked taking my proffered hand.

"Not unless news of our victories has been borne to him on wings. The gods have smiled on us so far. This is Vordemus, headman of Durovigutum. It's a fine town, Icel, you've done well. I didn't leave any men at Duroliponte. It's just an open town, there's no fort or town wall. If we left men there they would be as good as dead."

"There are ditches and walls at Durobrivae. I have left two hundred men there," Icel advised me. "They will be able to hold it long enough for us to get to them."

I looked sideways and caught Wulfstan's eye.

"Well that's our baited trap. That's where Cynfellyn will strike when he's ready. Have you heard anything of the Corieltavi?" I wondered.

"No nothing yet. But I wouldn't expect anything for a couple of days."

"Well, Icel, our friend Vordemus would like to present the leading townsfolk to you and show you around this fine town."

Icel spoke with his companions and the word was given for the army of the north folk to make camp outside the town walls. I accompanied Icel in through the great arched gateway, and followed wordlessly while Vordemus introduced him to the other worthies and discussed the town, the buildings and the business which was conducted at the market.

The day passed slowly as one after another, frightened traders and craftsmen explained their business to Icel and his reeve, Wygge, who would decide what taxes and services the town would have to provide. I invited Icel to a feast that would be hosted by Vordemus in the forum that very evening, to honour Tiw and to celebrate the arrival of the king.

It was a very grand but, at the same time, a very strange feast. Vordemus was our host in name only. He made every effort to welcome us to his hall and give the appearance of a man who was pleased to have us there. The other town leaders made a similar effort but, as Wulfstan drily noted, they looked like sheep feasting with wolves, and hoping that they wouldn't end up on the table. All of the lords of our army were there. Hygsic, Ithamar and Harald had come to me individually seeking forgiveness and pledging undying loyalty. They would each send one of their sons to join my household on our return home. It was a great show of their sincerity. They were confirming their own loyalty with the lives of their children. I accepted their obeisance and we were brothers once more.

Days passed slowly as we waited for a response from the Catuvellauni, but there was no sign of Cynfellyn and his army. I spent hours on the wall with Gram, Wulfstan and Oswine, staring out at the distant horizons. More worryingly there was no sign of our Corieltavi allies. I had expected Cynfellyn to take some time to respond. He would have to muster his army before he came at us, and if he struck at the Corieltavi first he might be defeated and be in no position to attack us at all. If that was the case we should have heard from our friends. If they had suffered a defeat at Cynfellyn's hands he would surely have been riding to our gates while his warriors were still afire with victory.

"Where are they?" I asked aloud to no one in particular as we stood on the western wall staring at any spot on the horizon that might or might not have just moved.

"They'll come," Ullr asserted. "What king could leave us to take his towns and not show some courage to fight us? He must come."

"No, my friend. I meant the Corieltavi, our allies. Where are they? What is happening out there? We can't just sit here forever we've got too many mouths to feed."

It was true. Icel had nearly five hundred men altogether and I had over two hundred. The wagons had been loaded high with provisions when we left home and we had bought or foraged for food from the local area, but we couldn't keep that up all summer. The locals would be left with nothing to take them through the winter. We wanted a battle and we wanted it soon, but still the empty days passed by. Doubts began to nag at me. Wulfstan had been right, but Icel wanted to trust in his friends.

When horsemen did eventually arrive, they weren't who we were expecting. The watchmen on the wall spotted four horses hurrying from the south, along the street from Duroliponte. I recognised Artorius' companions, Gaheris and Bors as they rode closer, and I dashed down to meet them. One of the other riders was also from Wolf Home, Triphun Namatius, but it was the last rider who was the important man.

"Bors, Gaheris, what news? Are we attacked? Why are you here?" I wanted to know why they had ridden here in such hate.

"Lord Wulfhere," Gaheris began. "This man is Ceneu of the Dobunni. He is a cousin of Artorius'. He has ridden hard to join us from the hall of Cynfellyn. He has news that Artorius thought that you would need to hear."

"What news?" I demanded.

"Lord, you have been betrayed," Ceneu began and straight away he began to confirm my fears about our 'allies'. "Cynfellyn has struck a deal with Tasciovarus of the Corieltavi, he has bought his loyalty with silver."

"Tasciovarus? Who is he?" I needed to know.

"He is one of the kings of the Corieltavi, lord Wulfhere." Gaheris informed me. "He rules Caer Lerion and wields considerable power."

"The men of Caer Lerion won't join their brothers in their attack on Cynfellyn," Ceneu continued, "and without Tasciovarus and Caer Lerion, the Corieltavi won't risk war with Cynfellyn."

So this was the truth of it. We would have to face Cynfellyn alone, cut off from our homes and help by the great fenland. There would be no escape if the battle didn't go well.

"So we have to face the Catuvellauni alone. When will they be here?"

"That I don't know, lord Wulfhere," Ceneu shrugged.

"Well were they preparing to march when you left? How long ago were you there?"

"I left Cynfellyn at Verulamium four days ago. Artorius sent me straight here, lord."

"You have done well Ceneu, and you shall be well rewarded. If you left four days ago Cynfellyn could be here at any time," I pondered aloud.

"No, lord. That is what I meant to say. I don't know when he will come but he isn't coming yet, at least he wasn't when I left," Ceneu continued apologetically.

"Not coming?"

"No, lord. There are rumours that the Cantware Sais, the hated sons of Hengest, are planning to attack Londinium. They have had word of your plans, and they are waiting for Cynfellyn to be drawn north. Cynfellyn won't leave while there is a risk to the great city. The wealth of Londinium is a thousand times greater than these towns, lord. Tasciovarus has told him that you won't be able to keep your army in the field for long. He will come when he is satisfied that Londinium is safe."

I stared at the stocky Wealh warrior and then clapped him on the shoulder.

"Come," I addressed all four messengers, "We'll find a stable for your horses and some ale to slake your thirst.

Leofmund, you'd better find Icel and ask him to join us!"

When Ceneu had repeated his tale for Icel and his companions we sat and pondered our next move.

"Obviously the half-Dane Cantware have friends at our benches," Wulfstan observed, drily. "On this occasion they've done us a favour. Where is this Caer Lerion?" he wondered.

"About forty miles to the west of north west. The kingdom is based around Ratae, the city of the Corieltavi," Gaheris pointed out in his sing song Wealh accent. "If you follow the street towards

Durobrivae, after four or five miles another street bears away to the north west and it leads to the gates of Ratae."

"We should take the army and seize the place," was Wulfstan's advice.

"We have what we came for," countered Icel. "I think that we should leave enough men to hold these towns and start sending more folk from back home as they arrive. We can fight off Cynfellyn but I don't think that we should start a war with the Corieltavi as well as the Catuvellauni."

"I want riches to reward my companions." Wulfstan asserted aggressively.

"I understand, Wulfstan," Icel continued patiently. "But think for a moment. Ceneu didn't say that Cynfellyn isn't coming. He said that he is delayed. We can't know when he will decide to come up here to face us. He might already be on his way! So what happens if we go to war with the Corieltavi and the Catuvellauni arrive while we're still fighting them? We are a long way from home. We can expect no help. We have nowhere to run to."

We fell silent. To attack Ratae would be an impossible risk, but Marcellus stoked Wulfstan's desire for a fight still further.

"I doubt whether the Corieltavi would go to war on Tasciovarus' behalf. He is the most powerful of the Corieltavi kings but, if he was brought low, they wouldn't mourn him. He has few friends. He has flouted his power over them for years. Several of them have been insulted by him in the past. I could go to the Corieltavi kings who first sent the messengers to seek your help, king Icel. They have been humiliated by Tasciovarus' change of heart. If I extend the hand of friendship from yourself and offer them a share of the spoils I would think that you will have a free hand with Ratae."

"With Tasciovarus out of the way, do you think that the Corieltavi kings will stand with us and face Cynfellyn?" I wondered.

"I don't know, but if we promised that we would still help them win back the territory that they wanted to fight Cynfellyn for in the first place, in spite of Tasciovarus' treachery, they would be shamed by our loyalty. If they didn't take the field against Cynfellyn after that the whole world would see them for cowards. I think that they'd have to fight or risk the contempt of their own people."

"Ratae it is, then," Wulfstan slapped the table to emphasise his certainty. "Icel, the city's wealthy, there'll be rich plunder. If you wanted you could make Tasciovarus' kingdom yours. It's only forty miles from here. We could send you men if you needed them and you'll be one of the Corieltavi. If we buy a few of the other kings they'll stand by us when Cynfellyn turns up!"

Icel pondered the situation for a short while. He could see that the rest of us supported Wulfstan's call to take the city.

"Very well. Marcellus, go to the Corieltavi. Take some of my Iceni lords with you for a show of strength. Tell them that the Corieltavi have been shamed by Tasciovarus' lack of honour and we have been greatly offended. We can't allow this sleight to go unpunished and Tasciovarus will feel the wrath of the Angelcynn. However, we recognise that the other kings of the Corieltavi acted in good faith and we still extend the hand of friendship to these great kingdoms. We will prove our good faith by granting them some of Tasciovarus' wealth, and also by supporting their attack against Cynfellyn to regain their lost lands."

Marcellus left straight away with his companions. Icel rewarded Ceneu handsomely and I told Bors, Gaheris and Triphun Namatius that I would be equally generous to them and Artorius when I returned. I gleaned what news of home I could from them, and they left us the following morning.

Once again we returned to waiting and watching from the walls. I made the south folk men practise their warcraft, and Icel followed my example with his army. I pondered the nature of the Wealh as I walked the grassy battlements. I understood Artorius' frustration with his people. I wondered how I would have felt if Angel lords had sided with the Danes, or the Franks, against their own kin, in order to gain silver or land. In the old land we could even depend on the Saxons and Jutes to stand by us in need, and they knew that we wouldn't leave them to stand alone. The Wealh tribes were so full of their ancient emnities that they couldn't recognise the threat from the newcomers.

Marcellus returned after eight days. The Corieltavi kings would be prepared to stand back and allow us to take Ratae. They sent demands that they wanted met in return for their indifference, none of which was as much as I would have wanted in their place. They were a timorous tribe. Wulfstan scoffed when he heard the list,

"We could send them some balls while we're at it!"

Our venture into the kingdoms of the Wealh was bearing fruit! It was promising to deliver us a far greater prize than we had hoped for when we set out from home. Best of all, as far as I was concerned, the adventure had completely restored Wulfstan's spirits.

I stood on the battlements with him, Oswine and Gram, staring out into the night.

"I can remember, years ago when I was just a lad, arguing with Anna at a feast at Wyfburrh," I told them in a reflective moment. "I told him that we weren't like the Danes and the Franks. I said that we didn't covet other peoples' lands, we just defended our own. That somehow made us more honourable in my tender, young mind."

Wulfstan chuckled.

"Now, here we are." I paused as I sought the words. "We're conquerors, like the Romans. We're changing the world. We are going to march, out there, surrounded by enemies, like wading out into a lake. There'll be no refuge out there. We win, or we die."

"Only the gods know our fate, Wulfhere, you of all people know that. Even if you stay safe in your hall, you won't live forever. Weigh the risks, boy. New land, wealth, horses? Who knows what we'll win. If we die, it's better than waiting for age and sickness to catch up with us, so why worry. Live by your wits, live by your sword. It's what we're best at, Wolf lord!"

CHAPTER 4: Tasciovarus' Reckoning

Icel sent messengers to Dubrovae instructing the warriors there to leave enough men to hold the town and maintain order, and join us straight away. He gave Durovigutum to one of the lords from the old land who had joined the north folk. His name was Godmund. The Wealh town and the surrounding land was truly ours. Durovigutum was now Godmund's Ceaster.

We marched out as soon as we were ready. It would take at least three days to reach Ratae. We needed to take the wagons, to carry our supplies, and to bring back plunder once we'd taken the city.

I walked at the head of the army, with Icel.

"We need to finish this quickly," I told him. "We'll have to send folk from the old country to farm the land and bolster our strength. We will also need to be able to hold all the bridges and the new towns. What about the fenland? Will the fen folk pose a threat to travellers? Are there outlaws?"

"There's no power in the fens," Icel assured me. "The villages are small, and suspicious of strangers. They resent outsiders but they pose no threat. They won't hinder us. There are a few decent sized places, like the Isle of Eels, but the living is poor. Watermen mostly, living off the marshes with a few beasts grazing the islands. You're right, we need to put all of our effort into building our strength and defending what we've taken from Cynfellyn."

We marched all day along the firm, dry street making steady progress. Spies would no doubt be carrying word of our march to Tasciovarus and the army of Caer Lerion would be mustering, if it hadn't already mustered.

We reached the Nen early on the secnd day. I crossed first, with the south folk warriors, to provide defence of the ford. The wagons crossed while the north folk guarded the rear, and then they followed on. Once over the river, I made sure that everybody was in the right place, and urged watchfulness.

After noon we saw a body of about twenty mounted warriors across the fields to the north. The flat lands closer to the fens had given way to a gently rolling landscape, and the horsemen looked down on us from a low ridge. Presumably they had come to investigate a raiding party and discovered an army. Their appearance was perfect, it reminded the men what they were here for, and reinforced my call for watchfulness. I laughed with excitement and anticipation.

"Do you see them? I want a horse! I want to ride home. What's their gear like lads? Good plunder here by the look of it!" I couldn't contain myself. The battle was almost here. In the rumble of the heavy wagon wheels I heard Tiw's bass laughter.

"I know your price, lord Tiw. Rivers of blood. I swear, lord that you shall have it!"

I saw Wulfstan watching me with that expression that he had worn so many times in the past when I talked of Tiw.

"Tiw is with us, Wulfstan, can you hear him laughing?"

"The only one laughing is you, you mad bastard." Wulfstan replied with his usual bluntness and I roared at his sour face.

"Don't you see Wulfstan? When Tiw is with us, we can't lose, we are invincible! It is decided by fate!"

My excitement was rubbing off on the men nearest to me. The waelcyrge started a reedy incantation. Many of them had heard the stories that Tiw appeared to me, and granted me victories. Now they were seeing for themselves my excitement at the impending slaughter. Battle is a frightening thing. Fear and courage, are both infectious. Fear can spread through an army and make them run. By the same token faint hearts will draw courage from heroes. My father had been a man whose strength and ferocity made the men around him braver. Wulfstan was such a man. He had told me when I was a lad that one day I might be such a man. That day was here.

I laughed and shouted as I drew my sword and hurled it high into the air, catching it neatly by the hilt and brandishing it above my head. My men at the head of the column were putting up the chant of "WOLF! WOLF! WOLF!" and it was taken up all along the column. It swelled and roared and must have carried a blood curdling warning of death all across the landscape. The horsemen wheeled away and disappeared.

"They are scared of a word!" I laughed. "How will they feel when you form the war hedge and offer them your spears, warriors of the Wolf?" A cheer went up as the horses disappeared, and the men believed that we were invincible. We surrounded our camp with sharpened stakes and kept a keen watch that night but the dark hours passed without incident.

All through the next day Tasciovarus' riders kept pace with our march. They made no attempt to attack or harry us in any way. They just maintained a watch. The day trundled by to the sound of our rumbling cart wheels and the murmur of a marching army. We made our camp long before dark in an open field. We surrounded it with the sharpened stakes which we had carried with us. We were closer to the enemy's heartland and the risk of a night attack was greater than before. I had fires prepared away from the camp, outside the wall of stakes, to reveal any attack, and we stood sentries at the stake wall all night. Once we had eaten we dampened our cooking fires.

After midnight we heard the Wealh, calling out beyond the firelight, trying to unnerve us. I laughed aloud and howled like a wolf into the night,

"What's this? Have you come for a chat, you mangy, goat-fucking, arse-holes! We've come to fight! Why don't you come over and find out?" The watchmen laughed at my challenge.

The Wealh were weak. They obviously weren't ready to try and stop us. They weren't going to attack. If they were they would have come on silently. This was just a tactic to unnerve us and deprive us of sleep. It was quite likely that they might try and creep in and cut a few throats though, so when the watch fires began to die down I called Gram, Marcellus, Odd and three of the Wolf Pack lads to come with me to feed the flames.

"Bring plenty of wood. I want those fires to burn brightly and show us all of the ground outside our camp. They'll probably try to take us so have your weapons ready!"

We had stoked up three fires when the Wealh erupted out of the night shrieking like demons, trying to scare us into weakness.

We threw down our firewood and backed together in a ring, all facing outwards, weapons ready. We only had moments to react but we were warriors, not nervous fyrdsmen, and our blades were sharp and waiting. In the eerie, flickering light I watched them come. They passed swiftly through the orange tinted firelight and became black silhouettes, demonic apparitions brandishing spears and shields, with the flames flickering behind them.

With a mad shout the lead warrior leaped high and flung himself bodily at me. It was a stupid mistake which made my attack easy. His thrust could only come from above. I blocked it with my shield, and opened his belly with the shining edge of my sword. The momentum of his leap carried him forward. He hit the ground hard. The jarring impact burst his guts from the gaping stomach wound, and he rolled into Gram's legs, knocking him to the floor. I lost my grip on the sword and quickly ripped my seaxe from its scabbard, looking to see that Gram was alright. A second warrior launched himself at me. I didn't have time to swing the seaxe. I punched my shield edge into his hate filled face, smashing his teeth and hammering consciousness from his head.

Gram didn't have time to regain his feet. Another Wealh warrior closed with him as he was pushing himself up. There was a hollow thump as Gram raised his shield and blocked the spear thrust but the foeman clattered into him and they crashed to earth, together, grappling desperately. The Wealh drew his knife and tried to force it down into Gram's face.

"Hold him, Gram!" I yelled, and with a backhanded swing I hacked my heavy seaxe into the side of his opponent's head. The blade bit deep and I twisted it with a flick of my wrist, flipping the top of the skull wide open. Skull, scalp and brain slopped onto Gram's face, making him curse viciously. I looked for the next attack but several of our warriors had dashed from the camp to help us and the Wealh were running for the trees and the safety of the night. Gram regained his feet spitting the revolting slime from his mouth with a good deal of hawking and cursing. He stalked back to the camp to wash the filth from his head and try to get the stink out of his war gear.

The Wealh had meant to mount a lightning fast attack and overwhelm us. They had been met with a savagery that they hadn't anticipated and melted back into the darkness. We stripped the corpses of gear and possessions and threw them onto the fires. The rest of the night was quiet.

Dawn came as a thin strip of grey at the eastern edge of the sky. The grey light strengthened, unnoticed. Creeping slowly around the trees and hills by degrees until, suddenly, it was morning. The air was fresh and chill, brand new for that day. Birdsong saturated the sky all around. Stars caught out in the half-light hurried away to catch up with the night and leave the day behind.

The sounds of the camp gradually swelled. The coughing, spitting, farting and cursing of an army waking up and emerging from beneath their cloaks. Amongst the low murmur of hoarse, morning voices came the sounds of cooking and eating. These were pierced by the shouted instructions of lords and captains, and men cursing each other for laziness, tardiness, or just out of bullying animosity. Pots were cleared away, fires doused, and wagons loaded. Then there was the grind of movement; the rattling and grating of wooden wheels, and the whisper of men on the march, the sounds of approaching death.

As much as I had enjoyed the night, it paled to nothing now that this day had begun. The web of wyrd would be made plain for many men today, a day of fate, a day of destiny. This day we would fight for a kingdom. This would be a day of excitement, fear, sorrow and elation. A day of noise and spectacle. Of horses, of men, of metal, of reeking blood and shining, stinking guts. A mind-rending day of wild, staring eyes, of shrieking hate, of blood filled mouths, red rimming white teeth. Of pale, waxy dead flesh, purple bruised, and livid red and black. It would be a day of shouting, of singing, of screaming and wild, demonic, uncontrolled laughter and tears. A few hours filled with every emotion a man can know.

Afterwards, there would be utter emptiness, exhaustion and limb-shaking weakness, which would feed the madness of the battle field. Strange sights: hands, feet, and heads, lying amidst thick, congealing blood. Lost and broken weapons. Whimpering, moaning, crying, proud warriors, dying hard, calling for wives or mothers who will never know how their last hours bled slowly away in terror and agony. The magpie, crow, raven and kite relishing eyes, or pecking their way in through the arsehole to the feast inside. Dead flesh in a field. So much carrion left bloated, stinking, rotten and decaying where it fell. Life ended, while life goes on.

My stomach fluttered, my legs felt heavy, my breathing and heart beat were hurried and I had that familiar sharpness of sight and hearing. I knew these feelings so well, I knew what they presaged. I knew when I reached the field my pounding heart would lend my limbs speed and power. My eyes would see things happening with stark clarity, allowing me to anticipate and counter my enemies as if they were moving in a dream.

As our march started I hurried up and down the column. I couldn't keep still, I couldn't speak with anyone. I was Tiw's swordsman, taut as a bow string, eager for the kill. All through the morning we marched along that wide, firm street, the blue sky above us half full with fluffy white clouds. In other times a pleasant day for a walk, but I didn't notice the weather, or the green grass or any of the colours and sounds of the day. I saw only the horsemen who thought they were shadowing us unseen all morning. I watched them working in groups to keep concealed pace with our march. Finally, I noticed when they suddenly turned from behind the hawthorn bushes that they thought were hiding them, and slipped away down the far slope. I saw that we were approaching a ridge and could not see what lay beyond. The street had led us into a spoon shaped depression with higher ground on three sides. I thought that there was only one reason why those spies would have left us at this particular place, having watched us so carefully all day.

"Attack! Attack! Form your wall! Bowmen on the wagons!"

The men rushed to their places, shields overlapping, spears bristling. A solid ring of limewood, and shining blades, all around our wagons. There was a rush of jostling and shouting as they fell into place and then, a watchful silence fell over the army as they looked for the enemy.

Nothing happened. Time stretched out, men started to look around for answers, what ambush? Lords and captains looked at me. I was standing at the head of the column, where my men took pride of place, where Odd had raised my standard of the Wolf.

"Renweard, you're fast, get up to that ridge and......." The sentence went unfinished. A great shout of many, many voices washed over us from beyond the ridges ahead and to the sides. With a thunderous rumble, which made the ground shake, horsemen came flooding over the top of the hill to our front. A hundred yelling riders charged into view, followed by a human tide of shouting warriors. The horsemen came on wildly, fearlessly, racing each other to get to us first. Leaning forward over their wide eyed mounts, eager for the fray.

Our arrows started to fly over our heads, hissing through the air. One horse swerved left and right and then tumbled to the floor bringing a second crashing down. The horsemen split as they approached the head of our column where my men held the ground. Living rivers of horses flowed down both sides of our column, the riders hurling their spears into our ranks. I saw some of our men go down, but the wounded were dragged back behind the shields, the gaps were closed and the wall stayed solid. In riding the length of our column the horsemen were exposing themselves to a constant shower of arrows which bristled in their horses' flanks, causing many of them to career wildly away from the terrifying source of noise and pain. Some of our men hurled spears and several horses crashed to earth or threw their riders as they veered away. Still the sweat slicked horse flesh thundered across our front in a magnificent but fruitless first thrust from Tasciovarus.

The attack was well timed. As the horsemen cleared the end of the column the shrieking foot warriors were closing the last few yards, throwing spears, hammers, rocks, all manner of objects in a bid to open a gap in the wall, but the wall stayed firm. Many of our warriors hurled their spears into the onrushing mass, bringing men crashing to the ground and breaking up the weight of the charge. Our captains shouted for their men to brace for the impact. Those behind leant their weight to those at the front. Arrows flew eagerly into the leading ranks of the Wealh. There was that last split second of anticipation and then the great crunching, booming sound of the armies colliding, shield to shield. The tumult became a solid wall of sound. Screams, shouts, and gasped roars of exertion became a continuous tide of noise, as waves of superbly fit men heaved at each other, all the time trying to stab, to butt, to bite, in short, to do whatever would ensure that they lived.

Our wall had held. It had creaked and bowed in places at the savage onslaught but it had held. The bowmen were firing down into the second and third ranks of the Wealh, inflicting hurt and chipping away at the will and determination of the attackers. My lads at the head of the column were solid as a rock. When the Wealh assault hit home our front rank held them and the second and third ranks killed them with brutal precision. The Wealh attack foundered and withered as their leading warriors were steadily slaughtered by the warriors of the Wolf, and they backed off, leaving a bloody high tide mark of dead and dying men lying broken before our shields. They stood, and yelled incomprehensible threats and insults which were met by a grim silence.

Elsewhere the fighting was furious.

"Stand firm lads!" I yelled, and left my men. I made my way back down the column, squeezing, where I could, between the wagons and the heaving lines of warriors, pausing to yell encouragement. A couple of times I got the chance to inflict a wound over the shoulders of our front rank against desperate opponents. Two thirds of the way down the column I saw that our wall had been pushed back against a wagon and it looked as if it was going to break. Bowmen were loosing their shafts almost directly into the Wealh who were concentrating at that point. I ran hard to get there and as I approached saw that a huge Wealh warrior was laying about himself with a great club, battering our men backwards. Three arrows were stuck in him but still he roared and bellowed and his fellows pushed forward around him. They had more or less opened a corridor to the wagons with our men forced back on each side. As I reached the breech the first of the Wealh was ducking down to go under the wagon and attack our shield wall from behind. He looked up as I reached him, realised his peril, and re-doubled his efforts to get through. Not quick enough. I stabbed my blade down into his exposed back, severing his spine. He gave a series of insane shrieks of pain and terror as I stood on him and wrenched the blade out, looking all the while for my next opponent. Angel and Wealh were locked together in desperate fighting. Two men were scrabbling about on the ground at my feet, each trying to force an opening for his blade. I kicked the Wealh on the side of his jaw, stood on the stunned wretch's head to hold him still, and drove my sword through his neck. He twitched and jerked on the floor, his legs kicking wildly. I heaved the Angel fighter to his feet and pushed him to my right to shield me as I cut down the Wealh warrior who was fighting on the other side of the breach. He had his back to me and with one weighty swing I virtually took his head off.

The breach was closed. The bowmen were still loosing their shafts, helping to hold the Wealh off us, but the great ogre was still roaring, half sobbing, and flailing around with his club. Now that I was close I could see that he was no warrior. He seemed to me to be a simpleton. He was crying like a terrified child, roaring words of temper, hurt and fear, rather than just animal sounds of exertion. He shouldn't have been here. His size and strength made him a formidable enemy, but he was plainly terrified, and confused by the noise and rage around him. Another madly shrieking Wealh hurled himself at me, and I dropped my shield and grabbed him by the throat. He slashed at my arm as I drove him backwards at the sobbing, snot faced giant. As he saw me coming the ogre swung his club, succeeding only in breaking the leg of the man I still held by the throat as a shield. I hurled him against the monster who was turning to face me, but too slowly. I swung my sword so hard that I almost fell, and hacked into the side of his knee. As the giant turned, all of his weight was on the half severed joint and the knee snapped, with a crack like cobble stones being dashed together. The huge simpleton collapsed with a bellow like a distressed bullock. He dropped his club and was wailing and crying like a child, clutching at his snapped leg which stuck out at a bizarre angle. As quickly as I could, I aimed two blows at his neck and left his head half severed.

I stared down at his wide, frantic eyes. Surely dead, his face betrayed the terror of his last moments. I felt sick at the fate of this enormous simpleton. I wanted to slaughter them all, every single one, for what they had forced upon this child-like giant. I gave a wild shout of wordless fury and stormed out in front of our shield wall, in amongst the enemy. I laid about me to left and right, severing arms and legs, splitting skulls, slicing through necks and throats, cursing the dogs for the filthy cowards they were and exacting retribution on any part of a Wealh body which was within my reach. I felt a blow to the back of my shoulder, but I didn't heed it. A dying man was stabbing weakly at my right leg. I swung my sword backhanded and cut his arm off, mid-way between elbow and wrist.

One moment I was in the midst of the Wealh, surrounded by the shrieking, terrified men that I had hacked to the ground, and then suddenly there were Angel warriors on either side of me. The Wealh were running from us, abandoning their wounded to our blades. I turned to my right and cut down an enemy warrior who was struggling against our shield wall.

"Get back, lord!"

I looked round and horsemen were careering back along our front, looking to try to exploit gaps in our ranks. I dashed back into our wall and somebody handed me back my shield. I nodded my thanks and stepped back behind the men who were closing up tightly again. I looked around, regaining my bearings, shaking with exertion and shock. I was drenched in blood. Mine or theirs? I couldn't tell. I jumped up onto the nearest wagon to get a look at the battle. All down one side of our column the Wealh were fleeing, but on the other the fight still raged. I crossed the wagon and leaped down onto the far side. I ran to the head of the column where my companions still stood unmolested by the daunted Wealh. I called Gram, Wulfstan and Oswine to me.

We pushed through our shield wall and tore into the Wealh who were attacking the men next to my fearsome warriors. Wulfstan was back to his old self, roaring curses as his blood slicked sword rose and fell again and again. Our enemies tumbled before us as we cut into them, until my arm was so tired I could barely hold my sword. The Wealh were trapped. If they turned to face us they were hacked down by our men in the shield wall, if they continued the fight to their front they were butchered by our eager blades.

There was another shouted warning as the horsemen made another charge to try to take us by surprise. I grabbed Wulfstan and dragged him back into the shield wall while our bowmen loosed what shafts they still had at the horses. The Wealh broke and ran from our spearmen, who started to give chase, but were quickly called back.

The savaged Wealh rallied on the surrounding ridges while their captains goaded them into another charge. I knew our bowmen must be almost out of arrows and I wanted to break the next Wealh assault before it careered downhill into our tired and battered shield wall.

"Lads, pick up the spears, stones, axes, hammers, anything you can throw when they charge!"

I strode out through our shield wall. I wanted to bolster our men so I hurled my sword high again with a great shout, catching everyone's attention.

"Well done my brave lads! You've fought hard! Your children and your children's children will tell the story of this day around the winter fire and you will live forever through their words. I am proud to have stood shoulder to shoulder with you this day. We will break the next charge, and the one after that and the one after that if needs be. Tiw is here with us my lads. The fates have decided that this day will be ours, so hold your line and cut them down. Their land will be ours! Their wealth will be ours! We are the Wolf! WOLF! WOLF! WOLF!" The chant was taken up and the men beat their shields in time to their shouts.

With a roar, the enemy charged again. I retreated behind our shields and waited for the impact.

Ten yards from our front the Wealh were met by a blizzard of weapons hurled by our lads, with the strength of desperation behind them. The impetus of the charge faltered as men fell, stumbled or avoided those who had fallen in front of them. Instead of hitting the shield wall like a hammer blow, the charge hit home piecemeal and failed, woefully, to break our line. Once again the ferocious close quarter fight was joined, but because the charge lacked force our men in the second rank could apply themselves to attacking the Wealh rather than just lending their weight to hold the press. Those bowmen who had loosed all of their arrows had seized spears and were now using them to stab over the front rank at the heads of the Wealh.

The fanatical courage of the Wealh had been subdued by the grim resolution of the shield wall. Wild eyed fury was now grim resignation. They had been outnumbered from the start and now their dead and wounded were piled before our shields. Injured men were limping, staggering or dragging themselves away from our spears. Their greatest and bravest lay broken upon the field. Our bowmen had taken a steady toll of their horses and only thirty or forty horsemen still remained on the field, on tired, bloody mounts.

On one side of our column the attack faltered and fell back. They rallied twenty feet away but attempts to get them to charge again had only roused them to a couple of hesitant steps forward. The odds seemed hopeless. A hero stepped forward. He had the dark hair of the Roman, like Marcellus. He wore mail, and wielded sword and shield. He brandished his sword, shouting a hoarse challenge in his own tongue. Then he turned away from us to face his men, berating them, praising them, urging them to greater courage, to one last mighty effort. One of our lads stepped forward and hurled a spear which pierced him like a spitted pig.

The Wealh were stunned by the blow, a half-hearted shout of anger and dismay went up as their hero fell to the cruel shaft. Some charged, some came on a few paces, others didn't move. As the few brave souls charged home and were slain, the rest looked on crestfallen. Then, in silence, they turned and started to lope from the field, first in ones and twos and then the whole army. On the other side of the column the sight of their friends running away up the far slope was too much. The broken army gave up the struggle and ran for home.

The horsemen could do nothing by themselves, but these were the lords of Caer Lerion and they were reluctant to hand us victory and power in the land. One young warrior kicked his mount forward and charged headlong at my lads at the head of the column, screaming his challenge and his hate, his face twisted with rage and anguish. The horse wasn't stupid though and, at the last moment, it veered aside from the shining spear heads. The rider lost his seat and sprawled over his mount's shoulder crashing to earth at the feet of the Wolf Pack. In a moment the dashing young warrior was dead, bloody flesh.

A large group turned their horses' heads and rode away to the west, ignoring the shouts of their companions. There was a brief argument and then the whole group broke up, with riders turning their horses and heading off in different directions. They were going home to their loved ones, either to abandon their halls and flee, or to wait and see what the future would bring. At the last, a group of eight horsemen sat together. The leader walked his tired mount forward and gave us a speech, which we couldn't understand, before turning to leave.

I ran to the head of the column while he was speaking and threw down a challenge. I thought that this man must be Tasciovarus, and I wanted to kill him there and then.

"Tasciovarus! Faithless coward! Fight me! Fight me here and die with some dignity!"

Although I could not speak his language the message was obvious. I left the shelter of our ranks, walking forward over the dead and dying, to offer my challenge. He looked at me, looked at his companions and then rode away. I sheathed my sword and picked up a spear in case this was just a ruse and he was going to come charging back over the ridge, but it wasn't. Eventually Gram ran past me and up the slope.

"They're leaving, lord."

A cheer went up from our ranks and once again the cry of "WOLF! WOLF! WOLF!" rang out.

"Gram, stay with me!"

I had to find Icel. This victory would count for nothing if we didn't sieze Ratae straight away.

Icel had made his way to the head of the column and he was talking and laughing with Wulfstan and his own hearth companions. Leofa, the guide, was on the fringes of the group.

"Leofa, how far is Ratae from here?"

"I don't know exactly, lord but it isn't far. Three or four miles I would think."

"Icel," I grasped his arm in order to hold his attention. "We don't want a siege, we must take it quickly. We've defeated their army here today and now they're scattered. I will take my army on to Ratae. You look to the wounded and the spoils of battle and follow on as soon as you can. Leofa, four miles, where?"

"North west, lord," Leofa indicated the direction. "Follow the street."

"Lord Wulfhere!" It was Icel. As always he had the sense of the poet. "This was a great victory. I salute you my war lord."

"We don't have the victory until we have the city. I must go. I will see you in Ratae." I ran back up the slope so that I could address the army.

"Men of the south folk! Quench your thirst, bind your wounds and then follow me. King Icel will take care of our wounded."

CHAPTER 5: Ratae Corieltavorum

Standing two thirds of the way up the slope I looked down on the scene of glory and triumph. Our men were tending to injured friends, or searching through the piles of bodies which perfectly ringed our wagons. Wounded Wealh were being slaughtered. I was becoming aware of the injuries I had picked up. The slash across my forearm I knew about and it would need stitching together, but I also had three long cuts on my legs, and a gash on my left shoulder which I couldn't even remember getting. They were stiffening now and I thought the run to Ratae was going to be uncomfortable.

As soon as the slope was filled with victorious south folk warriors I called them into order and turned and set off. At the top of the ridge I was stopped in my tracks. As I reached the crest and looked down the far side I was confronted by a scene of desolation. Dozens of wounded men were laying or sitting on the reverse slope and more were trying to make their way along the street towards Ratae. Amongst them were a few abandoned horses, too badly hurt to carry their riders to safety. When they saw us the wounded men cried out in alarm and many of them tried pathetically to struggle away.

I surveyed the dismal scene. Six feet in front of me a man with his lower leg hanging on by threads of flesh looked up at me with anguish and agony his face. Sitting at his side was another warrior with his jaw hacked away. I drew my sword, causing another panic stricken cry to rise from the Wealh.

"Let's get this done with lads. Be quick, we've got to get to Ratae."

The man with the ruined leg hung his head forward to make the killing stroke easier. His friend hesitated briefly but then followed his example. I finished them both quickly and cleanly. I didn't feel like chasing helpless cripples around the hillside so I left the men to it. I walked slowly along the street with Gram at my shoulder. When they had finished their bloody work and helped themselves to whatever trinkets their victims were carrying, the men fell in behind me. Once I was satisfied that we were all present I picked up the pace and we jogged on. The north folk warriors would no doubt be reaping the plunder on the reverse sides of the other slopes that fringed our battle field.

As we jogged along the track we periodically overtook injured fugitives who were unable to maintain the pace of their escape. Some pleaded, some made a courageous stand, some just accepted the end, all died where they stood or sat. After a couple of miles we had a real stroke of luck. I saw a horse standing beneath a tree, fifty yards from the street. I halted the men and jogged across to it with Gram and Leofmund. The horse was uneasy, and at first I feared an ambush, but as we drew nearer we saw that the horse's rider was dead on the ground by his mount. It looked as though a broad headed arrow intended for the horse had pierced his thigh, and he had bled to death from the wound. The horse's flank was drenched in blood as was the rider's leg, groin and belly and it was probably the smell of the blood and the rider's unusual reactions that were making the creature uneasy. We took the pale warrior's sword, shield and fine mail shirt. I examined the horse for wounds but, apart from a cut on its fore leg, it seemed unharmed. He was a strong, stocky beast. A dark brown colour with an even darker mane. I spoke softly to him and held his head, leading him calmly back towards the road. Once I was away from the tree and the blood soaked body I mounted the skittish beast. He danced and fretted at first but settled to my commands and I led the column away, sitting proudly on my new stallion. I decided to call him Victory.

We stopped briefly at an abandoned village by a ford where a couple of men washed my horse down. I told Marcellus to announce to the surrounding country that Icel was now the king of Caer Lerion and that all people would enjoy his protection in return for their loyalty. I had no doubt that the villagers would be watching us from nearby hiding places. As soon as the blood had been washed from Victory we were off again. I knew we must be close to Ratae and I wanted to hurry on before they were warned of our approach.

We ran through a landscape of low rolling ridges. The land was green and rich, with woodland and hedgerows breaking up the well-tended fields and pastures. We passed farms and villages at regular intervals but they had all been deserted. This was a good land. Our people would live well here, and make Icel wealthy and very powerful.

We jogged over another ridge and caught our first glimpses of Ratae between the trees. The city was on slightly higher ground only three quarters of a mile ahead. I hurried the men quickly down over the crest and out of sight of the walls but I was sure that they must have seen us.

We had to get into the town straight away. If they closed us out we would be in an awkward position. We didn't want to have large numbers of men killed trying to assault the walls, nor did we want to be stuck outside the gates mounting a prolonged siege. If Cynfellyn arrived while we were outside the city we would have to fight his army with the men of Ratae ready to flood out of the gates and attack us from the rear. None of us would see our homes again.

The Romans had known a thing or two about warfare. The city had been placed to command the surrounding country and I had seen, from our brief glimpse of the old walls, that there was no way that we would be able to approach unobserved. There was something that gave me hope though. As we reached the top of the next ridge and began our last dash towards the town I could see people hurrying for safety from all directions. Our appearance would spread panic amongst the fugitives and cause them to rush for the gates. With a bit of luck the press of terrified folk trying to get in would prevent the guards from shutting us out.

I urged the lads forward, yelling at them to get to the gate. They were running hard, pouring down the ridge, getting strung out as the faster men pushed ahead. There was less than half a mile to go. The Wealh were panicking, women screaming, all running for their lives. There were two or three carts with possessions loaded on board being driven towards the gate. I could see guards urging the fugitives to hurry and I kicked Victory forward. The horse was almost exhausted but he responded and I admired his spirit and courage. I could see the guards looking from me to the fleeing people and back again, trying to weigh up whether they should close the gate or get the last stragglers inside. I was a hundred yards away now, galloping hard, overtaking desperate families, who were looking wildly around, terrified and confused, so close to safety, so far from safety.

One of the guards lowered his spear and came at me. I leaped from Victory with my sword in my hand and went straight at him. The other guards were starting to pull the gates shut, urging the panicking fugitives inside. The Wealh watchman thrust his spear at me, but I parried it and crashed straight into him, hitting him high and knocking him to the ground.

I staggered and almost fell, but I was almost at the gate. I didn't stop to finish him, I had to stop them shutting that gate. The warrior nearest to me had laid his spear and shield aside while he helped to pull the heavy gate closed. He clutched at the hilt of his dagger but he was too slow and I cut him down. Two more guards left their toil and dashed to snatch up their weapons.

One of the gates was closed. I hurled my shoulder against the solid oak of the second one and forced it wide again.

The spearman who I had first sent sprawling had regained his feet and was coming at me. I glanced beyond him. My nearest men were about two hundred yards away and running hard. I parried his thrust but the spearman leapt back out of the reach of my counter stroke. The other two guards joined him and I was like a bear at bay. I turned first to one then to another warning them back. Then, with a shout to bolster their courage, they all rushed me together. I parried a fierce thrust with my shield but felt a heavy blow to my thigh which made me topple forward. The third spear was thrust past my shield and it thumped into my side causing an agonising, burning, bolt of pain. In a furious moment of fear and desperation I made a wild backhanded swing at the nearest spearman, cutting his face in half just below the eyes. Before I could swing again I was crushed to the ground as one of the remaining guards flung himself onto me. I felt my wounded side tear and a shout of pain was forced from my throat. The guard drew his knife and tried to stab down into my throat. I had lost my sword, and my left arm was trapped under my shield. I grasped his wrist with my right hand and tried to push him off but pain ripped through my side again and my strength failed. His face was inches from mine as he tried to force his blade down. I twisted, forcing his knife over my shoulder, and seized his nose between my teeth. He tried to pull away but I held him and got more purchase with my jaws. My mouth filled with blood as he screamed and clawed at my eyes. There was a sudden shout, a rushing sound, and I almost lost my teeth as he was hurled bodily from me.

 My men were sweeping past me into the city. The guards were dead and I was hauled robustly to my feet, causing me to cry out in pain. It was Gram. I grimaced and half spat, half dribbled the blood, and a lump of gristle, from my mouth.

 "Lord, are you badly hurt?" Gram was trying to look at the wound in my side.

 "A spear thrust. I don't think it's too bad, Gram," I growled through the pain.

 I leaned back against the gate, my right hand resting on his shoulder, my left arm held tenderly against my side. I was gasping for breath but my side was agony if I breathed too deeply. Marcellus cleaned my sword and handed it back to me. I sheathed it and asked him to bring my shield. Hunched over, unable to straighten, with my left arm tight to my injured side, I tried to walk through the open gate but my thigh gave me a stab of sudden pain. It felt as though a rock had been pushed between the muscles and the bone. I just couldn't pull my leg forward.

 "Gram, give me one of those spears," I pointed to the spears that the gate keepers had been wielding.

 Using it as a staff, I hobbled into the city, our city.

 The people of Ratae Corieltavum hadn't expected to see us so soon after the battle. Fleeing riders might well have spread word of the defeat but no doubt the folk would have expected us to halt and tend to our wounded before pushing on. Those who lived outside the town walls had been making their way in, to safety, along with people from outlying farms. They were trying to put up a fight. It was a mistake. They provoked a savage response from warriors fired by victory and their own invincibility. This time I couldn't stop them. Even if I wasn't hurt I would have let them plunder the city. This was Icel's city, not mine. The plunder of Ratae would be just reward for our spilt blood, and fitting retribution for the treachery of Tasciovarus' people. The screams of the tortured city filled the air and hammered at my ears. I closed my mind to the carnage and concentrated on limping through the town in search of the royal hall. Odd joined us with my banner. Wedda, Leofmund and Penda were with me. Wulfstan and Oswine came hurrying to find me and said the hall was a short way ahead. We made our way, painfully slowly, like a procession of mourners, along the stone paved streets between the houses.

The Hall was an old Roman building, like the forum at Godmund's Ceaster. The grandeur had been diminished by repairs and alterations, but it was still a wondrous thing. The roof tiles had been replaced with thatch, and in one or two places damaged stonework had been replaced with timbers covered in daub. The building was on a grand scale with stone columns, and a damaged statue, proclaiming its importance. We walked between high stone walls, through a gateway into a great courtyard. There was another statue in the middle, surrounded by a pool of green water. There were buildings to three sides of the courtyard and, directly opposite the gateway, steps led up to a large double doorway. Wedda pushed the eight feet high doors wide open and I hobbled into a room big enough to fit most halls inside.

A fire was smouldering in the middle of the floor. Abandoned tables and benches indicated that this was indeed the royal hall, but there were no guards, and no sign of the king. The only folk left at the hall were the men and women of the royal household, and they grovelled and wept on their knees before us, certain that their time had come. Tasciovarus had abandoned his people to whatever fate might befall them, and I spat in disgust. I needed to rest. I told Marcellus to reassure the wretches that they were safe and that if they had families in the city they should fetch them here for safety. I told Odd to find us some ale and I tried to remove my mail shirt which had been badly hacked and torn. Leofmund came to my aid, unfastening the straps and lifting the heavy shirt from my shoulders. Removing the weight eased the stress on my side, and, after an initial wave of pain as I adjusted my stance, I could breathe a little more easily.

We examined the wound. My left side had been cut open at the height of my navel. Three inches from the belly button the spear had pierced the skin, but luckily, as I had been moving rapidly to my right, the blade had cut across and out of my side rather than piercing my gut. Leofmund looked closely and said he didn't think that it had done any serious damage to my insides. This was a relief, but it didn't lessen the pain, which was a continuous throbbing, as if someone was holding a red hot iron against my side. He removed my leather arm and leg armour and my trousers, and we looked at the thigh wound. Again I was lucky, the wound was deep but it was on the outside of the thigh away from the big blood tubes.

"I need a healer. Tell Marcellus to find one. There must be one in the city"

Odd had returned with ale and we drank to Tiw and to our victory, which reminded me.

"Where's my horse?" I looked at the faces around me.

"Your man Haeddi has got it," Wulfstan laughed. "I reckon he's been waiting for this moment ever since you came here!" Haeddi had looked after my horses back in the old country, I laughed but it hurt my side too much and I ceased abruptly with a grunt of pain.

Marcellus was ushering another family into the safety of the hall. They were clearly nervous of my rugged companions in their war gear, decorated with fresh cuts and bruises. They caught sight of me, naked, bruised and bloody and the woman said something to Marcellus.

"Lord, this woman knows of a healer, we'll fetch her for you."

They left, and I told Odd to get our guests a drink. I felt cold, and shivered suddenly. Leofmund built up the fire before going off and searching through the hall. He returned with a cloak and some skins which I wrapped myself in, and sat by the fire like an old crone. Now that I was off my feet and the pain was slightly eased my thoughts turned to the plight of Ratae.

"We need to restore some order to the city. Let the men take what they want but try to stop the slaughter of the people. Icel will need them. You know what Tiw expects of my army," I announced to the assembled warriors. "Leofmund I want you to stay, Wulfstan, you do what you like. Penda and Odd, watch the door, Wedda take some men and go all through this hall, let's see what we've got."

CHAPTER 6: Magic and Myth

The men rose to their feet and went about their tasks. Wulfstan and Oswine joined me by the fire.

"We've seen it all before," Wulfstan said simply. "So what now? Do we return to Godmunds Ceaster or stay here with Icel?"

"My job was to win the battle. I've done that. I don't think I'll be travelling far for a week or two, but I think that we can leave this to Icel. The lords of the south folk will want to take their rewards and get back to their farms." I thought about the situation for a while. "There will be a lot of people arriving from Angel. We need to get home to sort them out."

"When's your next little one due? You'll want to be home so that you can put another one up her, won't you?" Wulfstan gave the conversation his usual earthy content, Oswine chuckled.

"Well can you blame me?" I countered.

"You've got a fair point there, young Wulfhere. She certainly is a beauty. I've often wondered why she chose to wed the mad, badly scarred, immensely rich and powerful, lord Wulfhere?" Wulfstan asked with false curiosity. Oswine laughed out loud and if my side didn't hurt so much I would have joined him.

Marcellus strode back into the hall.

"I've brought the healer."

A young woman was following Marcellus. She stepped out from behind him and stared at me. I stared back, surprised both by her youth and her appearance. Her brown hair was cut short and it gave her an elfin appearance, which was accentuated by her fine-boned face and large dark eyes. She was wearing a long green dress which disguised her shape but couldn't conceal her athletic bearing and lithe figure. There was something else about her, not physical, an air of superiority to the common herd. She wasn't a noble lady, but her clothes were clean and well cared for. Her skin was smooth and clear, and her short hair, soft and neat. She wore a bead necklace and bracelets. She was no common woman that was for sure.

Her attention was suddenly snatched by the Wolf Standard which Odd had brought inside and propped against the wall. The sight had an almost physical impact upon her and she caught her breath, staring at it with those wide eyes. After a distinct pause she tore her gaze from the standard and turned it in my direction, she whispered something to nobody in particular, still staring straight at me.

"What does she say Marcellus?" I asked, intrigued by her reaction.

"She says you have the mark of dragons on you, lord." Marcellus stated and shrugged. Wulfstan gave a shout of laughter.

"Tell her I am the Wolf lord, chosen sword of Tiw, the god of war and justice, and my victory over her people proves my power."

"And how would she like a bloody good seeing to?" Wulfstan was still laughing.

Marcellus translated my words and she looked at me and nodded slowly as if it was obvious and she should have known it all along. She gave Wulfstan a long icy stare before returning her attention to me. She started to mutter then as she floated, rather than walked, slowly towards me. She reached out to touch my face, still speaking in a low, almost musical, tone. I snatched hold of her wrist and her eyes burnt with rage for an instant before she smiled and bit her lip like a nervous girl. Her eyes widened and she looked at me in a manner which I took to be an appraisal, like a farmer looking over a beast he was thinking of buying.

"What did she say Marcellus?" I whispered.

"She says she carries the wisdom of the ancient times, before Tiw walked the earth. She has been waiting for your arrival since she first saw the wolf when she was a child, and that....that your children will wield unimaginable power." Marcellus told me hesitantly.

"Of course," I agreed. "They are Wolf lords."

"No, lord. I think she means your children.....with her."

Wulfstan roared with even more uncontrolled laughter.

"How does he do it? Smashed face, all cut up and useless, wrapped in some old rags, and he still has all the best looking stuff throwing themselves at him!"

I didn't laugh, I was looking into those deep, dark eyes, wondering what she was up to. I released her wrist and pulled my coverings aside showing her my wound. She was a healer again. She inspected the bruised and bloody gash, drawing in her breath, and then stood back. I took the chance to show her the gashes on my thigh and forearm. She looked at them unmoved and spoke to Marcellus.

"Lord she needs to get some things from her house. She says you should rest until she returns."

"Tell her I need to greet the king when he arrives."

Marcellus translated and she just rolled her eyes and turned and walked out.

"Get her an escort, Marcellus! I want her back safely with her things." I called as he followed her out.

"I'll go along with that," Wulfstan interjected. "I'd like to have a good look at her things!"

He and Oswine laughed out loud again, I was still seeing those big, dark, shining eyes.

More of the Wealh had come into the Hall while I had been captivated by my healer. I suddenly realised that I knew nothing about her, not even her name, was she genuine? Was I wise to let her tamper with my wounds?

One of the women was fussing with pots at the fire, and she was joined by two more who started preparing a meal. Wulfstan, with no knowledge of the language, had somehow managed to get one of the women to bring him mead. I laughed under my breath, it was going to be an interesting evening. I wanted to know what was happening in the town. I wanted to know where Icel was. I cursed my wounds and the dead Wealh that dealt them. I noticed Wulfstan staring at me.

"There's no point getting frustrated, Wulfhere. You can't do everything. Your job was to win the battle, you did that, you've captured Ratae. It's Icel's problem now. You've sent your lads to stop the slaughter. You've done everything that could be expected of you, now relax and have some of this."

He poured the last of my ale into the ash by the fire and refilled my pot with mead. He was probably right. There was nothing I could do that wasn't being done. I would have to rely on my companions, and they were good men.

I sipped my mead.

"These Wealh," I mused out loud. "They will be tricky to hold down. They can't get near us in a pitched battle but if they take to the country and wage a hit and run war, on their horses, they would be a pain in the arse. We would have to move everywhere in strength. Farms wouldn't be safe, people would be reluctant to settle. We will have to get them on our side pretty quickly."

"We need to get some horses," Wulfstan concluded. "Then we could get after them. You can't fight horsemen if they don't want to fight when you're on foot."

"I saw you take down that bloody great, big bastard", Oswine interjected. "That was good work. I thought he was going to smash the wall."

"What was that?" Wulfstan asked. "During the battle today?"

"Yes, there was an enormous Wealh giant, with a club," Oswine confirmed. "Wulfhere took him down, left the shield wall and waded into them. It was very impressive."

"Wulfhere the Mad, Giant Slayer!" Wulfstan raised his mead to me.

"No, that was wrong, all wrong. The bastards! He was simple, like Beorn, you know, Beadwof's boy. He should never have been there. He was crying like a little lad. I think he was just terrified."

Silence reigned for a while as we sipped our drinks. I remembered the giant's dead, staring eyes. Oswine raised a couple more incidents from the battle. As he and Wulfstan chatted I wondered which of my men had been killed, or badly hurt.

Marcellus returned with my elfin healer, he was carrying a cloth wrapped bundle.

"What's happening out there Marcellus? Has Gram got a grip on things?" I wanted to know.

"Yes, lord it's all settling down now." Marcellus confirmed. The girl had left us and walked off to look at the rooms at the side and back of the hall.

"What's her name? Do you know?" I asked Marcellus again.

"I'm not sure, she's very mysterious, probably Druid. The ancient knowledge, herb lore, healing. She was shocked by your Standard, lord. She has some sort of reverence for the wolf. She has brought a pot with her that's full of wolf teeth and claws, as well as all her herbs and healing stuff. I think your arrival fits in with some sort of prophesy. She's really excited about you being here."

She came back into the hall and started talking to Marcellus, giving instructions.

"She has chosen a room for you to rest in, lord. She wants a bed made for you and she will treat you in there. She wants a fire lit and she will prepare the room to 'cleanse' it."

"What's her name Marcellus?" I asked him again.

He asked this simple question and she paused and held my gaze as she gave a long, convoluted answer in a voice which was at once light and pleasant, yet breathless and worldly.

"She says she is the earth and the sky, the sun and the rain, the wisdom of ages and the hope of the future and her name is her soul," Marcellus informed me. She was still holding my gaze unblinking.

"Well that's quite a mouthful. I will call her Elf, for that is what she reminds me of, an elfin spirit of the woods," I decided with a smile, and Marcellus translated for her. Her hands flew to her face, her mouth and eyes wide with surprise and shock. She walked to me and sunk to her knees before me, staring wide eyed she spoke again in a hurried breathless voice.

"What's she saying now, Marcellus?" I demanded.

"I'm not sure what it's all about, lord. It's this prophesy business again, something about wild beasts ravaging the fold and the Wolf and the Elf coming forth from the forest to make known their power....and magic. I think it must be some ancient learning, lord. The healers and the followers of the old ways, they have a reverence for the earth and the forest and wild things. This must be something to do with all of that. You should be wary, lord, this is all to do with the old gods. Their ways are mysterious and unpredictable. They were overthrown by the Bishops of Christ. It is dangerous to have dealings with them."

I stared into those wide eyes and I couldn't help but reach out and stroke her short, soft, dark hair. She didn't flinch or draw away, she showed no reaction at all, she just held my gaze and allowed my caress as if it was my right.

"You forget Marcellus that I am Tiw's chosen sword. Woden's blood runs in my veins. My lore is as ancient as hers, and if she believes the Elf and Wolf are destined to rule this land with power and magic, the rest of these people might accept our rule as fate, unavoidable and not to be resisted."

I looked around the hall and saw that the other Wealh were all riveted by our exchange. This was good, word would spread through the city within days.

"Get the room sorted out as my Elf directs," I instructed Marcellus. I had decided to make the most of this surprising situation.

She left me abruptly and went to direct the preparations somewhere off to the side of the main hall.

"You lucky bastard!" Was Wulfstan's contribution. "I was a lord of the Wolf before you were even born but she didn't even look at me. She's lovely. I might cut myself open to get a bit of 'treatment' off that. You're unbelievable! Tiw's swordsman? More like Tiw's cock."

We all laughed but it was too painful. I tried to control the impulse and that only caused Wulfstan and Oswine to laugh all the more.

"Serves you right. It looks like your little Elf is going to have to wait to get her helping of Wolf magic doesn't it."

He drained his mead and called for more. Gram returned,

"The town is calmer now, lord. Our lads are keeping a hold on things. We're letting them take what they want but they're keeping the women safe for you, lord."

"Well done, Gram. Just keep a firm hand and watch for Icel."

He nodded and left us again.

"He's a good lad," Wulfstan averred when Gram left. "He was bloody good in that shield wall today. Your Wolf boys are all good. The Wealh didn't want to know too much about fighting your lads. They fell away and wouldn't go near them. They made plenty of noise, but when it came to it, they didn't have the strength, did they? They didn't stay with it. They just wanted a quick win, no stamina. Once the initial fire was gone they couldn't maintain the fight."

I smiled to myself, the mead was making Wulfstan talkative and he eased into his topic, starting to compare the different fighting styles of the peoples that he had faced down the years. Oswine chipped in with his own observations every now and then.

Elf and Marcellus returned and said that the room was ready. I tried to rise but my leg and side had stiffened, and I couldn't push myself up without a vicious pain which made the sweat stand out cold on my forehead and back. I shivered as Leofmund drew me to my feet and he and Marcellus half supported and half carried me through to the side room. The small room was bare, except for a bed which had been made up on the floor, and a fire which was burning happily away. The smoke was struggling to escape through the thatch. The walls were damp and bare and some of the plaster had fallen away leaving the brick and stonework exposed. I shivered again in spite of the fire. My Standard was propped against the wall at the head of the bed which I noticed was surrounded by the teeth and claws that Marcellus had mentioned. Elf had lit candles around the room and strange little lamps which were giving off a heavy, sweet scent as their fuel burned.

They eased me down onto the bed and Elf began to inspect my wounds, muttering her incantations the whole time. She washed them with some strange smelling hot water which she had heated on the fire, before stitching the wounds. They were very tender and I had to squeeze my fists tight shut as she worked on them to overcome the pain, but I couldn't take my eyes off her. Marcellus and Leofmund were watching her work, anxious for my safety, but

I was comfortable with her care. I just wanted to look at her. I was sure she didn't wish me harm and I made no effort to interfere or ask what she was doing. Even if I had asked her, I knew nothing of healing so I wouldn't have known if she was curing me or poisoning me.

She had covered the wounds, at my side and on my thigh, with scented cloths and, still muttering her incantations, she mixed aromatic ingredients in a head sized cauldron over the fire. I had started to shiver again and she covered me with skins and woollen coverings while she worked. The room was filled with more pungent smells of her woodland herbs and medicines as the pot warmed. She dressed the wounds with spider webs and eventually produced some strange grey paste from the cauldron, which she spread over the web dressings. The paste was extremely hot and I could only just bear to have it on my skin, but I accepted the treatment. I wouldn't let her see me flinch. Finally the paste was covered with tree bark and bound in place. She said some more words over the covered wounds, before returning to the fire to prepare another small pot of something. Beneath the bark the hot paste caused the pain of the wounds to burgeon and swell before gradually calming and easing away to almost nothing. She returned again and anointed the cuts on my legs, arm and shoulder. By the time she was finished I was soaked in sweat. I felt sick and very cold. She brought me a hot drink from the small pot, and as my shivering continued she got under the coverings with me and indicated that Leofmund should do the same on my other side. I soon felt warmer and much more comfortable but every time someone moved I felt a cold draught that caused me to shiver which in turn pulled at the stitches.

I awoke some time later to find Icel standing at the foot of my bed. Leofmund and Elf were standing at either side of me.

"Wulfhere, my friend," he seemed at a loss for words. "I was hoping to celebrate your victory with you but find you like this. I have healers with me if you would rather have our own people tend you?"

"No, the girl must stay with me. She has a Wealh prophesy. It's Druid magic. Marcellus knows, he can explain. I think it will help us. Icel....the town....I haven't....." I faltered, I was cold again, my head ached and the sick feeling was still there.

"Don't talk now, old friend, rest. We will talk when you have your strength back. I just wanted you to know that your victory will not be forgotten."

He left and I told Leofmund and Marcellus that they should have a drink. I noticed that Gram had stationed himself by the door and I was comfortable with him there. I lay back and Elf joined me again, sharing her warmth with me.

I was woken again by the raucous laughter coming from the hall. The pain in my side had subsided to a dull throb but I didn't think that I could move without setting it off again. It must have been late at night, and judging from the type of singing I could hear, the celebrations must have been going on for some time. I looked around the room and saw that Gram was sleeping in the corner to the side of the door, I was glad he was getting some rest. Elf was still lying at my side. I looked at her face and realised that she was wide awake, staring at me. She moved closer in to me and I raised my arm so that she could lay her head on my shoulder. She instantly sat up again, and I thought I had gone too far, but instead of scolding me she reached down and drew her dress up and over her head. In the flickering light there was a sheen on the soft, smooth skin sweeping from her neck and throat to firm, spare shoulders and delicate, beautifully rounded breasts. Her tummy was flat and lean, and her hips curved deliciously out from her taut flanks. The shadows and coverings concealed her thighs and the hair and cleft of her sex, heightening my desire for her. She waited, seemingly for my approval and I reached up and let my fingers brush lightly over her cheek and throat. Her head tilted back and she caught her breath as I caressed her breasts, feeling and watching the nipples tightening under my touch. I pulled her down to me and the touch of her skin against mine was the reason I had survived the battle. I tried to turn to her but the stiffness and pain in my side was too much. She placed her hand on my chest to make me still, but she didn't stop my eager hands.

I listened to her breathing, her little sighs and the soft sounds of pleasure and growing desire that escaped her. I caught the musky tang of her arousal and breathed it in savouring the powerful aroma. I absorbed the smooth, soft, warmth of her body, her delicately soft hair and the wetness of her sex. I teased and caressed her wet flesh until her breath was harsh and her hips were starting to thrust at my fingers. She suddenly moved my hand away and eased a leg across me. She reached down, grasped my prick and guided me into the heat of her belly. She lowered herself, painfully slowly, with catching breath. So tight that I knew I was her first. She stopped and raised herself and then eased back down, each time going a little further, pushing a little harder. Then with a small sob she forced herself down onto me. Her heat engulfed me and we lay still together for a long time before she started to move, keeping her weight on her toes and hands so that she didn't hurt me. She was softness and heat and quickening breath, curved hips, swinging breasts, lip biting pleasure and pain. I lay still, helpless and sore, as she moved above me. I watched, and savoured, every emotion and sensation that was written in her face. My world became her face, her scent and the heat and wet movement inside her. My release was a flood of power and emotion and I gripped her hips, brutally, as I spent my lust, my battle rage and my triumph inside her.

We lay, joined, for a long time. I was holding her, I could feel her hectic heart beat and I listened to her breathing, realising suddenly that she was mouthing another incantation. I lay there, and listened to the laughter in the hall and Elf whispering under her breath.

The next time I woke, the hall was quiet. The celebrations had ended, so dawn could not be far off. Elf was still beside me, watching me like a predatory cat. As soon as she realised that I had woken her fingers traced gossamer soft paths across my chest and belly and then her mouth and tongue rekindled my passions. Wulfstan was right, I was a lucky bastard.

When I woke again, many hours later, it was morning. Gram was gone and Elf was sitting on the chair looking at me. She smiled when she saw that I was awake and spoke to me in her own language before getting up and leaving the room. She returned in no time with a bowl of porridge, and when I had eaten she removed the poultices from my wounds, bathed them and bound them again with the same concoctions and invocations as before. I wasn't happy with the leg wound which was painful and hot to the touch, but once she had cleaned and dressed it with the hot paste the pain seemed to subside. I just hoped that it wouldn't hold any infection.

I decided to get up and go to the hall to find out what was going on, but Elf had made me another of her hot drinks and she sat with me as I drank it. She then forced me gently back down on the bed and, still muttering her breathless incantations, she eased the stress at my temples and shoulders with those delightfully light fingers.

I closed my eyes and lost myself in her touch. My belly felt warm and full and the room was filled with the sweet scent of her lamp oils. I felt weary, as though I had been awake for a week. I saw our battle field again. Horsemen whirled past, the giant was before me, crying and bellowing. There were shining blades and spear heads, shouting, screaming, turmoil and the rank stench of butchery. The slaughter of the wounded, blood on my blade and my hands, and then Elf. A darkened room lit by countless flickering candles. She slid her dress over her head and stood naked before me, but then she was kneeling on the bed, sweat glistened on her forehead and her hair was stuck to her wet skin, she gasped and cried out in the throes of childbirth, and something spewed wetly from her, bloody and slimy, covered in sodden, matted fur, muzzles drawn back in snarling fury, twin wolf cubs.

CHAPTER 7: Home

I awoke in the late afternoon and slowly opened my eyes. Gram was standing by the door, looking out. I could hear voices in the hall and I recognised Wulfstan, then Anna and Leofmund. I thought Icel must be there, it must be a council. I should be there. I tried to raise myself but my solid muscles wouldn't let me, and I subsided with a vicious curse of pain. Elf was sleeping on the bed, curled up by my feet like a hound. She stirred and was instantly wide awake, her dark eyes staring into my head. She said something I didn't understand.

"I need a shit," I said bluntly in reply. "Gram, get me some clothes."

He left us and I started to rise, Elf moved to restrain me.

"No!" I couldn't explain. I held my cock and made a hissing noise, she pointed to a bucket.

"No, I need to move about so that the muscles don't tighten and become stiff. I've got to keep them moving." I told her. She protested again trying to stop me, pointing to the charms she had placed around the room.

"NO!" I seized her hair at the back of her head and drew her hard to me. Her eyes were wide, staring into mine. I put my other hand on her belly.

"Don't worry, I'll put your wolf cubs up there." I released her and she stared at me as though I had ruined the whole middle earth. Gram returned with Leofmund, and a bundle of clothes. They pulled me to my feet and helped me to dress. Every movement was painful. I couldn't move my injured leg at all. With my companions half supporting, half carrying me, with my arms around their shoulders, we moved slowly to the door. My limbs felt heavy and reluctant to obey my commands. We left the room with Elf still kneeling on the bed and, slowly, made our way across the hall.

"Wulfhere. Good to see you up." Icel called from his seat by the fire.

"It's good to be up," I replied. "I'll join you once I've finished my weapon training."

I indicated a trip outside and received a polite chuckle. Out in the courtyard I was greeted loudly and warmly by my companions and Wolf Pack warriors who were obviously camped in the hall courtyard as a guard. They pointed out the midden which turned out to be a building with a stream running under it. A great idea, I thought.

The city was quiet. Apart from our army, who were relaxing in the streets in all directions, the people were, understandably, staying out of sight. The men called greetings and good wishes as I hobbled lamely past. I hadn't really noticed the place yesterday and I took in the odd mix of Roman and British buildings. There was a wide, paved road running from the great gate to the stone built palace. Other roads crossed it to form squares with a lot of houses, and a few byres and vegetable plots, fronting them. The town wall was stone, and the big Roman buildings were stone, but the houses, barns and work places in the town were mostly wooden framed, wattle and daub buildings. The Roman glory was fading, but it still dominated the place. Like Godmunds Ceaster there was at least one temple that I'd seen, and a bath house, and a lot of buildings still had tiled roofs.

Once I had relieved myself we resumed our slow, painful procession back to the hall. As we reached the gateway Haeddi hurried to see me.

"Lord Wulfhere, I have stabled your horse and tended its wounds. It's a fine beast."

"Thank you, Haeddi. I would be grateful if you would resume your old job of looking after my stable. I would like to establish a herd if I get the chance, oh, and his name is Victory." I informed him, and it was true, I was very keen to establish a herd so that we could fight the Wealh.

Back at the hall, under the pretence of adjusting my eyes to the light, I paused to rest for a moment. My leg, and side were throbbing painfully, and I thought I might have overdone it a bit. Wulfstan caught my eye and nodded at an empty seat. I crossed to him, trying to listen in on the conversation. Icel was establishing his plans for his new kingdom. Lords were being granted estates at the rivers that we had crossed on the way here, in order to hold the road open.

As the latest speaker finished, Icel stood and held up a hand for quiet.

"Lord Wulfhere has joined us. Wulfhere the Valiant, who won the gate to Ratae single handed and opened the town to our warriors. His wounds are marks of honour. Lord Wulfhere, who led our army, and defeated the Wealh, slaying the giant, before challenging Tasciovarus to face him in fair combat. A challenge which was shamefully declined.

Lord Wulfhere, I thank you for your loyalty. Your reward shall be in keeping with the service you have done me. Tonight we will feast in your honour."

Icel rose and the council was finished.

I sat with Gram and asked him which of our men were slain or hurt. It seemed the skill of the Wolf Pack had helped them escape too many deaths. The fact that we held the field meant that our injured men escaped the slaughter that befell the Wealh. None the less there was the sorrow of loss. Ingeld had been slain aiding his brother, Inwald who had been felled by a blow to the head and was about to be hacked by the Wealh. Ingeld had died beyond the shield wall, protecting his brother as he was dragged back to safety. Cissa, who had lost an eye fighting for me against the Franks, had been crippled by a cut to the back of his knee which had severed muscle and tendons. Six of the Wolf Pack lads had been slain and several more had broken bones or other wounds which would take time to heal. The lords of the south folk had suffered greater losses and would expect suitable reward for their sacrifice.

I returned to my room to find Elf still kneeling on the bed where I had left her. Gram lowered me onto the bed, beside her. My overworked wounds screamed their protests at me. I remained still, my breath as shallow as possible, as the pain slowly subsided. I looked up at Elf. She was staring at me with an expression somewhere between sorrow and bewilderment. I placed my hand on her belly.

"Elf," I spoke her name and then held up two fingers. "Two wolf cubs," I said and then touched the two fingers on her belly again.

She looked at me and questioned me in her own tongue which I didn't understand. I held up my fingers again.

"Two," I repeated and she echoed me holding up two fingers as I had and then pointing them at her tummy. I nodded and she looked long and hard at me before accepting what I was showing her. I wondered if it fitted in with her 'prophesy'.

"Now, let's just make sure," I suggested.

The feast was excellent. Songs had actually been written in my honour, much to the delight of Wulfstan, who made up a couple of extra, more colourful, verses. I was praised from all corners of the hall. I was soaked in sweat, and feeling sick, and the pain in my side was a constant, gnawing, burn but I wasn't going to miss my feast. Icel presented me with ten horses, a chest of silver, a very fine ring-mail shirt, a dozen swords, and a small bronze statue of a Roman warrior. I raised the clawed mead glass and made my speech, praising my king for his generosity. In the end I gave in to my wounds. Once the boasting and the retelling of battle stories began I made my slow, painful way back to bed. Elf was waiting. She stayed with me through the night, easing my pain, and when my rigid muscles at last relaxed, she rode me again, and drained my melancholy inside her.

I grew feverish, and for a couple of days it was uncertain whether my wounds would fester, but the fever broke, and I returned to middle earth. The first sight that I was aware of was of Elf, still kneeling over me, with Gram, Leofmund, and Wedda looking on. Wulfstan and Oswine came in when word was passed to the hall that I was awake again. They were followed by the waelcyrge who had a bleak greeting for me.

"Beware the witch, Wolf lord!" he mewed in his girlish voice. "Her magic is that of the old gods, the gods of wood and stream who hide from the Ese in their dark caves and stagnant pools. She will bewitch you, lord. She wil entrap you or poison you, beware!"

Elf hissed at him like an angry cat.

"If she was going to poison me I'd be dead by now. She wants my children. I've put twins in her belly. That's her payment," I told him.

"That is an abomination, lord. For your seed, the seed of Tiw's chosen, to bless the belly of a witch of the old religions. There is powerful magic at work here. Such a union would be a potent talisman of the old gods. When her work is done, when you are whole again, she must go to the gods. It would be a just offering, an acceptance of their power over the old ways!"

I looked into Elf's eyes all the while that he was speaking and she had held my gaze. She was nervous. She knew that the waelcyrge was a threat to her. I wouldn't see her healing rewarded with death.

"Leave us now, Waelcyrge. Make sacrifice to thank the gods for our victory and to bring fortune on Ratae. We will deal with the girl when I am healed. I'm too tired to talk now."

My leg was still too stiff and painful to move far, and I spent two more days in that bed before I was able to get up and take my place in the hall.

Each day I gradually built up the amount of walking I was doing, determined to keep the scars from stiffening up. Elf's potions, drinks and poultices gave me strength, and I paid her with my seed. After ten days I was fit enough to travel, although I couldn't exert myself at all. The slightest effort left me feeling drained. I had Marcellus warn Elf to hide herself. I gave her the wolf skin from my standard which left her awed. She was carrying my children, I knew it from my dream. She had her payment, I wasn't going to see her strung up and butchered. She had nursed me well. She muttered one last incantation and left the hall clutching the wolf skin. I wondered whether our paths would cross again.

The kings of the Corieltavi came to Icel and received their silver and pledged their friendship and loyalty to the new king of

Caer Lerion. They happily informed us that Cynfellyn had become involved in struggles around the great river Temes. The sons of Hengest had made a bid to take all of the south bank of the great river and put pressure on Londinium, Lundenwic our folk called it. Cynfellyn had granted land on the southern shores of the Temes to Sais warriors, in order to help him keep the Cantware at bay. They had made a stout defence of the river in the service of their Wealh king, but he wouldn't risk coming north while the war was still raging, and with summer wearing on it grew less and less likely by the day that he would attack this year.

Now that Tasciovarus had been overthrown, the Corieltavi wanted to act on their original plan with Icel's help, and take back their land from the Catuvellauni. They feared the might of the Angels more than they feared Cynfellyn, and had decided that Icel was the future. With Angel strength a little over a day away in our new towns on the western edge of the great fenland, Icel's kingdom was assured, for now.

We held a meeting of the Wise in the hall. The great lords of the people were there to discuss how we would rule our new towns. The feasting tables had been drawn around the fire pit to form a square and we sat around, listening to the opinions of the wise men. Icel was anxious to hold Ratae, as well as the towns at the edge of the fens.

"It would be foolish to return home and relinquish the land and wealth that we have won here," he argued with real passion. "Caer Lerion is more than land. It is the people that matter. Whoever rules here is a king of the Corieltavi. This is Ratae Corieltavorum, the city of the Corieltavi. The towns west of the fens are vulnerable. It will take time for us to come to their aid if Cynfellyn tries to take them back. With the Corieltavi as our allies……"

"They can't be trusted, king Icel. Tasciovarus would have seen us all killed in return for Cynfellyn's silver. How do we know that they would help us?" Heremod of the north folk wanted to know.

"No doubt they are as suspicious of us as we are of them, Heremod, my friend. They won't stand by us out of love! They see the strength of our blades. They see the skill of our smiths. They see ever more of our folk joining us from the old lands. They see a strong ally who will give them the might to take back what was taken from them, and help them push back the Catuvellauni to strengthen their borders. They have dreamed of Cynfellyn bowing, and grovelling, and sending them tribute and hostages. That is why they will stand with us. The kings who came to us to take their reward for leaving Tasciovarus to stand alone, have pledged their loyalty to me. Others will follow their lead once their appetites have been whetted. Together we can hold back Cynfellyn while we build our strength."

An unpleasant doubt suddenly occurred to me.

"So who will rule Caer Lerion, Icel?" I asked, softly. Half dreading the reply.

He paused while he framed his reply.

"I have spent a lot of time wrestling with that question, old friend. My first thought was to give you the kingdom," that was what I had feared, "but then I considered further. Ever since we came to this land you have led the way. You defeated the traitors amongst the north folk, you defeated Tasciovarus. I have come to wonder what my ancestors will judge my part in the story of our people to have been. I will rule this kingdom, Wulfhere. The more I have thought about it, the more certain I have become.

The king of Caer Lerion must be a war leader, and truly there is none better than you, but he must also be skilled at making treaties and building alliances. This is my destiny. This will be my kingdom and my monument."

"Then who will rule the north folk, lord?" Heremod smiled with the guile of a snake. We all knew who he had in mind.

"Wulfhere will rule all of the Angels in the east. I ask you, the council of the wise, to name him king. Who among us do the Wealh fear the most? All the time that they look jealously on Caer Lerion, they will know that the Wolf lord is a few days march away with the army of the eastern Angels. They will know that there will be no mercy if he marches forth. They will be fearful and that will help to stay their hand. I ask you now for your decision."

There was a sudden babble of voices as the lords discussed Icel's idea. Heremod looked as if the world had fallen around him. Icel caught my eye and I nodded in deference and thanks. Eventually the talking ceased and Heremod rose to his feet with the expression of a condemned man on his face.

"It is agreed, king Icel. In your absence, king Wulfhere will rule our people."

I rose quickly to my feet before anything else could be said.

"Thankyou, Icel, my lords. I accept, before all present and by all law, that I will rule only in your name, my king and that the land will be yours to order should you return to it. This is my first decision as ruler of the eastern Angels. I name Heremod, as my reeve amongst the north folk. You have served king Icel well and I want you to continue. Maintain the prosperity of the north folk, Heremod. Apply the law and see that there are men for my army when I summon them. The Golden Hall at the ceaster shall be your home and I will come there for the royal courts. Ask of me what you will, give to me that which is due. Tiw will be my guide in all things."

In the space of a few heartbeats Heremod had lost all hope of ever having the thing that he coveted most in the middle earth, only to see it given to him. He rose to his feet and just about managed to thank me for my generosity without jumping up and down for joy.

It was time for me to return home. Winter was all but upon us. We were into the tenth month, Winterfylleth, and the full moon would mark the start of winter. My men would want to be home before Blotmonath, the blood month, which followed Winterfylleth. In the eleventh month livestock must be slaughtered to ensure that there will be enough stored fodder to keep the rest through the winter, and the right beasts need to be selected. The weather was changing. The roads would soon be too soft for the wagons and there was a mountain of work to do. As well as organising farms and courts I would need to send new settlers to strengthen our new lands.

I got the chance to speak with Icel late in the evening when the ceremonies and speeches were all finished.

"Icel, I'll be returning to Wolf Home in the morning. The blood month will soon be upon us. I can't keep my men from their farms any longer."

"Wulfhere, my brother," Icel was tired, emotional and full of good mead. "Duroliponte has been troubling me. It will be a vital, vital place," he declared forcefully, and stared hard at me. "I am giving it to you, my brother, my warlord. I owe you everything, Wulfhere! And Esme! I owe her everything as well! Bring her to me won't you, Wulfhere? Bring her safely to me here. My new kingdom. We have two kingdoms! Aethelstan only had one, and now he's gone. He should have kept you, Wulfhere. But then I wouldn't have you so he couldn't! You are the greatest warrior of the Angelcynn, Wulfhere. The very, very greatest. You fought the giant for me..............", and on, and on he went.

Wulfstan was trying not to laugh but I let Icel ramble on. Even kings must be able to unburden themselves at times, and nothing he said here, in his mead, amongst loyal friends, would create offence.

We set off for Duroliponte in the morning. My wagons were loaded with provisions, and the spoils of war. I sat astride Victory, and my close companions were riding with me.

We made the return journey along the Roman street to Godmunds Ceaster and thence to Duroliponte. On the way I had a quiet talk with Aldwynn. He had been one of my first companions. His father had been one of my father's hearth companions and, together with his friend Cissa, he had stood by me since the time of the pirate raid in which my parents were killed.

Now Cissa was crippled and his fighting days were finished. I was not prepared to just leave him languishing on his farm, though. I had a job that they could both help me with.

"Aldwynn, old friend, I want you to be the lord of Duroliponte. It is going to be a hugely important town. Cynfellyn will want it back because it controls the road between the south folk and Icel. Traders, settlers or armies will all need to travel that street, so I will need someone that I can trust to hold it open. It will be a wealthy place in time. I will send people to join you, and Hygsic and Ithamar are a day's journey away.

In order that your strength is sufficient for the task I will ask Cissa to join you. I will grant you forty hides each and the bridge tolls, in order to make it worth your while."

He couldn't really refuse such an offer, and Cissa was overjoyed. He had feared that he would be trapped on his farm for the rest of his days, watching us leave him behind whenever we marched off to war, but now he would still have a very important job to do.

When we arrived back at the town we found it still partially deserted. Some of the people, the headman included, had opted to move to lands still ruled by the Wealh. The majority though were resigned to living under new lords. Their lives wouldn't change much, if at all, it would just be a different face and strange accent in the hall.

While I had the army present we set to work to build a burrh. We felled trees and dug the old ditches out again, ten feet deep and ten feet across, in three rings around the burrh. The dirt was heaped up to make a rampart which we strengthened with logs and stones, and topped with a wooden wall. A well was dug and gates hung on two mighty oak posts. The enclosed area would be big enough for the hall and all of the byres, barns and work huts the lord would need, but small enough to be robustly defended by as few as a hundred men. With two hundred men helping to build, it didn't take very long. In six days we had the site well established.

Aldwynn chose to stay and complete the work. Cissa was going to return home and fetch their families and possessions. I would return in the spring and begin the task of collecting a yearly tribute from the Catuvellauni lords who lived within raiding distance. There was nothing else to attend to now to keep us from home. I wanted to hold my woman and see my son again.

As soon as we reached my lands men began to leave the column to go to their farms. I shared the silver and the swords that Icel had given me amongst the lords who had served me so well.

Men, women and children who were working in the fields stopped what they were doing and came to the road to cheer us home. At Wolf Home fort there was quite a crowd, cheering, waving, or dashing forward to greet sons, fathers or husbands.

I sent the wagons on up the hill to Wolf Home and addressed my people.

"People of Wolf Home. Your men have won a famous victory. All day they held the wild charges of the army of Tasciovarus of Caer Lerion. They slaughtered the foe until they could stand our blades no longer and fled the blood-soaked field. Your men will be remembered as long as Angels tell tales around the hearth. Return to your homes and know that you have my thanks, the thanks of king Icel and that you will be revered among our people!"

A great cheer went up and my men made their way home. The Danes, the Frisians and the men from the Eastern reaches of the kingdom were welcome to stay at my hall for the night, and continue on in the morning.

As we left the fort a handful of people were hurrying down from the hall. It was easy to make out Asfrid carrying Togi, accompanied by the Danish guards. Running ahead of her were Wuffa, Sigurd, Eadric and Hildy. I rode ahead to greet them.

"Wuffa, he's going to need plenty of exercise," I dismounted, and held Victory's reins out for my younger brother and then half ran, half hobbled the last few yards to my lady. I was laughing with unrestrained delight at the beauty of her smiling face. I took in her great rounded tummy, and my son looking curiously at me over his shoulder. I crushed her in my arms, breathing her in, absorbing her laughter through my skin. I was home again, and there was nowhere else in the entire world that I would rather be.

CHAPTER 8: A Pause for Breath

She truly was the most beautiful woman I had ever seen. She was my world, dearer to me than my own warrior's life which I knew would one day bleed away from me on some field of slaughter. I just wanted to hold her, feeling her chest rise and fall against me, breathing in her scent, touching her hands and face, listening to her laughter and her voice. She showed me my son and I took him and swung him round, joining with his high pitched laughter which was pure merriment. I carried Togi on one arm with my other arm around his mother. I looked up at my hall and the surrounding buildings. I saw my land, my sheep and my workers and I breathed in the clean air of home.

I told Asfrid that we would have quite a few guests for the night and she looked back and waved to Wulfstan and Ullr. Wuffa had mounted Victory, he always loved to ride.

"You make sure that you take care of him," I called back. "He's going to be the founder of my herd."

"Don't worry," he replied in a deep, but wavering, voice. "I'll school him properly."

He kicked the horse and rode past us, up the slope towards home. I realised that I was watching a young man.

"He has been tremendous these last few weeks, "Asfrid read my thoughts. "He is becoming a man, Wulfhere, another Wolf lord. He and Sigurd are inseparable, they will make a formidable pair."

I watched them both, I would have to take Wuffa to war. He would need to understand the battlefield if he was going to be a true Wolf lord.

"You know Asfrid, we are now the rulers of all the Angels of the east. The north folk as well as our south folk," I told her with a smile.

She looked at me uncertainly, not sure what I was telling her, and then gasped.

"What has happened to Icel?" A frightening thought had suddenly gripped her.

I explained the situation to her as we walked to the hall.

"Icel's well. He is now the king of Caer Lerion, the western Angels. I am king in his absence. You are now a great lady of the Angelcynn, like Offa's queen, Thryth. All who gaze upon you shall die!" I told her with a grand gesture of woe, recalling the legend.

"Oh no! I never liked her!" She dismissed my nonsense.

"Well you shall at least have your own band of warriors who love you from afar, and dedicate their lives to your safety!"

She punched my arm.

"You're teasing me, Wulfhere!"

"No my love, I'm not. I do think that it would be a good idea for you to keep a few more warriors with you while I'm away. For you and the children." I had absolutely no doubt that there would be plenty of volunteers.

"Will we have to move to Ceaster?" She asked doubtfully.

"No, I can rule from here. I've made Heremod my reeve at Ceaster. We will have to travel to hold courts, but the north lands are safe. Especially now that we rule both sides of the great fenland! We have the streets for easy travel, or I can take a ship up the coast if I need to move more quickly. No this will do nicely, unless you would like to move anywhere?"

I suddenly wondered if she was bored, after all, her life had been pretty lively up until now.

"Oh no, Wulfhere. I love it here. It really feels like home, somewhere that I can have my family around me and feel safe and, home. Do you understand?" She looked at me with her, 'have I said that properly?' look.

"Of course I understand." I drew her to me again as I spoke and kissed her temple which was on a level with my mouth.

We reached the hall and she sent Hildy to start preparing food and drinks for our guests. We turned and waited for them by the door.

"Eadric, I know there must be lots of things to look at with you but we will leave them tonight and start at breakfast in the morning," I told my reeve who was looking very anxious and keen to catch my eye. He agreed with me and I asked him to join us tonight with his lady, we would have a celebration of my homecoming.

Asfrid made a short speech of welcome before bidding everyone enter and giving them all her greeting. Ullr was delighted to see her again, as was Wulfstan who flirted roguishly with her, making her light up with delighted laughter. Togi had caught the mood and giggled and smiled at all of these strangers who were happy to make a fuss of him.

Once inside Asfrid, as the lady of the hall, poured the mead for her guests and called for a song from the Danish skald, Bragi. He obliged with songs and poems which kept the company entertained as we sat and talked.

"So what now, king Wulfhere?" Wulfstan wondered.

"More of the same, uncle. We continue to build and welcome folk from the old land. I'll see what profit my ships make, and whether Coenred and Gyppe have caught any pirates. We'll grow our crops, and breed horses! I'll be on the lookout for more. I want more horses. I want to match the Wealh for speed.

Then there will be courts. We'll spend the winter on the move, making sure that everyone knows who's in charge."

The mead flowed freely, some of the men returned with their wives and we enjoyed a good, if rather basic, feast. It was perhaps less colourful than the evenings when only the warriors were present, but it was our homecoming. We could relax in the peace and companionship of my hall.

Later still, back in my own bed, I let out a long sigh and relaxed into the soft, dry straw. Asfrid made a fuss, undressing me, and reacting with dismay and concern to my vivid new scars. She laid me down and kneaded and rubbed my stiff muscles from head to toe. While she worked I told her all about the battles, my wounds, my mysterious, magical healer, Elf, and the bizarre dream of wolf twins. She wasn't very happy about this and gave me quite a stare.

"Don't worry, none of my bastards will ever rival Togi or your other children. How many are we going to have? Was it ten?"

"Don't make fun of me, Wulfhere," she was serious. "I don't want our children to have to run and hide as I had to."

"Our children will be kings, and the wives of kings. They will know greatness, wealth and comfort. My seed was merely payment for a service. There is no obligation to the Elf, or her bastard whelps!"

Later we cuddled close together, luxuriously warm under the heavy skins. Asfrid was clearly troubled by something, she kept investigating my scars with her fingers.

"One day, Wulfhere, you might not move quickly enough."

"No doubt! But that will be when I am old, and slowed down by my wounds. Fate knows my death. I can't hide from it. That can't stop our happiness, Asfrid. There will always be wealth and comfort for you, even when I'm slain. You'll be old and wrinkled by then anyway, and Togi can be the new king!"

"Wulfhere, don't make fun of me. I do worry when you go to fight. I want you with me to watch the children grow. It is cold at night. I want your warmth and your body. I want to ease your aches and your stiff muscles and listen to you telling your ideas. I love you, Wulfhere." She finished softly, almost apologetically, but her words almost made my heart burst and I crushed her to me again.

"We must live our lives like a king and queen from your sagas, Asfrid. In years to come they will tell the story of Wulfhere and Asfrid, and two stars will be named for us, I will order it. When I do get cut down, you can bid me farewell with a smile for fond memories, and I will wait for you in the mead hall of my family."

"Will you really order stars named for us?"

"Of course!"

"Oh, Wulfhere, that is so beautiful."

The next morning Eadric was in the Hall when I came down the steps for breakfast.

"My Lord, I need your authority to deal with all the newcomers and find them farms. I just don't know where we are going to put them all. The land that you told me to allocate has already gone and we have far more people waiting than we have already dealt with."

"Come, Eadric, I saw them at the fort, there are a lot but we can cope, surely."

"That's just at the fort, lord. There is a camp at Gyppeswic where they land. They are becoming impatient lord. What can I do with them?"

"We will move them on to the new lands that I have just conquered. Did you say all of my land has now been taken?" I asked again. I was surprised that there could have been so great an influx. That would mean that hundreds had arrived since I had been gone.

"All the land that you told me to grant, lord. From here to Gyppeswic and beyond, lord Wulfstan's lands, and your new estates to the west beyond Ithamar and Hygsic towards Theodford. The land that you selected for settlement is now tilled and tended by your people Lord."

I was pleasantly impressed,

"Aldwynn and Cissa are moving to new estates by the Granta bridge. Once we have enough tenants we need the new comers to take up the farms that the Wealh have abandoned to the west of the fenlands, or in Icel's lands."

Eadric stared at me in awe as all of this sank in.

"The world changes, my lord, our people begin a new journey." He said in hushed tones

"Yes Eadric, and you are one of the founders of our new story."

He sat down heavily as though the weight of this responsibility had just fallen onto him.

"You have done an excellent job so far, Eadric so don't falter now. Our people, and our king, need you to rise to this task and see it done."

He leaped up, suddenly full of zeal for his task.

"It will be, lord! It will be!"

"We'll have breakfast, and then we'll get to work!"

By mid-morning all of our guests had departed for home. I embraced Wulfstan and Oswine and spoke briefly.

"You will find new tenants at your hall when you get back to Rendels Home. Eadric sent them there while we were away. Grant them what land you think is best. Take what land you will, uncle, in the name of the Wolf. Our wealth will grow beyond measure. Rule with an even hand. They're all our people," I reminded him.

Eadric and I sent the settlers who were sheltering in the fort, to the Granta Bridge where lord Aldwynn would either grant them land or send them on to Icel to be given farms. The land they would be receiving was farmland which the Wealh had abandoned, so they wouldn't miss out on this year's crop. I told Gram to send a few of the Wolf Pack lads with the newcomers to show them the way, and once that was sorted out I went down river on Udela to Gyppeswic. I was staggered at the sight of the tented town which had engulfed the port. There were eight ships in the harbour, but whether these were traders or settlers I couldn't tell. As we approached the nearest jetty, Ine hurried to meet us. We threw him a line and he tied us fast.

"Lord Wulfhere, it's good to see you. As you can see we have a lot of people to deal with!"

I stood on a keg at the dock side and addressed the crowd.

"I am Wulfhere, king of the Angels of the east. There is good land here for you all. Follow the river to Wolf Home, and from there you will be directed on to your farms" I pointed up stream.

"What Farms?"

"Where?"

"When?"

I held up my hands again for quiet.

"Bring all of your possessions up river to Wolf Home and my warriors will lead you to your new homes. Lord Aldwynn, and king Icel himself, will be granting you land. Wolf Home is on the river, about five or six miles!"

CHAPTER 9: Taken and Lost

Before I left, I had a pot of ale with Ine and Gram. We stood alongside Udela and watched the port.

"Trade is good, lord. The Norse bring amber, ivory, furs and whale bone. They like our pottery and fine wool. We have tin from Dumnonia, Frankish blades, and glassware. This is becoming a famous port. It's safer than Lundenwic and well placed between the Norse, Danes, Geats and Svear to the east, the Franks and the old Roman trade routes to the south and the Wealh and the Irish to the west."

We sipped our ale and watched the people starting out on the last part of their journeys to a new home.

"A lot of folk didn't wait for your return. Some of the larger families have taken the river roads to find their own land. You might have to get on your travels again in the spring to make sure that they know where they stand in the grand order of things," he confided.

"None went to the south of the Sture did they?" I wanted to avoid provoking the Trinovantes before we were ready.

"They were all warned against it, lord. We made sure of that."

There were merchants with warehouses on the dockside, as well as craftsmen with their workshops, and a market was well established. I wandered amongst the traders, looking at some of the goods on offer; shoes and leather goods, jewellery and adornments, the latest fashion in brooches, apparently square headed brooches were very popular now. There was a smith, a tanner and of course the potteries. There was fresh fish, smoked fish, crabs and shell fish, pins, combs, pots, beakers and domestic goods, a wonderful array. There were taverns with ale, and women to comfort the sea farers.

I watched the noisy whores outside one of the alehouses. They shouted to the keel hands, punctuating their calls with lewd comments and harsh laughter. They hadn't bothered with too much clothing, and their swinging tits and wobbling arses made an eye catching lure. Their brash behaviour was encouraging a number of keel hands to the doorway. While I watched, a scuffle broke out between the sailors which resulted in two of them staggering sullenly away to find a more peaceful hall.

"Do you need some more reeves to keep order, Ine?" I wondered.

"Three or four more would be useful, lord. It gets quite lively at times, and the extra eyes would help me to make sure that all of the traders are paying their dues as well."

Looking around the port, I was sure that the levies on all this activity would cover the extra cost without noticing.

"Hire four, and let Eadric know when they start. Have Gyppe and Coenred caught any pirates while I was away?"

"Yes, one, lord, a Frisian. He'd taken Wealh slaves to the Irish and he was returning home with silver and four fine horses. Coenred fed him and his crew to the fish so we'll all be eating him when we tuck into our smoked herring, won't we?"

We chuckled at the thought.

"Irish horses? Now that is a prize. Where are they?" I was eager to know. I would reward Coenred well for his effort.

"At Ship Home. A stallion and three mares. All the silver is at your warehouse, with the trade goods."

We walked the waterfront, past the whorehouse, with its preening whores and sullen keel hands, to my warehouse. Business had been good. Merchants paid for the privilege of conducting their business, safely, at my port, in silver or in goods. I gave Ine five silver fingers and a glass beaker for his service. The glass was cleverly decorated with clawed feet and he liked it more than the silver. I selected a few choice items to keep for myself. He told the lass who kept his house to fetch us all another pot of ale, and I stood at the front of my warehouse and watched the activity at my port as I drank.

It was an overcast sort of day with a chill wind blowing in from the sea. The hollow sound of footsteps on the wooden boards mingled with the low background hum of half heard conversations. I watched the whores who were still encouraging keel hands inside. They would certainly help to bring ships to the port. Theirs was a strange existence. There was no pride in their lives. There would be no hall, they were just labourers. If they were prepared to let the keel scum hump away inside them then that was their food and drink and a roof over their heads, and who was I to tell them otherwise?

There were two of them in particular who fascinated me. To look at them they could have been mother and daughter such was the age difference. The older of the two was trying hard to draw the customers in, laughing and calling to the men on the dock. Her dress hung down from her right shoulder so that her breast swung free in a shameless invitation, but the other girl, a young girl of thirteen or fourteen summers, was silent, and nervous, and reluctant to make eye contact with any of the sea farers or passers by. She seemed out of place and I wondered why she had chosen to be there.

"Where do the whores come from?" I asked Ine

"Lord?" He replied dumbly

"Where do the whores come from? That little one there looks terrified."

Ine came over to where I stood and followed my gaze to the tavern door.

"Well that's Emma, she's a Dane. It's her alehouse."

"What about the other girl? The young one? Do you know her?" I wondered.

Ine was suddenly nervous.

"Well?"

He knew everyone in the port. If he couldn't tell me who she was it was because he didn't want to. I knew straight away why he didn't want to. Whores could ply their trade freely if that was all they had to make their living, but I wouldn't have girls kidnapped and sold into prostitution to be humped by every passing keel dog. Any girl could be snatched from her home, be she princess or bonded. It could have been my sisters, all those years ago. Or mother. I couldn't even think it.

I strode along the dockside. Gram fell in with me and, sensing trouble, called the lads from Udela, but I wouldn't need them.

"Emma," I shouted as I approached, "Emma the Dane." The keel hands quickly moved away when they saw me coming with my men at my back. Ine hurried to keep up. Emma said something to the girl who made to enter the tavern but I told her to stop.

I stood in front of the brash whore who, in spite of looking slightly nervous, stood her ground defiantly.

"Emma, who is this girl?" I indicated the other girl, and when no answer came on the instant I spoke directly to her,

"What is your name girl and where are you from?"

"She's a Pict," Emma cut in. "Caitlinn's her name. D'you want her eh? Like your reeve are you? Expect a free helping?"

I slapped her hard.

"She is a slave." I made it a statement rather than a question.

"Of course, my lord." Emma confirmed with a trembling voice, one hand on her reddened cheek trying to recover her composure. "Pretty girls her age are looking for a husband, not whoring. How else do you think I get young flesh? Oh I might find one or two, but not enough fresh young skin to turn heads and bring in the business that I can get at a port like this."

"Caitlinn, come here!" I ordered, pointing at the ground directly before me. The girl looked at Emma, and then came nervously to me.

"Can you understand me girl?"

She nodded, silently.

"How did you get here?"

She looked at me wide eyed, but blankly, not sure whether or not she was in trouble.

Finally, looking down, she recalled her fate.

"The Norse took me. They were strong. I couldn't get away. They laughed." She swallowed before continuing in her little girl's voice. "Emma looks after me. She won't let Gunndolf hurt me as long as I work."

"Does Gunndolf hurt the other girls?"

"Only Ilse. She's ungrateful. She won't work. She won't eat. He's wasted his money on her."

'Wasted his money', she had said. Slaves, taken by pirates. My mind went back to the raid. I remembered the women and girls of my home, and the pirates.

"Emma," I was breathing hard and my heart was thumping. "Fetch me Ilse, and any other girls that you own."

I wouldn't leave them here. We had failed that night, I wouldn't fail again.

"I'll do no such thing! She's ours! I paid a fair price for her! She'll do as she's told and then she'll eat." The Dane told me defiantly.

"Emma, fetch me Ilse, now."

She stared at me wide eyed.

"You can't do this! He said we could work here." She indicated Ine, "Gunndolf!" She shouted into the house. "He wants to take Ilse."

"Not just Ilse," I told her. "All of them!"

"What!" There was a roar and the doorway was filled as a huge man came out. He was so big that he had to bend almost double to duck under the door frame. He was enormous, a monster, the bully who threatened these girls. The one who hurt them if they didn't work. I drew my seaxe and the Wolf pack lads behind me followed my lead. The giant halted in his tracks and the anger drained from his face in an instant.

"King Wulfhere, I didn't know it was you, lord. I meant no offence. She didn't say who it was," he dropped to his knees as he tried to shift the blame onto his woman who remained defiant.

"I might have known I'd get no help from you!" She spat contemptuously before returning to the attack. "If you want those girls for yourself you can buy them off me. You can give me what we paid and then you can play with them as much as you want!"

She couldn't understand why I couldn't allow these girls to be kept here. I was king of the east Angels. If I allowed young girls to be snatched from their homes and forced to whore themselves what state would my kingdom soon be in. I had tolerated Emma the

Dane for long enough. I slapped her hard for a second time, sending her sprawling across the wooden floor.

"Ine!" I shouted for my reeve. "You were there, Ine when the pirates came. This could have been Esme." I waved a hand at the girl, Caitlin. "The whores can work here, but no slave girls!"

I seized Emma by the hair and dragged the suddenly cowed Danish whore to her feet.

"Your punishment for forcing slave girls to your work is that you will be bonded to the dock for the year. Everything that this house earns for the next year will be mine. You will not leave under pain of death. Ine will see you fed. After a year the house will be yours once more and you will be free to come or go as you please. If you ever force slave girls to your work again I will have you sold to the Picts, where this girl came from. Gunndolf! You will serve as Ine's reeve for a year and help to keep order here on the waterfront. You will do what he tells you, when he tells you, on pain of death. Now where's this Ilse?"

I shoved Emma inside.

There was nobody inside the house. There was a long table across one end with a barrel of ale and a number of abandoned pots still on it. Then there were a couple of benches and a number of straw beds. They must have all fled through another door. I followed Emma straight through the alehouse to a work hut in the yard at the back. The door was locked so she went back inside and fetched a key to push the latch up. There was no one in the hut but I expected that. She showed me where a barrel of smoked herring was placed on the trap door. I pushed the barrel off and opened the door. The stench drove me back. I coughed and caught my breath before returning to the dark portal.

"Ilse! I am king Wulfhere. You are free, Ilse. I am here to help you. They can't hurt you anymore." I spoke hoarsely into the darkness, trying to breathe as lightly as possible. I waited and then heard light, wet, muddy footsteps, and a girl came into view. She was naked, as thin as a spear, and her body was decorated with purple, black and green bruises. I looked at her haunted face and suddenly I was furious with myself for letting Emma off so easily. I held out my hands to her,

"Come, Ilse. It's over now."

She stared at me for a long time.

"Are you going to kill me?" She asked in the barest, accented whisper.

"No Ilse, you're free," I told her.

She raised her arms and I reached down to draw her up. I braced myself for the weight but almost threw her across the hut so easy was she to lift. She weighed next to nothing and once out of the hole her joints looked too big for her arms and legs. I told Emma to fetch some clothes.

"Where are you from Ilse?" I asked.

"Where am I from?" She seemed confused by the question and had to think about her answer as if she was remembering a half faded dream.

"My father was a lord of the Alamanni, a great warrior," she paused to try to remember. "He is dead. My mother also. The pirates brought me here. I could not stop the pirates from having me, they were too strong, but I would not let it happen again. I would die before I let it happen again." Her strength was staggering, I didn't know if I could have been that steadfast in her place.

"It will not happen again." I assured her. The whore returned with clothes and Ilse dressed.

"So what will you do with me?" She asked as she dressed, her voice was soft, almost distant and dreamy, but her mind was clear and sharp in spite of her trials.

"You speak my language very well," I told her.

"My mother was a Saxon. What are you going to do with me?" She repeated.

"I will take you back to my hall and when you have your strength back you may do as you will, stay in my household or go."

"With no wealth and no family there is not much of a choice."

"Fate will choose something for you," I stated, blankly.

"Fate will always choose." She said emptily.

She held herself with such pride and character. Even in her weakened state she stood as straight as her battered body would allow. She was truly the daughter of a lord. We went back through the house and out onto the dock. I sent the girls to the boat with a couple of the Wolf lads.

I watched them go, the young Pict girl nervous and frightened, the proud Alamanni unsteady on her weak legs. My anger rose again. I grabbed Emma by the arm and shoved her at Gram.

"Get Wyne or Odd to give her a flogging before we go! She needs a lesson in respect. Use willow wands from the hurdle maker, over there!"

They hauled her away. She had the sense not to protest.

The waterfront was quiet. People were still going about their business but they did so nervously, all the time watching to see what would happen next. The sound of Emma's thrashing drifted across the town while the lads loaded the goods and the silver that I was taking home. It didn't take long, Ine kept most of it for trading. We waited while the shrieks rose and fell and were finally swamped by her continuous wailing. When Wyne's powerful arm was tired they brought her back to the ale house and dropped her onto one of the beds. I left her with Ine, and the ogre, Gunndolf.

"Make sure that they work hard, Ine," I looked hard at the huge bully, Gunndolf who bowed his head and avoided eye contact. He would certainly help maintain order on the waterfront. "You only need two extra reeves for the year now, Ine."

We rowed out into the river. I tried to speak to the girls as we rowed upstream. Caitlinn was a young girl with little to say. Ilse told me that her family had been offered land by the Regni to defend their shores against pirates but they'd been waylaid by pirates on the way. A cruel twist of fate. I was pleased that my shores were being kept clear of that sort of keel scum. It was dark by the time we got back. Ilse couldn't cope with the exertions and I carried her virtually the whole way from the dock. Our arrival at the hall created a stir. Asfrid and Eadgyth helped Ilse straight off to wash and then get into a bed. I told them that she hadn't eaten for a while, but that isn't unusual in our world and they knew that she shouldn't have too much too soon.

    Hildy and Frigyth took care of Caitlinn. She was very young in character, and it was hard to think of her being a whore. Perhaps her child-like outlook helped her because she just took to being a housegirl as if nothing else had ever happened to her.

CHAPTER 10: More Work, More Reward

Following my visit to Gyppeswic there was a steady stream of settlers passing through the fort by boat or on foot, heading west. Some had livestock, most had handcarts, wheelbarrows and back packs loaded with their possessions. There were hundreds of them, eager to be on the move and start a new life. I told Hunberht to get a couple of labourers to clear all the dung from the streets and the waterfront, and spread it on the fields.

I had hoped to see Artorius, but he hadn't been at the fort since I got home. I needed to thank him for sending Ceneu to advise us of our betrayal by Tasciovarus. That wasn't all though. We had become an important part of the confused collection of tribes that was Britain. We had gone from being bewildered outsiders in our quiet backwater, to being a great power among the kings of Britain and growing stronger, quite literally, by the day. I wanted to know how the Wealh would react. What did Cynfellyn have planned? Would Ambrosius and the Combroggi join with the Catuvellauni to try and drive Icel out? Closer to home what was happening about Gwrgant and the Trinovantes? This was my land now, and I needed to understand it.

I left word with his people that I wanted to see him when he returned. Two days later he was back. His men informed him of my request and, in his usual forthright fashion, he rode straight up to the hall without even stopping to dismount.

I was pleased to see him again. I knew that his abrasive, single minded manner didn't please Asfrid, but I had a lot of respect for the young warrior. As Haeddi led the horses away I took his spade-like hand and asked him and Gaheris to join me inside for a pot of ale. In the hall, Asfrid greeted Artorius cordially enough but then left our presence informing us that she had a back ache and wanted to lie flat. According to her estimations of the moons the baby should have already been born and she was struggling to stay on top of the household and cope with the aches, pains and frustrations. Eadgyth went with her and Hildy fetched the ale.

I led them to one of the tables on which I had placed a pair of silver cups, arm rings and a fine drinking horn, all from Caer Lerion. They were my reward for loyalty.

"Artorius, I would like to thank you for your service here, defending Wolf Home while I was away, and for the timely warning that you sent regarding Tasciovarus. These gifts are well earned, my friend."

"I am your sworn man, Wulfhere. It was my duty," he said simply. "And besides you have done me and my people a great service, and there is more that I would ask of you."

I indicated that we should sit.

"Lord Wulfhere, I must thank you for the shelter you have given to me, and to my people. Our numbers here have been greatly swollen in recent times by the many folk who have suffered injustice at Gwrgant's hand, or who just cannot accept his rule any longer. The time will shortly be here when I intend to move against him."

He paused, half expecting me to make some sort of interjection, but I had known for a long time that this would happen in the end. I waited for him to continue.

"Although our numbers have grown, I don't have the strength to topple him alone. I will need your aid, lord."

"Go on," I prompted, neither accepting nor declining.

"His stronghold is the fortress in the great Roman city of Camulodonum. It is a mighty fortress and if defended it would take a long siege to break. I need your men, lord. Your warriors are a rock upon which armies break themselves. My horsemen will harry, raid, destroy a broken enemy utterly, but your army is like a great bear which closes with its enemy and uses its strength to crush and maul it to death. Gwrgant has mercenaries, Danes, Saxons, and Jutes of the Cantware, who fight as you do and can withstand my horsemen. I need your men to win my battle and to besiege Camulodonum." He finished and waited for my response.

I had known this request would come and I had often considered what my reply would be. If I helped him conquer Caer Colun I would have a friend on my border. On the other hand I could gather my own power and conquer Caer Colun for myself. Not only would I gain the wealth and strength of the Trinovantes, from Caer Colun I could seek to control the great city port of Lundenwic.

The trouble was that this chance had come too soon. Icel would need my support to defeat the threat from Cynfellyn. I didn't have the strength to wage war on the Catuvellauni, and hold the captured territory of the Trinovantes. It was bad luck, but it was fate. I would have to settle for a friend on my border.

"Artorius, I respect you both as a warrior and as a man of honour. You have sworn your loyalty to me and I have sworn you my protection. If you believe that this tyrant should pay for his crimes against your folk and wish to wage war on him, then you will have my support. When would you make your move?" I got straight to the point.

"As soon as possible, lord. The people of Caer Colun cry out for succour and with every passing day......."

"Once we have victory there will be time to help your people who are crying out. First we must defeat the tyrant. Now you say 'as soon as possible', but winter will soon be upon us and my men have only just returned from war. It is likely that I will have to take the army to defend our new, western lands come the fighting season after the harvest. I think that we should plan for a surprise war in the spring my friend, when Gwrgant's granaries are empty. Nobody expects an attack in springtime, and I don't want a siege. That never works. I want a short war and a quick victory, so we'll attack him when his granaries are bare and then he won't be able to retreat behind his walls." Artorius nodded, he couldn't argue with my reasoning.

"That doesn't mean we sit idly in the meantime. Use your horsemen to steal his harvest, and stop the feorm. Not only because our army will need the grain. If his granaries aren't full at the start of the winter, they will surely be empty by the time we are ready to wage war. If he is hiring mercenaries it would be good for us if he has nothing to pay them with. Mercenaries go home if there's no silver. So steal his grain and his money, my friend and he will be ready to topple come the spring."

"There is clearly much that I can learn from you, Wulfhere. There is far more to war than just fighting!"

"Far more my friend. Once Gwrgant is gone, what then? What of the other tribes? This Combrogi? Will Ambrosius accept your kingship of Caer Colun?"

"I will have an army, a kingdom and my ally, king Wulfhere at my back. Gwrgant's reputation is widely known. Ambrosius wants strong kings who can unite to defend our lands. No, I don't think that there will be a problem from that quarter. What will you want in return for your help?" Artorius wondered.

"I want peace my friend. I have my family, I am building my home. I need peace to settle my people and create wealth and well being. I will need to be able to reward my men, and I want horses, but after this war I will have a friend on my southern border and friends to my north and west, my lands will be secure." I told him truthfully.

I would have peace, and that would give me time to build up my strength and the prosperity of my kingdom.

"Wulfhere, once you have built your kingdom, will the Wolf be hungry for new lands?" Artorius looked at me quizzically.

"More land, or more influence? I can't see the future, Artorius, and I can't know my fate. Suffice to say that you're my friend. I won't covet that which is yours, and you can call on me in need. What of the Combrogi, Artorius? Do my people need to fear what you might become?"

"By your people are you talking of all the Sais?" Artorius wanted to know.

"I speak of my people, and of course those of my king, Icel."

"As you have sworn, and proved, your friendship to me, so will you have my friendship, Wulfhere. I am indebted to you, and I will always answer your call."

He stood and offered me his hand. I took that mighty bear's paw. There would always be peace between us, but I knew that there would never be peace around us.

"Now please stay my friend and I will tell you......" At that moment Eadgyth came back into the Hall holding Togi by the hand.

"Wulfhere, the baby's coming." She called in a state of excitement.

"It's time for me to leave you, Wulfhere," Artorius decided looking from Eadgyth back to me. "I will return to discuss our plans another day, thank you."

He left as abruptly as he did most things. Eadgyth sent Hildy to fetch Flaed, the wise woman, handed Togi to me and put a pot of water to warm over the fire. Then she returned to the private chambers to be with Asfrid. I followed her and found Asfrid kneeling on our bed on all fours, panting like a dog.

"Wulfhere! What are you doing here! You must get out at once." Eadgyth scolded me.

Asfrid looked round when she heard my name.

"See, this is what you do to me you pig! Now get out! I don't want you to see me like this." Asfrid growled.

I kissed her.

"I love you my Lady," I told her and then backed out of the chamber, fascinated by this glimpse of the female world. I returned to the hall where Gram looked at me inquisitively.

"The baby's coming," I told him simply.

I sat down with Togi on my knee. We sat in silence for a while. Hildy returned with Flaed and they went straight through the hall. Flaed bobbed me a greeting as she hurried past and I stood, then they were gone and I sat again. Togi wanted to follow them and got grumpy when I stopped him. I got some of his toys and rattled and shook them to keep him amused. I eventually broke the silence by telling Gram about the plan to attack Caer Colun in the spring. He made a few terse comments and when I finished we sat in silence again.

I got a whetstone and sharpened my blades, while Togi explored around the benches and tables. I went outside and realised straight away that there was no point and went back in. I paced up and down the hall carrying the little fellow while he dozed on my shoulder. When he woke again he was grizzly and fretful. I found some bread and I cut some of the crust for him to suck and chew. Realising that it could be hours yet before the baby arrived we went for a walk, the Warlord, the bodyguard and the toddler. We found ourselves down at the riverside where we gathered pebbles and sticks to throw out into the water. There were sheep in the water meadows which fascinated the little fellow at a distance but when we got close and I put him down so that he could look at them he got frightened and wanted to be picked up again.

We walked back to the fort and watched Leuthere hammering red hot strips of iron to make a scythe for one of the farmers. Togi liked the fire and the sparks and struggled to get down and take hold of them for himself. He then got irksome again when he couldn't and it was time to move on. Some of the ladies we passed came over and made a fuss of him which he enjoyed and after a couple of hours away we were back at the hall.

He had just about exhausted my paternal energy and he was crying and annoying me again. Luckily Hildy had left the other women in order to start preparing food for the evening and I handed Togi to her. She cleaned and fed him and settled him down for another nap. I went with Gram and we got out the practice swords but I struggled to concentrate and Gram managed to catch me with a couple of good hits. I apologised for not really testing him and I fetched a bow and had a go at shooting at a straw target, it occupied time but I would never have Wuffa's skill with a bow.

I thought of Asfrid kneeling on the bed trying to force the baby out from between her legs. I thought of the men I had watched helping to draw calves or lambs out of their mothers, and I wondered if Flaed reached in and drew the baby out, like a shepherd. I shuddered at the thought. I supposed that they knew what they were doing.

The day crawled past and still there was no news. I returned to the hall in the late afternoon and had a pot of ale while I watched Hildy prepare a broth, and keep Togi amused at the same time. She had penned him in to a small area with a number of playthings and by chattering to him as she worked she was keeping him quite happy. Some of the Wolf Pack lads returned to the hall, and I had men to talk to again which helped to ease the time a little more. A couple of them played with Togi and eventually the broth was ready and we ate.

The light was fading when, finally, a baby's cry from my chambers reduced the company to instant silence. I stood up and waited for Eadgyth to appear. After what seemed an age, the hanging was pushed aside and my sister beckoned me in. I hurried through to the back of the hall and up the stairs. They had cleaned the mess up, and Asfrid was propped up in our bed holding our new.......

"Boy," she stated baldly. "Another one, although this one is going to be a giant I think." She looked exhausted, the baby looked like any other to me.

"Look at him," Eadgyth urged. "He's huge, your poor lady needs a rest. She must be worn out."

"She looks as beautiful as she ever has," I told her with a kiss, remembering Aelfgifu's advice.

"You obviously need a rest as well then, your eye sight is clearly failing," she joked. "Here do you want to hold him?"

She offered him up and I took the wrinkled, snub nosed lump from her. He stirred, opened his mouth wide and raised his fists, before settling again.

"What are we going to call him?" Asfrid asked.

"I thought, Aethelwulf," I said simply.

"Aethelwulf it is," She agreed.

"Are you happy with that?" I asked.

"Aethelwulf is good. If the next one's a girl I will choose. You can choose the boys," She told me affably, and I thought that was a fair approach. Little Aethelwulf was determined to sleep and I handed him back to his mother. I escorted Flaed from the hall, paying her well for her services, and I announced to the Wolf Pack that I had a second son and told Renweard to go to the waelcyrge and tell him to make sacrifices in thanks to the gods and for a great future for prince Aethelwulf. They cheered and laughed and downed their ale in his honour, and I called for more. Life was good.

CHAPTER 11: Horses

My side was healing well, even though it was still a little tight, and daily weapon practise with the Wolf Pack was bringing back my speed and sharpness. Every night I lay awake, thinking ahead to my next war. In the deepest dark of the night, when I couldn't even see my hand before my eyes, I had no shape, no form, I was merely thought, and visions of slaughter filled my emptiness. The ghosts of the battles that I had fought, and the faces of the men and women who I had butchered, came back to remind me that my own place awaited me in the next life at Wolf's mead benches. When they left, the silence rang in my ears, disturbed now and again by a cough, or the breath starved snores from the men sleeping around the fire in the main hall below.

I knew that many would question my decision to give Artorius the throne of Caer Colun. Even though he was my oath giver he regarded himself as one of the Combrogi. The ancient hatred between the Wealh kingdoms had enabled our people to make this land our home. While they fought among themselves the Irish had taken the western coastal lands, Picts had raided from the north, and Angels, Saxons, Jutes, Frisians, Danes and Franks had won or been given kingdoms all along the eastern and southern coastland and river roads. The Wealh kings had welcomed our folk to their kingdoms in pursuit of conquest, or safety. Now many of those warriors were ruling the kingdoms that they had come to defend. The Combrogi wanted to see the Wealh kingdoms unite in order to resist any further advances by the Sais, as they called us, or the Irish and the Picts. Many would have seen this as cause for suspicion and animosity between us, but he was my friend, and I had promised him that I would do this. I knew that once he was king, my southern border would be secure. I wouldn't have to fear war or raids from the Trinovantes as long as he held power. It was also sensible to remember that my people weren't only Angels.

Many Wealh of the Iceni tribe were also east Angels. They wanted to see the tyrant, Gwrgant thrown down.

I decided to visit Artorius. We needed to decide how we would fight the Trinovantes. It would be a welcome change for Asfrid and the children as well. The journey was easy enough in spite of the lateness of the year. It was a steady ten mile walk, and with the ladies and children accompanying us progress was sedate, but the rain held off and we spent a lot of time pointing out birds, and plants to Togi. Asfrid laughed a lot, played with Togi, kicked leaves about, and skipped around like a spirit of the season. I was entranced by her, as were my warriors, and I thought again about organising a guard for her and the boys.

The land we walked through had changed hugely in a very short time. There were farms dotted about the country at regular intervals, and we actually passed a few people on the road. There was still plenty of room for growth, but my kingdom was well ordered, wealthy, and at peace with itself.

As we drew close to Artorius' home a group of horsemen rode out to investigate us. I recognised their leader as Artorius' companion Gawain. He dismounted and bowed a greeting.

"Lord Wulfhere. This is an unexpected honour."

"Gawain, we have come to visit our friends, that is all."

He sent a rider back to announce us and had the rest of his men dismount and walk with us to the town.

The track was well worn by foot, wheel and hoof, though the grass grew thickly at the sides. Ahead of us we caught sight of thatched roofs and a gathering of folk waiting to greet us. One hulking figure stood out from the crowd even at this distance, Artorius, at least a head taller than anyone else, at the forefront of his people. He strode forward to greet me with his arms wide. We embraced and then he greeted Asfrid, and little Aethelwulf.

"This must be the fellow who was making his arrival the day that I was at your hall. He's a bonny little Sais, has he started training yet my lord?" He asked mischievously.

"Not yet Artorius, he won't get a seaxe until he's at least two." I joined in the jest.

"You think he's joking don't you?" Artorius warned his companions, "They say that lord Wulfhere was eleven? When he killed his first enemy." He looked at me quizzically.

"They say all sorts of things my friend," I replied neither confirming nor denying his enquiry.

Eadgyth brought Togi forward and Artorius looked surprised.

"You will bring your entire family under my roof?" He looked at me with a staggered expression on his face. "Even though I am, Wealh?"

"I believe that you are a friend, Artorius. I am absolutely certain that you are a man of honour. If we stood as opponents on a field of battle I would still accept your word. I have killed many Danes and my family has suffered grievously at Danish hands, yet my wife is Danish, and I love her as I love my life. It is what is in the heart that matters, not what is in the veins, as I have said before."

"Then I am truly honoured to have you as my guest, my lord."

He announced something in his own tongue to the assembled people who raised a cheer and parted to give us the way to the town. We walked the bare track between the houses. Children played, chickens scratched and strutted, women spun yarn in groups in doorways where the light allowed them to work. We rested and enjoyed a pot of ale in Artorius' hall.

"It's not as grand as yours, lord, but then I don't intend to stay here for very much longer," he confided.

"That's one of the reasons that I am here," I said. "I wanted to discuss how we will defeat Gwrgant."

"Just one of the reasons, lord?"

"Yes Artorius, I am firstly here out of friendship and gratitude for your service while I was away in Caer Lerion. I also wanted to meet your people. I believe that we have much to learn from each other. I am sure that your people will have ways of doing things on farms or in the house which we could learn from, just as no doubt our people have some ideas that you could borrow.

I am also keen to learn the history of this land. I look at the great stone forts and halls and wonder how the builders and garrisons of those structures could have ever been overthrown.

There must be lessons in that story for everyone." There was a brief silence between us as he absorbed my words, and then he nodded.

"You know there is one lesson I brought straight home. I have my warriors practising their skills every day." he smiled broadly.

In the afternoon we went to an open field and Artorius and his warriors gave us an excellent show of their horsemanship. They rode in line, wheeling or charging as one. They hurled their spears at targets, at the gallop, and engaged posts with their swords. It was an impressive display.

"Is that what the Huns were like, Wulfhere? And the Wealh of Caer Lerion?" Asfrid asked me, wide eyed.

"They weren't as good as these men," I confirmed. "But it gives you a good idea. It isn't actually all that frightening when you are ready for them. Horses won't charge the shield wall. We can deal with them quite easily." I tried to reassure her.

We ate well in Artorius' hall and he had a, 'bard' who told heroic poems and sang songs, accompanied by a lyre. It was a good evening until I was asked about the attack on Caer Lerion. Marcellus took up the tale dwelling on my slaying of the giant, and then making much of my seizing the gate of Caer Lerion by myself. I knew Asfrid was watching me. I felt her hand on mine and I turned my head and looked into her eyes.

"I am very proud of you my love," she told me quietly.

Later in our dark, quiet bed she kissed me and told me what was in her heart.

"When I saw all those men in the hall looking up to you, I realised how lucky I am to have such a man. I love you, Wulfhere, and I will tell our children that you are the greatest man of our time, but don't forget that I am a Danish shield maiden. My father was Toglos Frostbeard. I understand that you have your duty on the slaughter field, and I understand that fate knows if you will return to me or go to your place at Wolf's mead bench. You have served your family well, don't fear for us."

We made love then, and though we couldn't know it at the time, our next child was conceived in that love.

We had a wonderful time as a guest of Artorius and the Wealh. They had a love of poetry and music and in the evenings they sang songs and we recounted our heroic tales. Asfrid told sagas of the Danes which Marcellus translated. We spoke of the Roman Emperors and the history of the empire, and tales of far flung places, and Rome itself, were recounted. I told them how Leofmund's grandfather had travelled to Rome and the sun burnt lands beyond and this news was greeted with great interest.

On our third night we sat with our companions around us and discussed the plan to conquer Caer Colun.

"When we spoke before, Artorius, we decided that the best preparation for the war would be for your horsemen to worry at Gwrgant's outlying country. Take his taxes, burn his grain and the like. How is that going?"

"For some time we have been waging a small war against the tyrant. We have been trying to hurt him while still defending the people. It isn't straight forward. He is," Artorius sought words strong enough to capture Gwrgant's nature. "Cruel," was all he could fashion at that moment. His companion, Bedwyr, stepped in. He was a swarthy, wiry fellow, possibly of Alan blood, I couldn't say.

"Lord Wulfhere, Artorius struggles to find words. You must understand that Gwrgant is a clever man. A man of words, a devious man. He didn't win his kingdom on the battlefield. Nor was he raised to rule. He has gained his place through, cunning, plotting and deception. He trusts no one and fears everyone. He doesn't even trust his own people to guard him. He has a warband of Irish warriors who are his guards. They are like beasts of the wild. They are beyond any law, they are his hounds. They are hated and feared in equal measure. That hatred binds them ever closer to the tyrant who pays them and encourages their excesses.

We have found that when we take food, livestock or silver which has been levied as tax from the people, Gwrgant blames the local folk for not protecting it, and unleashes his Irish men upon them. We have been forced to restrict our attacks to areas which are known to support the king, but they tend to be in the Southern lands of Caer Colun and they are harder to reach and further to flee home from."

I nodded acceptance of this explanation. They were clearly doing what they could.

"Do you know what strength he will be able to call on? How many men will remain loyal to the king?" I wondered.

"As well as his Irish he has some Sais who have been granted land on the banks of the great river Temes. They defend the land from the Cantware Sais, and pirates and raiders. They will remain loyal, of course. The southern lords of Caer Colun will follow his banner, if only out of fear. We have stirred up a broth of discontent and contempt in the northern half of the kingdom because it is easy for us to reach the folk there, and they have had our protection on a number of occasions. When the monster took bishop Gwilym into captivity he also turned many hearts against his disgraceful rule. I believe that no few lords will wait and see which way the victory is going before they commit their men to battle. I would think that he can probably muster an army of six or seven hundred with perhaps two hundred horsemen among that number."

"How many of the Trinovantes will muster to your banner, Artorius?" I asked quietly.

"I have some forty horsemen here and I can raise the same number of foot warriors. I have spoken personally to a number of lords of the Trinovantes and I am confident that another eighty horsemen and two hundred foot warriors will join me, as long as they know that you will be there with your army. I am also certain that almost as many again will come over to us if they see that we are going to triumph. How many warriors will the Wolf lord bring to war?"

"I will bring five hundred, warriors, not fyrdmen. Many of my Iceni lords are anxious to help your struggle. With the Wolf Pack at the heart of our shield wall it will be enough."

I was quite confident that if between us we could command over seven hundred men on foot and well over a hundred horsemen we would be able to defeat an army which didn't love its king.

We stayed for four more days, and hugely enjoyed the Wealh hospitality. We chose a dry day for our journey home and made it an excursion again. Asfrid had always been full of life and vigour but it now seemed as though she wanted to draw value from every moment. She sang and laughed as we walked, and started games of riddles.

I watched and smiled and joined in when I was required to, but my mind was elsewhere. I liked to know as much as I could about my enemies. I didn't want to leave anything to chance. I wanted to know how many Saxons Gwrgant would have to anchor his shield wall. Asfrid walked with me.

"What's troubling you, Wulfhere?"

"I need to know more about my enemy. There are many uncertain things about this war. I know that my men will stand fast and fight hard but I don't know how to best use Artorius' Wealh warriors. They don't fight like us, in the war hedge. The Wealh like to make great wild charges and then fight a broken, uncontrolled battle. I don't know that Artorius' men will be able to hold the line without losing their heads and charging out to meet the enemy. As for the horsemen, well," I shrugged, at a loss. "Do they just follow us and then chase the enemy when they flee? Do they dismount and join our wall and then mount up again and chase the enemy. It seems a waste somehow but I can't see how I can use them to break Gwrgant's charge."

We walked in silence for a while. I was stuck. If we used the horsemen as a screen in front of our wall they would be overwhelmed and slaughtered. They had speed but they couldn't defend.

"You told me once that when you fought the Danes in the old land, Wulfstan took his men round behind them while you attacked from the front," Asfrid suggested.

"Yes, that's right," I answered, a little distracted by her interruption.

"Well, couldn't Artorius do that? Horses are fast. He could dash round behind them." She looked earnestly at me, desperately trying to help.

I smiled and brushed her cheek with my fingers.

"Well they could I suppose, my love, but........"

There was no but. Nothing filled that long pause. Why not? If they were off the field why shouldn't they encircle Gwrgant while I held his head on assault. My lads could wear down his horsemen and his wild Irish and then Artorius could appear behind them. They would panic and run and Artorius would be amongst them and my lads would be at their backs. It was brilliant, the shield wall and the horsemen working for each other. It was just like the Romans!

"Asfrid, that's brilliant! That's just brilliant. I would never have thought!"

I picked her up and swung round with her in my arms and she shouted with laughter. She was wonderful, she was beautiful, she was magnificent! We had our plan.

Life was good, life was for living, for assaulting the senses with the sun and moon, wind, rain, or snow, song and laughter and loving, and, when it came to it, with the thrill and heart pounding exhilaration of battle. We had seized life between us and together we would devour it.

CHAPTER 12: The Wolf in Winter

The air cooled, the wind got up and blew rain across the land in waves. Typical blood month weather, which meant that the flies were being washed and blown away. All of the livestock that Hunberht wanted us to keep through the winter for next year's breeding stock had been selected. There wouldn't be enough hay to keep the rest, especially now that I had a herd of horses to keep. We sent sacrificial beasts to the waelcyrge to thank the gods for our rich harvest and then the hall yard was awash with blood and meat for three weeks. Hides were scraped clean, meat was smoked, salted and dried. The hall's rafters, up where the smoke gathered, were hung with flesh. Hams and tongues were cured and packed in ash filled barrels, buckets of blood were kept for black puddings and colouring paint and limewash. Bones and horns were sorted into carefully selected piles ready to be fashioned into tool handles, needles, combs, hooks, pots and all of the useful items that we would need every day. Intestines had to be rinsed for making sausage skins or stitching sails or tents together. This was really a time of overflowing plenty. The granaries and storehouses were full, the haylofts were piled high and winter was knocking at the door.

A number of young warriors arrived at my door seeking to join my household. No doubt, with another winter about to test their storehouses, their families had suggested that the time was right for them to make their way in the world and chance their arms with the Wolf. They were made welcome, but I wouldn't take any oaths until they proved themselves. Not only did they practise their battle play relentlessly, Gram and I expected them to live as warriors and to love the life. Every evening the talk was of battles, warlords, new skills learned at practice and the great stories of the heroes of old. The way that they'd fought in the war against Tasciovarus was proof that our way was right. Encouraged by Gram to live as Tiw's chosen warband they competed with each other to constantly prove themselves and drive standards ever higher. The arrival of a Norse warband who wanted to join us was proof that our renown was spreading far and wide.

Ottar Strong Arm, was the third son of a Norse jarl. As his name pproclaimed he was a powerful young warrior, not as tall as me, but as broad as a hall door, with a bull neck, thickly muscled arms adorned with sturdy leather bracers, and an impressive number of shining rings. He hefted a great war hammer which he called Skull Crusher, but before fighting, the thing that he liked to do most of all was laugh, and what a laugh. He came to the hall with his companions and from the moment he arrived and introduced himself his great bellows of laughter filled Wolf Home. I couldn't help but like him. There was nothing sly, or underhand about him. He didn't stand on ceremony and would speak to me, or one of my bondsmen, with equal frankness and complete honesty.

He arrived at Wolf Home aboard a neat, high prowed long boat, rowed by his twelve companions, and made straight for the hall. I had spent the morning with Haeddi, admiring my horses. He had brought the new Irish horses from Ship Home and we had given the herd a thorough inspection, deciding which stallion should be put to which mares to give us the fastest or sturdiest foals.

I had returned to Wolf Home and was drying by the fire, enjoying a pot of ale with Gram, when the hall door opened as if a gale had suddenly sprung from nowhere and flung it wide. The portal was filled by the young Norse man who looked around the hall before spotting me and calling, in a voice which made the beams ring,

"You must be lord Wulfhere, the giant killer! Well that's alright because you're taller than me!"

Perhaps something had been lost in translation because he bellowed with laughter as if this was the finest joke he had heard in many a long month, but we were soon to discover that if ever you weren't sure where Ottar was you just had to wait a short while and his laughter would give him away.

"I am Ottar Strong Arm, and I am come to here, to join the mighty Wolf men!"

He strode across the hall and clasped my hand as if we were dear friends.

"Welcome, Ottar Strong Arm. Bring your companions in and find yourselves a place in my hall. Frygith can bring us more ale and you can tell me your story."

Ottar told us colourful tales of his own prowess in battle, his sea voyages, his family's connections and renown and we discovered that tales of lord Wulfhere and his Wolf Pack had crossed the sea to the Norse lands. I was delighted to hear that the Wolf Pack had become a watchword for ferocity and prowess upon the slaughter field. I was even more delighted when Ottar recounted the tale of Wulfhere and the Wealh giant, even though it bore no resemblance to the actual event and made my lads chuckle and add their own embroideries to the fanciful story.

Clearly I was delighted to welcome the young lord to Wolf Home, and he proved his boasts of strength when we practiced our weapon skills over the following days. I warmed to the ebullient, forthright nature of the barrel chested Norseman, and would have asked him to join my household but Asfrid suggested that I should test him first, for very sensible reasons.

"I like him as well, Wulfhere, you can't dislike him, but we are feeding forty seven warriors, and the household, every day! Can't you find him, or some of the others, a task to do? What about courts, it must be time for you to travel soon, couldn't you start early?"

She was right of course. We would empty our storehouses by early spring if we weren't a little more careful with our supplies. It was too early to hold courts though. Courts were always held at the same time, at the same places during the winter months. Firstly because they wouldn't interrupt work or war. Secondly so that my household would be fed by the assorted lords and estates where the courts were held, and thirdly so that the people knew when they would be held and could gather at the appointed time and place to bring their petitions.

I did have an idea of my own which would give Ottar an ideal chance to prove himself. I took him to one side and explained my plan the following morning after practice.

"Ottar, in the spring we are going to war to take the kingdom of Caer Colun and kill the filthy tyrant, Gwrgant, who rules that sad land. When he is dead, Artorius will be the new king and the people will be much better off.

I know nothing of Gwrgant's strength and I want you to go to his hall, offer him your service, and return here in the spring with that knowledge."

There was a long pause.

"You want me to spy."

"Yes."

Another pause as Ottar considered my request.

"You are an outsider. As far as he is concerned you are just another sell sword. You will be able to get into his household where my men couldn't."

"Your men? So am I not your man?"

"If you do this for me I will take your oath, and you will have my gratitude. You will join my household and I will not forget your service. All of the warriors who come to my hall have to prove themselves before I take their oaths, you know this."

"Yes, lord. I know it. But it is not easy to be a spy."

"Gwrgant is a filthy swine. He rapes, he murders, he steals, he looses his Irish men on his own people. It is right that we should kill him. It is right for our people, it is right for me and for Artorius. The gods themselves would want us to do this. My god, Tiw, lord of Justice, will want this and he will be with me when I take the field in the spring. Our victory will be helped by the knowledge that you bring me." I had spoken my piece and I expected his agreement.

He sighed deeply, then shrugged his heavy shoulders,

"If it is your wish, lord, I will do it."

He left the next morning.

There was nothing to do now but to prepare to travel my kingdom to hold the winter courts. My heart sank at the prospect of sitting through the petty arguments of greedy little men, but it was my duty, and there would be hunting and entertainment at each estate to ease the pain. I began to prepare for the mind numbing ordeal.

Before we got underway, however, four rain soaked Wealh horsemen arrived at Wolf Home, sent by Icel to summon his wife, my sister Esme, and their son, Angeltheow, to join him in the Marches. I was to provide them with an escort. Here was a chance to escape, for a while at least. The messengers were sent north to the Golden Hall of Caer Went to inform my sister that I would meet her at Durobrivae in ten days time.

Eadgyth wanted to come, of course, to see her sister and have a look at her new home. She also wanted to bring her maids, Hildy and the new lass, Caitlinn, in order to make a show as much as for any practical purpose. As we would be skirting Catuvellauni territory all the way from the Granta bridge I would take twenty Wolf Pack lads to see us safely there without attracting too much attention from any curious Catuvellauni eyes.

Durobrivae, was the northernmost of the three towns that we had taken last year. It was the easiest one for Esme to get to, following the old Roman street across the great fenland. Since the war, Icel's Wealh lord of Durobrivae, Cadwr, had been very busy. The walls had been repaired and the ditches deepened and widened, making the fort a very tough obstacle to attack. The River fort, as it was now known by our people, was a hugely important burrh, standing as it did right on the border of Corieltavi and Catuvellauni land. Even though the land was truly in the grip of winter it was bustling with traders when we arrived, as well as Esme's strong company.

Esme was very excited to see me again, and full of questions about her new home. I answered as fully as I could from memory, and Cadwr made up for my vague descriptions with his own, more knowledgeable, observations. We spent the night in Cadwr's hall and were on the move shortly after dawn had crept across the land. I didn't want to waste any time, or give spies a chance to send word of our journey to Cynfellyn.

Esme had her own guard of twenty six warriors and their families, as well as her attendant maids and household servants who were accompanying their lady to her new home. We were all tied to the steady plod of the oxen which drew the four wagonloads of goods and belongings that she was also taking. I didn't relax for one moment of the entire journey. All through the daylight hours I was gazing southwards, watching for any sign of approaching horsemen. Throughout the night I was unable to sleep. Instead I drifted between the camp and the street, alert for the slightest hint of an attack.

The oxen were harnessed in the dark and we were on the move again before the world was fully light. Two nights were spent in the open and it was dark on the third day before we reached Icel's city of Ratae, which he had re-named Ligora Ceaster in honour of the Wealh king who had originally founded the city, before the Romans took it.

Icel and his companions met us at the gate. There were speeches of welcome and a long line of worthies waiting to be introduced, which was tedious, but necessary. Then we made our way through the city to the stone hall where my rumbling stomach was soon filled by the excellent feast which had been prepared to welcome Esme.

I had been given a place of honour at the high table alongside Icel. Even though he had only held Ligora Ceaster for a few months he was already assuming a leader's mantle amongst the Corieltavi. His kingdom was large and wealthy, and with my support he was as strong as, if not stronger than, all of the other Corieltavi kings acting together. Several of them had already thrown in their lot with the new Sais power, and accepted Icel's overlordship, sending him gifts in order to gain favour with the new strong man.

Looking around the hall it was obvious that the bulk of the folk present were Wealh. The speeches and entertainments were in our tongue, the tongue of the king, and in our presence all of the lords used the language of the Angels. But where the Wealh sat together in the quiet corners of the hall, the throaty language of the

Corieltavi was still more common. Icel seemed quite comfortable among his Wealh oath givers.

"They look to me as their lord, just as our folk do," he enlightened me. "The Wealh have fought each other for hundreds of years. The Corieltavi with the Catuvellauni to the south, Cornovii to the west and Brigantes to the north. The Romans kept the peace to a point. There were always tensions around borders but as long as the legions were here none of the tribes could wage outright war on their neighbours. The Romans wanted peace and prosperity. They wanted grain and iron for their armies and anyone upsetting the order of the empire would soon be put in their place.

Now that I am here the Corieltavi have the strength of two kingdoms to keep their enemies at bay, and possibly even to extend their wealth and power in the land. They see, in us, a great opportunity. The test will come when Cynfellyn marches north to reclaim his burrhs!"

"When will he come?" I wanted to know.

"One of the advantages of living among the Wealh is that they all know what the other kingdoms are planning. Merchants and travellers carry the news. I have a good position here, Wulfhere. It gives me an understanding of the other kingdoms. Cynfellyn is planning to come north with his army as soon as the land will support his war. He wants to take us by surprise!" We both laughed at that. "We also need to keep a close watch on our Western border. Ambrosius of the Cornovii is the main power behind the Combrogi."

"Oh, I know all about them," I stepped in. "Artorius is a great one for the Combrogi."

"Then you will know that they want us driven out!" Icel stated incredulously.

"He wants to hold what he has. He isn't against us. He will give me peace on my southern border, Icel. I will be able to watch Cynfellyn without fearing the Trinovantes, which will be no bad thing. As far as I have learned from the Wealh, the Catuvellauni and the Trinovantes have acted together in the past. With Artorius in Caer Colun I will halve the threat." I explained.

"So you're still planning to give our sworn enemy a kingdom then! Wulfhere, are you sure that this is wise?"

"I have no doubts about Artorius, Icel. When we take Caer Colun he will hold it in friendship. Our security will be certain."

"And when are you planning this war? I will need you here, ready to fight Cynfellyn in the spring. If I am going to hold on to this kingdom, and increase my power within the Corieltavi, we need to beat Cynfellyn and prove to the world that we are the strength in the land."

I paused before answering. I had to support my king even though I had told Artorius that we would attack Gwrgant in the spring. I had no choice.

"We will take Caer Colun once Cynfellyn is defeated, Icel. We cannot risk what you have gained here. We will fight the Catuvellauni, and then I will lead my men against the Trinovantes. Gwrgant won't ally himself to Cynfellyn. He is too uncertain of his own kingdom to leave it and march to war. Once he is overthrown Artorius will rule the Trinovantes. This will be an advantage for us in the long term."

"As long as your Artorius doesn't take up the Combrogi banner and join the Cornovii and the Catuvellauni to drive us out!"

"He won't attack us, Icel. He is sworn to this. He is a trusted friend."

I had no doubts about Artorius' intentions but I felt wretched at the prospect of having to tell him that I would have to deal with Cynfellyn before I could turn to Gwrgant.

CHAPTER 13: Loyalty

I only stayed with Icel for two days. I was running short of time if I was going to attend the courts of my kingdom and prepare for war in the spring. I stopped at the River Fort, Godmund's Ceaster and the Granta Bridge to warn them that Cynfellyn was planning to surprise us. I was particularly anxious to see if Cissa and Aldwyn had finished building the defences at the Granta Bridge.

Our reunion was genuinely friendly, and even though it was only early afternoon I gave word that we would stay here for the night. Osburga, Cissa's wife, invited us up to the hall but I wanted to inspect the wall and ditch, so I told the ladies to go ahead and promised to join them shortly. Once they were gone I spoke to my old friends, warning them of our situation.

"Icel has word from the Wealh that Cynfellyn will attack us in the spring," I told them straight away. "Have you finished the burrh's defences?"

"Come and see for yourself," Aldwyn said, leading the way.

The thatched roofs of the hall and the estate buildings rose above the stout walls of the burrh. Three ditches ten feet wide and ten feet deep ringed the burrh. The innermost ditch was defended by an earthen rampart, topped by a wooden wall of stout boards pegged and nailed to heavy beams. A couple of men watched our progress from behind the wall, indicating that there was a platform on the inner side from which defenders could fight off an attack, or hurl or shoot spears, stones and arrows at an enemy. The defences were sound. The only small improvement I could suggest might be some sharp stakes driven into the inner wall of the ditch to hamper attempts to climb up, but it was a minor point.

"A hundred men could defend the walls easily," Cissa explained. "We can gather that strength fairly quickly from our own people and by calling on the nearest lords and ceorls for assistance. It's better to keep the walls tight. I know that it won't house an army, but if we had an army we wouldn't be hiding behind the walls. This way we can man the walls with a relatively modest force and then wait for help to arrive."

It was a sound strategy.

"Make sure that your friends locally are ready for trouble then, so that they can muster here quickly. You can be sure that Cynfellyn is coming so don't leave anything to chance," I warned them.

Inside the walls the burrh had a real feeling of strength. Round sling stones had been stockpiled in wooden boxes by the gate. A well had been dug, and stone lined store pits constructed so that provisions could be brought into the burrh from outlying farms if an enemy was pillaging the country. They had done a good job.

There was a lot of laughter that evening as we talked of old times and remembered boyhood adventures. A hair raising encounter with a swarm of bees, wolf nights in the sheep folds, stolen fruit, and a lass named Ebba, who would give the boys a free hand, literally, to strip and explore her in return for delicacies like honey or sweet mice. Those were good times, when everybody was a hero, and the woods and fields around our town were our whole world.

Our sedate column crossed the bridge in the morning and rolled on towards Wolf Home. Along the way we warned the lords and clan leaders; Ithamar, Hygsic, Lafa, Caw, Morwain and Iuniavus of Cynfellyn's intentions and preparing the country for the muster that would be called in the spring.

I barely had time to catch my breath at home. I spent the night with Asfrid and departed to see Artorius the next morning telling Asfrid to prepare the household for our departure to the court at Theodford.

I took only Gram, Marcellus, Wyne and Odd with me as there was little threat of outlaws and I wanted to travel quickly.

Artorius guessed that something was amiss by my presence and I came straight to the point.

"Artorius, my friend. We have to make a change to our plan. Icel has word that Cynfellyn is going to march against us as soon as the season permits and he will need my strength to hold off the

Catuvellauni. I have to follow my king's wishes. I can't leave Aldwyn and Cissa without support, so there is no choice in this. As soon as that threat is dealt with I will bring my army to Caer Colun and honour my promise to you and your people." There was nothing else that I could do.

The tempestuous giant threw his chair back and rose furiously to his feet. He turned and stalked backwards and forwards across the hall, his anger simmering as he considered this news.

"If this is your decision then there is nothing more to be said," was his opinion once he had calmed down enough to speak.

"It is not my decision, Artorius. If I had a free hand I would march with you, as we had planned. You know the strength that Cynfellyn can bring against us. You know the peril that Icel and the Corieltavi will face. Aldwyn and Cissa will not hold him at bay without my help. We will deal with Gwrgant once our people are secure."

"I understand that, Wulfhere, but our support amongst the Trinovantes is at risk. There are many who want us to overthrow the tyrant but they fear him. They need to be sure that we won't fail them. They have..."

"We won't fail them, Artorius! I will come with my army to free your people. I believe that Cynfellyn is going to attack as soon as he can. We will deal with that threat and...."

"Can you be certain, Wulfhere? What if Cynfellyn doesn't attack straight away, what if he tries to break your towns by cutting them off from succour and supply? What if he triumphs, Wulfhere? What if you are killed, your army broken? What will I tell my people?"

"You will tell them that the lord who was going to free them, who was going to shed his blood and his mens' blood to free them, who expected no gain from the war but that his friend would wear the crown, will not be coming! That is what you will tell them!"

We stared at each other briefly before he visibly subsided and held up his hands.

"I'm sorry, Wulfhere. Of course you are right. You must answer Icel's call. I have been set on this course for so long that I reacted wrongly, my lord."

He paused briefly before his thoughts moved on.

"What will you need me to do, while you are away, lord?"

"I want you to guard my family and my kingdom while I fight Cynfellyn. As you did last year. You can reassure the lords of Caer Colun that we are coming, and that they haven't been forgotten."

He accepted my word without further debate. He knew that I was sparing him from having to fight the Catuvellauni. I knew that he had ambitions amongst the kings of the Wealh, and fighting for the Sais against Cynfellyn would have been disastrous for his reputation. I also knew that he had been prepared to do so if I had asked it of him.

He offered me his hand.

"Thank you my lord. You will always have my loyalty, no matter where our paths take us in years to come."

"I know that, my friend. I will never forget your service."

I hurried home and the next day I set out on my journey around my vast kingdom. For a month and a half I lived as a guest of the great lords of the east Angels at Theodford, Waelsingas Home, Heremod's Golden hall at the Iceni Ceaster, Dommoc Ceaster and a last stop at Wulfstan's hall, Rendels Home. I had travelled my kingdom north, south, east and west. I had hunted, feasted, granted and received gifts, held courts, and taken a dozen lads into the Wolf Pack. Most importantly I had met my people and they had seen me. Everywhere I went I had dressed in my finest gear, accompanied by my beautiful wife and my stern household warriors. I was every inch the king, and the people knew that they could have faith in my strength. They were safe, their farms were safe, the kingdom was strong.

We had celebrated modraniht, mothers' night, the feast that marked mid-winter and the lengthening of the days, at Waelsingas Home. The waelcyrge had made sacrifices to Frige, Eostre and Sigel, as is customary, for prosperity, fertility and the return of the sun. We had made good time since then and we would be back at

Wolf Home with weeks to spare before Eostre's own feast. The court at Rendels Home was an important one. This coastal region of the kingdom held a wide mix of peoples; Danes, Frisians, Wealh, Huns, and Angels all shared the land and all had to be treated fairly. I asked Ullr the Dane and Brega the Frisian to advise me and I took my time in passing my judgements, making sure that I knew all of the relevant details of rank and influence of the petitioners, in order to maintain the balance of nature. I didn't mind the slow passing of the days though because Wulfstan had made sure that we had good hunting and excellent mead to ease our burden. My younger brother Wulfgar had left Wolf Home to join Wulfstan's household and it was good to see him again, along with my old teacher, Oswine. Asfrid was happy to be re-united with Sigurd, the true prince of the Danes, and the Danish folk from their towns along the coast and at the Wooden Bridge.

Wulfstan, the scarred, fearsome warrior took a special interest in Togi. It was great to watch the old fellow playing with the toddler and carrying him around the estate showing him the sheep and swine. His own son, Wulfnoth, had been cruelly slain by the Danes, and he was assuming the mantle of grandfather for the youngsters. It was good that the family was drawn close around a new generation. We were the Wolf, individually we were strong, together we were invincible. That was the lesson that I had been taught ever since I was a little older than Togi. It was the lesson that I would be teaching my sons.

All around the kingdom I had spread the word that I would need the army to see off the Catuvellauni and defend king Icel in the spring before marching on Gwrgant. All around the kingdom I had been enthusiastically promised support. After the victories and fame of last summer the lords were eager for the chance of plunder and more glory. These folk had summoned a king from the old lands. Now they wanted to bask in the might and glory of the Angelcynn. It would be a good summer!

We spent over two weeks at Rendels Home but outside our happy hall the world continued to turn. We had to return to Wolf Home and prepare for war. We made our way along muddy tracks to the Roman street which would lead us all the way home. We left the wagons to follow at their own pace and pushed ahead, but it was late into the night when we reached the yard at Wolf Home.

Leofmund was waiting to greet us, along with Ottar Strong Arm's companion, Egil. I was pleased to see him, his presence meant that Ottar must be back. The knowledge that he would have of Gwrgant's strength would help me to plan our battle. Hunberht was organising men to take care of the oxen. Asfrid and Hildy were hurrying the boys inside.

"Leofmund! It's good to see you. Egil, where is Ottar? I will need to speak with him. We are in for a busy summer my friends. Sharpen your blades!"

The dark yard was busy with returning men and wagons.

"Wulfhere, Ottar is inside. He was badly beaten by Gwrgant's men," Leofmund told me grimly.

The news made me pause, badly beaten?

"Did Gwrgant find out he was spying?" I asked. That didn't make any sense. Surely if he had, Ottar would be dead. Leofmund looked to Egil.

"No, lord," the Norseman explained. "Ottar laughed at him!"

"What?" I wasn't sure that I had understood Egil's explanation.

"It was not a good place, lord," Egil elaborated. "The man, Gwrgant is mad with his own power. His hall is a place of fear and cruelty. He sets his Irish on prisoners for entertainment, it is a place of madness, his people fear to go there even to deliver food or feorm. He has wild tempers and, I don't know, it is just a bad place." He seemed to lose his train of thought.

"What about Ottar, Egil?"

"Ottar, yes, well, there is all this madness, all this rage and fear but he was scared of a spider. Gwrgant, I mean. He was scared of a spider which ran under his table, and Ottar laughed. You know how Ottar laughs, he just thought it was funny. Gwrgant flew into a rage and set his Irish on Ottar. We had no weapons. Only the Irish can have weapons in the hall. We were knocked down and beaten so we could not help, and they beat him until he didn't move, and then they cut his face. Gwrgant took a sword and forced it between Ottar's teeth and then back, so that he cut through both cheeks. He said his 'smile' will always be there to show everyone what happens to those who laugh at their betters! Their betters! Gwrgant is a coward, lord. A weak, mad, coward!

Lord, when we beat them, please, give him to us."

I looked into his fiery eyes.

"I will Egil. He is yours."

I followed them inside. Ottar was seated by the fire. He looked up, and in the low fire light the cruel scars, which striped his face from the corners of his mouth almost to his ears, were shining wetly. His nose was broken and, although his face was no longer swollen, there were still some fading bruises on his cheeks and the flattened bridge of his nose. He stood, and I crossed the hall to greet him.

"Lord Wulfhere," he mumbled, trying not to move his mouth too much. "I have the knowledge that you wanted."

"You will be rewarded, my friend. Your loyalty and courage have earned you a place at my hearth. I have promised Egil that after the battle, Gwrgant will be yours!"

CHAPTER 14: The First Blow

Ottar and his lads had been home for ten days. They gathered around and told me what they had learned. Ilse brought us ale and I greeted her warmly. She acknowledged my greeting with a nod and a momentary, half smile, before continuing to busy herself about the hall. Bjarni took up the tale for the Norse men. He had a good knowledge of our tongue.

"He has fifty six Irish madmen, lord. They do as they will and they have lost all control of reason. They are hated and feared and will fight to the death for Gwrgant, for without him they will be torn apart by the people. They are lead by a tall warrior they call Caoimhghin, which means 'gentle' in their tongue. They think it is a great joke! When they fight, or murder I should say, they eat the magic mushrooms so that they feel neither pain nor guilt. Their excesses have driven them beyond reason. They take girls in the street! Just when they want them! They beat or kill folk at the slightest provocation and they drive each other on to ever greater cruelties. It is a bad place, lord."

"I don't care about these men. They will fall beneath our blades. What of the Saxons to the South? How many are they?"

"They have been granted land, to guard against river raiders and the half Danes and Saxons who live on the other side of the great river. We didn't see more than a few of their head men at the hall, but from what we have asked we think that they might bring sixty or more to the shield wall."

I pondered this for a moment.

"And the Trinovantes themselves? Will they die for this beast?"

"Like all tyrants he bribes his most powerful lords to keep their loyalty. They will still fight for him because he gives them what they want; land, slaves, gifts. There are of course many who will join our side when we march on the city. Many of the people of the city have been cruelly treated and I think that they would rise as a mob if we were camped outside the walls and Artorius assured them of mercy. Many others will not join an enemy but neither will they help the tyrant. I think that his army won't be strong, lord!"

The Irish would fight hard and the Saxons would fight hard. His own people were likely to be less loyal! This was truly, 'a bad place'.

I asked Leofmund to fetch silver from my strong box to reward the Norsemen. For Ottar himself I had a fine, bone handled seaxe and a Wealh helmet, which I had captured at the war with Tasciovarus. It was in the Roman style. It had a domed crown, sweeping neck guard and cheek flaps which fastened with a leather thong.

"Thank you, lord." Ottar muttered, and I noticed that a few teeth were missing.

"Loyalty freely given deserves reward my friend. Now, I will take your oath."

He knelt, and clasped his hands over mine upon my sword hilt. Quietly he promised me his loyal service to the death and in return I promised him fair reward and my protection at all times. Ottar Strong Arm was now my man.

Now it was my turn to speak.

"Gwrgant will have to wait. I have spoken with king Icel since I last saw you and he knows that Cynfellyn of the Catuvellauni is going to attack our people as soon as he can bring his army into the field. He has called on us to lead the army again. We will deal with Cynfellyn and then march on Gwrgant."

The Norsemen were clearly disappointed with my news but they held their counsel while I continued.

"I have spoken with Artorius. He will guard Wolf Home while we face Cynfellyn. The king has summoned us. That is all."

It was Icel's will. Revenge would have to wait.

First of all we had to be ready. We had the Norse men and the new lads to test and to teach our way of war. We formed the shield wall, keeping friends at each other's shoulders. We practised fighting with spear, seaxe, sword and shield. We taught the newcomers the spirit of the Wolf Pack. We dedicated ourselves to Tiw and to battle and because we served a god we had to be proud of ourselves and each other, and live by standards of steadfastness and weaponplay that others could never hope to match. We weren't a fyrd rabble. We didn't torment captured women, we kept order and thought only of the next chance to go into battle. We were brothers. I told them of my visions of Tiw. I tried to explain how the emotions of the battle field, together with the strength of my god and my ancestors, could take me beyond the middle earth to a place that was both within me and above me at one and the same time. That mastery of death and fear was what they should all strive for. Gram said that he had felt it too and I believed him. He embraced war as I had done. The others wanted to find that place and they worked hard at reaching perfection.

As the festival of Eostre approached I was confident that the reputation of the Wolf Pack would flourish with these lads. They adapted well. Ottar's boys were no strangers to the slaughter field. Ottar himself wasn't taking a full part in practices yet. Gwrgant's men had broken two or three of his ribs and swinging his heavy war hammer was too much of a strain, although he was hefting it as much as he could, and I didn't think that it would be very long before he was back to his full strength.

There were sixty of us now and Asfrid was becoming concerned about our supplies again. I decided to move camp to the Granta bridge. If the Catuvellauni started raiding or testing our readiness before our armies were in the field I would be in the best place. I would also have a chance to venture into Catuvellauni territory and do a bit of raiding on my own account.

I didn't want to call out the whole army yet. I couldn't possibly keep them fed at this time of year. I sent messengers to Wulfstan to tell him that I was going to the Granta bridge and that I would summon him as soon as I had any word of the Catuvellauni. I sent Leofmund to stay with Heremod's household at Ceaster where he would wait for my summons to gather the army of the north folk and march across the fen causeway to join us. When I sent for the south folk, Artorius' horsemen would muster the army and Ullr would lead them to the Granta Bridge.

I was going to ride to war. I had eleven horses; three stallions and eight mares. Five of the mares were definitely pregnant and they would stay behind. Haeddi, my stable master, thought that two of the other mares might be pregnant so I would take three stallions and the remaining mare. For the first time I would be able to send riders to carry messages in haste. As my herd increased I would eventually have enough mounted warriors to be able to counter the Wealh horsemen, but that was a long way off.

Spring was upon us. Fields that had been ploughed during the winter were sown. The early flowers were showing their colourful heads, and lambs were chasing each other around the sheep folds. Gnats gathered in afternoon sunshine, and the birds were pairing and nest building. On the first day of Eostremonath I kissed my wife and led my men away from Wolf Home. I was riding to war, and Gram, Marcellus and Ottar also had mounts. Ottar was no horseman. He bounced along uncomfortably and soon decided that riding was hurting his ribs. I told Renweard to take the horse and he leaped up onto it with real delight. We had three wagons which were carrying tents, ale and smoked and pickled fish. Provisions were scarce, storehouses were getting low, but the fishermen would put to sea as soon as the weather was calm enough, and the sea fish swam into the broad mouth of the Arwe, so there was nearly always fish to eat.

Before noon it started to rain and once it had started it didn't want to stop. The skies were relentlessly grey and a chill wind blew from the east. For three days we marched, while the showers came and went. We reached the Granta bridge in the afternoon of the third day. We raised our tents inside the burrh while the rain held off, and I was glad that we were able to cook some hot grain broth in the hall. It was a welcome accompaniment to smoked herring.

"So do Icel's spies know when Cynfellyn is coming?" Aldwyn asked as we spooned the warming broth into our mouths.

"No. Just that he is planning to come early in the year. He wants to surprise us."

"So what are we going to do? Just sit here and wait?" Aldwyn was understandably concerned. We would soon eat him out of house and home.

"No. I'm going raiding. We want supplies ready for when the war does start, and I want plunder for my men. We'll get both from the Wealh towns and villages. Cynfellyn won't be here yet. Even if the local lords rally together we can fight our way back here."

"So this is it. From now on we must be watchful. We will never have peace once the raiding starts," Aldwyn announced with a resigned air.

He was right, of course. The price of a border estate is constant watchfulness, but that was the reason that I had given him this land. I wanted a strong man in charge here.

"I will make it worthwhile, my friend. Once Cynfellyn is beaten I will enforce a yearly tribute on the Wealh. You will be able to afford a strong household!"

The next day was fine and bright, but the ground was saturated and the camp was rapidly becoming a muddy swamp. It was time to go raiding. Once the men had eaten and filled their skins with new beer I gathered them together by the gate.

"We are going to take plunder, food and livestock. We won't be taking slaves, we can't spare the men to guard them. I'll choose men to drive any livestock that we come across straight back here. We need to fill the storehouse before Cynfellyn gets here so that we can fight him with full bellies. We will kill every man we come across. I don't want them swelling Cynfellyn's army.

The first town that we're going to take is about nine miles away to the south west, on the street," Aldwyn had told me where the best prizes would be. "We can't hang around. I don't know when Cynfellyn's coming, although I doubt he'll be dragging an army along wet tracks this early in the year, but they will be alert and they're on the edge of muster so their local fyrdmen might come after us. Just stay awake, watch for anything and don't get left behind. Follow me."

I turned and jogged out through the gate. I wouldn't ride on the raid for two reasons; firstly I would have to keep to the pace of the warband. The only time I might need a horse would be to flee, and I wouldn't abandon my men no matter the threat. Secondly horses were hard to hide, and much of our success would depend on stealth. Aldwyn and Cissa watched us leave from the wall by the gate. They would be busy while we were gone preparing the burrh for the battle to come.

The Roman streets were perfect for raiders and I set a good pace. The land was flat, but there were enough trees to hide our approach until we were half a mile from the town. I peered out from a small wood, across cultivated fields at a collection of Wealh houses. They were a strange mix, some round, some squared like ours. The small town had grown around the place where the Roman street that we were following crossed another street which ran north to south. I sent Ottar and his lads to skirt the town to the south and Wyne took a dozen men to the north. When I thought they would be ready, I started from the trees. The Wolf Pack emerged behind me in a line which stretched across the bare field. As silently as morning mist we drifted across the field, until a sudden female shout announced our discovery.

We lurched forward into a clumsy charge, stumbling over the sticky, tilled earth, and I realised straight away that I had made a stupid blunder. The recent heavy rain had soaked the bare earth and our progress was hampered by the clay which clung to our feet and legs in great clods. An arrow whistled past me, and then another, and then a stone bounced off my mailed shoulder, raising a stinging bruise. I cursed as I slipped and slithered onward, needing to reach the town as quickly as I could, but unable to gain any purchase on the soft, slimy clay. We were easy targets. Another stone hammered against my chest making me gasp at the bruising impact. A lad to my right cursed as an arrow struck home into the big muscle at the top of his left arm. We were at the mercy of their bowmen and slingers. I redoubled my effort to hurry forward but I lost my feet altogether and, luckily, slopped full length in the mud as another arrow whispered over my head. Almost mad with rage and frustration I slipped and slithered to my feet, expecting an arrow to thump into me at any moment. As my frustration boiled over into a mad rage I heard Ottar, Wyne and their lads yelling between the houses ahead of us. Our tormentors turned and ran back into the town to face this unexpected assault from my companions. They had enjoyed a much easier charge along the stony road, and I was glad that they had. I staggered to the grassy field border, gasping for breath, leg muscles burning, my whole body steaming in the cool spring air. I dragged my feet through the grass, wiping the heavy, cloying mud from my leather shoes and leg armour, before hurrying, on weak legs, between the haphazard collection of buildings.

There wasn't much fighting. There was a lot of cursing and the shrieking of women, and the heavy pounding of running feet. Dogs barked, fowls flapped around, men died. In a few heart beats the town seemed to be full of my warriors and empty of most of the towns folk save the old, the very young and their mothers.

"Take anything of value, especially food!" I yelled, heading for the biggest round house at the northern end of the town. It stood slightly apart from the rest with its supporting byres and storehouses in attendance. This was the lord's house. Two men and a boy lay dead in the yard. A woman knelt by one of the bodies, keening her grief.

Maccus emerged from the house with a mail shirt, helm, and sword, a magnificent haul.

"Well done, Maccus!" I praised him. "What else is in there?"

He left me the war gear and returned to the hunt. Having been a slave of the Wealh he probably knew better than any of the lads where they might hide their treasures. I chuckled as I examined the shirt, I would have to reward him well for this.

The woman screeched something at me before returning to her weeping. I stared at her. I didn't understand the words but the grief and hatred were clear. I looked around the town. There were several women and children weeping over fallen bodies and cursing my men as they went about the business of stripping the houses of anything valuable. I stared back at the screeching woman. I knew of raids where women had been taken and humped by the warband for days, and others where they had had their tits cut off so that they couldn't feed their infants, or been impaled on stakes shoved up inside them. We were the Wolf. We didn't wage war on women and children. I spat.

"One day you will know how lucky you were today," I told her.

Wyne found a cart, which we loaded with whatever food and fowls we could find or catch, and I sent it back up the street to the Granta bridge with twenty four sheep, and four lads to guard, and drive, the prize. Three of them had taken wounds which would hinder them in a fight but wouldn't stop them herding sheep. We slaughtered and bled four swine, and laid their carcasses on the wagon to be butchered back at the fort. This had been a good start. I gave Wyne the helmet and Gram the mail shirt. The sword was for Ottar. The men had also taken spears and knives, which I let them keep, and a fine hanging bowl decorated with a well worked pattern of wheels and swirls which went on the wagon with various other pots, knives and tools which would be useful back home.

We watched them go and then left the street and headed south east across country. Word of our raid would be abroad. We were eight or nine miles from the next village which I planned to raid. Aldwyn told me that there was a small village in an old Roman fort which stood at a ford where other streets met. The fort was the muster place of the local lords. With raiders abroad the Wealh warriors would gather there to deal with the threat. I was going to slaughter them at that place and deprive Cynfellyn of his local fyrdmen. This knowledge of the Wealh had come from the traders who visited the Granta Bridge. It was something that we would miss, for a while at least, after the war, but as long as there was a living to be made the traders would eventually return with their goods, and their knowledge of other kingdoms.

We got our first sight of the fort, or what remained of it, in the late afternoon. It wasn't particularly well defended any more, and I could see why. It was vast. It must have housed an army at one time. Now it was basically a huge open meadow, surrounded by three ditches. The earth that had been dug from each ditch had been piled up on the inner bank to form low, grass covered ramparts. A number of streets gathered at the fort like spokes on a wheel. The one on this side forded a river, which Maccus said was the Granta.

In the centre of the fort was a collection of houses surrounded by cultivated fields and sheep folds. A warband had made camp by the village. The warriors were standing or sitting around their cooking fires. I examined the old fort for a long time. A fort this size would require thousands of men to man it. It was almost impossible to imagine. How did they feed them all? Who could stand against them? I shook my head in helpless admiration. At the moment there were about thirty or forty men at the village, not enough to stop us crossing the ditches, but that wasn't the problem. The ground all around the fort was open for at least a quarter of a mile. By the time we had crossed that ground, negotiated the ditches and then the farm land within, the warriors would be disappearing over the further ramparts and away, leaving us with nothing.

The Wealh had first rate war gear, a legacy of the wealth and craftsmanship which flourished under generations of Roman rule. This Wealh war band would have swords, mail shirts, and helmets. Watching from behind the cover of a bramble thicket I saw something which I prized even more highly than the gear. Tethered, in the heart of the camp, were half a dozen horses. Above everything else, I wanted those horses.

We would have to wait until it was dark.

I slipped back to where the men were waiting out of sight. They gathered around and I motioned for them all to sit. I looked around the expectant ring of faces, some sporting dark bruises and pouting gashes from the earlier fight.

"It's right out in the open. There are three ditches round it but no walls and I reckon that there are about forty Wealh inside at the moment. They've got horses, right in the middle of the camp. I want those horses. If we attack now they'll be over the ditches and far away before we can get near them." I paused and ran through my plan in my head one last time before I told the lads. I didn't want to miss anything out.

"We're going to have to wait until dark. Then we'll march up and go straight in the main gate, pretending that we're another war band coming to help."

"Won't they see that we're not Wealh, lord," Hubbe wondered.

"That's why we're going in the dark." One or two laughed and Hubbe shrugged.

"I was just thinking, lord."

"Quite right, Hubbe. Some of you who laughed should remember that. It's always best to check."

Hubbe smiled proudly, and I continued.

"We will be challenged by the guards. If we're not it's going to be easy!" More laughter. "Maccus and Marcellus will be at the head of the warband with me. When we're challenged they will answer that we're men of, where do you think, Maccus? Where might help be coming from for these lads that they might not know?"

Maccus thought hard.

"From Cynfellyn, lord. From the van of the king's army. Cynfellyn will have Sais in his army. Even if they're not certain, they're not so likely to challenge warriors who might well have been sent by the king. With a bit of luck we'll be in amongst them before they suspect anything."

"That's excellent thinking, Maccus. Once we're in, Ottar, I want you and your lads to grab the horses. That's the biggest prize. They're right in the middle of the camp. The rest of us will split. We will march in two lines. Everyone on the right will go through the right of their camp, all those on the left will go left."

"Lord," Wyne had a question. "Why don't we split up again and attack from different sides like we did before?" He pointed his thumb back over his shoulder in the direction that we had come from.

"I thought about that, Wyne but this is a warband that we're facing, about forty strong. There's a quarter of a mile of open ground to cover all around the fort, and then the ditches. If we didn't all arrive at the same time they could slaughter the groups, one after the other. I think that it's too risky.

We'll all stay together which means we will have to move quickly once we're in. Speed will be vital. We kill everyone in that fort. If they go into the houses you wait outside and set them on fire, don't follow them in, you don't know how many are inside, or if they're standing by the door waiting for you. You set the thatch ablaze and wait for them to run.

Now get a bite to eat and drink and then we had better move. If we're going to claim to be help arriving from Cynfellyn's army, we had better march up the south road.

CHAPTER 15: A Hasty Retreat

The street that Cynfellyn would take from his royal city of Verulamium actually ran slightly west of south, and stayed on our side of the river until it reached the ford at the fort, which was very good news. We waited for darkness to cloak the land before joining the street about a mile and a half from the fort. Our approach would be open and unhurried and I wanted any observers to be convinced that we had marched up from the south. It was a strange feeling, just walking boldly along this street to meet our enemies. I felt that they must know straight away that we were foe men. Were they watching us? Were they preparing to launch a charge against us somewhere ahead in the darkness? Nothing happened and we walked on.

In a very short time we had reached the ford and splashed across, quite openly. We made no effort to disguise our approach and as we reached the gap between the ditches which marked the fort entrance, I told Marcellus to hail the defenders and announce our presence.

The reply drifted out of the darkness from the camp within the fort and a shouted conversation followed between Marcellus, Maccus and the Wealh guards. Stupidly, I was half expecting guards at the old fort entrance, but when I thought about it there really wouldn't have been much point. The old fort was vast and there was no possible way for them to man the whole boundary, so they had just set a watch around their camp.

I didn't know what Marcellus and Maccus were telling them but they clearly weren't alarmed by our approach. As we got closer I could see the guards on our side of the camp, black shapes against the fire light. Behind them men were sitting round the fires, talking, mending, cleaning, doing the things that all warriors do while they wait for war. None of them was at all concerned by our presence. One or two looked up in vague interest at the approach of the king's men, but war bands come and go all the time in camp, and nobody would expect the enemy to just stroll in!

Maccus was chatting amiably with the guards. There were four of them. Even though I couldn't understand the words I had to smile at the guards' demeanour. Here we were, supposedly the royal vanguard, so these four were strutting about, trying to show that they were every bit as tough as us, if not tougher. If it hadn't been for the situation I probably would have laughed out loud. As it was I was trying to gauge what was being said from the different reactions. My men were itching to strike, but I wanted to be in amongst the Wealh before I gave the word, so that they would have no chance to arm themselves. My heart was pounding as I looked for the right moment.

Suddenly one of the guards was asking me something and waiting for my response. I just stared at him, dumbly. I couldn't reply, I didn't know what to do. Was this it? Should I give the word to attack?

He asked again, an impatient tone in his voice. All eyes were on me, waiting for a reply. I would have to go, I would have to give the word.

Maccus was suddenly in my face, yelling at me and then slapping me on the front of my helm. He turned and shrugged at the guards, bemoaning something about 'Sais', which I didn't understand, but which was obviously exasperation at my stupidity. The guards laughed and then made some further observations which provoked more laughter. They stepped aside and indicated that we should join the camp.

Now this was it. I was walking forward. I had reached the first fire. The Wealh were looking up from their activities, taking in these newcomers, trusting, relaxed, about to die. I walked right through the heart of the camp.

"Kill Them!"

My sword was in my hand and I cut down two men where they sat before they even had a chance to stand. They were writhing on the ground, out of the fight, and I looked for my next enemy. As I turned, my vision was suddenly filled by flame. One of them had grabbed a burning stick, as thick as an arm, out of the fire and he thrust it at my face. I turned my head and swung my sword at the same time. The flames seared the right side of my face as I turned with the swing. Pain added desperate strength to my arm. I heard my assailant gasp as my blade bit home and I continued to turn, full circle, trying to escape the burning. The flames died but the stick was glowing red as he continued to press his attack. I used the momentum of my turn to put some power behind my sword and it whistled through the air as it descended upon his outstretched arm which was still thrusting the glowing stick at me. Arm and stick fell to the floor, and with a return back handed swing I half severed his head as he clutched at his stump with his remaining hand.

All around me the Wealh were falling to our sudden, unexpected attack. We must have accounted for half the warband in the first moments of the fight and the rest were hopelessly outnumbered. Ottar charged ahead, anxious to get to the horses with his men. The Wolf warriors rampaged through the camp, slaughtering the Wealh with great relish. Warriors were emerging from the houses into a scene of utter chaos. Outnumbered by at least three to one, they were hacked down from all sides. Flames lit up the night as one of the houses was torched. Before long, smoke and heat drove the inhabitants out to die on our blades. In the fear and excitement of the moment, women were killed alongside their men.

It was all over in a surprisingly short period of time. Two houses were burning as a watchful calm fell over the flickering scene. I could hear women shrieking and crying, and raised voices somewhere in the dark camp beyond the glow of the burning houses. The lads were shouting to one another, wary, uncertain, suddenly hurrying this way or that to confront perceived threats. They brought prisoners to me who had given themselves up to our mercy rather than be burned in their homes or slaughtered outside them.

The dismal group fell, or were pushed, to their knees before me. The pain in the side of my face was driving everything from my mind. It was coming in waves, as though burning sticks were being repeatedly applied to my sticky skin. I had explored the wound with my fingers but the increase in the throbbing burn had convinced me not to do that again. I forced myself to look at their wretched faces. They were draped in fear. Five men, eight women and their children.

"Kill the men!" I had already decreed that all the men should be killed and the pain in my burnt flesh removed any faint chance of me changing my mind and sparing them.

They were killed where they knelt, almost before the sound of my order had died on the air. The slaughter triggered a wave of hysterical screaming and crying from the women and children. Some of them fell, weeping and keening, on the bodies of their men. Others just wept and wailed in utter abject terror. I couldn't stand all of this noise, but what to do with them? My words, 'we don't wage war on women', kept swirling around my head. The obvious thing to do was enslave them. The raid ended here. We would be returning to the Granta Bridge in the morning and it would be easy to take them with us, but I didn't want a chorus of weeping and wailing all the way home. I had told the lads that there would be no slaves when we started on the raid. I didn't want to appear indecisive. If I set rules we all had to live by them. I couldn't be bothered with these wailing creatures, I needed to stop the throbbing, annoying pain that was driving me to distraction.

"Put these in one of the byres and bind them. I don't want my throat cut in the dark by some vengeful hag."

They were hauled to their feet, one woman had to be dragged, screaming, from her man's body, and pushed and pulled away to the byre.

I removed my helmet. I think that the cheek flap had saved me from a fair bit of harm but where the leather flap hadn't covered my cheek it had clearly been thoroughly burnt and my right ear was also a bundle of pain. There was a bucket of water close to the fire and for some reason I felt compelled to kneel and soak my burnt skin in the cool water. Just as water kills a fire, so it also helped to ease the burning in my skin. I stayed knelt over that bucket for a long time. The pain in my cheek eased, and I turned my head so that I could bathe my ear, but then the cheek started to burn again and I replaced it in the cool, still balm.

"Lord, Wulfhere."

It was Gram.

"Yes, Gram." I answered him without moving.

"The camp is ours, lord. Ottar has the horses. We've stripped the bodies of gear but we can't really search the place properly until daylight."

"Tell the lads to rest, Gram. Set guards all round. We'll leave once we've searched the place in the morning."

"Yes, lord. Is everything alright?"

I lifted my head from the bucket.

"I got a bit burnt, that's all, nothing serious. I'll be alright to check on the guards during the night."

The throbbing pain in my cheek and ear kept me awake. After a while it didn't nag quite so much, it was just there. I spent most of the long dark hours talking with the guards, trying to keep my mind from the burn. I got to sleep eventually and woke cold and damp, with the throbbing sting still there, but not enough to really distract me any more. The lads had porridge bubbling in a pot which helped to chase the cold from my bones, but everyone kept peering at my face which made me more conscious of the wound. Poor Asfrid! I thought to myself. Here I am with another scar for her to have to look at!

Daylight revealed that four of our lads had been killed during the chaotic fight. Three more were badly hurt and would need to be taken back to the hall at the Granta Bridge for rest, and treatment of their wounds. We had killed thirty two Wealh warriors, and a handful of women and children. I would leave the others behind when we left. They would have to meet with their fate as best they could.

Ottar had reached the centre of the camp in time to ensure that the Wealh didn't ride away with the horses. I had another six horses for my stable. I also had five swords, four mail shirts and six helmets as well as the spears, shields and knives carried by the bulk of the Wealh war band. The town hadn't been wealthy but there were a few nice household items and some nice rings, brooches and amulets.

It was time to leave.

"Gram, Ottar, Wyne get the boys to gather everything up. We're leaving. I want biers for the wounded lads. Come on now, we've got about ten miles to........"

"Lord Wulfhere!" My instructions were interrupted by Renweard who had been on watch at the fort's southern ditches. "Lord Wulfhere! There are horsemen approaching. Ten of them, from the south, along the street that we walked on yesterday."

Ten horsemen? That didn't make sense. There was no time to ponder it now though.

"Out of sight! Everybody get into the houses or byres and stay quiet! Ottar, get those horses into a byre. I want everything hidden. I want them to think the place is empty. Listen for my word. I will give the word to attack when they are close. Now go!"

The men scattered in all directions. Most ran into the empty buildings, a few laid themselves down amongst the dead. In a few heartbeats the town appeared to be deserted. I dashed into one of the houses with Gram, Odd and Inwald hard on my heels. There were already several lads inside. I made myself a small gap in the low thatch so that I could look out across the fields. The others hung back from the south facing doorway and watched from the shadows.

For a long time we watched, staring hard across the fields towards the street, looking for the horsemen. For a long time there was nothing to see. Had Renweard made a mistake? It seemed unlikely. But why would ten horsemen be riding this way. The local warriors mustering to fight raiders would have mostly been on foot. The only time that ten horsemen would have been riding abroad together would have been if they were lords out hunting, or scouts, ahead of an army.

I let out a low moan.

"No, not yet."

"What is it, lord?" Gram wanted to know, moving himself to try and see what I was looking at.

"Why would ten horsemen be riding together?" I asked nobody in particular.

"Because they're scouting ahead of a bastard army!" Gram answered grimly.

He was ahead of me. I looked at him and he held my gaze.

"Yes, that's what I thought too, my friend."

"So what do we do, lord?"

"We kill them and then we run like deer. If we don't get back to the burrh they won't know that Cynfellyn's coming!"

He was even earlier than we'd expected. He had decided to deal with us and be back in Lundenwic before the Cantware were ready to make another attack. It was a clever plan. He was taking a big risk. He would struggle to feed his army this early in the year but he had certainly caught us all off guard. We had to get away. We had to raise the alarm. I would send riders to Artorius, Leofmund and Icel as soon as we got back to Aldwyn's hall. If we could kill these scouts the Catuvellauni would be confused for a while, uncertain of what lay ahead of them. These scouts? Where were they? There was still no sign..........

Suddenly they were at the ford. I could see them now. They were moving slowly, cautiously. They would come on and then stop and look all round. They were looking at the ruin of the town. The burnt houses were still smoking. The bodies lying where they had fallen. They were careful, very careful. They split up. Four of them stayed by the 'gate' of the old fort. Two came straight on, two skirted to the left and two to the right. They were like deer leaving the woods to brave the meadow, constantly watching and listening. Ready to bolt at the slightest sign of danger. There was no way that we would catch them all, they were too careful.

At that moment there was a sudden rumpus from the byre where the women had been put. They had seen the scouts and were shouting at them. Warning them that we were here, presumably. I expected the horsemen to turn and run, but they didn't. They converged on the house. The women must have been calling for help! Six riders were gathering at the byre, fifty yards away. Two dismounted and were going to open the door. The last four had stayed by the gate, no they were coming forward as well. We had to go, it was now or never. In a moment the women would be out and they would warn the riders of their peril.

With a great shout of 'Wolf!' I dashed from the house and charged across the yard at the horsemen. Gram and the other lads were hard on my heels. Men came rushing from the other houses and byres, 'bodies' suddenly leapt to their feet and closed on the scouts. The six in the yard stood no chance. Two of the others kicked forward to try and help their friends. They were all surrounded and dragged from their mounts.

I had stopped short of the slaughter. I looked at Gram and we watched as the last two riders galloped away, back down the street. We had eight more horses but would I ever get to see them stabled at Wolf Home? I shouted for silence and Gram joined me in calming the men. When the excited crowd had calmed down I told them of their peril.

"Those men were scouts. Probably from Cynfellyn's army. That means he can't be far behind. I want two men to ride to Wolf Home and tell Artorius to send the army. The wounded lads and five more are to ride to the Granta bridge burrh and tell Aldwyn and Cissa that Cynfellyn is coming and to raise the fyrd. Load the plunder onto the other four horses and some of you riders can lead them home. The rest of you run with me. We have got ten miles to cover and a hundred horsemen on our heels. Come on!"

The dead scouts were stripped of their gear. The spare horses were loaded with our plunder and the riders cantered away, some riding, some bouncing. We ran north. How far away was the Wealh army? How long would the scouts take to reach them? It was possible that the smoke of our raids had drawn the curious scouts further ahead of the army than normal. On the other hand Cynfellyn might only be a mile down the street. If that was the case we would be overtaken before we were half way home.

I lengthened my stride slightly. It didn't matter much about saving strength. If we were overtaken by Cynfellyn's horsemen we were as good as dead. There would be too many of them. All that mattered was speed. I fell into a rhythm, my breathing fitting in around my footfalls.

Miles passed, the pace didn't flag. I could feel my heart pounding but I felt strong. I felt as if I could run forever. Running, breathing, running, breathing. After about five miles our street joined the street that ran from the Granta bridge to Ithamar's South Burrh. I knew the road well. We needed to turn left and it was about five miles more to the Granta bridge. I glanced back. There was no sign of Cynfellyn's horsemen yet, but they must be coming. Would we be able to get to the burrh in time?

"Get a quick drink, lads!" I needed to think.

They would be following the street. They knew that we were on the street. They would expect us to stay on it. I looked at the trees at the far side of the paved Roman street. We could go north from here. Leave the paved way and head north until we cut the street from Theodford. Then we would turn west and cover the last three or four miles. It was longer overall but the Wealh wouldn't be expecting us to do it. They would stay on this street until the Granta bridge burrh was in sight. It might give us a chance.

"Lads, listen! We are going to leave the street behind and head north, across country. When we reach the Theodford street we will follow it to the Granta bridge. Now go carefully straight ahead there. Leave no signs. Wyne, I want you to bring up the rear and make sure that our tracks are hidden.

The ground was still soft. Our horses' hoofprints were clearly visisble in the soft earth. Hopefully the Wealh would just follow them. The men melted from the open street. They trod on roots and stones to mask their tracks. Once we were into the trees and lost to sight we started to run again. We probably had about four miles to go to reach the Theodford street.

My burned skin was rubbing against my helmet. I cursed the Wealh, cursed Cynfellyn and the Catuvellauni. I wondered how long it would take my army to arrive. Would Icel and the Corieltavi be able to come to our aid? I decided that it would take twelve days for help to reach us. Could we hold on for twelve days against the army of the Catuvellauni? There was food at the burrh.

Aldwyn thought that he could raise a hundred warriors to defend the walls. We had the Wolf Pack. We would hopefully have about one hundred and fifty men.

How determined were the Catuvellauni? If they attacked, day after day they must break us in three or four days. We would run out of men to man the walls. They would have five or six times as many as us. They could take the losses. They would take the burrh if they were determined. There was little hope for us there, but even less in the open. Tiw knew what was going to happen. Our fate was spun. We just had to fight.

Pigeons flew up from the trees to our south west. Something had scared them. I listened as I ran. I listened for thundering hooves, for the crashing of undergrowth. The noise of running men drowned out any other sound. Keep going, just keep running. Once the Wealh reach the burrh they will spread out to look for us, they will come for us. Keep running.

Brambles and whip-like twigs scratched my face and hands as we ran. No more stops, no more drinks, just run. I slithered and slipped down banks, stumbled on roots, ran straight through beds of nettles. Don't stop, don't slow, keep running.

Suddenly the forest floor was replaced by the clear, straight Theodford street.

"Come on lads! Three more miles. There's ale waiting! Come on my Wolf Pack!"

Gram was with me. The nearness of safety gave us an extra source of strength. Running onwards, pace after pace, breath after breath. Rain started to fall, cold, heavy rain. Wet gear, wet shoes, rubbing and chafing, sweat stinging, cold air, muscles aching, need to stop, mustn't stop, daren't stop. Step, after step, after step, rhythmic words were running through my head keep moving, stay together, keep moving, stay together. Time passed with the miles. We must be close. Again pigeons flew from the trees somewhere behind us, startled by a sudden shout this time, not too close, but not far enough. No not now, we were so close, so close!

"Come on lads! Come on!"

I lengthened my stride again even though my muscles were tightening, stiffening, trying to slow me down. I had to run, run like a stag. They were coming! I could sense them. I could feel the drumming of their hooves through the ground. The deep drumming of a hundred horsemen.

There was the burrh! There were the walls!

"Come on lads! There it is!"

My lungs were screaming, my muscles were tight as drying leather on a rack. I could see men on the walls. Hooves thundering! I could see them waving us home, calling us home. I was gasping with each breath, rolling from side to side, my muscles so tight that I could hardly force my legs forward. The gate was at the far, western side of the burrh. We were so close, but not safe yet. Another fifty yards, around the corner of the wall, there it was, I was up to the gate and through. I was in. I looked around, dizzy, gasping for breath, waving my men in. My stomach suddenly clenched and I threw up, nothing. I was empty but still I heaved and convulsed.

I straightened up, wiping my mouth with the back of my hand. Wincing as I rubbed my burnt face. I was looking around. Looking to see that my men were safe, looking for the Wealh.

"Have you been fighting again, boy?"

I knew that voice. Only one man called me boy.

"Wulfstan? What…… are you……. doing here?" I panted.

"I heard that you were going to war and I had hoped to get here before you started raiding, but you can't have everything. What in the name of Woden's knackers have you been doing? You look like shit."

At that moment there was a shout of alarm from the wall.

"Wealh! Beware, the Wealh are here!"

Wulfstan looked from the wall to me.

"What have you done now?"

CHAPTER 16: The burrh

We hurried across to the wall. My lads were still arriving at the gate and staggering in to safety. Aldwyn was at the wall before us.

"Wulfhere, your riders are here. I have summoned the fyrd. I've sent riders of my own to Icel. This is a surprise," he indicated the twenty or so Wealh horsemen who were sitting a quarter of a mile down the Theodford street, staring at the burrh. "I didn't think that they'd be in the field yet."

"Neither did I. I haven't seen the army but they must be following on behind."

"So you're telling me that I brought my people here to do a bit of raiding and fill my coffers, and we're going to end up trapped in here by that turd Cynfellyn and his pox ridden, sheep humping army of in-bred Wealh bastards!" Wulfstan summed up our situation perfectly.

"Yes."

"Yes? Is that it? Just, yes? Some pissing warlord you are! Can't even organise a raid without getting your arse kicked and having to run for help!"

"These boys have got some good gear. There'll be profit in this if we hold fast, but if all you're going to do is moan, you can piss off now!"

He threw back his head and roared with laughter.

"Your father would have been proud of that, boy!"

"Wulfhere, what is happening?" I knew that voice, it was Ullr the Dane. I turned to face him but the greeting that I was about to give stayed on my lips.

Ullr was walking over to where we stood on the wall. With him were Oswine, Sigurd, and my brother Wulfgar.

"Wuffa! What?" I was stuck for words. Wuffa should have been safe back at Rendels Home.

"We did say that he needed to see the slaughter field," Wulfstan cut in. "If he's going to rule he needs to know about war."

"Yes, but." I couldn't say anything more. I had been meaning to start involving Wuffa in the more serious aspects of being a king. I just hadn't planned to start with such a harsh lesson.

"So how many men have we got?" I asked nobody in particular, glancing around the inside of the fort at the collection of tents and cooking fires.

"Well between me, Ullr and the Frisian boys, Brega and Hod, we've got over seventy men." Wulfstan advised me smugly.

"Over seventy! What were you thinking about? You came here to make a profit with seventy men? How much profit were you looking for? Half a grain of silver?"

"Alright, alright. We knew there was a war coming and Ullr and me decided to get here early, and when Brega and Hod heard they decided to come along as well. They wanted to show loyal. Here they are now, you can shout at them in person if you want. Let's face it, if we hadn't all come you'd be up to your neck in it! And you must have sixty? Yourself, so don't try and lecture me about profit!"

"Not now. I've lost a few and a few got hurt. Fifty, ready to fight."

Brega and Hod were crossing to the wall with their companions.

"Brega, Hod, it's good to see you. We have been surprised. Cynfellyn is already in the field. I have sent for help......"

"We know, lord Wulfhere," Brega stopped me. "What is your plan?"

"The plan is made for us, Brega. We stay here and wait for help to arrive. We kill as many of the enemy as we can and slaughter the rest of them when Leofmund and Icel get here."

"How long do you think that will be?" Wulfstan queried.

"Two days for the messengers to get there, six days to muster, four days to get here. I reckon about twelve days from now."

By the time Aldwyn's fyrdmen had gathered we would have well over two hundred men inside the fort. If we were careful with the food it should last until help got here. All we had to do was hold off the army of Cynfellyn, king of the Catuvellauni.

"I'm glad you're here, my friends. I'll get my lads sorted out and then we'd better look at what supplies we've got and how we're going to make sure that they last. Double the watch on the walls. Cynfellyn won't be here yet but we don't want to be caught napping."

I left the wall and crossed the fort to where Gram was sorting out the Wolf Pack, and my horses. The men were recovering from our desperate race. The bigger fellows like Wyne, Frithuwald and Odd had really struggled with the pace. Odd was flat on his back on the saturated ground, allowing his aching body to rest.

"Don't get cold and wet lads. Light the cooking fires and get some hot broth down you. We're going to have to sit tight and fight off the Catuvellauni until Icel gets here. Sharpen your blades, eat and get some rest, because once the fighting starts you won't get much."

I looked around for my right hand man.

"Gram, how do we stand?"

"Forty seven men fit to fight. The wounded are being tended."

"Right, you make sure that you get some food and rest as well. Where's Haeddi?"

"There he is. Haeddi! Over here!" Gram ordered.

Haeddi hurried over.

"Well, Haeddi. Fourteen new horses. You're going to be busy when we get home!" I laughed and clapped him on the back. "What do you think of them?"

"They're fine beasts, lord. Nine stallions and five mares. With this year's new arrivals the herd is really starting to build."

"Yes, and if I'm not mistaken we'll get the chance of a few more yet on this trip. And the next one for that matter! It's looking good Haeddi. If you need anything for them let me know."

"Yes, lord."

Fourteen horses as well as the four that we had brought with us. At this rate half of the Wolf Pack would be riding when we returned home. If we returned home, I smiled grimly to myself. I looked around the fort. What could we do, before Cynfellyn got here, to strengthen our defences? I started a slow walk around the inside of the walls. Within forty paces I was joined by Wulfstan, Oswine, Ullr, Sigurd, Wuffa, Brega and Hod. I looked around at them and chuckled.

"If Cynfellyn knew who was inside this burrh he would probably shit himself. Well done the south folk! We'll be ready for the bastards!"

They joined in my laughter.

"What are you doing?" Wulfstan demanded.

"Just looking. Seeing what we can do to improve things. If anything."

"Oh there's always something. Even if it's just collecting some rocks to throw at the bastards," Wulfstan suggested.

"How long would you say these walls are?" I wondered.

We had deliberately built the burrh to a size that could be defended by a modest sized army.

"About a hundred and sixty feet, the long walls," Oswine suggested. "And, what, eighty feet, for the short walls?"

We all agreed.

"About that. What length of wall can one man hold, when they attack? Six feet?" I wondered.

We all looked at each other.

"I don't know," Oswine was holding his arms wide. "That's about six feet. I think that you would have a job to fight here, and block another man from climbing over, here." He imitated a fighting man trying to defend a section of wall.

"You've got another man next to you," Wulfstan pointed out.

"Yes, but if you've both got six feet to cover and you're at this end of your six feet and he's at that end of his, you could have a five or six foot gap between you."

"Alright, let's say five feet for each man," I suggested.

"Two men for every ten feet. That should be plenty," Wulfstan suggested. "Any more and you'll end up blocking each other's swing."

"Right, so we'll need thirty-two men, let's make it forty men on the long walls and what's that, it's not twenty is it? Sixteen? Yes, sixteen men on the short walls. A hundred and twelve to man the walls effectively. That gives us roughly the same again to hold back in case there's a breakthrough. Perhaps we could put some bowmen on the roofs? They could shoot over the walls at the Wealh."

"Good idea. Right, well seeing as my lads are just sitting on their arses, staying dry, I'll get them out to gather rocks," Wulfstan ventured.

"Mine will join you," Ullr chipped in.

"And us," Brega and Hod.

They all went off to get to work. I went to find Aldwyn and Cissa. Aldwyn was still on the wall by the gate.

"Aldwyn!"

"Lord."

"How are we provisioned?"

"That's Cissa's job, lord. He's at the hall."

I left the gate and strode across to the hall. I was pleased with the way Aldwyn and Cissa had worked things out between them. Cissa couldn't fight any more, with his leg so badly injured, but organising our stores of food would be vital work. Inside, the hall was a hive of activity with a lot of work around the fire as food was prepared for the army. The wounded men were laid out nearer to the walls, out of the way of the workers.

Cissa was talking with Osburga. They looked round as I entered.

"Cissa, Osburga. How long will our food last?" I got straight to the point.

"We were just discussing that, lord," Cissa informed me.

"How many men have we got now, Wulfhere? My husband doesn't seem to have any idea!" Osburga asked with an exasperated tone.

I knew that she had been disappointed when Cissa was injured. They had only been married a few weeks when he had lost his eye to a Frankish axe, and I don't think that she ever got used to his changed face. The crippling leg wound upset her still further. Every woman wants a strong man, but she had chosen her man, and he had been a fine warrior before his injuries. She certainly enjoyed having the ordering of his household, and the position that he'd bought with his wounds. I didn't like her disrespectful tone.

"Until all of the fyrdmen are here we can't be certain, Osburga, that's why Cissa can't be definite yet. I hope that we will have about two hundred and thirty once they're all gathered. I think that we'll have to hold out for about twelve days. Now, we don't have to fatten them up! Just make sure that they've got enough strength to keep swinging their spears. The sheep and all of the supplies that my men brought back are yours. Once the siege is beaten off I will make sure that your storehouses are replenished. Don't fear Osburga, you won't suffer for your loyalty.

I'll leave everything in your hands Cissa. I've got every confidence in you, my old friend."

I left the hall and wandered around once again, taking in the scene. As well as the hall there was a barn, two houses, a byre, granary, ale house and a weavers hut. There were store pits, which had been recently dug and lined, behind the hall, and hurdles had been erected between the hall and the fort walls for a sheep fold. The closeness of the walls to the buildings was a bit of a worry. There was a danger that the Wealh might try to set the thatches on fire. If we had bowmen on the roof they would have to react quickly and throw any flaming torches back over the walls.

Some of my horses were inside the byre but it wasn't big enough to get them all in. Eight were tethered to the byre wall and Haeddi was erecting a hide cover to keep the weather off them. I hoped that they wouldn't be a nuisance once the noise of the battle started.

In between the buildings and the gate, the army had erected their tents. It seemed that we were ready. All we could do now was wait for Cynfellyn. I went back to the gate where Aldwyn was still watching the street.

"Are all of your fellows inside, lord?" He wondered.

I climbed the steps up onto the fighting platform next to the gate. The street was clear, there was no sign of the Wealh horsemen, and no sign of Cynfellyn. Just a lot of our fellows gathering flints or firewood and cutting stakes.

"Yes, Aldwyn. They're all in."

I nodded and watched men struggling in with bundles full of rocks over their shoulders. Under Oswine's direction they were making heaps at different points around the inside of the walls.

"Have you got many arrows?"

"Yes, lord. I've got a good stock of arrows. We've filled all the store boxes with sling stones," we watched a Dane tipping his bundle of rocks onto the pile below our position. "And now we've got piles of apple sized flints to hurl. I've placed sharpened stakes in the ditch walls, pointing down, as you suggested, to stop them climbing up. I've also put a lot along the bottom of the ditches in case they slide down in a hurry. I think that we've made it as hard as we can for them."

I looked at the houses of the town outside the walls.

"What about the town? Are they ours, or are they Catuvellauni still?"

"If we want them to be ours I will have to protect them. I am their lord."

"Then bring them inside the burrh, and empty the houses of anything that might be useful to Cynfellyn; rope, nails, tools, spades, anything at all. Don't leave any food out there. He's come too early. He was hoping to take us by surprise but we're ready. I wonder if he will be? If he can't feed his army they'll have to slink back home with their tails between their legs. Don't give the bastards anything."

"Yes, lord."

He left me and went to clear the town. I stood and watched the preparations continue and the fyrdmen arrive. Every now and then I looked to the South. Eventually the sun set and it was too dark to see. I made sure that the walls were guarded and that the warriors knew when they were going to have to take their turn on watch. It rained again. Watch fires faded and smoked. Men hunched inside their sturdiest travelling cloaks, breath smoking in the cold, wet night air. I went up to the hall to get something hot to eat. Gram was with me again. Battle was approaching and he wouldn't leave my side until it was over, or we were dead.

In the hall, the leaders of my army were sitting together enjoying a warming bowl of stew. I helped myself to a bowl and joined them.

"So what's the plan?" Wulfstan wanted to know.

"We take a section of wall each and then we hold it. You and I have the south wall, uncle. Ullr, Brega and Hod yours is the north wall. Aldwyn, you,ve got the east and west and I want you personally to hold a company in the middle of the fort and watch for any threat of the Wealh breaking through. If you have bowmen amongst your companions get them onto the roofs behind your wall to support your warriors. Organise your own watches, if you're hard pressed call for Aldwyn to support you.

Cissa is in charge of provisions. I've told him to make our supplies last for twelve days. Your men won't get fat but it's not Cissa's fault, he's just doing what I've told him. Have I missed anything?"

I looked around at the hard faces which were staring blankly back. It was straight forward really. Hold the wall, or we all die.

"Well, make sure your blades are sharp. We've got twelve days to kill as many of these bastards as we can. If Icel gets here before Leofmund we won't get the chance to clear up, so grab what plunder you can."

They laughed at that. They all understood war. They all knew that there was wealth to be had from war. They were good men and fine companions.

I was on the wall, staring south when dawn turned the world grey and then gradually added colour. The rain that had fallen through most of the night had stopped and the world was still. The torrent of birdsong always enthralled me and I let it fill me with a lightness of spirit. I thought of Asfrid and the boys and the dawn easing over Wolf Home. They were wonderful, this middle earth was wonderful. If my fate was to die here then I could have no complaints about the life that I had been given. I would hold my head up when I stood before Tiw and my ancestors.

As I thought about it, the prospect of death seemed more real. I had done Tiw's work. I had brought my people over the whale road to a new land, just like the dream that he had sent me. I had won them a kingdom here in Britain. There was no more. What were our chances of holding on for twelve days against the army of the Catuvellauni? Each attack would drain us, chip away at our numbers until we were too few to defend everywhere. How many would they have, eight hundred, nine, a thousand? Marcellus said that the Catuvellauni were the most powerful tribe. We could kill half their number and still be overwhelmed in the end.

I looked up to the sky. This was it. I would die here in a lake of blood. Every Wealh who fell beneath my sword would be my offering to him. It was suddenly staggeringly clear. I called to the war god. I had so much to thank him for. So much to celebrate in the hall of my fathers.

"I am ready, lord Tiw. Their blood will be yours, as it always has been. Their deaths shall be your glory, your victory. I have done your will. I am your sword, your messenger. I am ready to greet you, lord if the spinners are finished and my thread is to be cut here.

This victory will be my thanks, and my tribute. All middle earth will see your power, and fear your wrath. Be with me, lord Tiw, be with my men."

I sank slowly to my knees and wept. The power of the war god was with me. My fate was upon me. In the silence of that damp, grey dawn my warriors watched me in silent awe. They knew that Tiw was with us. They knew that they would have a place at his table. They knew that I was his sword, his messenger in this middle earth. They looked out from the walls and willed the Wealh to come to our blades.

CHAPTER 16: The Siege

Cynfellyn didn't arrive until after noon. That was a surprise. He couldn't have been far away when his scouts had found us yesterday. He knew that we were waiting. He knew that we had been raiding. Did he fear a trap? Did he think that we were deliberately trying to draw him on with our raid, and our wild dash for home? He was clearly very cautious, and yet he had launched this bold, surprise attack.

"He must have most of his strength with him," was Wulfstan's interpretation. "He is too wary. He daren't risk defeat for fear that his power will be broken. He has got Saxons to the south and us and the Corieltavi up here on his northern border. He's afraid. He wants to fight us but he is frightened of defeat. I doubt that this siege will last twelve days, Wulfhere. If he can't take us quickly, he won't want to have his army ground down assaulting these walls. If we can hold on for three or four days he'll piss off, you mark my words."

I thought that he was probably right. Three or four days? There was a glimmer of hope. We might be able to cling on for three or four days. Wulfstan had been fighting wars for a lot longer than I had. Cynfellyn was clearly wary. Perhaps this was not so much the plan of a bold warrior, but rather a desperate attempt to snatch a cheap victory. But I was being foolish. It was not sensible to tempt fate, or presume to guess the future. The web of fate would be spun and no false hope would change it.

Between Wulfstan and myself, the Wolf lords, we had sixty four men ready to fight. When the attack came there would be forty four of us on the wall. Eight bowmen, including Wuffa who was a deadly shot, on the roofs behind us. Wyne would hold the rest of our men behind the wall, ready to fill any gaps. I could hear them splashing about below us in the soft, muddy ground. The rain had continued to fall for most of the day. The ground was soaked. The ditches below us had muddy, thigh deep water along their lengths, which concealed Aldwyn's cruel stakes.

I stood with Wulfstan, Oswine, Gram, Marcellus and Wedda gazing out across the flat, rain-lashed land. The clay was holding the water in shining puddles. It took a little while to realise that there had been a change to the view. At the edge of my vision, the rim of the world, the street had darkened and, in the misty light, a dark shadow was running along the street, filling it as it went, like a trickle of wax running down a candle spike. I was looking on my death. A sudden lightness of spirit caused me to smile. Knowing that I was about to die had lifted a weight from me. Nothing mattered now. The harvest, the hall, the moaning, whingeing people were no longer my responsibility. My wife would be well cared for. My sons had a strong family about them. I would die with my dearest friends around me. The gods were good. I would make a good show of these last hours in middle earth.

"Here they come," Wulfstan muttered. "Filthy, sheep-fucking, stinking, whoreson....."

I missed the end of his description of the Wealh.

"Here they come!" A watcher called out somewhere along the wall.

The whole of our army stopped what they were doing and gathered to watch the enemy army march up the south street. The burrh fell silent but for the rain, and the sound of their approach gradually filled that silence. At first it was a whisper, like wind in the trees, but it became a murmur, and then we could hear voices. They were sounds rather than words but they rose in pitch and excitement as they drew nearer and looked on our walls, seeking out the shapes of the defenders. They were eager for the fight. The pace of their march quickened as they got closer. They weren't in columns. They had become a great bunch of warriors hurrying forward, all wanting to be first to hurl themselves upon the Sais. From a quarter of a mile away, with a sudden yell from hundreds of throats, the march became a mad headlong charge. There was no plan, no order, no decision. The warriors wanted to get at us and with a great roar of fury they raced each other across the saturated ground.

"Everyone back to your places!" I yelled, and the order was echoed by a dozen voices as our army prepared to defend the walls.

The distance between us closed staggeringly fast.

"Ready lads. Hit them as they climb the wall. Heads and hands whatever's first. You don't have to kill them, you just stop them getting over that wall. Heads and hands!"

We had banged home that message all day. Just hack them. Cut off fingers and hands or split their heads, whichever came into reach first, it didn't matter so long as they didn't get over the wall.

Our arrows whispered overhead. The first shots were too early, too eager with dampened strings and they fell short, but the Wealh were coming on like the wind, and soon the feathered shafts were striking home, picking out this man, or that, doing fate's work. As the onrushing horde approached the first of the ditches the lads started hurling the rocks that they'd collected. Lumps of flint the size of apples, with wickedly sharp edges hurtled down into the onrushing flesh.

Like a tide, the front of the army reached the first ditch and slithered down into the muddy water. There was a shock in store for quite a few. Beneath the murky liquid the sharpened points waited to tear unsuspecting flesh. Blood soon stained the filthy water with dark red blooms, and screaming, injured Wealh were crushed beneath the surface by the weight of the warriors sliding down the greasy banks behind them.

Arrows flew, stones arched through the sky above us. The boys on the wall hurled their spears and the Wealh army rolled and boiled and slithered across the first ditch and down into the second. Some of them began to hurl their own spears and loose arrows but behind the wall and with shields to cover ourselves we were hard targets. The banks of the ditches were steep, and slippery, and they were finding it difficult to climb up. Slowly they came on, gasping for breath, fine targets for the bowmen. Then they were at the foot of the wall. Some managed to climb up, helped by their friends, but there were too few to overwhelm the defenders and those who did manage were easily hacked down. Hands or heads, it didn't matter.

The army flowed around the fort looking for a way to get in. The gate was the obvious point. We had placed obstacles and driven more stakes into the ground before the gate to hinder attackers. We had also placed barrels filled with earth behind the gates so that they couldn't be forced. Aldwyn's slingers were positioned to the sides of the gate and they hurled their rounded stones into the mass of warriors with deadly accuracy.

In a short space of time the fort was beset on three sides, but without ladders the attackers couldn't climb up in sufficient numbers to carry the walls. Those warriors who had charged headlong down into the ditch now found themselves in a terrifying trap. The sides of the ditches had been reduced to slippery slime by the dozens of feet which had slid down into the water, and now they were almost impossible to climb out of.

The main body of the army had halted at the ditches. They were being tormented by our bowmen and there was little point in just standing and providing our lads with target practice. They broke away and fell back beyond bow range, leaving their companions struggling below us in the deadly mud trap. The ditch was red with blood, and the water had been churned into a thick, brown ooze. Some of the Wealh were trying to help their friends out by lowering their spear shafts to pull them up. We showered them with arrows, spears and rocks, felling them where they stood, or driving them back so that they couldn't save their doomed friends.

In the ditch below us frantic warriors splashed and tore at the greasy slope, but it was too steep. There was no purchase and after a couple of desperate steps they just slid back down. The lads on the wall were calling for more rocks, spears, anything to hurl down upon the helpless, desperate, mud soaked Wealh. Directly below me one of them had been pierced through the leg by a hidden stake. He was stuck, unable to pull himself off of the wooden spike. The boys on the wall called for the lads below to throw them up some more rocks. Laughing and making bets with each other, they hurled them down at the forlorn warrior until he was battered unconscious and his bloodied body sank into the filthy ditch water.

Blood spread across the surface of the thick brown soup, swirling and striping into flowing patterns. Bodies littered the ditch, and injured men dragged themselves back to their friends, away from those terrible walls, leaving smooth trails across the churned ground.

I left my place on the wall and jogged around the inside of the fort, checking on all the other points where the attack had been pressed to the walls. The result had been similar all around. Without ladders the Wealh had been unable to scale the walls and had fallen back, leaving their dead behind.

The attack on the gate had been fiercest and dead and dying Wealh were piled up on the causeway before the main portal. Men on the barrels behind the gate had been kept busy striking down heads and hands. The bowmen and slingers had wreaked havoc amongst the attackers as they tried to reach the gate, struggling over the stakes and barriers that had been placed in the way.

We had a number of injured men but only one killed. One of the defenders at the gate had been shot through the eye with an arrow. Many more had been struck by arrows, spears or stones but only a handful were too badly injured to carry on. We had repulsed the first attack for a loss of only eight defenders.

"I've walked along the wall and I reckon we got at least thirty," Wulfstan informed me when I returned to my place. "Not a bad start. It'll get better once they get some ladders," he added hopefully.

"They got the same again over at the gate," I announced to the men around me. "How many do you reckon there are altogether?" I asked Wulfstan and Oswine.

They both gazed out at the Wealh who were now spread across the fields to the south. They had started felling trees and it wouldn't be long before they had their ladders.

"Eight or nine hundred," Oswine decided.

"Yes," Wulfstan agreed. "It's like I said. He's brought his entire strength north to try and crush us. He'll put everything into the next attack. It will be the decider."

The lads were in good spirits after our initial victory. I heard Ottar's laugh rolling across the fort and couldn't help but smile. I walked around the walls talking with the men, laughing with them, but reminding them that this was only the beginning.

"That was easy, lads. They weren't prepared for the attack. The next ones will be harder. The next attacks will be the ones that we have to break."

They didn't come again that day. We ate and we watched. Their cooking fires spread across the fields before us. Some of them had crept into the town. The lads at the gate had heard them rummaging through the houses, but there was nothing there for them. In the middle of the dark, clouded, night some of our lads climbed out over the walls and gathered up spears and arrows, and no doubt helped themselves to goodies from the dead Wealh. They bundled the retrieved weapons and we drew them back over the walls. They did well, flitting silently back and forth among the dead for some time before their presence was discovered. Shouts of alarm went up from both the Wealh and the foragers, who dashed back to the ditch and scrambled up the knotted ropes that we had hung down for them.

We heard Wealh horsemen riding up but it was too dark for us to see them or for them to pick out the climbers against the dark fort wall. A few arrows thumped into the ditch wall and the wooden fort wall but I told our lads not to waste any arrows shooting back in the dark.

All through the night we heard the Catuvellauni making their ladders. The ringing thumps of axes on timber mingled into a continuous thunder as steps were cut in a hundred tree trunks. We had left a quarter of the men on the walls. We doubted that there would be any attack until their preparations were completed so we tried to make sure that the lads got as much rest as possible. There was porridge in the dark before dawn. The cutting had almost stopped. The attack would come as soon as there was enough light for them to see their way across the ditch. The men on the walls were reinforced, and we waited.

The lowest edge of the eastern sky was changing colour by cruelly slow degrees. Shapes were emerging from the darkness. The men around me were darker against a slightly less dark night. A whispering sound told us that rain was approaching across the fields from the west. A few heartbeats later it fell cold and heavy on our shoulders. The birds still sang, muffled by the hiss of the pouring rain. Clouds held back the dawn. Even when the sun should have been up we were still in twilight and the rain still fell. There were puddles forming in the churned up mud beyond the ditch. Magpies and crows kept the corpses company, and still we waited.

From the camp before our walls, a quarter of a mile away across rain soaked earth, beneath struggling wood smoke, the army of Cynfellyn emerged. There was no headlong rush this time. They made their way forward and then fanned out. They were going to attack everywhere at once. They were going to test our strength.

I jumped from the wall again and ran around my army.

"Don't hold back! Put as many men on the wall as you need to hold them. Aldwyn, make sure that you are watching for weaknesses. Ullr, Brega use all of your men if you need to. Aldwyn, the same with you. If you want to put more men on the walls, do it now. They are going to come with everything they've got."

I returned to my place. Our wall was bristling with warriors. Wyne had about eight men in support of the wall, everyone else was waiting for the enemy. I looked out at them, Gram pushed in beside me, telling the lad who was stood there to join Wyne.

My heart was pounding. Was this it? Was this my last day? I would give my lord Tiw rivers of blood today. I would hew every limb that came within my reach.

"Kill them! Tear them!" I yelled at nobody in particular.

"Wolf!" Shouted Gram, and then, "Wolf! Wolf! Wolf!" the rhythmic chant that I had heard so often on the slaughter field. It was taken up all round the walls. The lads thumped their shields and the wooden wall in time with the chant. They called the Wealh to their deaths, and the Wealh answered.

With another great shout they slithered and splashed forward, surging to the ditch. All around the burrh they charged. They were carrying tree trunks, some to bridge the outer ditches, and some that they had cut steps in to climb the wall. Arrows flew, and as they drew nearer, spears and rocks brought men crashing down to ruin beneath the feet of the army. The fallen didn't stop them. They came on across the tree trunks and planted their ladders, upright, on the far side of the ditch and then let them drop onto our wooden wall. Some of them bounced away and slid down into the ditch but where they rested on the wall, the Wealh were scrambling up before the trunks had stopped quivering.

"Come on then!" I called to the first warrior who was running up to fight me. I flung myself forward and he paused to avoid my swing, precarious on the narrow trunk. The man coming behind ran into him and drove him on, cleverly using the lead man as a shield. I swung again and this time my blow hit home and opened a great gash to the side of his head. His senses had left him but the fighter behind held him up and drove him forward before discarding him two steps from the top. The stricken Wealh fell from the ladder down onto the sharpened stakes in the ditch below.

His companion had been clever. He had almost reached the top by using the leading man as his shield but now he was exposed. He had a desperate race to get over the wall and make a gap in the defenders so that the man behind could run through to help him. The last steps took him above me to the wall top. I held my shield high so that he couldn't strike down at me and I aimed a great swing at his knee. An arrow whined past my head as my sword cut into the exposed joint and his leg collapsed under his weight sending him shrieking to the ditch below.

All along the wall the same scenes were being played out. A stone struck me, just at the point where my head and helmet met. The helmet saved me from serious harm but I was momentarily stunned, and straight away blood started down my face. Next to me Gram thrust his blade at the next attacker and I rallied my senses and joined him to send a third warrior down to the murky water. I don't know how long the attack lasted. Arrows and stones continued to whistle and thump around us. In all Gram and I sent six enemies down into the slippery, drowning ditch before the press stopped.

All around the fort the Wealh were pulling back, except at the gate. There was no ditch there and it was the most exposed point of the defences. Aldwyn's fyrdmen were hard pressed. The Wealh were swarming to the attack, throwing everything at that vulnerable place and threatening to overwhelm the defenders. Aldwyn himself had seen the danger and he was leading his company to help them. I was about to send Wyne and our lads to back them up but at that moment Gram shouted,

"Here they come!"

Cynfellyn was hurling his army in again. He had to keep us busy on the walls while he threw his finest warriors at the gate. He couldn't afford to lose. All the kings knew that he wanted to take back his lost towns. If he failed, then all the kings would see his weakness.

The Wealh came screaming back to the ladders. They came on as before, and we hurled them back, as before. This time the attack fell away sooner. As they ran back from the walls, beyond bow range, I looked to the gate. Aldwyn's men were all committed to the fray and still the Wealh were pressing. I looked round for Wyne and his company.

"Wyne! Take your lads to the gate! Hold the gate!"

The big man looked around at the gate. Then he acknowledged my order and led his men away at a run. I watched them clamber up onto the barrels and wade into the Wealh, who were swarming to the gate like bees to a hive. I could see Aldwyn rallying his tired fyrdmen who redoubled their efforts with the warriors of the Wolf alongside them.

"Heads and hands, lads, heads and hands" I thought to myself as I watched the vicious fighting. Wyne had listened well. He was wielding his seaxe brutally, simply hacking this way and that, at any part of any Catuvellauni warrior that came within his considerable reach. Still the enemy pushed forward, climbing over the bodies that had piled up before the gate, or slipped from the sides of the earth bridge onto the growing heap of dead and dying which threatened to fill the ditch below.

I looked out at the Wealh who were gathered in a leaderless mob, sixty yards beyond my section of the south wall. Below me dead men littered the ditch. Maimed and injured men were dragging themselves up, over the dead and dying, in order to keep their heads above the filthy, blood slicked water. These men weren't coming again. They clustered together like sheep. There were no leaders, no rallying cries. They had tried twice and twice they had been fiercely thrown back. The first men up the ladders would die. There were no more first men left in that beaten crowd.

The fighting at the gate was still ferocious. The Wealh were attacking with desperate courage. That was where I should be. That was where I could honour Tiw. Those warriors were a fitting sacrifice. I left the wall and sprinted across the fort. As I reached the barrels and started to climb Wyne suddenly crashed down beside me. An arrow was buried in the great warrior's throat and he was clutching at the blood soaked shaft. He recognised me and tried to say something but there was no sound. He fell back, but I couldn't stay with him. Above me the Wealh were clambering onto the gate. I leaped forward driving the lads in front of me hard against the foe. The impact toppled one of the Wealh from the top of the gate and bought me enough time to reach the timber bulwark.

I looked down at the crowded mass of warriors below me. They were struggling forward over the obstacles and the dead and dying who had gone before. The heap of slain rose to half the height of the gate and the Wealh could reach the top of the barrier by climbing on the bodies. An arrow whispered over my head. This was it, this was my time to die, but I wasn't going to stand here until a Wealh bowman hit his mark. I was going to die in the midst of my foes. I was going to make a legend.

"Wolf! To me!" I vaulted the gate and I was standing on the hill of slain in amongst my enemies. The 'bodies' were heaving and moving beneath my feet and it was hard to stay balanced but I was coming down, and my momentum helped me as I swung my blade left and right, hacking at arms, shoulders, heads, whatever I could hit. The blood and flesh of the Wealh was Tiw's tribute. I would win this fight and they wouldn't stand against me! They would be my slaves in the next world.

"Slaves!" I yelled, "slaves, slaves, slaves," the shout punctuated each savage swing as my bloodied blade hummed through the air, forehand to backhand, forehand to backhand.

Gram was at my shoulder, Renweard and more of our lads were following our charge and I was carried forward by the rush, splitting the crowded Wealh before me, punching with my shield rim, scything with my sword. Down from the gate we stumbled and staggered over the bloody heaps of flesh. I was in amongst my enemies but even as they drew back their spears to strike me down they were killed by the Wolf Pack warriors who were charging down recklessly behind me, desperate to keep me alive. I climbed onto a barrier of sharpened stakes and leaped down again, heedless of peril, hacking my sword into the back of a shirtless warrior who was turning to run. The Wealh were broken. Our charge had taken them completely by surprise. They turned and fled, scrambling beyond our reach but I couldn't stop. Still I wielded my blade and waited for my fate to fall. I wouldn't spare fleeing enemies any more than I would spare those who tried to fight me. My blade severed hamstrings, knee tendons and ankles, and carved its message of death into the backs and heads of beaten foes.

Suddenly we were off the bridge and there was no more flesh within my reach. No enemies left to fight. They were utterly beaten, their flight wild and uncontrolled. They scattered in all directions and I halted my charge. Gram was still at my shoulder. He was painted in the blood of his foes, his eyes as cold and deadly as mine were wild and burning. I punched my sword arm skywards,

"I am ready, lord Tiw! Here is my triumph!"

I didn't understand. Where were my foes? Where was my death? Had I been mistaken?

"Lord, come back now." Gram took my arm and drew me back, carefully, respectfully.

He was right. We had done our work here. We had broken the attack on the gate. I allowed myself to be led back up the ramp of dead and dying enemies. An arrow slapped into a body by my knee. Frithuwald, Renweard and some of the other lads closed behind me, raising their shields to protect me from the Wealh bowmen.

"Come on, lord!" it was Haeddi above the gate, reaching down to help me up and over. Another arrow whispered past, too high, but then we were back inside. I climbed carefully back down the barrels and onto the soft wet ground of the fort. I didn't understand. I turned to my faithful bodyguard.

"I was meant to die today. He has spared me for greater glory, Gram. He has spared me my fate. We are marked for even greater glory, my friend, even greater victories! Tiw has changed my fate!"

I embraced my hearth companion and clapped him on the shoulder. He shrugged and we laughed together. My brothers were all around me, my brothers of the Wolf Pack, painted with the blood of our foes. I embraced them all, laughing and clapping their backs. As we stood behind the gate I suddenly became aware of the world around us. A strange rhythmic pulse drew my attention and I looked around the walls, trying to work out what I was hearing. All around the burrh the chant of,

"Wolf! Wolf! Wolf!" had been taken up. From every section of every wall the men were chanting, punching their weapons to the sky. I raised my sword and shield, accepting their adulation, turning to acknowledge them all. The world slid out of view. My mind took me beyond this middle earth to the hall of my ancestors. Father and mother, my dearest, beloved mother, were standing at the door. They were waiting for me, their faces etched with pride. I was laughing and weeping at the same time. Someone shook me. Wulfstan was there, and Oswine.

"Come on boy. Let's get you cleaned up and find you a pot of ale. You've earned it."

He put his arm around my shoulders and we walked through the cheering, chanting army to the hall. The door closed behind us and Osburga gasped at the sight of me. I laughed and wept as they eased me to a chair and put a pot in my hand.

"I was meant to die today, Wulfstan. Why didn't I die?"

"I don't know, boy. You have a drink. Get cleaned up. The ladies here'll sort you out. There's no need to dash back. The bastards have gone for now. Come back out when you're ready."

He patted and squeezed my shoulder and they left.

CHAPTER 18: Tiw's tribute

I was alone. I hadn't died. I'd seen mother, though, and father, and they were both proud of me. Tiw had spared me. Clearly there was some greater purpose than even I had imagined. I gulped the refreshing ale. Gradually the elation of the battlefield left me and I felt hollow and almost too weak to raise my pot. Tears ran down my cheeks and my hands shook. I pushed all thoughts of the battle aside and looked for something to hold my attention. All around me the women of the Granta bridge were tending to wounded men. I recognised some of them and one or two of them called greetings to me. They were pleased that I was here with them. Pleased that I should see that they had earned wounds in my service. I smiled,

"This won't be forgotten," I assured them.

"Thank you, lord", "Thank you."

I watched Osburga busy about the hall. The sheen of sweat on her forehead and red cheeks stirred the savage lust that battle always left behind. She was a fine looking woman with a full, heavy bust, rounded hips and a strong arse. The fluid female flesh pushed and swayed beneath her dress. If she was mine she wouldn't be disrespectful. I watched her move. I imagined my hands on her soft flesh, pictured her reddened, sweat-slicked face looking up at me. I wanted to feel the warmth of her. I wanted to smell her soft, warm, female scent. I wanted a woman. I wanted her. I wanted to bend her over one of the tables and bury myself in her, spend my rage in her belly while she gasped and squealed. She turned suddenly and looked straight into my eyes. What she saw held her fast.

"That's a lot of blood."

"What?" I turned to the unexpected voice. A young girl was standing before me with a bowl and a cloth.

"That's a lot of blood. Should I clean it?" She asked nervously.

The words took a moment to sink in.

"That's good, thankyou," I decided, and allowed her to wash the dried blood from my face. When I looked back, Osburga had gone.

"It doesn't look too bad. It's just a cut," my helper told me.

"I know, it was a stone," I said stupidly.

What was I doing here? I looked around as if I had just woken from a deep sleep. I needed to get back on the wall. This was ridiculous. I drained the last of my ale.

"Thankyou for your help. I feel much better now," I informed my young carer who gave me a beautiful, girl's smile and nervous laugh.

I made for the door and went out into the rain. I was alive! I tilted my head back and let the cold water run down my face. I was still here. There was still work to do. I began to chuckle. By the gods she had a fine arse! I let out a great sigh and shook my head to clear the vision of Osburga's backside from my head. I looked around the fort before deciding to find Aldwyn.

"Aldwyn, what's the situation at the gate?"

"Wulfhere, good to see you back with us, lord. You were, I mean, thankyou, lord."

"You've lost me now, Aldwyn. What's happening with the gate? Do you need more men?"

"We've had a bit of a change round, lord. The Danes are holding the gate. They've been fairly quiet on the north wall and they wanted a chance to be more involved. My lads are on the wall with the Frisians. Ullr's got the gate."

"Well done Aldwyn. That was good work, and good thinking about the Danes."

I left him and hurried back to my lads on the south wall.

"Wulfstan! Anything happening?"

I stepped up onto the fighting platform and looked out. There was a lot of movement going on around Cynfellyn's camp, but the ground between us was deserted, apart from a few arrow pierced bodies.

My uncle gave me a searching look.

"Everything alright, boy?"

"Yes, it was only a small cut from a stone."

"Hmmm. That's not……..That's alright then."

We both looked out towards the Wealh army.

"They're deciding what to do next," Wulfstan announced, giving me the latest news.

I looked down into the ditch beneath us. There were dead lying two or three deep along the entire length of the wall. Wulfstan followed my gaze.

"Oh yes. What were you saying about no profit on this trip? We are going to be going home with wagons full of loot my boy! I've always liked the Wealh. A very generous people!" He laughed at his own joke. "Nothing is too much for them, so we'd better take everything they've got!"

"Except for the weather," Oswine suggested.

"You've got a point there old friend," I agreed.

The weather had been absolutely awful.

"If this keeps up we won't be able to plant any grain. It'll rot in the ground," Oswine continued his theme.

"This won't keep up," Wulfstan decided. "There can't be much left up there now. Besides, our mad Wolf lord can have a word with the bosses up there and get them to polish up the sunshine. He's on first name terms you know." He added conspiratorially to Oswine who smiled at the thought.

"Well it hasn't hurt our cause, has it?"

"Oh no! Don't get me wrong. I'm all for it, all for it! You keep bringing your god to our battles. You fight like a complete madman, the Wolf boys think that you can't lose, and everyone else is scared shitless. You should see the effect that you've had on some of the Wealh lads. Our boys are used to it, and he's our god of course. These new lads, well. Don't be surprised if they start burning virgins and such like. You've really got them thinking!"

I looked around at some of the nearby warriors. They were doing what warriors always did, sharpening and cleaning their gear, talking, watching, they didn't seem any different to me. I knew that they called me Wulfhere the Mad. That didn't bother me, it helped keep order and discipline if they were half scared of me. I left my companions and walked along the wall talking to as many men as I could. They all just seemed to be pleased to be here with me. It was all smiles and laughter, and 'well done lord', 'great work, lord'. They were my men. Ottar's great booming laugh as he grasped my hand, and the smiles of his Norse warriors convinced me that I was doing my job properly.

Wulfstan called to me from his place on the far wall.

"Wulfhere! Quick! Look at this!"

I was about to make a light hearted reply, but I saw that he was very serious about something outside the fort. I ran and joined him and looked out at the Wealh camp.

There seemed to be a lot of activity. I watched for a while before I realised,

"They're going! Aren't they?"

"That's what it looks like," Wulfstan confirmed.

"Yes, 'looks like'," Oswine echoed. "That doesn't mean that they're really going. That's an old trick. Pretend that you've had enough and then creep back in the middle of the night. Darkness hides all sorts of goings on. He's not just going to crawl away after one attack!"

Aldwyn, Ullr, Brega, Osburga and most of the fort were soon gathering at our wall to watch the Catuvellauni begin the long weary march home of the defeated. Cheers started, men were laughing, pointing, shouting insults at the beaten enemy.

"Quiet!" I shouted above the noise.

Gradually the silence spread and the army was watching me. I stood on the fighting platform and looked at the men before me.

"This battle isn't over yet. Not until I tell you. They might look like they're going but if any one of you wants to stake his life on it, step forward now and, if they return, I will kill you myself."

Nobody stepped forward. "That's wise. Now stay on your guard. This is probably a trick. We can stand down and rest. We'll leave a quarter of our strength on the walls, but there will be no drunkenness. No celebrations, not just yet. You will sleep with your weapons close and your gear on, until I tell you otherwise.

And do not shout at your enemy over the wall, like farm dogs barking at strangers. You are warriors. Respect yourselves. Have some pride. We fight! We kill! We are the warriors of the east Angels! Not farm dogs!

Now rest, look to your gear. Eat. There will be a time to celebrate, but it's when I say. You've made a legend here. The two hundred and fifty who held the army of Cynfellyn! You should be proud of yourselves because, by Tiw, I am proud of you. Now remember who we are. Go on."

Laughter and chatter broke out as the men returned to their places. The tone was happy, but it was restrained, and they all walked a little taller and straighter.

"What about plunder?" Wulfstan jerked his head in the direction of the bodies beyond the wall.

"They're not going anywhere, uncle."

The dead don't care who has won or lost. They are all united in death. Wyne would be with his ancestors. He lived bravely and died well, they would be proud to welcome him. Six more of our lads would be making the journey with him. I looked at their bodies laid out in the north east corner of the fort, by the sheep pen, and called upon the gods to welcome them to the mead benches. Aldwyn's lads had suffered harder. Twenty two of his fyrdmen had been slain, mostly holding the gate. The Danes and the Frisians had only lost five of their companions between them. The north wall had been furthest from the Wealh and had been lightly pressed compared to the others. When we plundered the dead I would make sure that Cissa and Aldwyn had enough to repay their loyalty and encourage more folk to settle here and replace their losses.

This day seemed to have lasted for years and it was still only mid-morning. The Wealh camp was dwindling as they marched away in their companies. The pressure was off for now and I had set men to dragging the bodies away from the gate. If the Wealh wanted a ramp they would have to build another one. Other fellows were gathering arrows, spears, rocks and sling stones from amongst the slain. I wanted to be ready for whatever happened next. Cynfellyn might be attempting to trick us into lowering our guard. On the other hand it was still early in the year and Cynfellyn's losses were severe but not disastrous. He could return home, regroup, and attack again when there was food to be had. He could be more patient then, and take his time with the assault. I wanted to be ready for all eventualities.

Nothing happened for the rest of that day. The Wealh left. By the time that the light began to fade the last of their warriors had marched back to the south.

I sat with the leaders of my army as we ate an excellent hot, filling stew of mutton.

"So what's our next move?" Wulfstan wondered.

"We wait here for Icel and the rest of our army. The decision will be his. He might want to take the war to Cynfellyn," I shrugged. "Who knows? As soon as we are finished here we're marching on Caer Colun. I've promised Artorius. Don't worry, there'll be plenty of plunder there. Not only will we be able to strip the dead, Artorius will want to reward us for helping him gain the kingdom. He won't want to be in our debt so you can expect a fine reward there."

It was true. I had made the offer to help Artorius out of friendship, but I knew that, as king of Caer Colun, he would want to be free of any commitment or debt to me. I had no doubt that our reward would be very rich indeed.

"What are we doing tomorrow?" Wulfstan persisted. "We aren't going to sit inside these walls all day are we?"

He wanted to gather the gear and goods from the bodies beyond the walls. We needed to get them burnt or they would start to stink and poison the ground.

"We'd better make a pyre for the bodies. We'll still keep a quarter of our strength on the walls just to be safe and keep a good watch. Everyone else can help clean up. But don't relax, any of you. Keep your men alert, at all times."

I spent most of the night on the wall. I made my way around the fort, talking to the guards, watching and listening for the first sign of any attack. Shortly before dawn I got the army out of their beds to man the walls. We stood there, in the inevitable rain, but the Wealh were gone. After a hot breakfast of porridge I went into my tent and got my head down for a well earned sleep while Wulfstan took charge of the body clearing, and searching.

I slept from the moment my eyes were closed until after noon. A deep, solid, healing sleep with no dreams that I could remember, and not an inch of movement from the moment I had drifted off. I rose straight away and went to the hall to get a pot of ale.

It was quiet in the hall. The wounded men were sleeping or talking quietly in small groups. Women were chopping vegetables and preparing the food. As usual at this time of year it looked like nettles. Osburga was in charge, she came in to the main hall through a door, which I knew led back to her private chambers and the back door to the work huts, carrying a large urn.

"Wulfhere, my husband's out with the others, burning the bodies."

"That's alright, I'll go and find them shortly. I just came in for a drink, a pot of ale."

"I'm sure we can find a pot of ale for you, my lord," she simpered. Osburga never called me, 'my lord'. We had known each other since childhood and I had always thought that she had resented my birth right.

"It's a bit mad in here. Come through to the ale house. I'll get you a pot from a new barrel." She put down the urn and made to go back through the door she had just entered, pausing to look back and wait for me. I hurried after her. We left the hall and made for a small building. Osburga quickly opened the door and went straight in. I followed and found myself in the ale house. She glanced out before closing the door behind us. There were barrels of new ale on shelves all the way down one wall. There was mead on the other side and great barrels where new brews were underway.

"Now, just let me find you a pot." Osburga went to where rows of pots were standing on a rack. "One of the good ones I think, for lord Wulfhere," she told me in a voice which was full of respect, bordering on awe, and which I didn't believe for a moment. She turned and bent to 'look' at the lower shelves, as languidly as a waking cat, giving me a very pleasant chance to admire her fine rump. I smiled to myself and stepped forward. I gave her behind a slap and then forced my hand between her thighs as she gasped in first mock, and then very real, surprise and arousal. She grasped the shelf for support, and squirmed against my hand as I rubbed her hot flesh.

"If you were mine, Osburga, you wouldn't speak to me the way that you speak to your husband. You're lucky that he cares too much to beat you the way that I would," she gave a little squeak and writhed at the thought. "But he is my oathgiver, and I will not tolerate disloyalty." I drew my seaxe, placed my left hand between her shoulder blades, held her still and smacked her backside hard with the flat of the heavy war blade. "He has won you a fine house," smack, "and a comfortable life," smack, "his injuries bought your position," smack, "honour him," smack, "and show him the loyalty," smack, "that he deserves," big smack. Now, where's that ale?"

I stepped away from her and, red faced and discomforted, she poured me a pot of new ale. I drained it in one and handed her back the pot.

"You're a beautiful woman, Osburga. I've always been jealous of Cissa."

I left her and went to see how things were progressing outside. Bodies were being heaped onto a huge pyre on the field to the south of the burrh. I crossed to the wall to have a clearer look. The ditch below me had been cleared of the dead, but a few lads were still searching the murky water for dropped gear. I left the wall and walked to the gate. The barrels had been cleared away and the scarred and battered gate stood wide open. Inside the walls, recovered gear was being brought in and laid out. Spears, shields, knives, belts, cloaks, purses, caps, all manner of possessions. Apart from the everyday goods there were items of real value. Twenty two swords, sixteen mail shirts, nineteen helmets and a sack for rings, arm rings, coins and other valuable items. I was shaken from my appraisal of the haul by Wulfstan striding happily back into the fort.

"Over a hundred and forty dead! What do you think of that? That's just the ones who died here. Only the gods know how many more will die or were crippled!"

"We did well," I replied, and we had done well, in every sense.

We left the fort and ambled through the gateway. The ground before the gate was heavily stained with blood, in spite of the rain. The barriers were still in place.

"We'll be taking them down shortly," Wulfstan stated baldly. "They did their job well."

"Don't take them down yet. They can stay there until Icel gets here. That's when the next stage of this war begins."

"But they're a bastard nuisance!" Wulfstan exclaimed.

"They're supposed to be."

Our feet led us to the street from where we watched the lads trying to set a flame to the great pyre. They had a job because everything was damp at best and it smouldered for a long time until it was hot enough to get properly underway. The flames spread, slowly but relentlessly, through the great stack of timber that was required to create the heat to burn such a huge amount of flesh. We turned away from the sizzling, spitting pyre and went back inside.

"How long did you think it would take for Icel to get to us?" Wulfstan wondered.

"Icel ten days. Our lads twelve."

"How long ago was that?"

"I don't know. It seems like years."

CHAPTER 19: Rivers of Blood

I stood on the wall again all that night. I made the men replace the barrels behind the gate once they had finished outside. There was some surprise but I reminded them that the Wealh could come again at any time. I still suspected, as did Oswine, that their retreat might well be a trick. He had stayed up as well, and Wulfstan had felt compelled to join us although he had complained constantly. We had already endured a couple of showers, which hadn't eased his mood, and now, in the depths of the night, thunder rumbled in the distance and the promise of another down pour was enough to finish the last of Wulfstan's enthusiasm.

"This is madness. If they were coming they would have come last night. They can't still be out there, they'll be running out of food. I'm cold, I'm wet and there isn't a sniff of the bastard Wealh bastards!"

"Well go and put your feet up by the fire, uncle," I suggested. "At your age it probably isn't healthy to be out here all night."

"At my age! You cheeky little shit! I've been........."

"Wulfstan, quiet!" Oswine hissed.

"Well don't you start......" Wulfstan broke off, realising that Oswine wasn't just complaining about the noise.

"Listen"

We listened until our ears were ringing. Another rumble of thunder, this time slightly closer, broke the aching silence.

"What was it?" I wondered.

"I don't know. I thought I heard a shout. Distant. Don't know." Oswine was still listening intently.

One of the Danes came running over from the gate.

"Lord, Wulfhere. We think that we hear movement. We can't be sure, but we think."

"It's what I thought. The bastards are trying to catch us cold. Right, go and get your lads up and get them on the gate," I told the Dane. "Gram, get everyone else up, now!" The two hurried away to the tents and men began climbing out and heading for the walls almost straight away.

From the endless darkness beyond the fort there came a clear voice on the night, shouting a ringing note. Before the sound had ended a great roar went up from hundreds of throats.

"They're going for the gate again!" I shouted, drawing my sword.

We had kept a quarter of our men on the walls. The Danes were dashing to take up their posts, many had already reached the fighting platform and others were climbing up the barrels to hold the gate itself. I was secretly pleased that I had insisted on our readiness. I had been proved right again and everyone would know it.

At that moment there was an answering roar from the eastern end of the burrh. They were going to hit us from both ends at once. I jumped up onto the platform and looked out to the south. Nothing. They were concentrating all of their strength on two smaller sections. They wanted to overwhelm the men on the wall by sheer weight of numbers. I jumped down again. The front, western, wall was, if anything, over manned with Danes longing for a chance to get to grips with the enemy. I couldn't see the eastern wall because it was largely hidden by the hall and the other buildings.

I was about to go and look for myself when one of Aldwyn's lads came running up, wide eyed and terrified.

"Lord Wulfhere! The Wealh! They've won the wall! North east corner! They're in!"

The fyrdmen! I should have known it. I should have given them more support.

"Wulfstan! Oswine! Gram! Ottar! Fifty men, with me now!" I ran across the fort.

"Brega! Give me twenty men, now! This way!"

I curved my run past the end of the hall and almost collided with three of Aldwyn's lads running the other way.

"Stand! With me!"

I dashed past them, hoping that they would turn and follow. In the dark I could make out shadows of men still fighting furiously on the wall.

"So we've not been swept aside yet then." I thought to myself. Hopefully only a few of the Wealh had got in and we could force them back out and hold the wall.

A screaming figure ran at me. It was too dark to make him out clearly but I could see that he was quite tall. I lowered my weight, crouching slightly, and drove forward behind my shield. I was in a strong, low position and the collision hurled him to the ground, smashing the air from his lungs. In the darkness it was impossible to see him clearly, so I just hacked at him seven or eight times. I stopped when he was quiet. Gram was beside me.

"Here, lord Wulfhere!" He shouted in the darkness to avoid confused injury.

"Shield wall! Wolf! Shield wall!" I sheathed my sword and drew my short, heavy fighting seaxe.

I knew Gram was on my left. A new warrior joined to my right.

"Who's there?" I demanded.

"Hubbe, lord!"

"Good man Hubbe! Come on Wolf! Shield wall!"

I wanted to trap the Wealh in this corner and stop them getting into the fort.

"Wulfhere!" It was Wulfstan.

"Here, Wulfstan!"

"What are we doing?"

"Shield wall Wulfstan! Across the corner! Trap them here and drive them out!"

"Good! Oswine, to the wall, with me." He hurried to close the shield wall to the fort wall. I could feel men joining behind us. I could hear our lads and Frisians.

"Right lads on my word we step. And. Step! Step! Step!"

One step at a time we started to move to the corner.

At that moment the storm broke directly overhead. Great, heavy drops of rain started to hammer down and a flash of lightning lit the scene for an instant. The Wealh were rushing over the wall. There must have been thirty or forty already on our side of the wall. There were five or six ladders up on the wall and with each passing moment more warriors were leaping down into the fort. We had to drive them out and regain the wall. They had to drive us back so that their army could climb in behind them and overwhelm the defence.

In the dark we couldn't see them coming, but we heard the yell, we sensed the rush, and we braced for the hit.

"Wolf, step!" On my order we took one pace forward to take the shock of the hit and throw it back at the enemy.

As always that impact was nerve shredding. In the dark it was even more so. I pulled my head down behind my shield and peered over it. I had to trust my helmet to save me from whatever might be coming my way because I couldn't see it. A wild Catuvellauni warrior hammered into my shield and if it wasn't for the lads behind me I would have been hurled back. Fortunately for me I think that my enemy had misjudged the crash and he was more dazed and winded than I was. Before he had time to gather himself I stabbed at him with my seaxe and felt the blade slide home. I had stood in the wall before and I knew that men were like beasts in this terrifying death trap. They never died easily. I stabbed again, and again, and again and kept stabbing until he slumped down in front of me to be replaced by another enemy.

"Step!"

More weight was coming onto my shield now. There must have been a lot more Wealh clambering over the wall. I stabbed under my shield this time, seeking the groin and the big blood tubes. My opponent was screaming, crying, my hand felt hot and sticky. Stab, stab, stab, twist and saw, and down he went, underfoot.

"Step!"

The lads behind me had got themselves sorted out at last and spears were being thrust over my shoulders at the faces of the Foemen.

"Step!"

Nothing, no forward movement. We were actually being forced back. No that couldn't happen. If we broke we were lost. We had to hold this corner. I brought my seaxe up so that I could lean my weight forward. I could see a round shadow amongst the other shadows. It was the head of the Wealh who was grinding, shoving, and heaving against my shield. I stabbed at his head, over and over. He screamed. Lightning momentarily revealed my victim. I'd stabbed through his left eye. I stabbed again, and again, the blade must have gone into his mouth because I felt it clashing against his teeth. Stab and saw, he was gurgling, coughing, drowning in his own blood.

"Step! Come on you bastards, step!"

My feet were sliding on the wet ground, trying to gain purchase. There was an almighty blow against my helmet. A spear thrust had glanced off. Behind me someone grasped the spear and pulled it to us. My attacker held on to his spear. I could see his arm darker against the dark sky. I stabbed at it, using the blade of my heavy seaxe, not the point. I cut hard across his wrist, severing tendons, flesh and blood tubes, until the blade grated on the bone. Perhaps his hand couldn't release the shaft now that his wrist was so badly damaged because I could still see his arm against the sky. I hacked at the elbow, again, and again, and again, until the man behind me had the spear, and the arm.

Lightning revealed a seething sea of heads. The Wealh were still clambering over the wall. The corner of the fort was a dense crush of Wealh warriors, crammed in like fish on a tray at the market.

"Step!"

It was all I could do to stay in touch with Gram and Hubbe. I couldn't fight anymore. I just had to push. The Wealh were in so tight that they couldn't fight us. They were so tight that they just stood and screamed as the lads behind me stabbed at their heads with their long spears. When they were killed, eventually, they couldn't fall. Their blood soaked heads remained part of the crowd as the spears picked on a new, helpless, terrified victim.

"Step!"

Ooh! The breath was driven out of me. Suddenly there was a big forward drive as more weight came on from behind. A lot more of our lads must have joined the crush. The noise was deafening. It had risen in pitch, the clamour of utter terror.

Lightning! I could see Wealh standing on the wall looking down at the seething mass of flesh below them. They couldn't get in. The fort was crammed with Tiw's tribute.

"Step!"

It wasn't me shouting, it was someone behind. By the gods! I couldn't breathe. I couldn't move! I no longer had any control over what I was doing. I was trapped, utterly helpless.

"Step!"

Another heave. Even the spearmen behind me couldn't move any more. A shaft was resting on my shoulder. The blade buried in a warrior's neck.

"Step!"

The noise of the trapped warriors was head splitting, unbearable, and suddenly it rose. The pitch changed again. It was frantic, desperate. There was a groaning, tearing noise, not of this world. A crash, not thunder, and we were carried forward, irresistibly. I couldn't stop, I couldn't get out of the unstoppable rush. We were driven together, and down, in a great crushing dance of death. No breath. The lads behind had fallen on top of me. We were down in layers. The Wealh had somehow collapsed.

I raised my eyes and looked up and in that moment lightning showed me Tiw's plan. The wall had gone. Just gone. The press within the wall had been too much. Days of rain must have saturated the ground. Softening and weakening the wall of the ditch. The wall had given way and hundreds of warriors had collapsed on top of each other.

Strong hands dragged me to my feet. Before us the Wealh were trapped. The dead Wealh who had been closest to us were now on top of their trapped companions. They were crushed, suffocating, helpless.

"Kill Them! Quickly!"

Before they could struggle out from under the corpses of their friends we had to kill them, every single one. I climbed onto the dead bodies in front of me and started stabbing down between them. The Wealh were screaming, my men rushed to the slaughter. My seaxe wasn't long enough to reach them. I snatched up a spear from dead hands and stabbed down between limbs, or through them, at the living flesh beneath. We climbed up the living, writhing, hill of doomed men, and we killed. Blood sprayed higher than our heads, and ran down between the bodies where it mingled with the torrential rain, and drowned the Wealh trapped by the crushing weight of the bodies above them. Outside the fort the enemy tried to rally to help their friends, but we had the wall again. Our lads hacked their way back along the fighting platform until they held the walls at each side of the breach. The ladders were hurled down. Where the wall had given way the ditch was steep, and slick with blood and rain. They couldn't climb up. They just had to watch and listen to the screams while their friends were butchered like tethered swine.

Wulfstan had rediscovered the battle madness. He was laughing and roaring curses and hatred as he killed. Gram was cold and precise. I stumbled over the heap, repeating,

"Your tribute, lord Tiw!" to myself, over and over.

The screams of the dying Wealh, suffocating and drowning at the bottom of the crush, were smothered by the bodies above them and the undulating heap of flesh gave off a low drone like a beehive. That vision of the underworld, the humming sound, the laughter and curses, the constant movement of dying men beneath my feet and the dread and horror as I climbed the living mound, stabbing and hacking at the helpless men beneath me who had been driven mad by terror, was lit up with each crackling flash of Thunor's lightning bolts.

I reached the edge of the abyss and looked down with the next flash of brilliant light at a sea of horrified Wealh faces beyond the wall. I raised my blood soaked spear above my head and by the light of the next bolt I cursed them and offered them all to my god. The next time the night was pierced they were running, running from the end of the world. In the total and utter darkness following the flash I could hear the bloody water running in rivulets down into the ditch beyond the ruined wall. Rivers of blood.

CHAPTER 20: The Smell of Glory

I peered all around at the bodies shining wetly beneath my feet. None was moving, the screaming and shouting had stopped. I had no one else to kill. Around me my lads were still casting around, hunting out any Wealh who were trying to stay silent and pretend that they were already numbered among the dead. We had held the wall.

Ullr! What was happening at the gate?

"Wulfstan. Make sure that this breach is stopped up. Gram! Ottar! With me, to the gate."

I ran back round the side of the hall and the byre and was nearly bowled over by a flock of sheep running loose, and panic stricken, in the burrh. Obviously the hurdle walls of their pen had been broken down. I couldn't do anything about them now so I avoided their mad scrambling dashes and splashed across the fort to the gate. There was no fighting.

"Ullr!" I shouted into the darkness.

"Wulfhere! By the gods," the old Dane's voice came back. "Wulfhere, what was that noise?" He came down from the wall to greet me. "Are you hurt?"

I looked down at myself. I was painted in blood. My hands and arms and the front of my mail were coated in thick blood which shone wetly in the near darkness. The sticky feeling around my eyes told me that my face was similarly coloured. But I didn't think it was mine.

"No, Ullr, I'm not hurt. How have things gone here?"

"They've come twice so far. I don't know what they're doing now, they've dropped back into the trees over there." He pointed to the unseen woods on the far side of the street beyond the town.

"Well done, Ullr. Stay alert. I don't think that they'll come again at the eastern wall. If you're hard pressed we can probably spare you some men from elsewhere."

"I think that we'll hold, lord. If you hear me shout for help, send those men!"

We both laughed. I didn't think that the Danes would shout for help if they were facing odds of ten to one. I left them and visited the other walls. The southern and northern walls were both dangerously undermanned. I left Ottar and his lads on the south wall and hurried back to the east wall to find that Wulfstan had blocked the breach with Wealh bodies. I left Aldwyn with twenty five men to hold the shortened wall. I told the rest to return to their places. Dead and wounded were taken to the hall. We went back to watching and waiting.

I no longer had any men in support of the walls. Every man was in place. We would just have to hold. The night passed slowly. The rain finally stopped and we stood and shivered in our soaked gear. I had the excuse of checking the walls to keep moving and try to stave off the cold, but it was still bitter. With the dawn we had the chance to relax a little and I called the leaders of my army together.

"A quarter of our strength to remain on the walls. Everyone else to rest. Get some hot food out to the guards."

I couldn't desert my lads who were still holding their places, so I waited while porridge was brought round by their friends, and stood watch with them. Gram fetched me a bowl and we stood together as we devoured the filling grains.

"Do you think they'll come again?" Gram asked between mouthfuls.

"I think that we've gutted him, Gram. I don't know how many men we've killed here but it must be hundreds, and that's not counting the ones who limped home. I don't think that he can risk losing any more men. I don't even think that he can stay here and face Icel when he arrives. When Leofmund gets here with the rest of the south folk, and Icel and the Corieltavi turn up, if they turn up, we'll easily outnumber what's left of the Catuvellauni. He'll have to stay out of the way and give us a free hand with whatever we want." I waved my hand broadly over the south and west.

"So are we going to take more towns?"

"We're not, but Icel might. This would be a good time for him to increase the size and power of his kingdom. Cynfellyn will have to think twice about coming north again, even if Icel and the Corieltavi claim every farm, village and town between here and Ligora Ceaster. Icel can take what he wants, and buy the loyalty of the Corieltavi. Our swordplay has made him secure. Aldwyn and Cissa, too. This has been a great victory for our people, Gram. Wyne and the boys can hold their heads high in the next world."

"I hadn't ever thought that there was so much at stake," Gram admitted. "I just thought that we were coming here to help Aldwyn and Cissa."

"Well we were, my friend. The rest was decided by Tiw and the fates. He sent me a dream, years ago, and at the time I didn't know what it meant. But it has become clear since then. He wanted me to win a kingdom for our people. He showed me a vision of fire and war and a new land across the sea. The way the gods work is beyond all of us. I didn't know what this fight would lead to. I have won the new kingdom as he ordained. I thought my time was over. I expected to die, but Tiw stopped the spinners from cutting my thread, Gram. I have been spared by the gods. Who knows what is in store for us now, my friend."

Cynfellyn was gone. He didn't come that day or all through the next night. The following day we cleared the bodies from the east wall and I sent riders to Icel.

"This is your message to Icel from me. 'Cynfellyn is defeated. The lands of the Catuvellauni lie open.'"

Once they had repeated it back to me I sent them on their way.

The great heap of dead Wealh was thrown down through the breach in the wall. The bodies were searched and then heaped up onto another great pyre. At the gate the Danes were doing the same with their defeated foes. Two hundred and twenty bodies altogether. Cynfellyn had lost the best part of four hundred of his warriors and many more must be dying of their wounds, or be too badly injured to fight again this year, if ever.

The haul of plunder was magnificent. I had enough swords to equip the entire Wolf Pack, if I so desired, and still have some to give to friends. Once our smith, Leuthere, had repaired the mail shirts I would also have enough of those to equip the Wolf Pack. Spears and shields were so numerous that we hardly knew where to store them. Helmets, two beautiful torcs, more coins, and another horse was found running riderless in the fields to the east of the fort. Presumably his former owner was sizzling on the pyre.

The smell of burning flesh clung to us everywhere. My hands were wreathed in the fatty, cloying smell of blood as well, which added to the slightly unhealthy feeling. We were alive and we had won a famous victory. That night I allowed the men to celebrate. We packed ourselves into, and spilled out of, the hall. The mead flowed and our songs were roared out, making the rafters of the hall quiver with the ear splitting din. I tortured myself watching Osburga's healthy curves test the fabric of her dress as we sat in the hall that evening. By the gods I needed a woman to take the rage from me!

In the moning I sent riders out to scout and watch for any Wealh return. They sighted nothing for two days and then two of them cantered into the fort to announce Icel's imminent arrival. His army was splendid. Icel rode at the head of his horsemen, but he had foot warriors, wagons and strange, fluttering banners which fanned the air above them and looked wonderful. I remembered my Wolf banner and decided that I would definitely take it to war in the future.

"Wulfhere! My lords! What is this news of a victory? Cynfellyn defeated? Catuvellauni lands lying open? What does it mean?"

We took Icel and the lords of the Corieltavi and showed them our battlefield, explained the events of the past days and pointed to the smouldering pyres which were covered in flocks of squabbling carrion birds.

Back in the hall they were still incredulous.

"So you honestly believe that Cynfellyn is broken?" Icel asked, yet again.

"Icel, I would not brag idley about something like this. And I certainly wouldn't give you advice that would place you in danger. You and your Corieltavi lords will have a free hand in the northern marches of the Catuvellauni kingdom this summer. We have killed, killed mark you, almost four hundred of his warriors. And I'm talking about the men who led the charge and were first over the walls. How many more were wounded only Tiw himself knows. Their northern lands must be defenceless.

He has the Saxons to his south who will be watching on, and waiting for a chance like this. He won't dare to risk losing any more of his strength up here. He will want to make sure that he can hold his southern heartlands. Not only can you take what you like, I don't think that he will be strong enough to try to risk taking it back for years.

Look at the strength that you will be able to call on if he did decide to return. The Corieltavi, the west marches and the eastern Angels. By the gods, that's a thought. What an army that would be!"

I could see Icel's excitement rising.

"If this is all true, Wulfhere, I will reward you beyond wealth, my friend. Yours will have been the greatest victory since Offa of Angel single handedly slew the Myrging champions on the Eider. This is beyond songs, Wulfhere. This is the stuff of legend."

"It is so, Icel. You have my word."

"Then I will have to return to Ligora Ceaster and prepare for the summer. We rode here to help you only to find that you have won us a great victory. I want you to hold this place for two more weeks, my friend. Then my army can return to the field and make the country between here and Ligora Ceaster ours. The Corieltavi will no doubt ride with me then, in their full glory. Do you think it not so, my lords?" This was directed at the Corieltavi lords who were with him. Clearly not all of their kin had been prepared to follow Icel's banners. It seemed that with this victory, and the gift of wealth and land at his disposal, they were all now likely to be Icel's men to command.

Riders were sent to stop Leofmund and the north folk and send them home. I did the same with the south folk and sent a message to warn Artorius to prepare for war in six weeks time.

Icel stayed with us for the night and marched away beneath his banners the next morning. He left us most of the provisions that his army had brought with them.

I had a meeting with all of my companions.

"So, in two weeks Icel will return. You have served me well, my lords. Return home if you will, and in six weeks, the third week of Thrimilci, we will muster at Wolf Home to fight Gwrgant."

"Wulfhere," Ullr spoke up. "Icel said that we were to hold the fort for two weeks."

"I don't think Cynfellyn will return, my friend. I will see you in six weeks time."

I shared the plunder with my friends. The lords of the south folk would all be riding home, and their men would be well equipped when they returned to Wolf Home. Ullr, Brega and Hod rode away. Wulfstan decided to stay with me. Most of his men opted to return to their farms with Sigurd. They would be at Wolf Home in six weeks time. Six of his lads who didn't have farms or families to worry over stayed with their lord.

"So what are we going to do for the next two weeks?" Wulfstan wanted to know when he had eaten his stew that evening. Our reduced company sat in the hall, enjoying a little more space and comfort than had been the case lately.

"Well first of all we've got to mend the wall."

"And then?"

"Well once the burrh is whole again, I think that we might call on some of the neighbours."

"Go on."

"well, Icel is going to be claiming the land to the west."

"It looks that way."

"As trusted servants of the king of the Marches, I think that the lords of the Granta bridge should expect feorm from all of the farms and villages within, let's say, ten miles, of here?"

"I would think that would be just and fair."

"Well, if this feorm had been granted in law, by the lord of the south folk, before Icel's rule was established, then it would have to stand, under the new king."

"I never knew that you were learned in law, Wulfhere," Wulfstan observed with a smile.

"I am learned in battle, uncle. I was taught by the best. I think you'll find that men who are strong in battle are also very learned, and much respected, when it comes to applying the law!"

We roared at that. I was the strongest. I was the law. Aldwyn and Cissa were going to do well out of their sacrifices. I would see to it.

Leofmund reached the burrh early the next morning having sent the army of the north folk back to their homes. He was racked with guilt at having missed our battle, but none of us had known that Cynfellyn was going to attack so soon, and he could hardly be blamed for following my instructions. There was still a lot of fighting ahead of us and he would get chances aplenty to win plunder and earn reward.

We all returned to the hall and over a pot of ale I explained our situation to the returning warriors.

"I have decided to march into Catuvellauni lands and demand feorm from all the lords who could be deemed to come under the protection of Aldwyn and Cissa, here at the Granta bridge," I announced. "They lost many men during the battle and I think that it's only right that they should gain some advantage from their sacrifice."

The men all around me nodded enthusiastically.

"So who are you going to take with you?" Wulfstan wanted to know. "Bearing in mind that we can't leave the burrh here undefended, and we need to repair that back wall."

It was a point well made. I had to venture forth with enough strength to impress, and intimidate, the local Wealh, but we couldn't leave the burrh unguarded. I wanted daily life in the town to return to normal as quickly as possible. I wanted to see merchants and a market. It would happen, but only if the place was safe and well ordered. A strong burrh was the heart of the town. I needed word to be carried abroad that we had beaten off Cynfellyn's attack and that a powerful lord held the burrh in safety.

"Has the army of Cynfellyn gone?" Leofmund wanted to know. "Are they all gone or are any of their warriors still in the field?"

"That's something that we can't know," I shrugged. "That's why we need to take a strong warband." Silence descended on the present company. The Wolf Pack had taken losses. I no longer had enough men to take a strong warband with me and leave a strong warband behind, and we all knew it.

"What about riding out?" Oswine hazarded. "I think that you've still got eleven horses. If eleven of us rode out, in our finest gear, we would look impressive enough and if there are still Wealh out there we can ride back here to safety. If we take eleven we will leave sufficient strength here to give an appearance of power and to repair the wall."

We pondered Oswine's suggestion and agreed that it was sound.

"So who's going and who's staying?" Wulfstan got straight to the point.

I would lead, of course and, as a lord of Granta Bridge, Cissa would have to accompany me. He would take the oaths of the lords of the Catuvellauni or I would have their heads. Wulfstan wouldn't want to miss anything so he and Oswine would come. I decided that Marcellus and his lads would make up the eleven. It would be good to have Wealh voices in our company as well as Angel, and not just because they could speak with the local people. Their presence would show that we were here to rule for all the folk in our kingdom, not just the 'Sais'.

CHAPTER 21: A Beaten People

I had never experienced anything like it in my life. I was leading a mounted warband. I had dressed like a king. I wore my mail shirt, crested helm and wolf skin cloak. My arms and legs were encased in leather and I carried my great war shield with its ravens and dragons. The rhythmic beat of the horses' hooves and the rush of their breath, were accompanied by the creak of leather harness and the occasional rattle and thump of spear on shield as riders shifted their burdens.

We left the gate and turned to the south. I wanted to journey through the land in a great arc, starting in the south and finally returning home from the north. We followed the street for about a mile, and in that time we discovered the bodies of two warriors who must have died of their wounds after fleeing our battle. They had been stripped by their companions and feasted upon by carrion eaters, both furred and feathered. We left the street and headed first eastwards, making always for the higher ground from where we could look for farms or villages. We started to discover farms almost straight away. Border lands are often deserted, but we had only held the Granta bridge burrh for a year. Since we had taken the town there hadn't been any of the raiding or slave taking which often follows, or heralds, war. As a result there was no tradition of hatred in the borders. I hoped that this would make it easier for us to assume lordship.

At the first farm that we rode up to, two men came out to meet us. There was a collection of five round houses without any defences. The fields were well tilled and neatly kept. We reined in our mounts and Marcellus did the talking. He announced me as 'Wulfhere the Grim', which apparently was what the Wealh called me. He told them that Cynfellyn was defeated and that I was now king of these lands and that Cissa held my authority. They looked from me to Cissa who looked very forbidding with the long scar disappearing beneath his eye patch. Marcellus demanded to know what tribute the farm was required to send to their king. They told him everything that they were expected to send. He then added a little, because the farmers would obviously tell us less than they actually sent. In this way, as we rode from farm to farm, Cissa was soon able to build up a keen understanding of what the land yielded.

At the seventh farm we were directed to the 'great house', where their lord lived. Marcellus explained that the 'great house' would have once been the hall of a great Roman estate and would now be the home of the leading clan of the area. The great house was a long building with a tiled roof. Stone steps led up to a large door at the very centre of the building and I longed to go inside and see how they lived within that long structure. It was very impressive. There were new wattle and daub built, thatched additions on each end of the great house, and the tiles on the right hand end of the original building had been replaced with thatch, but it was still a wonderful sight.

The houses of servants and workers clustered together by the road, a short way from the great house. An old man and a boy were watching over a flock of sheep in a meadow alongside their small village. The boy was holding a half full pale of frothy ewes milk. They didn't run, there would have been little point. After a brief discussion with the old shepherd, Marcellus told me that Drudwas had been lord here, but he, and his son Dyvyr, had been slain at the recent battle against the 'Sais wolves' from the east. His second son Dyrmig was now the lord. We rode forward and halted a respectful distance from the hall. Marcellus announced me and demanded that Dyrmig come forth to meet his new king.

Time dragged past with no sign of anything happening. I guessed that there were hurried debates going on within the silent walls. What should they do? Could we be trusted? Was it a trap for the new lord? I started to grow impatient. I didn't like being kept waiting. They were beaten, they had to understand that I was their king now. If these dogs wouldn't offer me their oaths I would use them to send a message to all of the Catuvellauni who might be thinking about defying me. I was on the point of ordering the thatches fired, when there was a sudden commotion of activity. I heard horses and men, and six riders emerged from a door in what must have been a stable at the right hand side of the great long building. They approached us at a trot and came to an uncertain halt, about twenty yards before us. I kicked my horse's flanks and closed the short gap with my warriors fanning out to both sides, half encircling our worried hosts.

Dyrmig was just a boy. His attendants were old men, with only one warrior amongst them. I guessed that most of Drudwas' warriors had been burned on the great pyre at the Granta bridge along with their lord and his son.

"That's close enough Sais!"

The old man on Dyrmig's right could speak our language, heavily accented, but perfectly understandable. I stopped six feet before the lad and slowly removed my beautiful, crested helm. I sighed heavily, looking at my men fanned out around their prey, and then back at the Wealh before us. We all knew that I held their lives in my hand.

"Dyrmig, I am Wulfhere, king of the east Angels." I waited while the old man translated for his lord. "This land is mine," I waved my hand over the surrounding countryside. "But like all kings I need men to husband the land. As your king I offer you the protection of my sword arm and my laws. As a new lord, young in years, you will need a powerful protector to ensure that you hold your lands from those who will look jealously upon your fortune. In return you will be expected to provide warriors and service when they are required and to yearly send feorm to lord Cissa at the Granta bridge." I indicated my old friend and, once more, I waited while the old advisor translated for his young lord and their companions. When he had finished he turned back to me.

"King Wulfhere, you will understand that these are matters which we must discuss a little further."

"No, I don't think they are. There are two choices before you. You will accept my rule and agree to send feorm to lord Cissa, or I will pile your heads by the gate and burn the hall and everyone in it. These lands will never again be ruled by the Catuvellauni. This will be Angel land from now until the end of days. King Icel will be lord of the lands to the west. You will do well to learn our tongue and our ways. The old ways are gone! Now, make your choice."

They all looked to the older man who stared at me with a shocked expression on his face. He translated for his companions but their talk was hesitant and punctuated by more glances to me and my companions. Finally the old fellow spoke once more.

"King, Wulfhere. We regard your offer of friendship as just and generous. What are the terms of this 'feorm'?"

I let Marcellus deal with the details. When it was all agreed I took Dyrmig's oath, translated by the old fellow, Morwain. We would meet again at the winter court at the Granta Bridge. In the meantime Dyrmig could call on me for protection, and when king Icel's men came here he had only to utter my name to guarantee his hold on this estate.

So we continued our journey through Cissa's new lands. The folk had no choice but to accept our terms. They were my people now. They looked at our horses, our gear and our scarred faces, and they believed that we were the new power in the land. We learned that alongside young Dyrmig the most powerful men in that country were Halwn, Cilydd and Anwas. We visited their halls in their turn.

We found that Halwn had been slain at the great battle with the Sais and his son Henwas had assumed his estate. Henwas himself had a long gash from the back of his shoulder running down his arm to the elbow.

"The sort of wound a fleeing man might suffer," I thought to myself.

He was extremely hostile, but he had no choice but to swear loyalty and accept our terms.

I didn't like Cilydd in the slightest. He was sly and falsely friendly. He was exactly the sort who would always escape a battle unharmed. He assured us that he had never trusted Cynfellyn and was honoured to be numbered among my folk.

Anwas' hall was the furthest north and he would be surrounded by Icel's Corieltavi once they came south to seize the land. He had more distrust of his blood's ancient enemies than he had of me, and he threw himself wholeheartedly onto my protection. Once feorm was agreed he swore his oath of loyalty and then called for ale. While we drank, a young girl of about fifteen years was ushered forward by the women of the house. Anwas stood aside, smiling and gesturing open handed as the lass came and stood before me with her head bowed.

With a sudden sense of uncertainty I looked to Marcellus. "What's this?"

Marcellus spoke quickly to Anwas who bowed and gestured at the girl with both hands, palms open in a gesture of giving.

Marcellus looked at me, considering his words, but I had already understood the obvious gesture.

"She is a peace weaver, lord. Anwas wants the security of a connection with king Wulfhere. She's his daughter, he's giving her to you, as a bride."

I looked from Marcellus to Anwas, and then to the girl. She was a pretty thing. Not beautiful, like Asfrid, but her dark eyes were bright, her long, dark hair looked soft and warm, and her skin was smooth and clear with the soft sheen of youth. Hunger for a woman stirred within me.

"Why hasn't she been married before?"

Marcellus asked the question.

"Her betrothed was killed at the burrh, lord. 'The great battle against the Sais'. He was the son of a great lord of their folk, from the southern lands."

"What do you think, Marcellus? Would it help my position with these people?"

"With these people? Of course, lord. Anwas would be delighted to have marriage links to the king of the east Angels. It is way beyond what he might have expected from life."

"Wulfhere, what are you doing?" Wulfstan asked, incredulous. "You don't need this girl, and what about Asfrid? Are you really going to share your hall with both of them? You can't seriously be thinking about replacing her at the head of your household with this little thing, so you'll end up annoying your first wife with a second wife that you don't really care about either way! This old goat is just out for what he can get. He's just chancing his arm. He wants the connection to your household, you certainly don't need it."

He was right, of course.

"Marcellus, thank Anwas for the honour that he has paid me. Tell him that the girl is very beautiful but I already have a wife who makes me very happy."

Marcellus entered into a long discussion with Anwas which went back and forth far more than was necessary to decline his offer. Finally he turned away from the older man and faced me again.

"He understands that, lord. He doesn't expect you to raise her above the lady Asfrid. She is his youngest daughter and he wants her to have a life of comfort. He knows that the Sais take more than one wife and he wants you to take her. He believes that she will have a good life in the royal household and that she will be a boon to you when your lady isn't, 'receptive'."

Wulfstan appreciated that and guffawed roundly.

"He's got a point there!"

I looked to Marcellus who merely shrugged. I looked at the girl. What would I say to Asfrid? I would say that the girl was a gift. That I had been away from my love for a long time and I wanted a woman. What about the girl? I looked at her home. She would certainly have a more comfortable life in my household, and taking Anwas' daughter would ally the old Wealh more firmly to Cissa and Aldwyn. It wouldn't hurt our position here with the Wealh.

"Alright, tell Anwas I'll take her. What's her name?"

She was called Arwen, a pretty name.

She walked alongside my horse as we headed back to the Granta Bridge burrh. She had a bundle of possessions that she carried over her shoulder. She was fit and agile and didn't flag at all in spite of her burden. We spent the night in the open and she fussed around me, fetching my food and drink and waiting on my instructions. She settled down for the night, snuggled tight to me for warmth. The smell of her, and the warmth of her, were too much for my lust. It was too cold to strip and explore her but my desire for her was overwhelming. She lay, unresisting and breathless as I raised her skirts and sought her wet, eager opening. I prised her apart with my fingers and guided myself in. She was tightness and heat and gasping, whimpering, discovery.

Afterwards I lay on top of her, spent of my passion. She was still and quiet beneath me, completely submissive, awaiting my pleasure. The thought stirred me again. I swelled inside her and rode her to a second release.

When I woke the next morning she was up and preparing porridge for breakfast. For the next two days she walked alongside my horse as we visited the last of the farms to the north of Granta Bridge. At night I humped away inside her quivering, eager, body as she lay panting and acquiescent beneath me. On the third day we made our way back to the burrh. The jokes about Arwen being unable to walk to keep up with us had ceased, and been replaced by respect for her uncomplaining attitude and willingness to do her fair share, and more, around the camp.

We had made good time around our land and there was still five days to wait for Icel to return. There were traders at the burrh and I bought Arwen fine clothes and jewellery which made her bright eyes sparkle all the more. The time passed heavily. Arwen's lack of our language became a bit of a barrier. She was learning, but it was hard to have any real conversation with her yet. She had become more of a servant than a companion. I still enjoyed having her in my bed, and the comfort of the hall had enabled me to enjoy her without freezing, but familiarity had eased my lust, and she was a part of my household rather than my lady.

We rode for miles. Every day we rode abroad, constantly watching for the return of Cynfellyn or any of his raiding warriors. All the time we were meeting the people, our new people, showing them that we were ever watchful, always present. Most importantly we assured them that we would protect them from the Corieltavi.

They were wary of us, distrustful but, with the exception of those who had lost loved ones in the great battle, not hostile.

Riders arrived from Icel to announce that he had left Ligora Ceaster and would be with us tomorrow.

Icel arrived like the spring.

"Wulfhere! Well met old friend! And Aldwyn, Wulfstan, so good to see you all again my friends!"

At his back came the army of the west and the Corieltavi. Well over two hundred horsemen and close to four hundred on foot.

"This is strength, Icel," I said simply, looking over his warriors.

"Wulfhere, this is barely half of my strength! I haven't left my home unguarded! Just think, Wulfhere, imagine the army of the east Angels marching with this host! We will be unstoppable!"

"One day, Icel. For now we must safeguard what we have and put down strong roots for our kingdom. The Wealh lords close by to the south and east have sworn their loyalty and will gather feorm for Aldwyn and Cissa here at the Granta bridge. There is no resistance, Icel. They know that Cynfellyn can't hold this land. From here to Ligora Ceaster it's all yours. Buy the Corieltavi my friend. Reward their loyalty with the wealth of the Catuvellauni. Build a kingdom for the sons of Icel that will last forever."

That night the mead filled our pots, and the songs flowed like a tide. Icel rewarded the valour of the south folk. He gave me four more horses, two stallions and two mares, a coffer full of coins, and a magnificent sword. The blade was beautifully crafted. The balance was such that I would be able to swing it for hours and hardly notice, and the spirit of the blade twisted along the face of the sword like writhing serpents. The deadly edges gleamed cruelly, and the hilt was topped with a vivid, garnet encrusted pommel. The red stones gleamed with an inner fire, and I named the sword 'Blood Seeker'. I had never named a sword before, but this blade was mine and it sang to me, danced for me, and the name just came to my lips.

The battle craft of the south folk was praised in song. Verses were given to Wulfhere, grim Wolf lord, Wulfstan steeped in sword craft, the Danes of brave Ullr and sea faring Frisians, Hod and Brega. The songs were so moving, so powerful, and I wept when I remembered the shield wall, the dark rainy night, and the screams of the trapped Wealh. Arwen kept my pot topped up all night. I saluted my warriors, I embraced Gram like a brother, I joined in the verses of praise, I raised my pot to the slain, to fate, to victory to anything that jumped into my mead weakened mind. I cut my hand and offered the blood to Tiw. I didn't remember how the night ended, the only thing I remembered was Ottar's great booming laugh.

 I woke the next morning with the worst mead sickness that I had ever known. My head split with every exertion, and I threw up half way through sword practise with Oswine and Gram. Arwen was mercy embodied. She brought me a drink which helped to ease my gurgling stomach, and when I was sure that I could keep it down, she brought me bread and cheese.

 Icel was still in a fine mood. The feast hadn't had the same meaning for him and he had maintained a dignified, kingly presence.

 "Wulfhere, who's the girl?" He wondered.

 "Arwen. She's a gift from the Wealh," I explained. "Icel, I need to return to Wolf Home. It is time for me to march on Gwrgant. The lands here are won. You won't need me for what you have to do now, and I have given my word to a friend."

 "Very well, Wulfhere. I will trust your judgement of Artorius. You are my brother. I won't make you break your word. May Tiw stay with you, brother and bring you a swift victory!"

 I embraced Icel, I embraced Aldwyn and Cissa. I kissed Osburga and complimented her on her hall and hospitality. I jumped up onto Victory and rode for Wolf Home with Arwen walking beside me.

CHAPTER 22: Queen of the Hall

"Oh I see, so she's just your whore!"

Asfrid was very pregnant and very angry. We had returned to Wolf Home in triumph. The march had been slow. As always we were tied to the pace of the wagons, and even though we had fifteen men on horseback we had to stay together. The folk had cheered us home. From Ithamar's estates onwards the people stopped their work in the fields and the houses and work huts and came out to cheer us as we passed. Ithamar and his son, Inga met us personally and I told them that the army would muster at their South Burrh in three weeks time.

We forded the river at Wolf Home, and the river front and the traders in the fort were deserted as everyone came to welcome us home. The senior Wolf Pack men returned to their homes and families, Wulfstan and his lads, and most of the Wolf Pack accompanied me up the track to the hall. The household was waiting at the gate to greet us. I could see Asfrid, of course, unmistakeably pregnant and Togi, jumping around excitedly. Eadgyth was there, Hildy was holding Aethelwulf. There was Caitlinn, and Ilse was with them, tall and angular. Hunberht would have been out working on the estate so I didn't expect to see him. I called over my shoulder to Haeddi,

"Take the horses to the byres and get Aelle and his boys to help you. We're going to need a lot more stable room. When Hunberht gets home you'd better think where we are going to build them." Aelle was one of my bondsmen. He wasn't bright but he was a good worker. He had thrown himself and his family on my generosity when times were hard and they had been facing starvation. I didn't think that he wanted to leave my service now that he had a safe home and I was pleased to have him, and his boys who were also a great help.

"Welcome home, men of the Wolf. Wulfstan, Oswine, Snorri, welcome. Bring your men under our roof and I will see that you find comfort here," as lady of the hall Asfrid observed the formality of welcoming our guests.

She was beautiful. Her face was lit up with happiness at my return. I slid down from Victory and embraced her, holding her tight and bathing in her scent and her warmth. Her rounded tummy was a little awkward and we chuckled and I placed my hand upon it.

"How is he? Kicking?"

"He? Another boy is it? Well it could be, he's certainly making enough fuss to be a boy! He's very lively, this one."

Togi was demanding my attention. He was around my feet, tugging at my leg and pointing and shouting about the horses. I removed my helmet and Asfrid drew her breath sharply and touched the pink, smooth, beardless burn scar on my cheek.

"Is that a burn? How did that happen?"

"A very inhospitable Wealh. He took exception to me joining his camp! It's nothing," I quickly snatched up my excited boy. "Yes horses! Lots of horses. And look at this!" I showed him the shining pommel of Blood seeker.

"Wulfhere, it's beautiful!" Asfrid observed.

I eased the magnificent sword from its red-stained-leather covered scabbard, which hung below my left arm.

"Icel gave it to me, and some of the horses. We won a great victory, Asfrid. The south folk, I mean. We defeated Cynfellyn by ourselves."

"What? Where was Icel? And the north folk?"

"Come on. Let's go in and I'll tell you the story. How's my other little man?" I crossed to Hildy and greeted Aethelwulf with a chuck under the chin and a ruffle of his straw yellow hair.

"And who's this, Wulfhere?"

I turned to see Asfrid standing before Arwen, waiting for an introduction.

"I am Arwen, lady," the youngster spoke for herself in a small, but confident, voice.

"Arwen is a peace weaver, Asfrid. She was a gift from her father, lord Anwas, to ensure that I kept his best interests at heart when the Corieltavi took the field."

There was a long silence while Asfrid digested this news. She silently appraised the young Wealh lass who held her ground, not defiantly, but just because this was her place.

"Good!" Asfrid decided with a voice like a frozen pond, and turned and swept into the hall.

I let her go.

"Hildy, this is Arwen, Arwen this is Hildy, and Caitlinn, and Ilse. It's good to see you looking so well, Ilse. Arwen is joining our household. She has been sent by her father to build friendship between our houses. I want you to show her the hall and set out a bed space for her in our private chambers. She is one of us now. Arwen, go with them."

I took a deep breath before following them inside. Of course Asfrid was upset, what with the pregnancy and the worry while I was away and managing the household and the estate. She would see reason. She had been raised by a jarl. She of all people should understand that these arrangements took place between houses.

Inside the hall, the company was settling down. Eadgyth was making a fuss of Leofmund, and Asfrid was ordering the hall, getting the men to arrange the tables and seeing that ale was fetched out. She didn't look at me. In fact she didn't look at me for some time.

"You've upset the hive boy. You can't have two queens in one nest," Wulfstan observed, stirring the pot nicely.

Arwen was doing what she always did, knuckling down and helping to serve and feed the men. Asfrid was extremely tense. I could see the mixed emotions in her face. I got up and, taking her hand, I led her from the hall to our chamber.

"Now then, Asfrid. There's no need to be like this......" I began

"Like this! And how is that exactly? I thought that I was doing what you wanted, tending to our guests. That's what I'm for now isn't it? I know how these things work, Wulfhere. I dwelt in the halls of lords and kings for long enough. Once a lady gets old and stretched and worn with care and childbirth, you find yourself another young girl and push her aside! I will run the hall with grace and generosity, but don't think that our sons will be pushed aside, Wulfhere! They will not!"

"Asfrid! No one's pushing you aside, my love. She is a peace weaver. A gift. I accepted her to cement the peace with the Wealh. I was far from home and we had fought a great battle. I needed a woman. I needed release!"

"Oh I see, so she's just your whore!"

"In a way, I suppose you could think.........."

"Don't you dare! Don't you dare!" Having turned the argument completely on its head she stared at me for a long time. "I know what is happening to her. She has been given to you like, like a dog or a horse! She had no choice! She is not allowed to feel, or to think. This is her duty. She has accepted this for her family. She has taken your seed, taken your passion, your desires. It's not for her that she must take you inside her! Not for how she feels! Don't you dare talk of her like that. I know!"

"Asfrid, I took her to make peace. Because I needed a woman when I was far from home and death hung around me like a cloak. Because I needed to spend the rage and the fear of battle inside her. She is a good girl, a good worker. I told her father that I already have a wife, that she would never be the lady of the Wolf, but he just wanted a better life for her, a safer life.

You are my lady. I love you, the men love you. They would all die for you, each and every one. Our children stand above all others, Asfrid. No one will ever, could ever, replace you."

"You told her father this?"

"Before witnesses."

"And he sent her, to be safe?"

"He wanted her to live in my hall. To be comfortable and live well. Beyond what they could give her."

"But that is...........She must be............Oh Wulfhere!"

Tears rushed down her cheeks and she flung her arms around me.

"Now why are you crying?"

"I don't know. Because it's........Because you frightened me. Because I missed you. Because I am confused, my mind is......." She waved her hand around in a wildly spinning motion.

"You're my lady, Asfrid. My only lady."

She clung to me and wept, then laughed, and then wept again.

"I had better get back to the hall," I decided.

"Yes," she sniffed. "I'll be through shortly."

"Wulfhere?"

I paused and looked at her glistening eyes.

"You will come to me tonight? Won't you?"

"Every night, lady."

I returned to the hall. Arwen caught my eye and I smiled reassuringly. She would be safe here.

"You're a braver man than me, boy!" Wulfstan announced when I sat down at the fire with my hearth companions. "Two women under one roof. Give me a battlefield any day!" He was enjoying this.

"They'll be fine. Arwen's young, quiet and hard working, Asfrid is the boss."

Togi leaped onto me.

"I'm killing you with my sword!" He cried, 'stabbing' me with a short piece of fire wood.

"Oh you would, would you?" I wrestled him into my arms and held him tight. "Now what are you going to do?" We fought quite happily for a while, Togi pleased to have me to himself.

"So what's the plan for Gwrgant?" Oswine wanted to know.

"We muster in three weeks at the South Burrh. I expect Artorius will be over to see us as soon as he hears that we're back. He'll gather his men and stir up the Trinovantes who want Gwrgant out, and we'll go from there. March on Caer Colun, draw him out into battle, and hopefully smash him in the field. I don't want him to hide up inside his citadel and dare us to come and get him. It all hinges on drawing him out."

"Do you think he'll come out then? If this citadel is so strong surely he'll just sit tight until we've gone away."

"It's possible. He is a cowardly swine. But if he does he'll lose his kingdom. He is not liked, in fact he's hated, in many quarters. With Artorius in the field, with strength enough to challenge Gwrgant, we think that a lot of the Trinovantes will turn against him. Artorius' power will grow as Gwrgant's dwindles. His only hope really will be to nip the rebellion in the bud and then come down hard on any would be rebels."

"Cowardy swine!" Echoed Togi, and we all laughed. "Who's a cowardy swine?"

"Gwrgant! The king of the Trinovantes."

"Will you fight him with your new sword? And the....Tivantes?"

"I certainly will. I'll chop off his head!"

The answer delighted Togi who dashed off around the hall, waving his stick and shouting 'cowardy swine!' At imagined enemies.

"Are you going to return to Rendels Home or stay here?" I asked Wulfstan.

"We'll go home. I can't keep the lads away from their wives for the whole summer, and there are always things to sort out. You know how it is. Someone's pig will have eaten someone else's apples or some such."

I grinned knowingly.

"What about you, Wuffa. Are you staying or going back with Wulfstan?"

"I thought I might stay here. I can practice with the Wolf Pack and improve my sword play. And I haven't seen Eadgyth for a long time. If that's alright?"

"Of course. It will be good to have you back for a while."

We supped our ale. I watched Arwen. She was busy, as ever, helping to prepare a meal for the assembled horde. She was a good girl, brave to come all this way, uncomplaining, with a war band of ruffians, most of whom didn't speak her tongue. I admired her spirit, and I recalled her firm young flesh as I watched her work.

Asfrid returned to the hall. I stood and beckoned her to sit by me but she declined and took charge of the cooking. I watched the two women being extremely considerate and courteous to each other all through the afternoon. The effort clearly took its toll on Asfrid and eventually she put her hands on her lower back and straightened herself up stiffly. I saw Arwen say something to her in her faltering tongue. Asfrid looked hard at her and for a moment I thought that she might be angry. But then she shrugged and, half smiling, made a reply. She glanced up at me momentarily and then straight back at Arwen.

They chatted together while they worked. It wasn't easy of course because Arwen's Angelish was very halting, but they made the most of being flung together. After we had eaten we all sat together. It was a long time since our household had shared the hall. I enjoyed that evening. Asfrid sat by me and rested her head on my shoulder. I put my arm around her and listened to the riddles and laughter, and the flickering fire. I decided that I liked Ilse. She had a wonderfully dry sense of humour and deferred to no one. From her position of strength, Asfrid made a point of including Arwen in the evening's fun and chatter. She spoke to her the way that a big sister might address a younger, less mature sibling and the message was clear. She would tolerate the young girl who found herself in a strange household, far from home, but she was very definitely the queen in this hive.

Much later, as we lay together in the warmth of our bed, she said,

"Don't hurt her Wulfhere. She's a nice girl, but she's very young. It's a shame that her father didn't find her a young man of her own people."

"He did. I killed him."

"What?" She gasped, shocked for the young girl.

"Well, I don't know if I actually killed him myself. He was killed at our battle."

"Oh that poor child! Did she know him?"

"I don't know. I just know that Anwas told me that her betrothed was killed in the battle. He was worried about the Corieltavi taking the land all around him so he thought that she would have a better, safer life with me. I told him that she couldn't be my lady, but he still felt that it would be best for her, and for him, of course."

I sensed her thawing.

"Yes, a better life."

She was silent for a while and I was on the edge of sleep when she spoke again.

"Wulfhere."

"Yes, my love?"

"When you have her, I don't want to know."

There was nothing to add which might have picked at the wound. I let the night engulf us both.

CHAPTER 23: The Trap

Wulfstan returned to Rendels Home the next morning. With just over two weeks until the muster at the South Burrh there was no point in delaying. After a brutal practise session I rode to Gyppeswic to see my ship masters and discuss their plans for the summer. Wedda told me that Gyppe and Maelgwn were going to spend the summer trading around the coasts of Britain and Gaul, but Ceolfrith and Ceolwulf had far more ambitious plans that they wanted to discuss with me. Coenred and Torht were going to hunt pirates along our coast. I had more ships but I just didn't have the man power to crew them all, yet. Gyppeswic was growing all the time though, and I was sure that it wouldn't be long before I would be able to put all of my ships to sea at once.

Wedda himself was coming to the war. I knew that he loved the sea and I was proud of his loyalty to me. He was a powerful warrior, a bear of a man, and his presence in the shield wall with his fearsome axe hammer would strike fear into the enemy and embolden the men around him. I walked around the town with him and Ine, proud with what we had started on this bend in the river. Gunndolf's alehouse was busy.

"No slaves there now, lord," Ine assured me.

The port was alive with activity. Ships were being loaded and unloaded, traders called out their wares, gulls keened, the hollow boards of the waterfront boomed and thumped under the step of sailors and the unloading of heavy goods. The smell of smoking fish mingled with the dank smells of the waterfront. It was a wonderful place. I rode on to Ship Home and spent the night with Ceolwulf, Ceolfrith and Aelfgifu. They certainly had some exciting plans.

"Africa?"

"The Roman Sea, Wulfhere. Think of all the wonderful things that we trade for that have come from there. Why should we buy them from others? We can sail to the Roman Sea. We will take tin, amber, ivory, the things that their traders always take back with them. We will come home with decorated plates and bowls, glassware, blue stones, all the finest things that they make down there." Ceolfrith had clearly been giving this some thought. Ceolwulf was right behind him.

"Anna wants to come too. You know what he's like, he just wants to see all the different places."

"Well, if you've both decided that it's a worthwhile venture then, fine. I'll leave all the planning to you."

We talked way into the night, and the hall around us was awash with the imagined sights and smells of the Roman Sea ports. They would leave as soon as they were ready.

There was a sense of excitement back at my hall. I arrived back in the early afternoon and handed Victory's reins to Haeddi who was waiting in the hall yard. Eadric was fussing around preparing our supplies for the war.

"Eadric! How are you getting on?"

"Lord Wulfhere. Yes, everything will be ready, lord. We have six carts. We have the tents. We have the pots and the cooking things. We have pickled herring. We have smoked fish, we have new ale. We have the extra spears and arrows that you asked for and Leuthere has been repairing the mail shirts that you brought home from the war. We have........"

"Well done, Eadric! When you've finished do you want silver or livestock for your richly earned reward?"

"Livestock would be better, lord."

"Livestock it will be, my friend."

I left him and went into the hall for a drink. As usual my household were all hard at work. Asfrid was to the fore, organising the food preparation. She looked up as I entered and sent me a weary smile. She reckoned that she still had three months until the baby arrived but this pregnancy had been a lot more burdensome than the others. I noticed that Arwen wasn't present.

Hildy was carrying a pile of pots out to be cleaned. I went with her to open the door. Once outside I asked,

"Hildy, where's Arwen?"

"Weaving, lord. She's quite nice isn't she? A bit quiet, but she doesn't know a lot of our words yet, does she?"

"No that's right. Thanks, Hildy."

She carried the pots round the side of the hall to where a tub of water and wet sand waited for her to scrub them clean. Once she was out of sight I took a casual walk to the weaving hut. The door stood wide and I watched Arwen nimbly working the coloured threads. She was good. She worked quickly, and kept the thread tight.

"That's very good, Arwen."

She looked round, startled, and stared up at me with wide eyes.

"I said that's good," I indicated her work.

"Good, yes, I think."

She knelt silently, hands still, eyes on her work, waiting for me to do, or say, something.

"Are you happy here, Arwen?"

She looked up again, uncertain.

"Please?"

"Do you, like, here? You, like here?"

"Yes I like. Big hall. Very......" She waved her hands wide to indicate big and bigger.

"Yes, very big," I smiled. "Do, you, like, the others?"

She smiled and shrugged.

"Hildy? Ilse? Caitlinn? Asfrid? You like?"

"Ah, yes, very kind."

"Come here," I indicated that she should come to me.

She smiled, and stood, nervously. I stepped into the hut.

"Come here, Arwen," I held my arms wide.

She looked into my eyes and started to slip her dress from her shoulders.

"No, no. Not." I stopped her and slid the straps back up. My hand brushed over the soft skin of her shoulder and I continued up and cupped my hand round the back of her head, stroking her cheek with my thumb. I kissed her forehead and held her to me. Finally I sat us down in the doorway and held her hand, She looked into my face like a puppy. Trusting, nervous, but eager to please.

"Arwen, I, want, you, to be, happy."

"Happy? I know this, yes. I am happy, lord."

"Wulfhere. Call me Wulfhere."

"Wulfhere, yes."

"I will make you your own hall. A hall for my lady Arwen." I decided it there and then. I would keep the two ladies apart. They could both keep their dignity. I would arrange a household and an estate for Arwen where I could visit her without upsetting Asfrid. She could live well. It would be fairer for both of them.

She was looking at me a little confused.

"A hall? For Arwen?" She repeated.

"That's right. Your own hall, with your own household, yes?"

I think that she understood. She gave me a huge smile which lit up her whole face. I hugged her and planted another kiss on her forehead. She tilted her head and we kissed long and deep.

I had her in the hay barn. We lay there for a long time after. She rested her head on my chest and I stroked her hair while I told her all about the hall that I would give her. I didn't know if she understood any of it, but it made me feel a lot happier.

When Caitlinn came looking for her I explained that I had been showing Arwen around the estate and it was my fault that she hadn't finished her work. We walked back to the hall and I kissed her before she hurried in, with a spring in her step, to help feed the returning Wolf Pack.

I didn't want to go into the hall hard on her heels. I turned and walked to the stables to have a look at the horses. I talked with Haeddi and Aelle about the individual animals, when hoof beats coming from the lane drew us outside.

Artorius was riding up the track from the river with four of his lads. I recognised Gawain, Gareth and Birinius but couldn't make out the fourth. I jogged across the yard to greet them.

"Artorius, my friend! It's good to see you. Is your blade sharp? Are you ready for war?"

"We are ready, Wulfhere. When do we march?"

"The men of the south folk will muster at the South Burrh in two weeks. Gwrgant's days are numbered. Have you planned ahead for the days after we take the kingdom?"

"I have done little else for a year, Wulfhere."

"Come inside my friends. Who is this?" I indicated the fourth horseman.

"This is Coinneach of the U'Niall. He was of Gwrgant's household until the feast of the lengthening days in the mid Winter. Gwrgant's, er what would we say? Celebrations? Convinced him that a true warrior shouldn't be part of that 'noble' household."

Artorius turned to the Irish man and said something in the Wealh tongue, to which the dark haired warrior replied in a deep slow voice. He looked at me as he spoke and waited for Artorius to translate.

"He says that Gwrgant's hall is a place of madness. A place where men seek to outdo wolves, or dogs, with their cruelty and depravity. It's a place that must be destroyed, burnt from the world.

I have spoken about all of this before now. You know it all, my friend."

"Come inside and we can talk."

Aelle and Haeddi took the horses and we stepped into the hall, Artorius ducking to get through the door.

I asked Ilse if she would fetch ale for our guests and then realised she was already doing so and apologised, which made her smile.

"Lord Wulfhere, the world of men is a strange place. You kill who you like, when you like, but apologise just for asking me to do something which is already done." She said in her strong Allamani accent with a wry smile.

I was surprised into a speechless silence for a moment by her reply. I wasn't used to Ilse's humour yet. She was a very intelligent woman, but she still walked under the shadow of the fate that she had been woven. I didn't know her well enough yet to judge her mood.

"Yes, Ilse, but we have to make sure that we get those things the right way round or it can be very messy." I answered, teasing.

"And so, this is what is in your minds? It cannot be very hard I think to get things the right way round." She smiled and handed Artorius a pot of ale.

She handed the drinks out in silence.

"Thankyou Ilse."

"Artorius! It's a pleasure to have you in my hall again!" Asfrid had just come into the main hall and seen our guests, who stood to greet her.

"Good, Ilse has brought you ale. Will you be staying with us tonight?"

"Yes they will, my love. We have a lot to discuss," I told her with a smile. Then I had an idea.

"Join us." I indicated a place on the bench alongside me and she sat, eager to be part of our plans.

"Those Irish will wish that they had stayed at home once their protector is dead." Artorius swore darkly. He had obviously been brooding on Gwrgant's warriors since our earlier conversation.

I saw Ottar sitting by the fire, watching us, and I called him over.

"Ottar, join us. I want your knowledge of the enemy."

"Artorius, this is Ottar, Strong Arm. A great warrior of the Norse. His scars were inflicted on the orders of the coward Gwrgant. He will be lending his strength to overthrow the tyrant as a trusted and highly valued member of my household." They clasped hands, and Ottar nodded his thanks in my direction.

The Irish warrior, Coinneach, was whispering urgently in Artorius' ear.

"Coinneach knows your companion, Wulfhere. From Caer Colun!"

"Yes that's right. He was there at my bidding. He's no common sell sword. Now my friend," I returned to the matter in hand. "How have your raids on Caer Colun affected the tyrant's strength?"

Artorius thought for a moment before he spoke.

"In two ways. We have been busy in the northern country of Caer colun. We have seized silver and supplies that were destined for Gwrgant's coffers and store houses. In this way we have weakened his ability to sustain his army. We gave our plunder to the lords of the northern country who had suffered Gwrgant's greed and spite. In this way we have gained the trust of the lords that we helped, and their neighbours who saw what we had done.

We have given the people a rallying cry. I think that they believe that Gwrgant can be toppled, and therefore they will be more likely to come to our banner when we make our move. If they doubted our strength they would be loathe to risk the cruel vengeance of their 'king', and our task would be all the harder. Your victory over Cynfellyn has helped us as well. The Trinovantes have ancient ties with the Catuvellauni. In the past they often made common cause against their enemies. There were a number of Trinovantes with Cynfellyn's host. Your victory at Duroliponte has staggered the tribes, Wulfhere. There are wild stories about your victory. They say that your priests used all sorts of foul magic against the Catuvellauni, that you wielded thunder bolts to crush Cynfellyn's army and that you and your wolfmen slaughtered hundreds of the strongest warriors under a blanket of darkness and drank the blood of the slain. They fear you and respect you, 'Wulfhere the Grim', in equal measure. They aren't certain that they can trust you, but they don't doubt that if you and your wolfmen take the field then we have a mighty ally indeed."

"Wolf men?" I was pleased and flattered by Artorius' news.

"Yes indeed, 'wolfmen'. I expect that many Catuvellauni will be scaring their children into behaving themselves with the name of Wulfhere the Grim and his wolfmen. Probably scaring themselves as well I shouldn't wonder. Reputation is a powerful thing! Your name resounds far and wide, throughout even the lands of my people in the west, as a mighty war leader and dreadful adversary. All know how you slew the giant and took Caer Lerion, capturing the gate single handed. They say that you consort with witches, and that your gods have given you the strength and cunning of the wolf and that you drink blood with your gods and witches at the full of the moon." We all laughed at these revelations but Artorius continued, "I'm serious. The stories of Wulfhere the Grim are many and colourful my lord. I just felt you might like to know."

"Wulfhere the Grim! That's not really fair!" Asfrid protested on my behalf.

"It is from the point of view of Caer Colun. The prospect of you and your wolfmen coming for Gwrgant has created a deal of unease I can tell you," Artorius smiled.

Ottar nodded,

"It is true my Lord, it was debated at Camulodonum quite regularly what your ambitions would be. They discussed sending tribute but felt it might be seen as a sign of weakness and encourage you to attack."

"It wouldn't have encouraged me to attack, but it would have told me that they lacked the strength to attack us, which I was never really sure about." I confessed.

"Well he is weaker now than he was then," Artorius went on. "He still has his Irish and his Sais, though. He also has a Danish warlord in his hall at the moment, called Swein of the Mountain, but we know that he will be leaving to fight for the Franks in Gaul. I think that sell swords jumping ship tells us a good deal about the strength of Gwrgant's support. Of his own people he can probably raise four or five hundred of which seventy or eighty will be horsemen."

"Do you know how many will come to your banner yet?" I asked the would be, future king, directly.

"Most of the lords who dwell in the north of Caer Colun will join us when they see your men taking the field. I expect about Three hundred foot and horse to join us from there. I will lead about two hundred foot and eighty horsemen into Caer Colun. There is no telling how committed the southern lords will remain when they see others of their people prepared to overthrow the tyrant."

We supped our ale as the numbers sank in. Artorius would command about four hundred and fifty foot and one hundred and twenty or thirty horsemen. Once it was united, the kingdom of the Trinovantes would be a powerful neighbour.

"We can outnumber him together, can't we, Wulfhere?" Asfrid's mind was working hard on numbers.

"Easily, my love," I sought to reassure her. "When we first spoke of war, Artorius, I proposed raising about four hundred and fifty men. I have thought long and hard since then about how best to combine our warriors. My men fight best in the shield wall, while your warriors yearn to fight an open, free moving battle. I wondered at first if we could train your men to the shield wall, but I think it would be a risk and perhaps a waste. My warriors will stand and hold the enemy at bay. We can loose your foot warriors on the enemy's flank and while we hold them I want you, and your horsemen, to encircle them. There will be no escape for the tyrant."

The plan was like the filling of a grave. No one ever planned the total destruction of an enemy. No one ever thought beyond the first clash of weapons. Once battle was joined fate and bravery decided the outcome, that was understood. This proposal of mine was brutal and chilling. This would truly be seen throughout the middle earth as the work of wolf men, and I gave Asfrid a proud look. The company was quiet for a while as they took in the cold brutality of the plan.

"Who will lead your foot warriors Artorius?" I finally broke the spell.

"It will be Gwernach, hero of the Crecgan ford. A famous warrior, and a lord of Caer Colun. He can be relied upon to inspire his men and be steadfast in the fight, and he gives us a strong connection with the people." Artorius assured me.

I was pleased that it would be an experienced warrior.

"I would like to meet him and share my plans with him if that's possible," I said, uncertain whether, as a lord of Caer Colun, Gwernach would already be with Artorius, or if he was still holding his lands under the tyrant.

"I don't think that you should meet him before we make our move," Artorius said, carefully. "Word would be bound to reach Gwrgant's ears and it would alert him to his peril I think."

"So I'll meet him when we muster at the South Burrh. From there we can dominate the north of Caer Colun. We can rally the support of the northern lords and drive any supporters that Gwrgant might still have, back to his citadel. He will have to march out and offer us battle or slowly watch his strength drain away. It also puts us in a position from where we can march on Camulodonum if a chance to surprise our quarry presents itself, or if we need to move quickly to seize the city."

"I am reluctant to spill the blood of my people, Wulfhere. This war has been forced upon us. We can't avoid battle but I ask you to remember that these are my people, lord. I would sooner have them yield if we can give them a chance, than slaughter them without mercy."

"I will remember it, my friend," I reassured him. "But it will be best for your kingdom if the war is won in a day. We must cut off the head of the serpent. We must draw him out to a field of our choosing where I can hold his forces while you encircle them and stop their escape, so here is my plan. We let it be known that I am going to march from the South Burrh and meet with your forces at a certain place on a certain day. He will want to crush me before your strength is added to mine. He will attack and we will spring our trap."

After a short pause for thought Ottar had a further contribution to make.

"Lord Wulfhere, there is a ford, about eight miles downstream from the South Burrh. If you name it as your meeting place it would surely tempt him out to attack. It would be impossible for him to ignore you that close to his hall. If you accept battle there, Artorius could cross the ford at the South Burrh and thus come upon the tyrant from behind."

This was it, our plan was laid. I would camp at South Burrh for a few days, long enough for Gwrgant to get wind of our plan to meet at this other ford. When I arrived at our meeting point a day and a half early it would be foolish of him not to try to seize the opportunity to defeat me before my ally arrived. Once he left Camulodoum he would have about eight miles to cover to reach us.

Spies would warn Artorius of Gwrgant's attack. Artorius would cross the Sture at the South Burrh and close the trap behind the tyrant.

CHAPTER 24: The Muster

It was all so neatly prepared. We had the numbers, we had the perfect plan. Our enemy was weak and he couldn't trust the loyalty of his army. It would be a straight forward victory. Yet something about this venture disturbed me. There was something unnatural about every aspect of this war. As the muster grew near, Gwrgant and his citadel filled my dreams. Vivid scenes of depravity in a flame lit hall came to me every night, in which the writhing, tormented victims were always my loved ones. Monstrous Irish warriors with fangs and horns ravished and tortured while I was forced to look on, helpless to intervene. I sent for the waelcyrge to interpret the dreams.

"This is clearly witchcraft, my lord. The witch of Caer Lerion has put her mark on you. You are going to war to drive out more Wealh evil. I expect that this Gwrgant is also in league with witches and the ancient Wealh gods. These monsters in your dreams are clearly the ancient gods, lord. They fear you. They fear Tiw. The threat is clear, lord. You must be cleansed. You have also brought a Wealh girl into your hall. She must also be cleansed. The spirits of the Wealh gods will cling to her otherwise and use her to bring evil to your hall."

I wasn't certain that the dreams had anything to do with Elf. She had got the payment that she wanted. Her gods would be happy. As for Arwen, the only spirits that might have clung to her would have been hard working cofgodas, household sprites. That might explain why her weaving was so good, and why she was always so cheerful around the hall.

"Tiw spared me, Waelcyrge. At the battle of the Granta burrh I was supposed to die. It was my fate. But Tiw spared me. He changed my fate. How can that be so if I was marked by ancient witchcraft?"

"You are Tiw's chosen. The old gods have no power over the Ese, lord. This shows that Tiw sees that you need his protection more than ever. We must have a cleansing ceremony without delay."

The household, and all of our workers and bondsmen and their families, were summoned inside the hall for the night. They huddled close together on the bare floor. Charms and symbols were placed around them while the waelcyrge and his priestesses made their chanting supplications. Arwen and I had to rise before dawn and stand naked in the hall doorway at daybreak, while a ram lamb was sacrificed. We were bathed in its pure blood to wash the witches' sprites from us. The sprites were prevented from entering the hall by the chanting and the symbols. They were forced to enter the nearest unprotected creature, which was a second lamb. This wretched creature was then hurled into a fire with its legs bound, so that the spirits couldn't escape. It was very sombre and it all seemed to make sense.

After it was all finished I thanked the waelcyrge and paid him for his work. I was still fearful that the dreams were warning of a threat to my family more than me, but if the evil had been driven out then hopefully all would be well. I was right to have been worried. My fears were confirmed that evening when Asfrid announced that she was coming to the war.

"What! You can't mean it, my love. Look at you. The baby!"

"I know, and I have thought about all of that. Hildy will come with me. The baby isn't due for more than two months. If the war isn't over with by then I will deliver the baby at the South Burrh. I'm sure that Ithamar can find the room!"

"But it isn't safe, my love. It's a war!"

"If you win it will be fine. If you lose and you are slain then what will it matter if I die with you."

"It's not that straight forward, Asfrid. There are sicknesses, assassins, sometimes the camp is looted by fleeing enemies, or sly ones. What about the boys? You're not thinking about bringing them along as well are you?"

"No. They're going to stay with Aelfgifu at Ship Home while we're away. That's already been sorted out."

She wouldn't be dissuaded. She had clearly been planning this for a while. She had suggested coming to war with me in the past, and I suspected that Arwen's appearance after the last war was really behind this determined decision. It was mad, stupid, it was reckless in the extreme, but she had made up her mind that if I didn't take her she would just follow anyway, so arrangements for her comfort and safety were put in place. She would share my tent, obviously, and I told Gram to choose four men who would remain with her throughout the whole time that we were away. They were not to leave her unattended at any time. I knew that this wouldn't go down at all well with the chosen guards, who would clearly prefer to be in the shield wall where reputation and plunder would be won, but I made it plain that they would be well rewarded for their service.

Apart from this shock the preparations were well in hand. I made a point of discussing the plan with Eadric, on the waterfront at Wolf Home in front of all and sundry. I repeated the exercise with Ine, up and down the waterside at Gyppeswic. If my plan to muster at the South Burrh before marching to meet Artorius at the downstream ford didn't reach Gwrgant's ears I would be amazed.

It seemed that reputation wasn't only useful for mothers to scare their errant children. More would be 'wolfmen' presented themselves at the hall. They were welcomed and sent along to Gram to be introduced to our life and our expectations. They were all tough, proud young men who were inspired by the challenge of travelling to an unknown hall to join a famous warband. That, in itself, was a good start, as long as they weren't too full of themselves. I valued commitment to the group far above self glorification. I didn't want a hall full of warriors who wouldn't fight together. By the time we were ready to march to war a further nine young men had taken up a spear and joined my household. They would be sifted by the war, and those that didn't meet Gram's high standards would be either killed in battle, or sent home. It was interesting to note that as well as the Angels, Danes and Frisians from east Angel land, there were also three Corieltavi warriors who were keen to join us.

The army was summoned and the lords and their chosen companions from their estates, from Gyppeswic, and from the towns, villages and farms of the south folk joined me at Wolf Home. I made sure that they all had good gear. Any of the hopeful young men from the farms or ports who were poorly equipped were given spears or shields from among the captured weapons that I kept at the hall. I wanted my men to be confident in their gear. In spite of our recent losses we had two hundred and ninety four from the kingdom and just under fifty in the Wolf Pack. As always they practiced fighting in the shield wall for two days before we marched for the South Burrh.

I marched with the men. Perhaps one day I would be able to put all of the Wolf Pack on horse back. Until that day, I would walk. I was particularly proud of the fact that Wuffa was marching with me at the head of the column. He was a young man now, a Wolf lord in his mail shirt, helmet and wolf skin cloak. As well as his sword, father's old sword, and seaxe he carried a bow. He was a master of the weapon and he would be responsible for organising our bowmen throughout the war. It was a good place for him to start learning to command men in battle. Eadgyth had seen us off and she was quite emotional about her 'little brother' leading the army to war. It was a proud day for all of us. Gram walked beside us and Odd followed hard on our heels carrying my banner with its new wolf skin. The people cheered us off and we smiled and waved as we forded the river and followed the street away from home. After a mile or so I told Odd to rest the heavy iron banner on one of the wagons.

Asfrid and Hildy, rode in one of the skin covered wagons with her four guards Tatberht, Styr, Dynne and Bosa walking two at either side. I know that they regarded their new job as a rather dubious honour, but I was absolutely certain that, in time, they would come to love their lady, and their duty. I was confident in their ability to guard her, and knew that they would die before allowing any harm to befall her. They carried themselves proudly, like the warriors they were, and watching them I decided that a specific design upon their shields, or a certain colour of cap, would add distinction to Asfrid's guard.

The march was tedious. War is mostly tedious. You walk, or row, you camp, you cook, you wait. Then there's an unbelievably mad few moments or perhaps hours and then it's back to walking and waiting again. The walking and waiting are almost as important as the fighting. The men have to be fed, sheltered and trained and they must, above all, believe that they will win, or the battle will be an uphill struggle before it even starts. The Wolf Pack was different. They always believed that they would win. They knew that we were favoured by the gods and they saw battle as their greatest trial. They trained for it, they lived for it. It was their destiny. The Wolf pack was our family, our household, it was where we belonged. I knew that Gram would die for me without a moment's hesitation and as their lord I had to be prepared to risk my life for each and every one of them if I had to.

It was twenty miles from Wolf Home to the South Burrh. With the slow pace of the wagons it was a day and a half's travel. Oxen wouldn't be hurried. We spent a night under our cloaks and approached the South Burrh at late morning. Ithamar was out to greet us with his son Inga.

"It is good to see you, Ithamar. Thankyou for your welcome."

"Yes, thankyou, Ithamar," Asfrid had joined me.

"My lady. I didn't know that you were travelling with the army. You must be exhausted in your condition. I will make room for you at my hall, of course."

"Ithamar, I'm not sick. And I have travelled with my husband because I want to be with my husband. It's very kind of you but I'll be fine in the camp."

"If you say so, of course, my lady."

I had forgotten, perhaps what Asfrid had lived through. A little hardship would be nothing to her. She made me smile, particularly so when I looked at the bemusement on Ithamar's face. Laying together beneath the skins in our tent that night I told her how I felt.

"The gods were wise and generous when they brought you to me, Asfrid."

"Yes, they were!"

"No I mean it, seriously. You're the most beautiful lady in the east Angel land. You're wise, generous and brave. You are the perfect lady"

She was up before dawn, with Hildy, to prepare hot porridge which melted the morning chill from within.

The north folk lords began to arrive throughout the morning; Iceni, Angel, Frisian and Dane. Conan, Inwine, Bald, Siferth, Conmail, Byrhtferth, Iden, Oswy, Aldhelm, Cadog, and Hygeberht were the first to greet me and many more flooded into our camp by the ford at the South Burrh. The ford where I had first met Artorius. The numbers exceeded my wildest expectations. The fame of my victory over Cynfellyn had spread abroad and all of my lords wanted to be counted beneath my banner. They wanted to be part of the victory, they wanted to be part of the songs and the glory. We were the army of the East Angels, nine hundred strong. I was staggered.

The task now was to make this host into an army. We had three days to practise before we marched to our 'meeting place' with Artorius. I had the army cross the ford and practice our battle on Gwrgant's land. Luckily our warriors were no strangers to the slaughter field. Some of the lords had followed my lead and practised their shield wall before they came to the muster field.

Together with Wulfstan I had worked out our battle line. The Wolf Pack would be at the centre, with Wulfstan on my right. Prince Sigurd and the Danes would hold the extreme right flank, and the Frisians, the far left. Then we filled the line between us, trying to keep friends side by side in order that they would stand firm and support each other. Once the lords all knew their place in the line we formed our shield wall, initially three lines deep, with a body of about fifty bowmen behind. I had decided that we would use the wagons once again as platforms for the bowmen to loose their arrows over our heads into the enemy. We practised building a line two, three, four or five rows deep to give us a longer or a narrower front. I wanted to be confident that we could adapt the length of our line to fit any battlefield.

We formed the men into line of march, and once on the move I gave the order to form the shield wall and watched the army fall into place. We repeated the process until it was fast and strong. I wanted every man to know who he would be standing beside so that we could form up in the dark, with our eyes closed if we had to. Then we circled the wagons with our shield wall in case we were ambushed in the open. When they could do it quickly enough I climbed onto a wagon and addressed the army.

"East Angels. I have fought alongside you before. I know your courage and your battlecraft. But even I am in awe of the strength that I see arrayed before me today. We will wait here for two more days. On the third day we are going to march downstream to a ford where we are to meet Artorius and his army of the Trinovantes. Once he arrives we will march into Caer colun and draw the coward Gwrgant into open battle. Our deeds will make songs for the scops to sing. Legends for our children and our children's children to remember around the hearth. I will be proud to stand with you!"

There was a great cheer and the men took up the chant of, "Wolf! Wolf! Wolf!"

I allowed myself the briefest of glances at the trees away from the river, and hoped that there were spies hidden there somewhere, ready to carry my words to Gwrgant and his captains. We marched back across the ford and into camp. It was late afternoon and the men set about cleaning and repairing their kit, bragging excitedly about the part they had played in today's practises and laughing at others' mistakes.

Back at the tent I removed my helmet and accepted a pot of ale from Asfrid. I was about to ask her what she thought of the army when somebody called my name.

"Lord Wulfhere!" I looked round for the source of the call. "Lord Wulfhere!" It was repeated again. Three warriors were approaching. They were plainly Wealh, dressed for war. The leader was clean shaven with dark eyes and chestnut hair. He was wearing a long red cloak over his light woollen clothes, and carrying a large oval shield. He had a long sword at his waist.

"What is it?" I asked, making myself known to them.

"Lord Wulfhere, we have a message."

The three focussed on me and strode quickly forward.

"What message? Have you come from Artorius?" I asked.

Something wasn't right, they were hurrying, almost running, their faces set in attitudes of grim determination. They weren't here to deliver a message. They had come to kill me!

"Gram!" I shouted throwing my drink aside.

I drew Blood Seeker and stepped forward in front of Asfrid. The assassins broke into a run, drawing their weapons as they came. All around us men were reacting to this sudden danger, but they were too late. The Wealh had been able to get too close. The leader of the three was focussing totally on me and I prepared to receive his charge, he raised his sword and I shaped to parry the blow, but it never came. Gram had been standing slightly to one side, talking with Odd about the day's practise when my shout had alerted him to the threat. With virtually no time to react he had spun round, taken two steps and just hurled himself bodily at the leading assassin. With both feet clear of the ground he smashed into the warrior, his left hand reaching across the man's front as they collided, trying to seize his sword arm. The attacker was hurled sideways to the floor, Gram still desperately clutching for his sword arm while the Wealh tried to keep his blade clear of Gram's reach.

Their tumbling fall brought down the second Wealh attacker. He tried to run around them, but was caught by Gram's flailing legs and crashed heavily to the ground. The third warrior ignored the melee and came straight at me, his face contorted with rage and hatred, his sword raised for the strike. Odd didn't have time to draw his sword. He was holding the Wolf standard and preparing to plant it in the ground before my tent. Instead of that, he gave the heavy iron standard a short two handed swing, smashing the shaft into the face of the killer. All of his attention was on me and he didn't see the blow coming at all. His legs took another couple of running strides as his head and upper body were thrown backwards. He landed flat on his back with a thump which drove the air from his lungs. His face was a mask of stunned surprise. Blood welled from his nose and a deep cut above his right eye. He was still dazed when Odd drove the pointed end of the Wolf standard right through his chest and into the ground beneath him.

Gram was still grappling on the floor with the first attacker as our men closed in. They seized both of the assassins, overpowering and disarming them, before beating them to submission and dragging them before me. I was still holding my sword although I hadn't been required to use it. I rested the blade upon my left hand as they were forced to kneel and await my judgement.

"Marcellus!"

"Lord?"

"Find out who they are and who sent them!"

A dagger was produced and Marcellus soon had the answers that I wanted.

"They are nobody of any consequence, lord. They have been convicted of crimes by Gwrgant. Their lives, and the lives of their families, were to be spared if they killed you."

I took the leader's sword, fine red cloak and brooch and gave it to Odd, in thanks for his swift action. I had the other men's gear placed in my tent.

"Hang them. Over that side of the river."

They were raised to their feet and hauled away. We watched the lads hurry them across the river, and hoist them up, kicking and twisting on their ropes.

Marcellus turned to me, his face drawn with disappointment and confusion.

"I know what you are thinking, Marcellus. It is unjust that those men are dying over there at the end of a rope, and you're right. It is. But it was their fate to die here today. They came here to murder me and, whatever the cause, that means death. These men were doomed whatever happened. If they had killed me here today where would they be now? Would they have just walked away?

They would still be dead. Gwrgant is guilty here. It's their families that you should feel sorry for."

Marcellus dwelt briefly on this but the logic was inescapable.

"Yes, lord, I hadn't thought of it like that."

"I know, now let's have a drink."

I turned and realised that Asfrid was still standing, wide eyed, behind me.

"Shall we have a drink my love?" I asked her.

"Of course, Wulfhere."

"I'll fetch it, my lady." Hildy hurried off to fetch some ale from the wagon.

"Wulfhere, you could have been killed. If Gram hadn't......" Asfrid was visibly shaken by the attack.

"No my love, I wouldn't have been killed. Gram reacted smartly yes, but I would have killed that lead man, and there was no way the other two would have reached me. Even if they had got to me they weren't warriors. I would have killed all three. You mustn't fear, my love, don't dwell on this. We all have our fate, and my death will come when it comes, but it won't be as easy as that half- baked effort." I hugged her to me and then laughed raucously. "What fools! Thinking that they could run half way through the camp waving their swords around!"

The men around me joined in the derisive laughter as Hildy returned with the ale.

"Let's get those fires stoked up and some broth going. I quite fancy a pot of ale and a song this evening!"

I took Asfrid's hand and led her into the tent and held her again. She was pale and shaking like a frightened child. It wasn't like her to react like this.

"Come here," I said, sitting down on our bedding. I turned her around and sat her on the coverings between my knees and started to knead the tension from her shoulders.

"This isn't like you to get so tense over a silly thing like that." I spoke softly. "I expect it's the baby making you overwrought."

She gave a low moan as I continued to ease the stiffness from her neck and shoulders,

"Wulfhere, I suppose there is so much more to worry about. When it was just me I........"

She trailed off and focussed on my hands.

"Oh, that feels good, Wulfhere."

"I should think it does, you're ever so tight. If you get as tense as this over a little camp incident what are you going to be like after a battle! I'll be rubbing you all over for a week!" I exclaimed in mock outrage. She thumped me and smiled weakly.

"I'm sorry Wulfhere, it was just a shock."

Once she had relaxed I helped her up and we rejoined the camp. The weather held up and we had a good evening by the fire singing, riddling and telling stories. Spirits were high and that was good.

Early the next morning Artorius rode into camp with a dozen horsemen. We greeted each other warmly, and I invited him and his men to eat with us. He introduced Gwernach, the Wealh hero who would be leading Artorius' foot warriors. Gwernach was a warrior, pure and simple. Heavily scarred, he radiated hostility and aggression with his wild staring eyes, and he contributed absolutely nothing to the discussion except his bristling presence.

"So, Wulfhere. When will you march?" Artorius, as always, was straight to the point.

"We are going to complete the muster tomorrow and strike camp at dawn the following day. We will make camp at the ford and wait for Gwrgant's reaction."

"Have you thought what we will do if he doesn't come forth?" The young giant wondered.

"We will take the war to him. We will march into Caer Colun, gather the support of all the folk who will support your cause, and then march into the south lands and either persuade the lords there that your cause is just, or destroy them in battle. Once the tyrant is cut off from all help we can close on the city and finish him."

Artorius pondered my plan. It was a vision of death and destruction for the people that he already regarded as his own, but there was no other way. I placed a hand upon his shoulder.

"Let's hope that he takes the bait, my friend."

"Yes, that must be our wish."

His manner suddenly changed as if he was rousing himself from a dream.

"Since our last discussion, Wulfhere, I have been considering your plan. I would like to make one more suggestion. I want to give Birinius a hundred and fifty men to keep back from your army so that when the tyrant comes forth they will dash to Camulodonum and seize the city behind his back. Birinius is well known in the city. His family were long established there until Gwrgant ousted them as possible rivals for power. He has friends inside the city who will throw the gates open when he arrives. I want to deprive Gwrgant of any bolt holes, my friend. This will all end here and a new story will begin."

This was a good idea, it made perfect sense, but it meant that I could be shut out of Camulodonum. My men were going to win this war. I wanted to be sure that we would be well rewarded for our blood. Artorius would have his kingdom. The Trinovantes would be free from their oppressor. I wanted my share of the prize. The thought gave me a moment's pause, but only a moment. Artorius had never given me cause to doubt his honesty

"That sounds like a good idea, Artorius. We don't want the filth to lock himself in and force a siege."

"Then I will return to my army. Gwernach will return later today with his men. I will leave Gareth with you, with three riders. Send them to me when Gwrgant comes forth and the trap will be sprung."

He waved his companions to their horses.

"Wulfhere my friend, I have not forgotten the shelter and help you gave me and my companions when we were fugitives from the tyrant. When I have the kingdom I will be generous to you and your people."

He turned on his heel and in an instant he was on his horse, riding away with a high wave of his arm. The horsemen splashed through the ford and dashed away across the open meadow. The horses' rumbling hoof beats and snorted breath added drama to their passing as they disappeared between the trees.

Chapter 25: Withermund's Ford

I lay awake for a long time, excitement and anticipation flooding my veins, images of battle in my mind. Our time in camp had been well spent. My army was ready. I was confident that they would give as good an account of themselves as was possible. Around me Asfrid, Hildy, Wuffa, Gram, Leofmund, and Marcellus lay sleeping, close together for warmth. We were a family, we were the Wolf.

I rose and donned my mail shirt in the darkness. I kissed Asfrid, who had woken with me, and left the tent, managing to tread on an arm and a leg as I tried to step over my sleeping companions. Gram followed right behind me. I followed my nose to the sewer pits, managing to beat the early morning rush, and returned to the tent, breathing the smoke from the newly lit cooking fires which were flickering to life all about.

Asfrid and Hildy had made their way up to the hall to visit the midden rather than be confronted by the glories of the army cess pits first thing in the morning. On their return they soon had a cauldron over the fire to prepare some good, hot porridge. I finished dressing, fastening on my sword and seaxe and finishing my battle gear with my wolf skin cloak.

I looked out, across the camp to the ford which marked the way to Caer Colun. I recalled Artorius and his lads riding away two days ago. My mind went back to the first time I had seen Artorius at this very ford. He had killed a man in a wild rage, and it made sense to me now that fate had revealed the hot tempered warrior to me that day in order that I would understand him better now.

As I pondered that point I realised that our fate was intertwined far more deeply than I had realised. Marcellus had been sent to guide me, and Marcellus turned out to be a friend of Artorius and a reason why the young giant had sought my help. I sank to my knees, suddenly overwhelmed at the thought that the gods had not only chosen me and ordained my entire life to lead me to this point, they had also been guiding everyone around me. Everything that had happened in my life, the raid, Wulfstan, Oswine, Acca, Icel, Yrre, Asfrid, Ullr, Marcellus, Artorius all seemingly unrelated events and people who had come into my life, all to fulfil Tiw's purpose. I could hear him chuckling now. In my head I could feel his laughter, amused that the truth had finally dawned within me. The fates were weaving threads of legendary proportion. So many lives, so many fates, all woven together.

"Lord? What is it?" Seeing me sink to my knees Gram had hurried over, a concerned look upon his face.

"Wulfhere!" Asfrid cried out, alarmed by Gram's sudden concern. She dashed across and knelt with me. Behind them Wulfstan, Sigurd and a number of the lords had gathered, ringed by Wolf Pack lads, all staring at my strange antics. I dropped my gaze to my hands and thought how I would explain what the gods had just revealed to me. When I couldn't keep them all waiting any longer, I pushed myself to my feet, raised Asfrid, and addressed them all.

"So many threads have been woven into my fate. So many lives, so many deaths. The gods have been planning it all. They have been choosing the threads, all of them. They have guided the three sisters since my birth. It was Tiw, all of it! He intended it all to happen. He has been behind everything. He has just shown me, opened my eyes, to what I should have seen all along."

I paused for a moment to be certain that I was right, but I had to be, everything made perfect sense.

"We can't lose this battle. We are the very instruments of the gods and if I am chosen by Tiw, you must also be favoured because he brought you all here to be with me. Tiw is with us, we cannot fail. So many threads! My parents killed, Acca, the battles against the Franks. Icel, Yrre, Heremod. Marcellus and Artorius. Threads so varied, so unpredictable and yet they have all been spun to create one story. The destiny of our people!"

I realised that it would take them a while to see what I had seen, but I knew that in time it would all become as clear to them as it was to me.

There was a silence, while my words were absorbed by my audience. They must know that what I said was true.

"Strike camp. It's time to go!" I ordered.

As the warriors started to go about the task of moving camp Asfrid was still looking at me with genuine concern and I kissed her.

"It will all become clear to you, my love," I promised her.

"Does that mean we'll be marching or flying on winged steeds?" Wulfstan enquired caustically.

The camp was struck and we marched to our destiny. Word of my premonition from the gods had spread through the army, and I was aware of eyes on me the whole time as I walked up and down the column. Everyone knew the stories that I was favoured by Tiw but hearing that the god had spoken with me in camp, this very morning, was both inspiring and unsettling. Wulfstan wasn't particularly concerned about my latest experience.

"Why couldn't the gods just strike Gwrgant down with the pox and save us all this walking? I don't suppose you even asked them that did you?" He asked in his best world weary manner.

"I don't know Wulfstan, but it all makes sense to me now. Just think of the road that we've travelled to get here. This is all the gods' design, it has to be."

"I know all that. Don't forget I've seen all this before. I'm just getting a bit too old for all the marching. I just hope you remember what a strain this has all been when you're sharing out the goodies!" He called hopefully as I made my way to the next company.

The Sture flowed through a wide, flat flood plain, with gentle hills rising away from the valley floor on both sides. The miles fell away almost unnoticed, and suddenly the Wealh horsemen who had scouted ahead for us were indicating that we had reached our destination. The river had wound its way to the edge of the plain where the valley side rose up with deceptive vigour. The ground there was more stony, so the river was shallower with firm banks.

A well worn track crossed the ford and ran along the far bank for a short way before climbing the slope where it was slightly easier. Anyone at the top of the slope could have held the ford against all comers. The only trouble was that Camulodonum lay on that side of the river, and Gwrgant would be approaching from the top of the hill. I swore, but then reflected that it probably would have been too strong a position for Gwrgant to even risk attacking. If I were faced with a solid shield wall on that slope I would have thought better of confronting it head on.

On our side of the river the ground was flat and wet. There was a farm right in the middle of the valley about two hundred yards from the ford. I told the men to set up camp on the far side of the farm away from the river, where the ground rose slightly and would be a little less boggy. The army marched off along the farm track and I summoned the lords to me in order to survey our battle field.

The curve which took the river close to the valley side gave us an obvious defensive position. We could place our shield wall so that each flank ended on the river bank like the string of a bow. It would make it impossible for Gwrgant's horsemen to outflank us. I just hoped that the position wasn't too strong. We needed to tempt Gwrgant to commit his forces to all out attack. The fact that he had come marching out of Camulodonum with his army all ready for war would put pressure on him not to back down, but he wouldn't want to launch a suicidal assault through the ford against a bigger army in a prepared position.

Once all of the lords were present we walked the ground looking at distances and putting a plan together. It was good to have men like Wulfstan, Oswine and Ullr in the camp who would pass blunt and frank opinions, and we gradually approached what we thought would be the solution. We decided that we would form the army into the shield wall and get them into the strongest possible position between the 'bow' of the river. Then we would mark each company's place in the line with coloured stakes. With the position marked out we could delay forming up until Gwrgant was committed to attack. If we left the wagons in place as well, the bowmen would also be able to lend their support to the defence.

The farmer came across from his home to greet us.

"Lords. I am Withermund. Welcome to my home. It is a humble place, but I place it at your disposal. Whatever aid I can give, you shall have!"

I knew he really didn't have a choice in the matter, we were here and that was that, but his noble and patient manner deserved recognition.

"Thankyou, Withermund. I am Wulfhere, king of the east Angels and I'm grateful for your support. On my authority this ford will forever be known as Withermund's ford. It shall be yours to maintain, and in return you, and your family, may charge whatever toll you see fit."

"Thank you, king Wulfhere. That is most generous, lord. Thankyou." He called as we left him and walked to the new camp.

I told Gram to send a couple of lads to collect bundles of sticks about three feet long from the trees on the valley sides. When the camp was pitched we called the men to the ford, and formed our shield wall in the strongest possible point, with our flanks protected by the river. I then had the wagons drawn into place immediately at our backs.

Using the sticks which Gram's lads had gathered, we marked the positions of each of the companies of warriors in our line. Caps, strips of coloured cloth and other items were tied to the staves so that the men would recognise their own markers and be able to form up, exactly as they were now. We told the men to return to camp, but after they had walked a hundred yards we called them to return quickly to the line. There was a fair amount of milling around but they got the idea and we repeated the process until they could find their places almost at the run. Then they were sent back to their tents.

All the activity had churned up the soft ground, but that fitted in with another idea that I had stumbled upon, quite literally. While we were walking the field I had turned my ankle on the edge of a rut. After I had cursed the ground and rubbed the sore joint I started thinking. I called my warriors back to to the expanse of ground between the ford and the staves which marked where our army would be. The ground was a muddy mess, but that was ideal because it would disguise what they were going to do.

"Right lads, I want this field riddled with small holes, as if a tribe of moles has been set loose with spades. They mustn't be much more than a foot's length wide and deep. Just enough to bring down a horse or make a runner stumble. And I don't want the Wealh to know that they're there, until they've tripped in one of them. When you've finished get back to the camp and rest, but keep your weapons to hand. The battle will arrive suddenly, with little warning, so be ready all the time from now on."

I left them to it. It wouldn't take them long to complete the task but that field would be deadly for Gwrgant's horsemen.

Gareth and his companions left us. They were going to ride closer to Camulodonum so that they would have early warning of Gwrgant's approach. Once the tyrant's army marched out they would ride to Artorius and bring his horsemen along the far bank of the Sture, like the hammer falling upon the soft iron on the anvil.

The mood in the camp was tense. Everyone had been told to keep their gear on, if they possessed any, and their weapons to hand. I had given Gwernach the privilege of organising a watch on the hills beyond the ford. His men were to raise the alarm when Gwrgant approached. Once battle was joined I wanted him to hold his warriors behind the shield wall. They were to prevent any break through and reinforce the line if it was in danger of breaking. If Gwernach sensed that the enemy were wavering, he was to unleash a charge to push them over the edge.

The Wealh wild man hadn't liked the idea of 'hiding' behind the Sais. He wanted to meet Gwrgant at the ford and fight toe to toe. I could understand his desire to get to grips with our foe, but there was no point in just enduring a slaughter on a front which gave us no advantage. My warriors were deadly in the shield wall. I wanted the enemy to have to charge, across a muddy field, which was riddled with holes, at a broad front of shields. The charge would be weakened by the distance and the obstacles and our bowmen. Once across the river, Gwrgant's only retreat would be through the bottle neck of the ford which, hopefully, Artorius would close behind him. My plan stood.

Cooking fires were lit and broth was soon bubbling in pots all around the camp. I walked between the tents, drawing in the smell of cooking, pausing at every fire to talk to the men. I wanted to reassure them, to build their confidence. I answered all of their questions with complete frankness and hid nothing; we would outnumber the enemy, yes they would have horsemen, but horses would never charge home against the shield wall, yes Gwrgant was as evil as they said. Most frequently of all, I was asked about Tiw.

'Yes, he sends me signs. I have been chosen as his sword arm in middle earth. He is our god, and he watches over our people. He first came to me when our people had been defiled by pirates. I have no doubt that he will give us victory over Gwrgant. Be brave, stand firm, trust in your spears and the battle will be ours.'

I received mixed reactions to my belief in Tiw's interest in our doings. Some of the men were fired by the idea that the war god was with us and that I was his chosen representative in the middle earth. Others clearly thought that I was mad and were unnerved by such talk. Most didn't really seem to know what to think. We had our gods and the Wealh had theirs. The question was, whose gods were stronger? Those men were probably happier with my reputation for winning battles and gaining plunder than the presence, or otherwise, of a god in the camp.

We ate, blades were sharpened, and men sat in groups talking and laughing a little too loudly. I had guards watching up and down the valley as well as Gwernach's men on the hills across the river. I wouldn't be taken by surprise. We discussed the enemy as we were eating.

"He'll have to come with the dawn," Wulfstan was adamant. "His horsemen will lead the charge, just like in Caer Lerion. They'll want to break us up and then get amongst us. That's how they work."

"That is the way they like to fight," I agreed.

"Yes. So they'll want some light, otherwise the horses will be frightened. They won't charge in the dark, will they?"

We didn't really know whether horses would charge in the dark or not, but it seemed unlikely.

"We'll wake the men before dawn and make sure that they're ready to run to the ford. They might come in the dark, I don't know. Either way Gwernach's men should give us a warning."

It was Asfrid's turn to knead my neck and shoulders. I lay awake for much of the night, trying to think of anything that I might have missed. How would we react if Gwrgant tried something other than the obvious strike from Camulodonum. What if he crossed the river lower down and attacked from our side of the Sture? I made quick plans in my mind for all the possible situations that I could think of, and dozed fitfully through the night, eventually deciding that I might as well be up and outside.

CHAPTER 26: The Cloak of Darkness

I gathered my sword, seaxe, helmet and shield, and left the tent. Straight away my companions were up and they followed me into the night. It was still dark and the camp fires were barely flickering. Through the night they were just about kept going by the guards, who put more wood on the glowing embers whenever they passed. There was no sign of dawn yet and the night was cold with a light, but chill, wind blowing from the east. We walked through and around the ghostly camp, speaking quietly with the guards, who had neither seen nor heard anything unexpected.

There were more watchers hidden within the dark shadows of Withermund's farm buildings. From there they could spy on the ford and the hills beyond, listening for anything unexpected or out of place. I announced our approach. I didn't want to be killed by an alert guard on the eve of battle.

"I am king Wulfhere," I half whispered into the blackness. "Anything to report."

"No, lord. It's all quiet. But we're a bit concerned about the Wealh boys over there."

"Why is that?"

"Well they should have been back by now. The relief went over a while ago. I don't know. Perhaps they're having a job finding them in the dark."

I looked across to where I knew the ford to be. That wouldn't be right, the relief wouldn't need to look for them. The guards would have been looking for the relief. They would be thinking about a few hours sleep. Once they heard their relief coming they wouldn't have to be asked to get back to camp.

In an instant my heart was pounding and a cold sweat stood out on my brow. We were in terrible danger. Our guards on the far side of the river had already been overwhelmed. Gwrgant's army might already be creeping down the hillside towards us. If we gave a general alarm they would attack and they would be at the camp before we were ready to receive them.

"Wuffa!" I whispered again. "Take these guards back and raise the camp, but listen! All of you! It must be done quietly, do you understand. Tell them to move up in their lines, as far as the farm. As quickly and quietly as possible. And Wuffa, get the Wolf Pack to me."

They hurried swiftly, and almost silently, back to the camp. I wanted the army here without alerting our enemy to the fact that we were aware of his presence. I waited by the farm with Gram, Leofmund and Marcellus. We crouched against the granary wall so that we were invisible against the blackness, but we would be looking up at anyone approaching in the dark. That way their shadow would be plain against the night sky. I strained my eyes and ears in the darkness towards the hillside two hundred and fifty yards away, but there was nothing to give alarm, just the silence of the night which was soon ringing in my ears, making me think that it would drown out any sound that Gwrgant's men might make. Time crept slowly by.

Odd appeared out of the dark with the first of our lads. I took his arm in the dark, and led them into the farmyard with me.

"Stay out of sight in the shadows. When the army gets here we will form our line, up at the ford."

In an instant I was alone in a dark, silent yard. I made my way to the side of the farm as more of our lads arrived and I sent them to hide themselves around the work huts and byres. I crept back to our dark shadow at the front of the farm and waited for my army to rouse itself.

My battle hung in the balance. I fretted and cursed at the tardiness of our men. If Gwrgant's men had surprised our watchmen would they have also discovered Gareth and prevented him carrying his warning to Artorius? We might be fighting this battle alone. That's if the army got here in time to fight! Where were they? An attack now would catch us all in the open. Exactly the kind of battle the Wealh wanted.

I thought of Asfrid, back in our tent, and I cursed the decision to bring her with us. She was in the camp with Hildy and four bodyguards. She was so vulnerable. Asfrid! Why did I let her rule me? The thought of what Gwrgant would do with Wulfhere's pregnant woman, if he captured her, just couldn't be faced. I hoped that if we were overwhelmed she would have time to kill herself before they took her. I should never have let her come!

I had to get a grip on myself! I was whingeing like a child! The battle hadn't been lost, it hadn't even begun! It was just because Asfrid was here. If Asfrid wasn't here I wouldn't be panicking like this! Tiw was with me! Victory would be mine! I took a deep breath and focussed on the hillside.

But what price was I going to have to pay? In the dark with the sense that there were unseen warriors all about me, and a deadly enemy close by I was suddenly reminded of the night my parents had been murdered by Danish pirates. There was that same sense of powerlessness. Asfrid's peril brought my mother's death jolting home to me, and I was almost overwhelmed with the feeling that I had to get to Asfrid and keep her safe. I was wrestling with the urge to run from this dark place and find her, when a sudden sound from the further side of the ford seized my attention.

I focussed every instinct and sense that I possessed on the source of the sound. I knew it was too late to go back. I knew that it was just time to kill the enemy. Kill them here, by the river, and they couldn't hurt Asfrid. It was too late for mother, too late! She had died as I held her and they would pay for her pain! These men coming to hurt Asfrid were no different from the pirates who had killed my mother. The gods wanted me to punish the filth, Gwrgant who tormented the helpless and weak just as those pirates had done. This was the task that the gods had set me. This was why Tiw was with me now as he had been back then. He wanted me to give help to the helpless and to punish the filth who would defile nature. The gods were revealing their purpose to me!

The sound of the voices came clearly again, and this time the sound was recognisable. It also confirmed that the enemy were upon us. The speaker was using our tongue, and quite openly and casually as if he wasn't worried whether we heard or not.

It was a courageous act from this small group. They were coming forward to see if we were ready for them. I expect that they would signal the Trinovantes on the far bank if the way was open and then they would sweep down to the attack. They had overwhelmed the guards in deadly silence, and were passing themselves off as our men returning to camp. It was quite brilliant, except our guards hadn't been the hated Sais whose tongue they were now cleverly using. They had been Gwernach's Trinovantes!

I listened to them coming closer.

"Would you make that much noise coming back from guard?" I asked Gram in a whisper. "I don't think I've ever heard men chatting coming back from guard at this time of night, let alone laughing and joking."

It was true, most men would just walk wearily back to a well earned sleep. These men were far too casual and happy after a long cold night on the hill side. We listened to them now, laughing and talking without a care in the world, the words were ours, but the accent? They were Saxons! These must be some of Gwrgant's Saxons! Trickery and cruelty! Webs within webs! This new world was bewildering! I had Danes, Wealh and Norse in my army and I was about to fight Saxons! I hated the thought of having to kill Saxons. I thought of my old companion, Edgar, who had fallen at my side fighting Danes at Wolf Home, and Wilfrid, Wurt and Oxa, his nephews, all Saxons, hidden somewhere close by in the dark yard. I hardened my nerves and prepared for death.

I waited until they were only yards away and discernible as darker shapes in the dark night.

"Do you want to wake the whole camp you fools? Where have you been? Lord Saeberht was expecting you back some time ago, he's not very pleased." I demanded gruffly knowing full well that there was no Lord Saeberht in our camp.

"The relief couldn't find us in the dark." The men had stopped and I could see that they were searching hard, trying to spot me, but I stayed in the shadows for the moment. "So you can tell lord Saeberht to send guards who don't piss themselves with fright in the dark next time. We're with Ithamar anyway so Saeberht can take his complaint to him."

"Ithamar's men?" I stepped away from the wall so that they could see me, "I spoke with his companion Oslac the Dane earlier, he didn't tell me that Ithamar was organising the guard across the ford."

There was a pause as the men considered their answer, of course there was no such person as Oslac the Dane in Ithamar's household. They would be able to see my mail even in the dark, so they would know that I was a lord and probably aware of the arrangements for guarding the camp.

"I wouldn't know about that, lord. We were told to keep watch across the river and that's what we've been doing."

"Fair enough," I replied. "Come on then you had better bed down here in the barn."

I turned and walked between the buildings and the four followed on. They had done a reasonable job. Ithamar would have been one of the few names that Gwrgant would know. His hall at South Burrh was right on the border of Caer Colun.

I guessed that Gwrgant wasn't quite certain whether or not to attack in the dark. Would we be ready for him? He wanted eyes on our camp. Sadly for these men, the ruse hadn't quite worked. Once between the buildings I strode ahead and said firmly without raising my voice,

"Wolf Pack, kill them!" In an instant the farm yard, which had appeared deserted, was full of movement. Overwhelming, sudden, half seen, half sensed butchery. Then deathly silence, punctuated by the muffled curses of a man whose forearm had been sliced open by one of the doomed Saxons. I sent him back to find Asfrid at my tent and get her to have a look at his wound. Another fellow went with him so that between them they could carry the Saxons' war gear to safety.

The eastern rim of the sky had a lighter edge to it where it touched the earth. In the lessening darkness I could hear the hushed sound of the army moving up as 'quietly' as they could. The lords of the army found their way into the yard to seek my direction.

"Get your men into position! Quickly! Gwrgant is just across the river! Gram, get the Wolf Pack in line!" They hurried away.

Now we needed to bring Gwrgant's men to battle. I expected that the Saxons would have been told to signal Gwrgant if the way was clear. I could only think of one signal that men would make in the dark. I knocked lightly on the farm door and it was opened instantly by Withermund, who must have been standing behind it, listening to all the activity in his yard.

"Withermund, I need a flaming torch." I told him,

He was about to ask why, but disappeared and returned a short while later with burning cloth wrapped round a stake of some sort. I thanked him and walked to the front of the farm, facing the ford. The army was moving into place, the light was growing on the horizon, and I gave a signal which I hoped any group of infiltrators would be expected to send to their friends in the dark. I waved the flaming brand steadily from side to side several times above my head and then returned it to Withermund who had followed me to see what was happening.

"What are you doing Lord?" He asked, bemused.

"Signalling the enemy to attack!" I answered optimistically.

He stared at me slack jawed and I left him there and ran to my place with my army.

The wagons, the bowmen, the army, the sky and the hill side were all different shades of grey as dawn approached. I clambered up onto one of the wagons nudging my way past the bowmen so that I could look over the unfolding scene. Our men had formed up and hemmed in the curve in the river with a solid wall of warriors a little more than one hundred yards wide and three, in places four, ranks deep. The eight wagons behind this thick barrier of muscle, limewood shields and sharp spears, were spaced evenly along the line, with about half a dozen bowmen standing on each of them peering into the gloom. Beside the wagons, Gwernach's men were milling around like eager hounds. Odd had planted my standard behind the ranks of the Wolf Pack slightly to my left, and Gram was standing in front of the wagon that I was standing on, clearly intending to stay with me throughout the coming battle.

The army of the east Angels stood, solid, like a vast living creature, bristling with spears between its scales of rounded limewood. A silence had descended on the ranks. Breathing hard, with their hearts pounding as if they had run ten miles, the army fell silent. The men were watching and listening for the enemy. The rumour of their approach carried across to us from the other side of the river. Horses snorted, men were speaking in hushed voices, spears bumped against shields, and hundreds of feet whispered through the long grass. In the grey pre-dawn light of a morning in early summer, the very hillside appeared to be alive with movement, like a crawling mass of maggots on a summer carcass. The army of the Trinovantes flowed down the hillside but the dawn halted their slow progress. They had become aware of our shield wall and their advance was faltering as they waited for direction.

They had to come on, we had to destroy them here and now and seize the kingdom in one day. Their army would be led by wild men. The hot heads, and the Irish warriors who ate the mad mushrooms before they went into battle. We had to give them a challenge and they would come charging to meet us. Once the wild men charged the army would follow in their wake.

I thumped my sword hilt rhythmically against my shield, and set up our war chant,

"Wolf! Wolf! Wolf!"

The familiar chant was taken up by the whole army. In that silent, grey landscape the sudden crash of spears on shields and the shouted words were like the roar of a waterfall. A savage statement of pride and contempt. An unavoidable invitation to battle.

No warriors on earth could ignore that blatant challenge, and from the slope opposite there came a great answering shout from the throats of an army. The might of Caer Colun rushed down the valley side like an avalanche, still grey in the dawn, a wild headlong rush of a host of spectres. But there was nothing spectral about that outpouring of aggression and hate. The sound rolled down upon us, crashing over our line like a wave on the shore. Our army maintained its unwavering challenge. It was a rhythmic heart beat, vital, unstoppable, the pulse of an army.

CHAPTER 27: The Battle of Withermund's Ford

Gwrgant's warriors careered down the slope with their horsemen to the fore. The first of them were soon splashing across the ford, white spray flying up in great drops, like startled fish leaping from beneath the pounding hooves. They reined in their mounts on our side of the river and waited for their full strength to gather. Forty yards from our shields they wheeled about, struggling to hold their excited mounts. The horses danced and reared, puffing and snorting, their eyes wide and white, milling around, tensed to breaking point. Wealh footmen waded through the thigh deep water which shattered high above them in startled white jewels. They spread across the field, jostling for space, nervous and white faced, eyes staring wide, like the horses. Their courage swelled with their numbers, burgeoning, flooding, growing louder, feeding on itself until men and horses couldn't be held. The fear broke, the moment was here, a handful of shouts became a roar of hate and shared courage and the battle began.

The horses leaped forward, desperate for release, charging forth in a fountain of pure power and energy. I shouted for our bowmen to loose their arrows. Almost immediately horses began to tumble and cartwheel to the ground, crashing headlong to the turf and hurling their riders, flailing and sliding across the soft earth. Arrows split the air above us, hissing over our heads, seeking their targets while horses crashed to the earth all across the field. Our bowmen were excellent, but it wasn't their arrows destroying the charge. The pitted ground was wreaking havoc. Some of the riders had realised the danger, but they were warriors, and we were close. They had to ride in close and hurl their spears with the weight and speed of the charge behind the throw. Their job was to tear holes in our shield wall and they came on valiantly. Their courage was their ruin. As more horses fell there were fewer targets for our bowmen. Those steeds that avoided the wicked little pits attracted flights of white feathered shafts which stuck from their shoulders and flanks like wheat in a field.

The attack faltered in flailing hooves and vivid clusters of white feathers. It was time for our bowmen to turn their attention to the footmen. Too few horsemen reached the wall to do any serious damage. Once they'd thrown their spears they were reluctant to ride back across the deadly ground and in a few places some of our men left the wall and ran out to drag the warriors from their steeds and slaughter them on the ground. One or two horses were actually led back through the shields.

The bowmen had lifted their aim and many of them were pouring arrows into the mass of men still crossing the river. They were packed densely and shots which missed their mark would slash into the flesh of a man behind. On this side of the river, warriors were charging, wildly towards our shields. They had seen their horsemen crashing to the ground but most hadn't comprehended the danger, thinking the horses were being felled by bowshot. Soon some of the charging men were tumbling to earth, bringing down the warriors behind them or causing them to slow and swerve. It was only forty yards to the river, and they should have hit us like a hammer blow, but the little holes did their job magnificently well, breaking up the charge of the Wealh army. We had stopped the enemy's main strength, his wild, crashing charge. They closed piecemeal with our front rank and the battle became one vast heaving trial of strength and courage. This was the war of the Angels, the shield wall.

To stand in the shield wall requires a different type of courage than facing an enemy in the open field. I have killed many men. I practise my weapon craft every day and have done since I was a boy. I am fast and strong, but in the wall it counts for very little. You are hemmed in, crushed by the press of men before and behind. There is no finesse, no glory. You stab at any part of your enemy you get a chance to stab. The chances of making a clean kill are virtually none. You just try to hack, slice, stab and do as much damage as you can. I once tore a man's eyes out with my fingers. It is a desperate, terrifying struggle, reeking of blood and steaming entrails, populated by screaming, spit flecked faces with eyes and veins bulging with the strain, pain and terror.

It was what the Wolf Pack spent their lives perfecting, because a well prepared shield wall is a merciless killer. The men in the front rank hold the enemy. They stab, gouge and heave but they have to hold. The men behind them use their long spears to stab over the shoulders, or in between the legs of the men in the front rank. They say that men killed in the shield wall never see the thrust that kills them. It's cruel, it's brutal and no matter how fine a warrior you are, you have to trust your friends around you to be your eyes and your protectors.

The army of Caer Colun was across the river. A cluster of mounted men still at the ford had to be Gwrgant, and his companions. Clearly the press of battle wasn't for him. I looked around at our bowmen and thought of directing their arrows at the cowards, but they were aiming their shafts at the enemy warriors close to our shields and I didn't want to stop them helping our hard pressed companions.

The sun peered over the trees as if it was nervous of what it might see. Its spreading light revealed two armies wrestling like stags, one side trying to force a way through the shields, the other trying to hold them and hurl them back. My head swung left and right along our line, constantly searching for any points where my men were struggling to hold their ground. From my vantage point on top of the wagon I realised that Gwrgant was massing his greatest strength on his right. He was making a determined effort to crush the far left of our line where it reached the river. Brega, Hod and Halfi held our left with their tough Frisian warriors, but the enemy had sent his mad Irish men against them supported by his Saxons and a great strength of his own folk. Clearly his plan was to break through there and then pour men round behind us. I jumped down from the wagon and, with Gram at my side, I called several of the lads at the rear of the Wolf Pack to follow me.

"Gwernach! Gwernach!"

I shouted for my ally but I couldn't wait to look for him. We kept calling for him as we ran, jostling our way through the supporting Wealh warriors. Either he heard us, or he was told that I was calling for him, because he ran up behind us leading a surge of warriors. Gram tapped my shoulder and alerted me to their presence and I waved them forward pointing towards the hard pressed Frisians. Gwernach, the veteran of many fights, instantly weighed up the situation and led his men into the fray. Brega was at the rear of his men. He saw us coming and waved madly to attract my attention. As we got closer I saw that the front of his slashed leather shirt was mired in blood. He was breathing hard,

"Lord Wulfhere!" He shouted breathlessly, "We are hard pressed my lord, we need..." I cut across him.

"I saw, Brega, we are here." I said simply and led my men straight into the carnage.

I drew my seaxe, the shorter, heavier blade was better suited to this close quarter slaughter than my long bladed sword. This would be stabbing work. The Frisians were fighting ferociously but our line was starting to give ground. If the Irish broke through, our whole line would break and run for fear of being surrounded and slaughtered.

I could see Hod fighting desperately in the front rank against the Irish. They were launching mad, uncontrolled assaults against the Frisians' shield wall. I guessed that their magic was making them reckless of danger and pain because I had never seen men fight in such a frenzied manner. I could understand why they had terrified the people of Caer Colun. An Irish warrior was raining a torrent of blows on Hod, intent on battering down his lime wood shield. I rushed forward, forcing a way through the Frisians in my haste to help my friend. The man behind Hod seemed to be overwhelmed with terror at the Irish. I shoved him aside and leaped on to and over Hod's back, swinging my seaxe at the head of the unsuspecting Irish warrior. The heavy slaughter blade hummed through the air and into the top of his head with a sound like splitting logs. I levered it from side to side, twisting his head and splitting his skull apart to free the blade. My sudden assault had taken the foe by surprise and gained me those few, precious moments, but then they were on me. Three of them rushed at me, but Gram stepped in to even the odds. One of the Irish warriors turned his attack on my hearth man. He went at Gram with his shield held high for protection. Holding your shield up leaves your legs exposed and Gram hacked into the leading limb between ankle and knee. The leg broke, the Irish man crashed to the floor and Gram looked for his next opponent. The other two were upon me, but their magic made them mad and reckless. They were intent on the kill and they left themselves wide open. I leaped forward and punched my shield edge into the face of the first attacker, surprising him and beating him to the strike. Without pausing and with barely a glance at my enemy, I swung it backhanded to the left, smashing the rim into the face of the other assailant who staggered away from me like a drunken man, before falling and bringing two more of his countrymen crashing to the floor where they were quickly stabbed to unresisting flesh. My first assailant, with his nose and cheek crushed in by my shield, stood before me, senseless. I gave a short jab and drove my blade into his throat. The keen-edged seaxe eased through the soft flesh till it grated on bone. I was back in my defensive stance before his body hit the ground. The men around him literally hurled themselves at us, growling and shrieking like animals, under the power of their ancient magic. I was shouting encouragement, rallying the shocked Frisians. Gwernach and his boys were wading into the fight, keen to make Gwrgant's hated companions pay for their crimes.

The battle was unbelievably savage. In their demented, unnatural state of mind the Irish warriors weren't even heeding their wounds. They hurled themselves forward with complete disregard for their own defence, utterly uncontrolled, swinging their weapons with staggering strength. Even with terrible injuries they just kept coming and I understood why the Frisians had been so hard pressed. We had to go beyond ferocity to defeat this enemy. I hacked, I stabbed, I heaved and punched with my shield, until my muscles were screaming for a rest and I was drenched in the blood and flesh of my enemies. Alongside me Gram was fighting like a mad dog, grunting with the effort of swinging his sword and shield, gasping for breath.

Then, with a sudden tumbling smash of flying bodies, Ottar clattered into the middle of the fight bellowing like a stag in the rut. Frisians, Wealh and Irish were hurled to the ground as he crashed into the heart of the fray swinging his dreadful war hammer like a man possessed. In a lull in the fighting further along the front he had spotted the Irish men out here on the flank and had hurried to exact his revenge. His rage increased his already great strength, and he swung his blood slaked hammer with savage hatred, smashing shields, arms, heads, shoulders and chests. If I thought fighting with a blade was messy, the gore which clung to him made him look like some hideous creature of the underworld, and I laughed aloud. Even our demented foes wavered before his onslaught. The mad, sorcery fuelled battle lust deserted some of them, and left them lost and confused in a nightmarish world of dismembered bodies and terrible, relentless foes. One of them staggered about amid the fray, mad and terrified, ranting incoherently, until he was hacked down. Another just stood and wept as our lads closed on him. We were in a world of utter madness. Wild men still bellowing and growling like demented beasts, fighting on with horrific wounds; one with a severed arm, another with his mouth and jaw smashed to bloody pulp by a hammer blow. This was beyond the realm of sanity. The last of the Irish men were given no mercy. They fought on through the nightmare of their forest magic but they were surrounded and cut to pieces.

They may have been butchered on the field, but they had done their job. Our wall was in ruins. We weren't a well drilled army, we were a crowd. A crowd of Frisians, Angels, Wealh and Norse and before us the Saxons were grinding forward in their shield wall. The battle mad Irish had weakened our men for the Saxon hammer blow, and now the hammer was falling.

"Shield wall! Shield wall!"

I shouted the order and the courageous Frisians formed up again, bolstered by my men. Gwernach's lads stood around us, and he was summoning more of his folk over, but they didn't know how to fight with us. They would just have to charge alongside us. This was going to be a close run thing. The whole of the battle now hinged on us holding the line.

The Saxons edged forward over the pitted ground and the butchered bodies of their allies. I didn't want to kill these men, but this was their doom. I lapped my shield over Gram's. Thick, sticky, sick smelling blood was drying on my face and neck, and I brushed my itching cheek with the back of my hand as I prepared myself for this last act. I was looking at the colours of the shields approaching us, only eight yards away. It suddenly struck me that the day was fully light. I hadn't noticed the final arrival of daylight and I had no idea how long we had been fighting. I gave the cry of "Wolf!" This was the signal for the men to be ready for the command to step forward one pace just before the impact of the two lines. That step would prevent us being driven back. It would knock the enemy out of their stride, and perhaps open their guard, but the command never came.

To our right the Wealh were breaking and starting to run for the ford. The Saxons halted their advance, suddenly uncertain about what their allies were doing. The men at the far end of their line nearest the river didn't realise straight away. They briefly closed to within striking distance and a few blows were exchanged before they pulled back with the rest of their kin. Our army was pursuing the broken enemy across the soft, pitted and churned ground, which was littered with the bodies of wounded and dead, men and horses. Gwrgant and his companions had already fled back across the river and now I could see why. As I looked to the ford, and beyond at the green hillside, I saw Artorius and his men riding along the hill top, dark against the sky. Obviously the Trinovantes had seen them. If Artorius took the ford they would be surrounded on our side of the river and slaughtered where they stood. They were running for their lives with a vengeful army behind them, and merciless horsemen before them. As I watched, Artorius split his force. Most of the riders wheeled down the slope toward the ford which was choked with fleeing Wealh warriors. The rest of them continued on their path along the ridge top endeavouring to cut off Gwrgant's escape.

Our bowmen were loosing what shafts they had left into the mass of bodies packed into the ford. Our army was at the backs of the routed enemy, hacking them down as they ran, or fighting with those at the rear of the crush.

The Saxons were pulling their line round into a crescent, with each end anchored on the river, preparing to fight to the death. There were too many of our men between them and the ford for them to consider escaping. They were proud warriors and they knew that their time had come. The Wolf Pack were hurrying to join me at this end of the battlefield and with them came Wulfstan, Oswine, Wuffa and their men, followed by Sigurd, Ullr and a fair strength of Danish warriors. The Saxons were hemmed in but I still did not wish to kill them and I did not want to lose any more of my men in what would undoubtedly be a tough fight.

"Hold!" I strode between the forces with my arm aloft.

"I am lord Wulfhere, and I tell you to hold!"

I was so drenched in blood and gore that I wasn't sure that our men would recognise me, but my command held firm and both sides stood and waited to hear what I had to say. I faced the Saxons.

"I am Wulfhere, king of the east Angels and victor on this field. Who leads here among you?"

A tall, fair haired warrior stepped forward from his place in the front rank. He was a similar age to Wulfstan. He carried his round shield and war spear and was dressed in plain woollen clothing with a blue cloak about his shoulders. He wore no cap or helm and his blond hair and beard reminded me of Edgar. I stood before him, a blood soaked king, master of the battlefield, attired in my mail shirt, crested helmet, leather leg and arm guards, armed with sword and seaxe, and carrying my decorated Wolf shield. At that moment Odd hurried up and planted my banner behind me. The contrast was cruel.

"I am Eorcenwald, say what you would say and then let us finish this day's blood letting."

"Eorcenwald, I stand here to offer you the protection of the new king of Caer Colun, Artorius. The battle is over. You are not disgraced. You didn't run, nor should you throw your lives needlessly away. Artorius will take your oath. It is clear that you have stood by your lord, and done your duty by him. Your reputation is enhanced by your actions here. Your homes are safe."

"If this is all you have to say, lord Wulfhere then save your breath. I thank you for your offer of mercy but I must refuse it." Eorcenwald replied, resigned to death here at the water's edge.

"This is not all I have to say Eorcenwald. Saxon and Angel are as brothers in this world of peoples. We should not be shedding each other's blood. I have fought alongside Hwaetberht your king. I stood shoulder to shoulder with your kin against the Franks. I have no wish to fight you, nor do I see why your men should die needlessly."

"It's true, Eorcenwald. I was there at the battle of the thorn ridge," one of his companions weighed in.

"That may be so, lord. I don't doubt your honour, and I certainly admire your battle craft. You and your men are no strangers to sword play! But I also have my honour. I have sworn my oath........"

"To whom Eorcenwald?"

"To king Gwrgant!"

"Oh!"

I made a great play of looking around the battle field.

"Where is this king Gwrgant? No wait! I did see him. He sat at the ford, out of danger, while his men threw their lives away. I did see him, fleeing for his life, leaving his men upon the field to face their fate without the protection of their lord. I am a lord of men, Eorcenwald, as are you, plainly. We know that it is our duty to protect our men, each and every one, or die trying. How can a lord send men to die for him when he doesn't risk everything for them in his turn? This man is no king? Don't you have ears Eorcenwald? Don't you hear the tales of his greed? His cruelty?

Have you ever been invited to sit at his mead bench? You have been given land but kept from his door. You are expected to die for him while he flees the field, and he treats you like lepers. He is no king. Artorius is your king. Meet him, talk with him, give him your oath and serve him, an honourable king, with honour."

"There is much truth in what you say, lord," the old warrior admitted. "Yet even so I have sworn my oath and my fate has brought me to this field and never intended me to return to my home. I have lived a good life and I am content to end it here. But my men need not suffer for following a fool into folly. I release them from their oaths to me. They will bow the knee to the new king. My death will ensure the honour of my people. No man will say that we didn't hold to our oaths!"

"If that is your wish I will send you swiftly to your ancestors. But listen to the wisdom in your own words, Eorcenwald. 'A man need not suffer for following a fool into folly', is what you said. If one man should be forgiven, then surely another who fell into folly in finding a home for his people, should also deserve forgiveness. You swore your oath to a man that you thought was a king. It turns out that he was a dog, disguised as a king. Do you know how he got the king's helm Eorcenwald? He poisoned the confused mind of the dying king with honeyed words. With false promises and lies he tricked a dying man, with a weakened mind, into granting him the name of king Gwrgant. He didn't win kingship. It wasn't his by right. He had no right before the law or before the people to take your oath. He was nithing, less than a man. It cannot hold you for it was wrongly given my friend."

He stood, unswerving, before me. He knew that I was trying to conjure with words. He knew that I was trying to spare him, but I was cheapening his leadership of his folk. In silence I drew Blood Seeker. He put down his weapons and turned to his men.

"You are released from your oaths. Artorius is your new king. My time on middle earth is ended. When the fates led me here today it was to make amends for bad choices. Farewell, my friends."

He knelt on the damp turf and in silence I cut his head from his body with one clean blow. On a day of blood letting, one more death bought peace for the Saxons of Caer Colun.

"Who speaks for you now?" I asked of the solemn warriors.

They looked to one another.

"Ecgfrith," one of them stated boldly.

"Yes, Ecgfrith."

The chosen man stood forward.

"Observe the funeral rites for Eorcenwald, Ecgfrith. Join our camp and await the return of your king, Artorius."

CHAPTER 28: Life and Death

The battle had gone. It had passed out of sight beyond the hill. The tumult of battle was replaced by the cries of the wounded. The bodies of Gwrgant's army were heaped on the battlefield and scattered across the hillside where they had been overtaken by Artorius' horsemen. The rout had crested the ridge like a wave and raced away towards Camulodonum. I hadn't seen whether Artorius had caught up to Gwrgant, but no doubt we would learn soon enough. My army was spread between our battle line and the far hill top, searching the bodies, picking the best pieces and gathering the gear and valuables.

I looked up at the sun and realised that it was still early morning. We hadn't toiled for long upon the slaughter field, but I felt heavy limbed and thirsty. Now that the excitement was finished I was discovering my wounds. Sweat stung a cut that looked like a mouth on my upper sword arm. My left leg and shoulder were badly bruised, presumably by some impact on my shield that I couldn't remember. I would be stiff in the morning. My lower lip was swollen and I could taste blood in my mouth.

These were no more than the marks that I might get from a hard practise session. I had been lucky. The line of battle was clearly marked by those less fortunate. The row of dead and dying stretched across the field. It was the wounded who needed us now.

I walked the field with my closest companions. Odd carried the Wolf standard behind us. Asfrid came hurrying up from the direction of the camp with Hildy and her four guards.

"Wulfhere!" She couldn't say anything else. She just stared at me and I realised that I must look a fearful sight.

"It's alright. It's not my blood. I'm barely hurt."

"Oh, Wulfhere! I wanted to watch, to see that you were alright, but I couldn't! I couldn't watch! It was too terrible."

"It's finished now," I said, simply.

All around us men were helping wounded friends back towards the camp. The dead were heaped on the dead where our shield wall had stood and rebuffed the Wealh attack. Men were dragging the bodies of friends from the heap. Many a brave man wept that morning as he discovered the corpse of a friend among the slain. They were being laid out in a neat line. We would bury them and send them to their ancestors in the morning.

Between the battle line and the ford were numerous bodies of men and horses. All of the wounded Wealh that were unable to flee the field had been slaughtered by our warriors, along with those men who had been overtaken by their pursuers. The ford itself was full of bodies. I could have crossed it with dry feet by stepping from corpse to corpse. A thick red bloom was blossoming downstream on the choked current.

I made my way to the centre of our line and looked on the faces of my men who had been slain. Men of the Wolf Pack lay on the blood soaked turf, torn asunder by the blades of their foes. I stared at the pale, blood flecked and bruised faces which stared back at me, but the stares were distant, the eyes were looking on another world.

"Go to your ancestors with your heads held high. You have won a mighty victory today. Your ancestors can be proud of you, my brothers."

There was a lump in my throat as I finished the words. Asfrid squeezed my hand and I looked at her. Tears were streaming down her cheeks and I knew that in these battle torn bodies she had seen my fate.

"We had better get back to camp," I decided. "There is no more for us to do here."

We walked back among wounded men who were either making their own painful way or were being helped along by friends. We helped a Frisian warrior whose broken shin bone was sticking through the bruised and bloody skin. In spite of the pain he had managed to drag himself most of the way to the camp. He had been terrified that he wouldn't be able to escape if the Wealh broke through our line, and that he would be butchered, as their wounded had been. His hair was stuck to his head with sweat, and his skin had the pallor of the dead. He was completely exhausted. Odd handed my standard to Wuffa and he and Gram carried the fellow to his tent, where his friends would help him when they returned.

Asfrid took the arm of an older fellow who turned out to be of the Finningas and only lived a few miles from Wolf Home. Fighting in the shield wall, he had taken a blow to the side of his face which had shattered his cheek. He had fallen unconscious and had regained his senses only to discover that his arm had somehow been broken as well, though he had no idea how. He was wandering about in a confused daze and we ushered him to the camp where he was recognised by a couple of his companions who were carrying captured spears back from the battlefield. The injuries would heal with care. Others would not be so lucky.

Hildy was already busy tending the injured and Asfrid was soon helping to stitch and splint. I told a couple of Wolf Pack lads to get a fire going and start a broth, or porridge. I was still coated with dried blood and nameless filth. I walked to the river with Gram and Leofmund and we stripped off our gear and washed ourselves in the slow, muddy flow. We cleaned our gear and then stood naked on the bank while it dried. We watched the melancholy scene in silence for a while until Leofmund suddenly broke the mood.

"Wulfhere, there's something that I've been meaning to talk to you about for a while. I thought that it would be best to wait until the wars were behind us, but now I think that I should ask."

"Yes, what's that?"

"It's Eadgyth, Wulfhere. I would like to ask if I may wed your sister."

I stopped and looked at him. I was taken aback for a moment. Here, in the middle of all this? But then, why not? I had just been dwelling on life and death. Perhaps the closeness of death had made Leofmund think of life. I cleared my head and tried to think of Eadgyth and Leofmund. I would be very happy to see him wed my sister. I knew that they had strong feelings for each other and I would be delighted to see them both happy. Mother and father would have been pleased. I had done well by my sisters. I would have to think of a fair bride price and when they were wed, I would grant Eadgyth and Leofmund an estate where they would be able to help me keep order in the kingdom.

"Nothing would make me happier, Leofmund but," I paused here and enjoyed the sudden look of fear that came over his face. "Well you see, I promised her that she would be allowed to choose her own man, just as her sister did. So I can't allow it unless she agrees." We both burst out laughing and I clapped him on the shoulder.

All through the morning we watched our men returning to the camp carrying armfuls of plunder. Weapons, shields, a few helmets, fine cloaks, coins, brooches and jewellery. Best of all, seven more horses were tied to posts driven into the ground behind the camp. A few rings, brooches, coins and the like no doubt disappeared into the small leather purses that most men had attached to their belt for carrying fire strikes, combs and such like. I wouldn't begrudge them trinkets.

Wulfstan and Oswine were sitting outside my tent talking with Wuffa and Ullr when we finally dressed and returned to the camp for a pot of ale. I noticed a proud bruise below Wuffa's left eye and scrapes on his cheek where the blow had left its mark.

"You've earned that Wuffa, and several more besides!" Wulfstan declared as my brother finished his drink and held the pot out for another. "He was better than you were in your first fight," he informed me with a broad smile. "You were hopeless first time out! That scrap by the river wasn't it?"

It was indeed, and I had been like a puppy in a sheepfold, not knowing which way to go first, while everything rushed around me.

"He did the family proud, held his place in the wall and killed six or seven with his bow before that."

"Well uncle I'm not sure........" Wuffa began but I jumped in.

"What do you mean, held his place in the wall? I thought you were up on one of the wagons, directing the bowmen."

"I was, but then we were running low on arrows. I'd shot all of mine, and the lads in the wall were struggling, and you'd taken several with you to help Hod and Brega hold the Irish so I had to go in. It wasn't for long though. They ran away almost as soon as I was in there," he shrugged.

"Now then Wuffa, don't do yourself down! Wulfstan has seen enough battles to know something about it, and if he was impressed with your first showing then that's something to be proud of. Here's to you."

I raised my pot to my brother and Wulfstan and Oswine joined me.

The lords of our army joined us during the rest of the morning. The mood was subdued as it always is after a battle. The pain of loss, weariness and the return to sanity leave you drained. We had won a great victory but we were tired in spirit as well as in body. A few were sporting vivid wounds, bruised and shining red between stitches. Others had swollen purple and black faces caked with dried blood. Hod would never join us again in this world, and nor would Oisc and Iden, both of whom had fallen in the shield wall, dying bravely at the front of their men. We drank and talked through the afternoon while our men, some of whom must have chased the enemy almost to Camulodonum, continued to return with their plunder.

Riders trotted up to my tent, messengers from Artorius who would expect us at Camulodonum on the morrow. They hadn't caught Gwrgant. He'd managed to give them the slip somehow, but his army was destroyed. Artorius would take the throne and he had sent messengers to Ambrosius to pledge his friendship.

By late afternoon our army had returned, as far as we could tell, but by then the mead had taken away our worries. Tomorrow we were going to Camulodonum. We were going to send the wounded home with our plunder, and we were going to see Artorius become king. I had taken a look through the captured weapons and I was very pleased with the quality as well as the quantity. Gram had a tally up and I was staggered to discover that we had captured forty three swords! I had never imagined that I would see so many in one place, but that was just the start. We had three hundred and sixty two spears, four hundred and forty eight shields, four hundred and twelve knives and daggers, thirty two mail shirts, twenty six helmets, thirty fine cloaks, and an impressive collection of torcs, arm rings and brooches.

I selected eight swords, and a wagon load of knives, spears, shields, mail shirts, helmets and cloaks, and still had plenty of gear to richly reward the lords of the East Angels. Amongst the many gifts that I gave to my oathgivers it was Wuffa's turn to get a horse, I gave Odd, my standard bearer, a mail shirt and a helmet, Ottar a mail shirt and a beautifully decorated knife and I granted Oswine the lands that Oisc had held, near Gyppeswic. This last act pleased me more than most. I was glad to be able to reward Oswine, who had been my teacher as a lad, and who had been a faithful servant of my family for longer than I had been alive. He was lord Oswine now, and it suited him.

After everyone had received their gifts, we sat round the fire and talked of the battle and various exploits of the day. Eventually the conversation turned to what would happen next.

"Well, we'll march to Camulodonum in the morning and there will be even more reward for our trouble," I answered, glibly.

"I didn't mean that," Marcellus protested. "We've defeated Cynfellyn and Gwrgant. Icel is king of the far west Marches and the Corieltavi. You are king of the east Angels. We have a friendly king in Caer Colun. Where next for the Wolf Pack?"

In the silence that followed Marcellus' question the fire crackled and spat, a wounded man cried out above the murmur of the camp and one of our companions coughed and spat. It was a good question and I thought about the answer, but I was tired and mellow with mead.

"We build up our wealth and our strength and we see what fate brings. Hopefully the south folk can enjoy some peace and see their herds grow and their children flourish. As for the Wolf Pack, we will be doing Tiw's work, so it will be bloody, but there will be great rewards. Don't worry about what we're going to do next. It will come and we will face it. That is all."

Much later, when I stumbled into my tent and crawled to my bed, Asfrid was already sleeping. She had worn herself out tending the wounded, and with the baby being close I had insisted that she should get some rest. It was a strange night. After the long build up to the battle, the excitement and intensity of the battlefield, and the melancholy of victory, I felt empty, absolutely spent. Wounded men cried out at intervals through the night and it was the sound of those cries which would stay with me from this war. I had seen this battle as an act of judgement on the tyrant Gwrgant. Until he had been sent screaming to the next world our triumph wasn't complete. I fell asleep with this on my mind and awoke in a strained mood before dawn. I almost woke my men to strike camp, but calmed down and decided that they deserved their rest. It wasn't our fault that Gwrgant had got away, my men had done all that was asked of them.

    I got up and walked the camp, greeting the guards. I found myself walking to Withermund's farm, and the field of carnage beyond. The dawn was lighting the rim of the eastern sky and the battlefield was ghostly in the half light. Eyes stared at me from the grey faces of the vanquished. I was their conqueror and their ghosts couldn't hurt me. I walked among them wondering where they were from. They were a tragic people. Courageous, poetic people, who had been failed by self-serving masters. Not just the Trinovantes. The tale was the same all over this land. I followed my feet around the fields, listening to the gentle river and the bird song which accompanied the dawn. Gram and Odd came hurrying up, concerned for my safety. They walked with me in silence as the camp woke and prepared for the new day.

    I was hungry, and the sounds of the morning set my stomach rumbling. I hadn't eaten much yesterday and suddenly a bowl of hot porridge seemed the most inviting meal in this world. It was a bright, early summer morning with the promise of a beautiful day ahead. The wood smoke rose straight up above the cooking fires and I had to stand close to the flames to pick up the delicious mixture of smoke and cooking porridge which teased my senses. This was wonderful; the bright, softly warm sunshine, the bird song, the smell of the cooking and the low noises of the morning camp. This was the perfect medicine for my melancholy. I closed my eyes and let my other senses absorb this wonderful life. Soft hands kneaded my neck and shoulders and Asfrid's beautiful voice flowed like honey into my ears,

"Good morning my lord, conqueror of Caer Colun, what great deeds do you have in mind for this day?"

I chuckled and turned and took her in my arms.

"Just to live my lady. Just to gaze on your beauty, and to breathe in the marvels of life which surround us. Which my enemies will never taste again."

I held her close for a long time feeling her warmth against me and breathing in her scent. I finally stood back and looked at her face.

"How are you? Is that baby kicking you this morning, keen to get out and march on Camulodonum?"

"He was earlier but he has settled down now." She told me with a smile.

We ate porridge together and then she left to have a look at some of the wounded men she had treated yesterday. The camp was struck except for the tents of the men who would be digging graves for our fallen companions. Eighty three of our men had been slain in the short but vicious battle. We would bury rather than burn them, it was a custom we had picked up from the people of the Northern Marches of home, and it made more sense in this situation. The wounded would depart for home with the plunder, and an escort made up of those men whose lords had died, and others who needed to return home. I would continue to Camulodonum with over six hundred men, which would still be enough to reinforce any negotiations which might be required.

Ecgfrith the Saxon was waiting at the ford with his warriors and they joined the end of our column. We crossed the ford in near silence. The bodies which had blocked the crossing yesterday had been dragged out, searched, stripped of gear, and left in a great heap, twenty yards from the river. In spite of this token of our victory there was no elation, no gloating sense of triumph. We followed the track which climbed the valley side in a south easterly direction, leaving Withermund's ford behind. The ground was littered with the bodies of the Wealh who had been unable to escape their pursuers. The number of bodies with wounds around the head and shoulders showed how deadly horsemen were amongst scattered foes. I paused at the top of the slope with Asfrid, allowing the column to march past us. The army hailed me, and saluted my victory as they passed. I enjoyed watching the long column of men and wagons snaking up the slope and heading towards Camulodonum. Across the river a second column of wagons and its escort was heading for home. The wounded men, slipping away, unseen and uncelebrated.

CHAPTER 29: Camulodonum

The journey to Camulodonum was strangely quiet. The road was deserted. The fields were deserted. The villages and farms were deserted. Yesterday a beaten army had fled through these fields and woods, pursued to death by a storm of horsemen. Now an army of Sais was marching past. These were dangerous times. I had instructed the lords of my army that there would be no plundering on the road, and my word was respected enough to ensure that none would risk it. Our pace was steady. There was no need of hurry, and many were feeling their wounds. We marched through the empty landscape and approached the great city after noon.

Camulodonum gradually came in to view between the trees and the rolling landscape, and grew until it dominated the world. It was quite simply breathtaking. The city was imprisoned by a massive stone wall, solid and imposing, with red tiled stripes running along its entire length. The precision of those straight red lines was set in deliberate opposition to the forest and the field. The builder wanted to show his mastery of this world. He was controlling the land, controlling the earth, not of it like the earth and timber halls in which we and the Wealh dwelt. As we approached from the west we were rendered silent by the power of the huge gateway which proclaimed the greatness of this place. Two dark, arched portals fashioned from solid stone were the entrance to the city, or were they the way to another world? They were so outlandish, so utterly foreign to me that I wouldn't have been surprised if we had walked under those archways and discovered that there were giants living within. Such wonder, such power, skill and craft. What manner of men could have fashioned this? Surely they should be all conquering, all powerful, immortal, and yet they were gone, swept away by the tides of history. I just sat on my horse and stared. I realised that my army had stopped behind me, but I didn't move for several minutes. I wanted to absorb this sight, I wanted to wonder and shake my head in awe and admiration. This was one of life's special moments.

As I sat in open admiration I realised that I was one of the masters of this great city. My army had won it. I was really the one who wielded the power of this majestic place and even though I was about to hand it to my friend, it was mine. I was Wulfhere, master of history, heir to the might of Rome. I took a deep breath and rode forward chest puffed out and shoulders square. A lord of war come to accept the spoils of victory.

We marched onto a stone street, and it was fitting that we should complete our journey to the great city along this paved way. From half a mile away I could see that our approach was causing consternation amongst the people entering and leaving through the great gate. Even at this distance I could hear faint shouts as the folk reacted with alarm to the approach of an army of the Sais. I wondered how much the ordinary people of Camulodonum and the surrounding villages knew of the events of the last couple of days. Had Artorius and Gwernach seized the town? Had Gwrgant been completely overthrown? I halted and glanced back at the relaxed column of warriors. Suddenly cautious, I ordered the army into columns at both sides of the road with the wagons between them. The message to the men was clear, be ready for anything. Then we continued the last stage of our triumphant march.

Mounted men clattered out of the city and rode towards us. I recognised the powerful figure of Artorius and I halted the march again. The young warrior dismounted with a huge smile on his face and, removing his helmet, he briefly dropped to one knee before me, he then stood with arms flung wide as I slid from my own mount, and we embraced like brothers.

"Wulfhere it is all ours, thanks to your courage and the skill of your men. You have won the undying gratitude and friendship of my people. I greet you as lord of Camulodonum and king of Caer Colun. I trust that there will always be friendship between our two kingdoms. As we have started, so may we continue. You will always be welcomed here. Now come and gaze on the fair city of Camulodonum."

He walked with me as we completed our journey into his city.

The great arch seemed to move forward as we stepped into the cool echoing shade, giving the strange impression that we were being eaten. I gazed at the brick and stone all around me, my head swivelling round and leaning right back on my neck as I tried to take it all in. Voices, footfalls and hoofbeats echoed all around until we were suddenly in daylight again as the city emerged and opened up before us.

The people of the city lined the way, having emerged cautiously to see us pass their homes. We had been the enemy until this morning. An entire generation had lived their lives fearing and despising both us and their own leaders who had brought our people to these lands. They had been preyed on by Angel raiders. They had fought civil wars. They had grown up with conflict and the constant threat of danger, and now it was being said that there would be peace and, as if to confirm it, here was an army of the hated Sais marching into their city as allies. They watched us pass without making any noise, neither in welcome nor in animosity. They just stood and looked upon us as you might look upon a captive wolf, curious to see it but still not anxious to get too close.

I stared all around at the sights of the city. The streets were laid out in straight lines, just like the roads through Ligora Ceaster, but it was far more prosperous and better maintained than Icel's city. I looked right and left at each crossroads at the rows of houses stretching away on both sides past further crossroads. As well as houses, there were great buildings which reminded me a little of the great hall at Ligora Ceaster where Icel and Esme now lived. They had mighty stone pillars supporting high roofs. There were figures carved in stone decorating the face of the buildings beneath the angle of the roofs. Elsewhere there were buildings with domed roofs, or roofs that were curved rather than angled. Finally, after passing about six crossroads and the houses in between we came to a place where the houses stopped and gave way to a wide, open space paved with stone. Across this great square, to our left, we were confronted with a huge building. Perfect stone columns all around it held up the massive stone and tile roof.

Artorius looked at the expression on my face.

"Impressive, isn't it? This used to be the great temple of the city in the old heathen times when the Roman emperors were proclaimed gods by their people. Now that we follow the one, true God, it serves as the royal hall. Our church is in that building."

He pointed out a smaller, but still impressive, building at the far side of the square.

The army filed quietly into the great square, hushed by the sight of the temple with its carved figures on the stonework above the pillars, and statues on great blocks of stone before the entrance. This truly was the home of the emperors, a place of legend and timeless splendour.

"Artorius, this is an incredible place. You can sense the greatness of these people. Surely they must have been giants!" I was truly overwhelmed by the splendour.

"Giants among men, perhaps. Come my friend," Artorius bade me. "We have business to discuss, and then I will show you more of the wonders of this place."

I gave word for the men to rest in the square and called Asfrid, Leofmund, Marcellus, Gram and the lords to join us. We followed Artorius up the steps and into the huge royal hall. Inside there were more statues, pictures on the floor and beautifully shaped columns around the broad open space where I could imagine benches and tables arrayed for a feast. Behind the columns there were shadowy walkways, and in the walls beyond were doorways leading invitingly off to mysterious rooms. At the far side of the hall a series of great steps led up to another grand archway through which I could glimpse the lower parts of a great statue on a stone plinth. Ale was brought out by servants to slake our thirst, and Artorius instructed them to take ale to our warriors as well.

"This is where the tyrant held his perverted orgies, and had prisoners tormented and tortured for the amusement of himself and his weak willed followers. Gwrgant escaped, Wulfhere. He managed to get away from us at the river. We were trying to cut him off, thinking he would try to get back here. We lost sight of him and he must have doubled back and crossed the river where we couldn't see him. I have got men out hunting for him but we haven't heard anything yet."

"Until we have him Artorius it's a hollow victory. He must answer for his crimes."

"I agree my friend, but look here, Wulfhere. I have taken from the treasury such wealth as we can afford to give you in recognition of your courage."

He led the way to the side of the great hall, and through a modest doorway into a small chamber. The floor was a plain white colour except for a black circle, about six feet across, which was somehow inlaid amongst the floor tiles. The walls were bare and although some of the plaster was cracked, the black rim of the circle was stark in that strangely featureless whiteness. The blandness of the room contrasted with the treasures that were laid within it. There were three chests of coins, glass vessels, ornamental bowls, small statues of bronze in the form of animals or human figures, spoons and other decorated domestic goods, some wonderful red cloaks and a selection of knives. Specifically for me Artorius had a bronze statue of a wolf but clearly a she wolf, ready to suckle her litter. He also gave me a magnificent helmet with a red horsehair crest, cheek flaps, and a sweeping rear neck guard, in the Roman style. I thanked him and told Asfrid to choose what she wanted. She selected some glass vessels, ornate gold and silver bowls and a couple of knives with decorated bone handles. One chest of coins was mine. I left Leofmund, Wulfstan and Marcellus to share everything else between the lords of the east Angels.

"Thank you for this old friend, it will make good our losses. You have enough to secure your own Kingdom?"

"This all came from Gwrgant's treasury," Artorius told me. "He was diligent in procuring his wealth."

"So what now, Artorius? The people seem quiet, Are they resentful? Is your position here secure?" I wanted to know what our next step might be.

"You didn't see them yesterday old friend. When we rode in here and announced that Gwrgant had been defeated and they were free of his cruel yoke there was excitement and merry making all through the city late into the night. It is your presence which has made everyone nervous and quiet. Gwrgant had Sais warriors at his call and our folk are nervous of you anyway. We have suffered much from the Sais, Wulfhere. You can't expect people to forget overnight."

"Those same Saxons are with us, Artorius. They are good men, ready to swear loyalty to you."

"How is it that they survived the battle?" He wondered.

"They wouldn't flee the field. They would have fought to the death as loyalty demanded, but I called on them to set aside their oaths to a crazed tyrant. Their leader accepted death rather than be an oath breaker, having first released his men from Gwrgant's service. Their new leader is a man called Ecgfrith. My advice would be to take their oath, Artorius. They are honourable men, they made a mistake in trusting a dog that they thought was a king. At least speak with them before you make a decision."

"You have never given me bad advice before, Wulfhere. I will speak with this, Ecgfrith."

"So what happens next, will you send an envoy to Ambrosius?" I wanted to get this all tied up.

"Gwernach has already gone. He has fought alongside Ambrosius several times. He is the best man to explain the situation here, and to assure Ambrosius of our best intentions. Whatever happens now, the die are cast, Wulfhere. There is no turning back. I believe that Ambrosius will accept my right to rule here in Caer Colun, and that with his acceptance my rule will be recognised by the kings of all the tribes. What else can they do? A civil war would be too destructive with all of our enemies poised to sweep up the pieces. I will go to see him when Gwernach returns and assure him personally of our peaceful intentions. I don't think you'll be rid of me as a neighbour for a while yet." We laughed together.

"Let's drink to that Artorius! Where do you get a pot of mead round here?"

For the rest of the day Artorius showed us his city. There were some wonderful sights; the baths, statues of old emperors, gods and heroes from legend, carved scenes of battles, or gods and goddesses drinking, laughing and dancing with strange creatures. There were beautifully crafted likenesses of animals and birds and brightly coloured pictures painted on the walls. Carved columns, stone steps, tile pictures, everywhere you looked there were such stunning sights.

That night we feasted in the great hall. Sitting in the hall felt like wearing borrowed clothes. It was magnificent, but it was utterly foreign and unnatural. Speeches of praise and friendship were made on all sides. Songs were sung, lakes of mead, ale and even wine were drunk. It was not only the start of a new reign it was a change in the very nature of our world. Two kings, one Wealh and one Sais, creating a new order in an ancient Roman hall. Where would our paths lead to next? Had I served Tiw's purpose? Would he have more work for me? Only the spinners knew the answers.

The next morning I struggled to escape the clutches of sleep. It was the first time that I had really been able to sleep without any worries in a long time. Even when I woke I felt as though I could shut my eyes again and sleep on for days. Asfrid brought me a pot of ale and led me to the hall where breakfast was being enjoyed by the lords of Angel and Caer Colun who were sitting in very distinct groups this morning. I sat with Artorius and helped myself to bread, hard cheese and pickled herring. I ate in silence until the food had filled my stomach and lightened my spirit.

"Well, my friend, if you are sure that you have everything in order it might be best If we take our men home straight away," I suggested. "It's the wrong time of the year to be feeding an army, and aside from clearing out your storehouses, I wouldn't want anything to upset the friendship that has been forged between our folk. Too many well armed young warriors in one place can only lead to strife!"

"I agree my friend, though I would like to speak to your men and thank them for their valour on our behalf. I made many friends whilst I lived amongst your folk and I would not want those friendships forgotten, Wulfhere." Artorius assured me honestly.

"Nor I, my friend, nor I."

"You will have to return here in the summer, Wulfhere with your family. I will show you all of the wonders of this place and we can talk of the future of our kingdoms. Such a visit would surely help to cement peace between our people."

He was right, and I would love to have more time to explore the city so I readily agreed. We walked out of the great door of the temple and stood at the top of the beautifully cut and shaped steps, looking across the square where my army had been told to prepare to head for home. Flanked by the mighty stone columns, with the roof projected over our heads, and the beautifully carved stonework behind us, I felt more like an emperor than a war lord. I held up my hands and hailed the men, and waited for word to spread that I was waiting to talk. When I had their attention I began.

"My brothers. You have forged a legend, a tale which will be told round hearths for a thousand years. King Artorius of Caer Colun wishes to thank you."

The men cheered and then fell silent as Artorius stepped forward and addressed them in his powerful voice.

"Men of the east Angels. Your king gave me and my people shelter when our own king wanted our heads. He gave us hope. He lent us his strength and now we have thrown down the evil tyrant. We have freed the people of Caer Colun and won a kingdom. You have shown that we may live and fight side by side. Your fighting skills are legend. You will be remembered in songs for a thousand years. I extend the hand of friendship from Caer Colun to the east Angels, my brothers."

He proffered his hand and I took it with a genuinely warm smile before he continued,

"May we enjoy a future of friendship, trade, prosperity and peace."

With that the men gave him a rousing cheer which continued for quite a while.

I drained the last of my ale and told Artorius that we would leave as soon as the lords had received their shares of the reward that he had set aside for us. I spotted Ecgfrith and his men in the crowd and beckoned him to the steps with a wave. I introduced him to the young king, left them talking, and went back into the temple to see how Leofmund and Marcellus were getting on with the treasure. Leofmund had gone to bring the wagons to the Temple steps so that we could get them loaded, while Marcellus watched over the hoard. I told him that as soon as it was all loaded we would head for home. The war had only lasted a couple of weeks and we were going home with chests full of coins, and the war gear from the battle field, before the first cut of hay had even been gathered in. I had a broad grin stuck to my face. I would be home for the summer, Asfrid would be delivered of our next babe, and then we would return to visit Artorius and explore the Roman wonders of Camulodonum. Life wouldn't get much better than this.

I suddenly thought about horses. Before we left I would approach Artorius and ask him if he would sell me some mares which we were short of. Most of my captured horses were stallions. I emerged from the cool interior of the temple looking for my friend but I was confronted by a sight which momentarily confused me. As I came through the doorway all faces turned to look in my direction. From their expressions something was clearly amiss. Asfrid, Wulfstan, Oswine all rushed up the steps towards me following Leofmund and Hunberht, who looked as if he had run all the way from Wolf Home. I suddenly felt cold. What had happened? Why was Hunberht here?

"Hunberht what is it?" I asked.

I took in Leofmund's deathly pale face and wide shocked eyes.

"It's Eadgyth isn't it? What's happened?"

"My lord, they came to Wolf Home, mounted warriors. The Wealh." he paused as if steeling himself to tell me, "They took the lady Eadgyth, and Ilse. They slew lady Arwen and Willa and the other household servants!"

"Took them? Who took them? Took them where?"

"They carried them off on their horses, lord. I was in the field, I saw them and I knew that they were Wealh, but I thought that they were lord Artorius' men. Then the screaming started. We ran back from the fields, but they rode away before we could get back to the hall. Eadric was badly injured, he tried to stop them leaving but they rode straight over him. I think there were eight of them, and Eadric tried to bar their way by himself but they just rode over him and then away westward."

"Hunberht, what of my sons? Are they taken? Or slain?" I had to know, my heart had sunk to my feet, my blood was ice.

"Neither, lord" the earnest farmer replied. "They are still with lady Aelfgifu at Ship Home. She doesn't know yet, unless word has reached her from others."

It had to be Gwrgant. He had escaped the battlefield and ridden to Wolf Home. He had Eadgyth. The sickest, most cruel, depraved....he had Eadgyth.

"By the gods! I'll..I'll." I could barely contain myself. Horror and rage were battling one another, but it was no good being like this. I had to act. I had to find them, before.........

"Hunberht, when did this happen?" I was forcing myself with all of my strength of will to try to stay sane and think. We had to try to find them.

"Last evening, lord. I borrowed your horse to try to find you and I came across some of our men returning home and they sent me here."

Last evening, last evening, think! What did that mean! It had to be Gwrgant that much was obvious. He had had them all night. No, please no, not Eadgyth, taken alive! That thought weakened me and I almost collapsed.

"Aaaaaaaaaaaagh!"

My shout, the incoherent roar snatched me back. Forced me to think. Eadgyth! I had to find her. I called on my mother and father for strength, thinking of my blood, Eadgyth's blood. This was family, not war, not kingdoms, this was Eadgyth. But it crept back in and screamed inside my head, 'Taken alive by Gwrgant!' It was going round and round my head stopping me thinking and I roared aloud again to clear my mind, an incoherent sound of anguish, fear and blind fury, I was shouting, thinking out loud, dragging my mind onto the problem.

"Last evening! He must have ridden from the battlefield! Horses! The horses will be tired! How far could he have gone, Artorius?" I was making myself think, he hadn't killed them, he had taken them alive, he was going to.......He was going to use them to punish me, he was going to exact his revenge on them. I had to think. Would they still be alive? Would he have had his fun with them yet? He would want to be safe, surely, he would want to get away to somewhere that he could take his time, to exact his revenge.

Back in reality again and Artorius was calling for horses, men were running.

He would have to head west to try to get away, he was fleeing from Wolf Home with tired horses, where would he be?

Artorius was thinking aloud, my friend was with me.

"If he left Wolf Home yesterday evening with tired horses, and carrying two women, he will be moving slowly. If he goes west from Wolf Home he will be crossing hostile country all the way to the Granta bridge and beyond into Icel's lands with hostages who could be recognised at any time. I think he would go south."

"South? Why south? West surely?" I put in.

"No I don't think so, Wulfhere," Artorius rejoined. "Not everyone in Caer Colun knows he has been defeated and what support he did have was in the south of the kingdom away from Camulodonum, where they didn't see his depravity and cruelty at close quarters. He won't be able to stay there long. He will have to go west eventually, whether by sea or by land, but initially I think that south would be his best choice. It is the way I would go in his place."

I had been thinking as a lord of the Angels and my immediate thought had been of flight to the west. Artorius was probably right. If we were to catch Gwrgant we had to think from his perspective, a Wealh perspective with the Wealh knowledge of their own country. I was lost. I was Wulfhere the Grim, I controlled armies, I ruled the battle field, I ordered my people, their laws and their lives but now I had no control over any of these unfolding events. I had to trust Artorius on this matter.

I was failing my sister. I had promised that I would never fail my people again but I had failed to protect her and now she was in the hands of this monstrous creature, along with Ilse. Noble, tragic Ilse, how much more could that woman suffer? Why were the fates so cruel? Surely she had proved her strength, proved her character!

Plainly then this must be my fault. Lord Wulfhere, haughty and over proud, chosen man of Tiw. I had got above myself and I was being punished. No, far more subtle than that, those that I cared about were being punished because of me! I had seen myself as an emperor. I had questioned Tiw's further purpose for me. Tiw would decide when my service was ended! I was being punished but at the same time my mettle was being tested. Was I still worthy of Tiw's generosity? We are judged by the way we react to fate's twists of the thread. I had wavered, I had stood on the brink of weakness and despair, but I had caught myself in time. I drew myself straight, I remembered who I was. I thought of Eadgyth and Ilse. I had been weak. I had to be strong and clear headed to give them a chance, any chance.

"So we will look to the south, Artorius."

I bled myself of emotion, by the gods I would give vent to my emotions once I had captured the bastard, but now I had to be cold. This was a hunt. I had to keep a clear head in order to make the right decisions.

"We will ride to Wolf Home to try to pick up the trail. Can you send men out into the countryside to raise the people against him, and look to discover his flight? We will chase like wolves from Wolf Home, and your riders can try to get in front of him. With luck we might catch him between us."

"We will do all we can my friend." Artorius gripped my shoulder in a clear show of friendship and support.

Gareth ran across the square and up the steps,

"Artorius, the horses are ready!" He called breathlessly.

"Then let us take provisions for our hunt and get underway as quickly as may be," Artorius decided. "Speed is vital if we are to help those ladies."

I had seven horses.

"Prince Sigurd, the army of the south folk is in your hands. Wedda, Odd, Ottar and my men will help you to get the army home. Keep the treasures safe lads, take them directly to Wolf Home. Leofmund you're with me, of course, and Gram. Wuffa, we need a hunter. You must find their trail and keep us on it. Marcellus, Wulfstan, Oswine. Quickly now! There is no time to lose. Hunberht, you did well. Return home now with the army. Tell Aelfgifu to keep the boys until our return. Tell her that we are on their trail!"

Glossary

Arwe; River Orwell
Atheling; A prince
Atrebates; An ancient British tribe
Baldric; A belt, worn over one shoulder, to hold a sword.
Blot monath; Blood month, November.
Caer Went; Post Roman British kingdom centred on Venta Icenorum. The ancient realm of the Iceni, modern day Norfolk.
Cantware; The people of Anglo-Saxon (AS) Kent.
Cofgodas; Mythical beings/sprites peculiar to a household or place who could be called upon to protect/bring good fortune to that place/household.
The Deep River; River Deben
Durobrivae; Water Newton
Duroliponte; Cambridge
Durovigutum; Godmunds Ceaster; Godmanchester
Ese; The pagan gods of the Anglo-Saxons
Hwaet!; A call to order – Listen! Quiet!
Icelingas; Icel's folk
Iceni: An ancient British tribe.
Jutes; A Germanic tribe.
Ligora Ceaster; Leicester
Maxima Ceasariensis; A province of Britain during Roman rule
Modraniht; Mothers' Night. The mid-winter festival. The birth of the new year.
Neorth: AS god of the sea – Norse Njordr
Neorxnawang; Heaven. A blissful meadow.
Offa of Angel; Venerated prince of Angel who famously defeated two warriors in ritual combat and thus won their lands for the Angels.
Picts; Confederation of Celtic tribes from modern day East and North scotland

Sais; Saxons. Still the Welsh word for an Englishman.
Seaxe; Single bladed knife typically of Germanic peoples ranging in size from pen knife to machete type implements.
Sigel; Goddess of the sun
Spinners; The three sisters who weave our fate. Life stretches before us unknown, like the bare vertical threads on the loom. As we move forward the design is filled in and our tale is told. The future pattern may vary but what has been is there for all to see. The first sister chooses the pattern, the second weaves and the third is ready with the scissors to cut the thread.
Sture; River Stour.
Thrimilci; May. The grass grows so strong and lush in May that, apparently, it was necessary to milk three times a day.
Thryth; A princess who had men who stared at her beauty put to death. She married Offa of Angel and became a 'model' queen.
Tiw; God of war and justice.
Wade; Mythological sea giant said to help sailors in need
Waelcyrge; The valkyrie, a priestess.
Wahenhe; River Waveney
Wealh; AS foreigner – from which we derive Welsh
Wergild; The value placed on people/property which would, by law, have to be paid in restitution for loss or death.
Winterfylleth; Winter full moon, October. Presumably Winter started from the October full moon.

TO BE CONTINUED……..

WYRD
BOOK 4 OF THE ANGELCYNN SERIES

Printed in Great Britain
by Amazon.co.uk, Ltd.,
Marston Gate.